MW00779530

Deadly Stillwater

DEADLY STILLWATER

ROGER STELLJES

ISBN 10: 1-59298-307-3
ISBN 13: 978-1-59298-307-0

Library of Congress Control Number: 2009935596
Printed in the United States of America
First Printing: 2009
13 12 11 10 09 5 4 3 2 1

Cover design by Judd Einan / ED-design.biz
Interior design and typesetting by Ryan Scheife, Mayfly Design

Beaver's Pond Press, Inc.
7104 Ohms Lane, Suite 101
Edina, MN 55439-2129
(952) 829-8818
www.BeaversPondPress.com

To order, visit www.BookHouseFulfillment.com
or call (800) 901-3480. Reseller discounts available.

For Roger & Mary Steljes.
A son couldn't ask for two better parents.

acknowledgments

The process of publishing a book starts with the author's written word. However, only with the help of many others does a book ultimately see print. I am indebted to a number of people who helped make this second book possible.

I'd like to thank the good folks at Beaver's Pond Press for their assistance in bringing this book to print. In particular, I'd like to thank Amy Cutler for her assistance in guiding this book through the publishing process, Kellie Hultgren for her editorial guidance, and Ryan Scheife for the book's set-up.

Dr. Jennie Riley provided invaluable assistance on certain medical matters in this book while being just days away from giving birth for the second time. Thanks, Doc, for your help.

The distinctive cover design is due to the creative genius of Judd Einan. Other authors would be wise to make use of Judd's immense talents.

My appreciation is extended to my ever-expanding reading crew, which includes: Mike Webb, Sue Stelljes, Matt Stelljes, Chad Stelljes, Jill Stelljes, Mary Stelljes, Roger Stelljes Sr., Sue Hall, Lisa McGinn, Gloria Williamson, and Sandee Byrd. I'd also like to single out Jeff Borowicz and Jim Snodgrass for their early and stellar editorial assistance with the book. I can't thank you all enough for your time, thoughts, and encouragement. I hope you enjoy the finished product as much as you did the rough one.

Finally, I'd like to thank my wife Sue and my children Julia and Jack for their infinite patience as Dad pursues his dream.

1

"Fifteen Seconds"

SUNDAY, JULY 1ST

Dictionary definitions vary, but "retribution" is typically defined as punishment imposed for purposes of repayment or revenge for the wrong committed. For Smith, retribution simply meant payback. He'd waited sixteen years for it, and now he was three hours away from starting to get it.

Smith turned the panel van left into the alley and pulled three-quarters of the way down toward Western Avenue. He stopped and then backed in behind a small office building housing an accounting office with a storefront facing Western. From this position, the back of the café was visible at a forty-five-degree angle to the right. Smith had watched the area and this parking spot in particular every Sunday for the last month. Nobody ever came to the building or parked in the back on a Sunday afternoon. He expected this day would be no different.

His watch said 2:03 PM. The office building's parking lot was elevated two feet above that of the restaurant across the alley. This allowed for a somewhat unobstructed view of the restaurant's back patio, which was surrounded by a six-foot-high wood fence. He could only see the tops of heads or upper torsos of patrons and staff from his position. Nonetheless, the spot provided a needed clear view of the café's small parking lot outside the fence. The target's car, a new Prius, occupied the second to last space in the back of the lot, located close to Western.

Smith set his gaze on the back of the restaurant, Cel's Café, a little bistro on the corner of Western and Selby avenues. The café was a busy hub in St. Paul's Cathedral Hill neighborhood, an area of turn-of-the-century Victorian homes encircling the majestic Cathedral of Saint Paul. The stately mansions of Summit Avenue lay a mere three blocks away. The café was a busy post-church lunching spot. By the mid-to-late afternoon, it changed over to a light crowd of book or newspaper readers, drinking coffee, iced tea, and, for those living on the edge, maybe a bloody mary. Cel's also employed a young waitress named Shannon Hisle, the daughter of St. Paul's wealthiest and most prominent lawyer.

Smith pulled black leather gloves tight over his hands and turned to the back of the van where two large men, brothers Dean and David, fiddled with duct tape, masks, and gloves of their own. There was also a gas-filled plastic milk carton with a detonator taped on the side for later. Each had a .45 lying on the floor. Smith turned his attention to the passenger seat and the police scanner, which reported little activity on this sleepy summer afternoon.

Smith had spent fifteen years in Leavenworth Federal Penitentiary. Because of who he was, the beatings started his first day. He had fought, but hadn't had a fighting chance. Those first few years, he suffered broken ribs, fingers, and wrists more than once. In one of the last and most brutal of the assaults, he suffered a broken nose that left him with a large and permanent bulbous knot just below the bridge and a shattered eye socket that blurred the peripheral vision in his left eye. He spent long tours in the infirmary, recovering from the abuse, only to be put back into the general population to be unmercifully beaten again and again. He had had no allies, no protection, and no hope in those early years.

If it wasn't for the arrival of the two hulking brothers in the back of the van, he wouldn't have made it. Three years into Smith's sentence, David—six-foot-three and 240 pounds of bulging muscles—moved into a neighboring cell. David saw firsthand the results of the beatings. He didn't like what he saw. Along with his equally large and skilled brother Dean, three cells further down, David used skills honed in the Golden Gloves to put a stop to it.

David and Dean had saved his life. Smith would do anything for his two friends. It was one of the reasons why he now sat behind the wheel and had masterminded what was about to take place. Before he could get his, Dean and David needed to get theirs.

Monica sat at her table at the front of the bistro, sipping her iced tea, alternately reading her Harlequin novel, watching the target, and making calls on her cell phone.

Dressed in a frumpy floral blouse, faded black spandex pants, and black heels, sporting a 1960s bouffant wig of black hair, she had the look of a mid-forties woman whose social life revolved around reading about romances she would never have. It was far from her normal, stylish look, but it was the look she wanted for today. She had used it the previous three weeks when she came in on Sunday afternoons to scout the movements of Shannon Hisle. The mark was sitting at the bar now, closing out her tables, sipping a Diet Coke. She would be leaving soon.

Taking one last sip of her iced tea, Monica put the receipt in her purse, popped a complimentary mint in her mouth, and discreetly wiped down the table and the arms on her chair. She'd never been arrested nor had her prints taken, but she didn't want to take a chance.

Hisle finished the last of her tabs and handed them to her manager, who gave them a quick look and approval. Monica checked her watch—4:56 PM—and placed a call as Hisle put her purse over her shoulder. Smith picked up on the first ring.

"Fifteen seconds."

As Hisle pushed the back door open, Monica slung her purse over her shoulder, walked out the front door and turned right, casually strolling east along Selby Avenue and away from the action beginning to unfold.

Dean, a black ski mask over his head, was out of the van now, crouched down behind a parked pickup truck three cars to the right of Hisle's Prius. David, his mask down as well, was stationed at the van's side sliding door. Smith focused on the back door and saw the pretty brunette push her way through. He pulled the van into the alley and turned left, driving slowly down the alley, watching Hisle all the way.

Shannon hustled to her car with her head down and digging with her right hand across her body deep into her black purse, searching for her car keys.

When she reached the back bumper of her car, she halted and dug with both hands, leaning down and peering in.

"Where the heck did they go?" she muttered. *Ah ha*, there they were, buried in a corner, under her cell phone. She grabbed the cell phone and keys and sensed the sudden flash of movement from her left. She looked up in time to see a mammoth black-masked man barreling toward her.

"NO! ... NO! ..."

Dean scooped Hisle, putting his hand over her mouth as she screamed and thrashed against his iron grip.

Smith quickly turned right out of the alley and pulled up along the curb. David slid the door open and grabbed the struggling Hisle out of his brother's hands. He dragged her inside, sat on top of her, and pinned her arms down. Dean jumped in, closed the door, and grabbed the duct tape as Smith punched the gas and took a hard right turn on Selby and accelerated east to Summit Avenue. Dean and David duct taped the girl's hands, ankles, and mouth. They then put a pillow case over her head. Hisle squirmed and tried to scream through the duct tape pasted over her mouth. A brief look in the rearview mirror and Smith could see the horror in her eyes. It was only beginning for her.

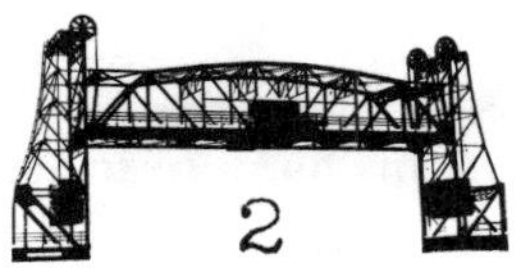

2

"How Do They Know She's Coming?"

Mac McRyan swerved his Ford Explorer through traffic in Spaghetti Junction just north of downtown St. Paul, flasher and siren going strong, as it had been since he left Stillwater and his boat fifteen minutes earlier. It had been a wonderful Sunday up until now. With his sister, Julia, her husband, Jack, and his girlfriend, Sally, he had spent the day on his family's boat on the St. Croix River, picnicking and soaking up the sun. It was the most relaxing day that he and Sally, a busy Ramsey County prosecutor, had experienced in months—at least until now. As the group was tying up the boat and deciding where to go for dinner, the call had come. Now he skidded to a quick stop just short of the patrol car parked across the intersection of Selby and Western.

Mac's full name was Michael McKenzie McRyan, but for all of his thirty-three years he'd simply been known as Mac. He'd been in the McRyan family business—the St. Paul Police Department—for eight years. A fourth-generation cop, Mac had relatives sprinkled throughout the department.

He rolled his athletic six-foot-one frame out of the Explorer. Ruggedly handsome, Mac had short blonde hair, icy blue eyes, and a taut face with a dimple the size of the Grand Canyon in his scarred chin.

A former captain of the University of Minnesota hockey team, he was still at his 190-pound playing weight and worked hard daily to keep it that way. Sliding on his Oakley sunglasses, he walked toward a uniform cop who waved him through. Mac took in the scene, with squad cars and Crown Vics everywhere. He saw two techs from County Forensics taking pictures and prowling around the parking lot behind Cel's. And, of course, the Chief's Boys stood just behind them.

The Boys were Detectives Pat Riley, Riley's partner, Bobby Rockford, and Mac's own partner, Richard Lich. When St. Paul Police Chief Charles Flanagan needed results—when the shit hit the fan—he turned to his Boys. Lyman Hisle was as high profile as it got in the Twin Cities, and his daughter had been abducted in broad daylight. Not to mention, Hisle was a close personal friend of Charlie Flanagan. Needless to say, the chief needed his best cops on the case.

They were a motley crew.

Pat "Riles" Riley was a sizeable man, well over six feet tall and two hundred pounds. The veteran detective had dark eyes, a heavy Nixonian five o'clock shadow, and a thick mane of black hair, which he combed back. A sharp dresser, Riles looked like a mobster in his pinstripe suits, perfectly pressed shirts, and stylish ties. Loud, boisterous, and loyal, Riles was like a brother to Mac, having served with Mac's father, Simon, when he first became a detective years ago.

Bobby "Rock" Rockford was even larger than Riley. He was black, dark black, with his eyes deeply embedded in his large, shaved head. When he smiled, he showed a gap between his two front teeth. He'd been a college defensive tackle and wasn't averse to getting physical when the circumstances warranted. Rock, given his size, appearance, and growl, could be downright frightening. Mac had watched him scare a guy into shitting his pants once.

Then there was "Dick Lick."

Richard Lich was short, squat, and balding with a bushy porn-star mustache in constant need of trimming. Twice divorced, he spent plenty of time lamenting his perpetually dire financial circumstances. He blamed both ex-wives not only for his financial difficulties, but also for his inability to fix his wardrobe. Perhaps the worst dresser ever to carry a shield, Dick donned a pitiful series of old soiled suits, all some shade of brown, whether it be gravy brown, dirt brown or shit brown. He topped each ensemble off with scuffed shoes, faded shirts, chewed-on cigars, and, in the winter, either a black or brown fedora. While Riles and Rock scared the hell out of people, Lich was comic relief, a true piece of work. But he was a piece of work that people tended to underestimate. Few realized that he was a damn fine detective. Possessed with a quick wit and an easy manner, he was a perfect partner for Mac, smoothing out his younger partner's abrasive edges.

With Mac as the catalyst, the Boys had earned their reputation on the PTA case. Their work had brought down a small band of retired CIA agents and their corporate employer, PTA, a St. Paul military and intelligence contractor. PTA, and its various players were behind the murders of an investigative reporter, a U.S. senator and the company CFO, while trying to cover up illegal arms deals. Since that case, the chief often had the four of them work cases together as an unofficial special investigative unit.

As Mac approached the Boys, Lich called out, "Nice outfit."

Mac still wore his boating gear: tan cargo shorts, navy blue Polo golf shirt, and leather sandals—all of which was at odds with the badge hanging around his neck. His blonde hair stood up just a bit more than usual, wind-blown from a day on the river.

"You're the last person who should give fashion advice," was Mac's ready response. Lich had matched his shit-brown slacks with a faded orange golf shirt, untucked and fully open at the collar. Mac turned to Riley.

"What the hell happened? Are we sure this was a kidnapping?"

Riley exhaled, running his hand through his large mane of black hair.

"Let me run it down, and you tell me what you think." Riles walked to the back of the Prius. "Cheri Hisle got off work at 5:00. She walked out the back door. Her car is this Prius. It looks like when she reached the back of her car somebody grabbed her. The positioning of her keys and phone on the pavement away from her car at least suggest that."

"And then what happened?"

"We think whoever grabbed her jumped into a white van that pulled away and turned right on Selby. From there..." Riley's voice trailed off.

Rock jumped in, rubbing a hand across his shaved head, "Our witnesses ... well ... kind of...."

"Suck," Lich finished.

"Suck, like they didn't see anything?" Mac asked.

"Regular Havercamps," Riles replied, never one to pass up a Caddyshack moment. He pointed across and to the south along Western Avenue. "An old couple was walking along the sidewalk down there, maybe a hundred yards away, and they think they saw a guy dressed in black pick her up and throw her into the van."

"Think?" Mac asked.

"Older couple, in their seventies, maybe early eighties, vision is a bit of an issue."

"Anything about the van?"

"White. It comes out of the alley, and turns right. The guy in black throws her in and off they go," Riles said.

"Anything else?"

"Another witness, female," Riles turned and pointed to the southwest corner of Selby and Western, "was waiting on that corner, facing north, about ready to cross the street when she thought she heard a scream. She turned around and saw the van slow and then quickly pull away, turn right and go east on Selby."

"So then what happened?"

"Confusion really," Lich said. "The elderly couple came walking up and spoke with the woman on the corner, asking, you know, 'did you see that?' They're not sure what they all saw, so they walk across the street into the parking lot and see keys and a cell phone lying on the ground. They go inside the café and explain what they saw. The café workers come outside, see that Hisle's car is still in the lot, and call 911."

"How long did all that take?"

"Three or four minutes at best, maybe more," Lich replied. "Nobody saw it all happen, just bits and pieces."

"So anyway, a squad gets here maybe a minute or two later," Rock added. "They ask some questions, get basically what we're talking about now, and make the call."

"So before we even have an alert out about a white van, it's what?" Mac asked.

Lich shook his head, skeptical, voicing what everyone else was thinking.

"At best, eight to ten minutes, probably more."

"Maaaaaan," Mac groaned. "That's a lot of time to get away before we even *start* looking. Did we get anything on the van? Plate, make, model, anything?"

"No plate, white van. It looked like a typical delivery or repair van, panel type, no lettering, maybe slightly dented behind the driver side door, but that's it."

"Nothing striking that would draw attention," Lich added.

"Where did the van come from?" Mac asked.

"The older couple said it came out of the alley," Rock answered. "We're not entirely sure, but we're thinking it was parked behind the office building." He pointed across the alley and to their left. "From there, they would be able to see her come out the back door and take her."

"How many people?"

"Driver, guy to take her," Riles answered, counting on his fingers.

"Maybe another guy in the van," Lich added.

"Why do you think not just two?" Mac asked Lich.

"The older couple thinks he threw her into the van. I'm thinking there might have been someone in there to take or catch her. We don't know for sure, just speculatin'."

"Any surveillance cameras or anything?"

"Nada," Rock replied. "Nothing outside. Hell, nothing inside the café."

"We're askin' the café people," Lich asked.

"Was there anyone unusual inside or outside today, last few days, anything like that," Mac added.

"Not that anyone can recall," Rock answered. "It was busy early in the afternoon with the post-church crowd. However, after that rush, the staff says there were just regulars sitting around reading, having coffee. Pretty mellow."

"In other words," Mac said, summing up, "we got shit."

"Hell, we ain't even got that," Lich replied, looking down, shaking his head.

The group stood in silence for a minute before Mac asked, "Where is the chief?"

"In a sad irony, already at Hisle's," answered their captain, Marion Peters, as he ducked under the crime scene tape and joined the group. "The chief was out there for Hisle's annual barbeque when the call came in."

"I assume they haven't heard from the kidnappers yet?"

"No," Peters answered.

"Are we on the phone?"

"Yeah, both landline and cell," Peters replied. "I've been setting that up. We're watching the phone at her place. We have someone at his law firm watching the phone. But we expect he'll get the call at home, and we have people and the chief out there."

"What about the Feds?" Rock asked. "Will they be coming in?"

Peters shrugged. "At some point they will. Kidnapping is one of their gigs. Hisle's a prominent guy, politically connected, so the bureau will be involved at some point and somehow."

"We don't know that they took her over state lines," Lich replied.

"True. But again, we're talking Lyman here. He'll probably want them in and the chief will accede to his wishes, they being friends and all."

"Yeah," Mac added, "and given what we have thus far, we'll need their resources."

Riley's and Peter's cell phones chirped, and they walked away from the group. Mac left Rock, and he and Lich and walked over toward Hisle's car.

"So did her old man piss someone off?" Lich asked.

"Possibly," Mac answered. Lyman had made the big time both financially and politically. You do that and you've made some people mad, very mad, along the way. He'd made millions on class-action and discrimination cases, fighting businesses for years. On the criminal side, he'd tussled with the police departments around town for years. Yet, given his practice, he was still popular with the local police departments. He often waived his hefty retainer and fees to help the men in blue. Consequently, there would be no "what goes around comes around" feeling that cops might have for many of the lawyers they dealt with. The cops would have Lyman's back on this one.

"It could be a nut, or...."

"Or what?" Lich asked following Mac back toward Hisle's car.

"Maybe not a nut," Mac answered blandly as he walked over to the yellow numbered evidence tags by the keys and cell phone. They were lying on the ground, to the right of Shannon Hisle's car, strewn toward Western Avenue. The way the keys and phone had spilled suggested that whoever grabbed her had come from the left, and with force. The cell phone was a few feet from the car and the keys a good ten feet from the car, nearly reaching the sidewalk separating the parking lot from Western.

Mac pivoted to his left and scanned the cars parked to the left of Hisle's. There was a Ford Focus and Chevy Cavalier, both compact cars. The third was a black Ford F-150, a hefty pickup truck. The pickup was parked with its back end pointing out. Mac walked around the truck to the driver's side and crouched down. There was little of interest on the asphalt, beyond gravel and litter. It would be collected and analyzed but was unlikely to be of any help. However, there was a definite fresh footprint in a bare patch of black dirt between the alley and the parking lot. Mac called a crime scene tech over. The print looked fresh and was big, probably size twelve or thirteen, Mac thought. The tread of the impression looked like a hiking boot. "Get a picture of that," Mac directed, "and dust this side of the truck, especially the back quarter panel, for prints."

"What do you have?" Lich asked, walking over.

"The keys and cell phone landed toward Western, to the right of the rear bumper of the car?"

"Yeah, so?"

"So it looks like whoever took Hisle came from this way, by the truck here. Scooped her up and ran to the van on Western. This is a big truck. You could hide behind it and wait for her. There's a fresh footprint in that bare spot between the alley and the parking lot. If you line it up, the footprint is coming straight, as if the guy came from right across the alley." Mac pointed toward the back of the office building on the other side of the alley. "The van was across the alley. They know Hisle's coming out, one guy hides here, the other drives the van from behind the building, down the alley and pulls up along the curb."

Lich picked up on the thought. "Yeah. I see what you're gettin' at. Our guy comes from this spot. It's three cars to Hisle. She comes out; he pops out, scoops her up."

"Right. Three cars to here is nothing. He'd be on her in an instant," Mac replied. "I bet that's what happened."

They stood in silence for a moment, and then Mac asked, "But do they know when she's coming?"

"Huh?" Lich asked.

"How do they know she's coming? I mean, their timing was pretty good."

"Beats me. Guy sits and waits for her."

"Yeah, but if the guy is hiding behind the truck here, he can't wait all afternoon can he?"

Lich nodded, "I see what you're saying. They had to have an idea of when she was leaving."

"So how do they know?"

"Maybe she always leaves at 5:00 PM."

"Maybe," Mac answered. "But that could be four fifty-five or five ten, depending on her schedule and what not. This is a good spot, but you wouldn't want to be exposed for too long here. Somebody might still notice if you were here more than a minute or two. No, you'd want to know *exactly* when she was coming."

Lich's eyebrows went up. "Someone inside?"

"That's what I'm thinking," Mac replied, already walking toward the back door of the café.

Smith peered in the rearview mirror as he slowly backed the van into the garage of the safe house. Once parked, he killed the engine and let the garage door down, not getting out until the door had closed. Once down, he donned a mask to match the ones worn by David and Dean. He climbed out of the van and opened the sliding door for the brothers.

The safe house was a small, nondescript white 1950s rambler located in a working-class neighborhood a few blocks off of West Seventh Street on St. Paul's south side. While there were houses on either side and across the street, there was a large wood privacy fence surrounding the back of the property as well as railroad tracks running behind. They'd only been in the house for two days, although it had been rented since June first.

A stairway in the garage led down to the basement. Smith led the way down as Dean and David, still masked, followed carrying the pixie-sized Hisle. The basement had a small family room, a bedroom, and a full bath. In the bedroom, there were two twin beds with metal frames as well as steel-barred head- and footboards. A piece of plywood was screwed into place over the small egress window. A solitary low-watt ceiling light lit the bedroom.

The two brothers set Hisle down on the bed, and Dean pinned her down. The girl began fighting, perhaps fearing she was going to be raped. But rape wasn't part of the plan. David pulled the hunting knife attached to his belt and cut the duct tape from her wrists. He then used two pairs of handcuffs to secure each hand to a metal post on the headboard. David then cut the tape around her ankles and manacled each to the footboard. Once the girl was fully secured, Dean pushed off, and she struggled against the cuffs, grunting and pulling to no avail. The men, masks still on, watched the young woman struggle and flail. Smith wanted her to get the last of it out of her system. He wanted and needed her calm. After a few minutes, Hisle began to settle down, exhaustion setting in from fighting her restraints. She wasn't getting away, and they weren't doing anything more to her.

Smith nodded and Dean and David backed away as Smith sat down on the side of the bed and removed the pillow case from her head.

"Settle down now, Shannon," Smith said quietly. "We don't want to harm you. Neither these men nor I is going to rape you or anything like that, so you needn't worry about those kinds of things."

She lay still, but fear showed in her eyes. Smith wanted her calm for what he needed from her. He sat silent for a few moments and let her settle down.

"I'm going to take the tape off your mouth, okay? But don't yell," he said, holding his hand just over her mouth, "If you try to yell, I will have to hurt you. Do you understand? And I really don't want to do that."

Shannon nodded slightly. Smith slowly removed the duct tape, trying not to harm her. She breathed deeply before speaking.

"What are you going to ... do with me?"

"We have taken you for a specific purpose Shannon. A very *specific* purpose."

"Money? Is it money you want?"

"*Of course, of course,*" Smith answered. "It's exactly why we chose you, Shannon. Your father has a lot of money, and we want some of it. Now, if you play ball with us, and if your dad plays ball...." Smith patted her lightly on her thigh. "Well, everything will work out just fine."

"What does that mean?"

"It means, if you do as we ask, your chances of making it out of this are a whole lot better. If you don't help us out, well ... it certainly could go much worse."

"So this is *just* about money?" she asked.

"Absolutely," Smith replied, patting her thigh again. "That's all we're looking for. If you're hurt, it makes it harder for us to get paid. So, I assure you, we do not wish to harm you."

"How will you convince *him* you're not going to harm me?"

Smith smiled under his mask. The girl was smart, but what would you expect from the daughter of a lawyer—a good lawyer for that matter. "Don't you spend time thinking about that," Smith answered. "I don't have to harm you to make sure your father is motivated to pay what he's going to have to pay."

"How?"

"Because you're his little girl and you're going to help us."

The café manager was Mike Haines, a balding, soft-spoken man in his late twenties. He placed the original 911 call and did a good job of holding the scene, having all of the patrons and staff stay until the police arrived. Shannon Hisle had worked for him for two years and normally worked Sundays. Pulling the schedules for the past two months confirmed that she'd been scheduled for every Sunday until 5:00 PM. Haines said that she liked to work the shift, which was fine by him because it usually wasn't a busy day and he often had difficulty scheduling staff for it.

"When she got off at 5:00, was it always right at 5:00, or could it be earlier or later?" Mac asked.

"She might leave a little early on occasion, maybe at 4:45 or so, but usually she would leave right around 5:00 PM."

"What does she have to do when it's time to leave?" Lich followed up. Haines ran a hand over his balding head.

"Close out her tables, which are usually just three or four at that point. Make sure her transactions balance, tip the bartender, and that's pretty much it," Haines explained.

"How long would it take her to do all that?" Mac asked.

"On a Sunday, not long. Five, ten minutes tops."

"Where does she do that, settle up?"

"If we're busy, it would usually be in my office in the back. But on Sundays we're a little more informal, and I don't mind if they sit at the bar and drink a soda while they're doing it. Most of our wait staff does that, and Shannon did it this afternoon."

"So what happens is, she sits at the bar, closes everything out, and that's it?" Mac said, moving toward the bar.

"Yeah, pretty much," Haines replied.

Mac sat on the bar stool, his back to the bar, looking out over the restaurant. He looked to his right, where a small hallway led to the back door, the patio, and then the parking lot where Hisle was abducted. He looked back out into the restaurant, where there were sixteen tables in four rows. To Mac's left a row of tables sat along the front windows of the restaurant. There were two rows down the center and then a row along the wall to his right. He looked at the back door again.

"How many people in the restaurant about the time Hisle left?" Mac asked.

Haines tilted his head, squinted, and pondered for a minute, "I'd say we had maybe four or five tables going at that point."

"How about in the half hour before she left?"

"Give me a minute," Haines said. "I can go through the receipts and get a count."

"What are you thinking?" Riles asked after Haines walked off for the receipts.

"They had someone on the inside."

"How do you figure?" Rock asked, puzzled.

"She leaves at 5:00 PM or thereabouts on Sundays, right?"

"Yeah, that gives them a time to be ready."

"Fine," Mac replied, "But let's assume for a second that our guy is waiting behind that truck for Shannon to leave. He can't just sit there for five or ten minutes with a mask on and not risk drawing some attention."

Riley picked up on the thread.

"So they know when she's generally going to leave, but they need to know when she's heading out so as to be ready."

"Right," Mac said. "Somebody sits in here, eyes the situation, and calls out when she's getting ready to go."

"And this person knows when Shannon is getting ready to go, since she sits up at the bar, having a soda and closing out her tables," Rock added.

"Probably because the inside person has been in here on Sundays, watching the pattern and knew when she was getting ready to roll," Mac finished.

Just then, Haines came back.

"In the half hour before Shannon left we had eight tables active."

"How many closed out between 4:30 and 5:00 PM?" Lich asked.

Haines reviewed them quickly, "I have four closing out in that time period."

"Which is the latest?"

Haines flipped through the four that closed, looking for the time along the top of the white receipt, "Last one was at 4:52 PM. Shannon closed it out."

"How'd the person pay?" Riley asked before the others could spit it out, all thinking the same thing and knowing the answer.

"Cash."

Not a surprise. A credit card would have made it easier, Mac thought.

"How much was the tab?"

"$18.76," Haines replied. "A few iced teas and a sandwich."

"Which table?" Mac asked.

"Four."

"Where's that?"

"Over by the front door."

They all walked over to the table. It was empty, except for the ceramic sugar holder and the glass salt and pepper shakers in the middle. Mac stood on the side that backed up to the front door. He could take in the entire restaurant, including the bar and the hallway to the back door.

"Mr. Haines, do you recall who was sitting here?"

"Vaguely. Black hair, flowery blouse. She was here for a while, reading a book."

"Was she ever on a cell phone?"

"I think she was from time to time."

"Had you seen her in here before?"

"Yeah, a few times."

"Over the years? Last couple of months? What?" Mac asked.

"Probably more recent," Haines replied.

"Do you recall when she left today?"

"Not exactly when."

"Do you think it was before or after Shannon left?"

"I really can't recall. I do know she wasn't here when the patrol car arrived. She wasn't here when I asked everyone to stay. She was gone by then."

"You think she went out the front door?" Lich asked.

"I don't recall her going out the back."

"We need forensics to work this table over," Mac said.

"I'll go get them," Lich said and left the group.

"Your entire staff has to remember this woman as best they can," Riley told Haines. "We need a name, full description, anything and everything they can think of. Call anyone in who has worked Sundays for the last month. We'll get a sketch artist down here as well."

"Why?" Haines asked.

"Because," Mac replied, "this person may have sat right here and let the kidnappers know when Shannon bailed."

Riley's cell phone went off again.

"Riley," he answered. He nodded his head a few times. "Where?" He took out a notepad and started writing. "Okay ... thanks."

"What's up?" Rock asked.

"We might have the van."

"Where?"

"River Falls."

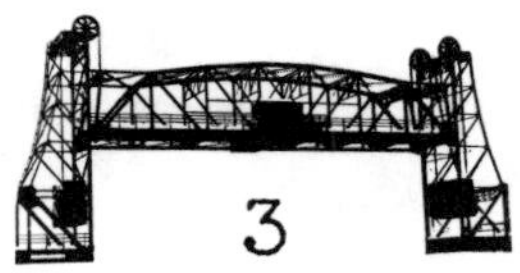

3

"Who's the guy?"

River Falls, Wisconsin, was a sleepy community half an hour from downtown St. Paul, fifteen miles into western Wisconsin. Mac pulled up to the crime scene tape in front of a bland industrial park. Mac, Dick, Riles, and Rock all filed out of the Explorer and walked up to the officer on guard standing in the opening between two one-story buildings and flashed their shields. The officer took a quick look at their badges and waved them through. Behind the building on the left, they found a burned-out van, a Ford Econoline Cargo. It was white, or at least used to be before it was torched. It was now massively disfigured with the frame and body distorted by the extreme heat of the fire. The van now listed to the right over the slag of melted tires. As they walked around it, Mac noted a distinguishing feature: a dent that ran for two feet just behind the bottom of the driver's side door.

A stocky man in his mid-fifties approached, a large dip of tobacco in his lower right front lip.

"You guys from St. Paul?" he asked. Everyone nodded. "Paul Fletcher, chief here in River Falls."

"Thanks, Chief," Riles replied and then introduced everyone. "How'd the call come in?"

Fletcher pulled a little black notebook out of his chest pocket, "Call came into us around 5:45 PM. The woman over there made the call,"

Fletcher pointed to an older lady holding a small terrier, "heard an explosion. She walked around to the back of the building here and found the van in flames."

"Did she see anyone, any other vehicles pulling away, anything like that?"

"Says no," Fletcher answered, spitting tobacco to the ground. "She was just walking along the street with her little dog and then heard the boom."

"How long for you to get here, Chief?" Riles asked.

"We got here about five minutes later, and the fire department just after that to put it out," Fletcher said, spitting again off to the side. "It was blown up intentionally. There's part of some sort of detonator in there and what might have been part of a plastic milk carton. The van has a Minnesota plate. And then we started hearing the radio traffic out of St. Paul about the kidnapping and to keep a look out for a white van, maybe dented. We thought this might be of interest."

"Not much left of her," Lich said.

"Nope," Fletcher replied, spitting again. "They did a pretty good job blowin' 'er up."

"I don't imagine we'll be able to get any prints or anything out of it," Rock said.

"I seriously doubt it," Fletcher replied. "The blast and fire probably took care of all that. Then us pourin' that water on it." Fletcher scratched his head. "Well shit, there probably isn't much left. Once we realized what might be going on, we left 'er alone. But at that point...." He squinted and shook his head. "It was probably too late."

"You run the plate?" Mac asked Fletcher.

"Yeah, the plate is for a van in Willmar. But, the VIN number matches a van stolen in Breckenridge two weeks ago." Willmar was a town in south central Minnesota, and Breckenridge was in far western

Minnesota, along the North Dakota border, two hours from Willmar. Mac snorted.

"These guys are being very careful."

"I'll say," Lich said. "So they dump the van here and use a pickup vehicle?" Lich asked.

"I imagine that's the case," Mac replied. "However, I suspect that, in putting out the fire, any tracks and anything else was washed out."

"Probably so," Fletcher sighed, resignation in his voice.

"Not your fault, Chief," Riles replied. "Safety first ya know. Gotta put out the fire. I'll make a call and get some forensics help out here. You never know, we might get something." He walked away from the group, cell phone already to his ear.

"So, they're being extra careful," Mac said. "They drop the van well out of the city, it's a stolen van with stolen plates, and they blow it up after the abduction. Smart."

"That it is," was Fletcher's reply. A local cop called to Fletcher and he walked away.

"You know what this means," Lich said.

"What?" Rock said. Mac finished off Lich's thought.

"Shannon Hisle went over state lines. If the Feds weren't in already, they'll be in now."

Smith and the others came up out of the basement, leaving Hisle bound, cuffed, and gagged downstairs in the bedroom. She'd been cooperative and gave them what they needed. "So, you're off?" Dean asked.

"Yeah," Smith replied, "I'll be a couple of hours. Keep your ears on your scanner as well. Call if anything comes up," he ordered.

Smith went out into the garage and jumped in the van. They'd dumped the Econoline in River Falls. Now he was driving a Chevy

Express Cargo. Within five minutes he'd maneuvered his way via Shepard Road to a Park & Fly lot for the Minneapolis-St. Paul International Airport. He dropped the van next to a light blue Chevy Impala. On a quiet Sunday night leading into a holiday week, the lot was quiet; most of the people intending to fly out were long gone. Nevertheless, he quickly scanned the lot before leaving the van. Noticing nobody nearby, he hopped out and slid into the Impala.

He maneuvered the Impala onto Interstate 494 and made his way through the southern and then western suburbs of the Twin Cities. When he reached Maple Grove, on the northwest side of the metro area, he took Interstate 94 toward the college town of St. Cloud, sixty miles to the northwest.

Lyman Hisle lived just north of Stillwater, a burgeoning suburb fifteen miles northeast of St. Paul. Perched above the picturesque St. Croix River, Stillwater looked like a town right out of a Norman Rockwell painting. Of course, in a Rockwell painting the shops would be used by the locals, but that was not always the case in Stillwater. On its main street, two-story storefronts of aged red brick and sandstone housed shops filled with antique furniture and trinkets. The narrow sidewalks teemed with antiques' shoppers from all over the Midwest, who milled through the maze of shops and ate at the small bistros. Stillwater was also a popular place to begin a cruise on the St. Croix River. Mac had his boat docked in the marina on the north side of town.

It had been a quiet ride to Stillwater from River Falls as the four detectives silently contemplated the case. As they idled at a stoplight in the midst of the town, Mac broke the silence. "Whoever is pulling this off is smart and ballsy."

"Is it someone Hisle pissed off or just a random grab for money?" Riles asked.

"Good question. It could be either, I suppose," Mac answered. "Lyman's apt to have some enemies we'll need to get to know. At the same time, this could be about money and nothing more. A sharp set of kidnappers decides to take Shannon and see what they can get."

"Could be a nut or a group of nuts," Lich added. "Some sex pervert who took Shannon for reasons other than money."

"That doesn't feel right," Mac disagreed. "This was too well-planned and thought out to be a nut. Shannon was picked out for some reason. The key will be whether, as I said, it was random in the sense that the kidnappers just picked her because Lyman was wealthy, or...."

"...they picked her because they want to hurt Lyman," Riles added.

"Right, or maybe both. We'll see."

"So," Lich asked Mac, "what's your bet? Financial or personal?"

"Hell if I know," Mac said, exhaling. "Lyman's rich. He's got lots of money, but it's not like he's the wealthiest guy in town. There are a lot of people with far more, so...."

"Personal," Lich finished.

"If I had to lay a two-dollar bet, yeah. At least personal in the sense there was a reason, a *specific* reason, to pick Hisle's daughter. It wasn't just random. There must be some reason to pick her. We have to figure out the why and maybe that'll gives us the who."

"That would mean we're looking at his client list," Rock said. "That's apt to be a fuckin' long list."

"You practice law for thirty years and have his level of success..." Mac whistled. "It'll be long indeed. We should probably look at his opponents as well." Hisle had hundreds, maybe thousands of criminal clients over the years, not to mention clients in his civil practice, discrimination cases, and class-action suits. "We'll have to get that list going in a hurry."

"Wonder if we'll run into any issues in looking at his files."

"Possible. Attorney-client privilege will be something of an issue, I suspect," Mac responded. He was a licensed lawyer, but he'd never practiced before deciding to be a cop instead. "He'll undoubtedly have a client or two who doesn't want us rifling through their files."

"I imagine that's the case," Lich answered, as he looked to the marina on his right and changed the subject.

"Isn't that where your boat is docked?"

"Yeah. Sally and I have to get you and Dot out sometime soon."

"She'd love it. Besides, I'd get to see Sally in a two-piece and that would be *quite* a sight," Lich replied with a dirty grin. Dick knew his comments about Sally's shapely body got under Mac's skin just a little. Rock and Riles laughed heartily in the back.

"I'll make sure she wears a one-piece for you," Mac snickered.

"Asshole," Lich said.

"Pervert," Mac retorted.

Hisle's house lay a mile or so north of town on a high bluff overlooking the river. Normally you wouldn't think there was a house on the bluff, as it was set back from the road behind a ten-foot-high wall of thick bushes and a line of mature trees. Beyond that natural barrier, well-tended flower beds dotted an expansive and finely manicured three-acre lawn that gradually sloped down from the road toward the river. The house itself was a wide, prairie-style home that looked like Southfork from *Dallas*. However, tonight the house, or at least its location, was easy to spot, given the collection of police cars and media trucks with lights flashing, parked at the gated entrance to the winding driveway.

Mac pulled up and waited for the sheriff's deputies to clear the cars blocking the driveway. Lich had his window down, and they could all hear Heather Foxx from Channel 12 starting her report fifteen feet to the right.

"Thanks John. Right now, we're in front of the Stillwater home of prominent attorney Lyman Hisle. At this point, we don't know if Mr. Hisle has been contacted by the kidnappers. What we do know is that his daughter Shannon was abducted outside Cel's Café on Selby and Western avenues in St. Paul. It is believed there were three men involved, who appear to have abducted her behind the restaurant and left the area in a white van."

There was a pause in Heather's report, although she didn't take her eye off the camera.

"That's a good question, Sheila. What we do know is that the van may have been dropped behind an industrial park in River Falls. Apparently, the kidnappers dropped it there and transferred Shannon to another vehicle. However, before the van was found by the police, it was burned, apparently through the use of an explosive device."

A uniform cop moved one of the cars blocking the driveway, and Mac pulled through while Heather finished her report, her voice trailing away behind them.

"Man is she aptly named," Lich said, his mind ending up where it normally did. Heather Foxx was a leggy brunette with inviting green eyes, a perfect little ski-slope nose, and a dynamite smile. One come-hither look from her and men melted. She'd been covering crime in town for two years and had developed many a good source, which she'd obviously already plumbed for information.

"Man, what I wouldn't give to throw a fuck into her," Dick said, his eyes shut, dreaming of the lovely Heather. Riles laughed from the back.

"Forget it, Dicky-boy. Your only hope is if your partner made a move on her and then gave you the post-game recap."

"Jesus Christ, not this again?" Mac said, shooting Riles a disgusted look.

"Whatever," Riles replied with a big grin, "I saw her try to get in your pants that night. What I don't understand is why you didn't let her."

Heather had been at the pub a few months ago with a group of friends. Mac was there after work with Riley, Lich, and Rock, but not Sally, and the two groups eventually found themselves together. Heather was well served and, at the end of the night, horny. As they were getting ready to walk out of the pub, she made a less-than-subtle pass that Mac was forced to decline in front of the Boys. Of course, with these guys around to see it, he never heard the end of it.

"Hey Mac," Rock said, "There are worse things to live down than having Heather Foxx want to screw your brains out."

"This is true," Mac replied with an evil grin. "It's one problem I have that you all never will."

"Fucker," Lich replied.

"Prick" and "Smartass" were added by Riles and Rock, respectively, as Mac parked the Explorer at the edge of the circular drive. Theirs was the last in a long line of cars, both police and private. Inside the front door, they found Chief Flanagan and Captain Peters awaiting their arrival. The group quickly ducked into a small, well-appointed study.

Charlie Flanagan had been chief of the St. Paul Police Department for nine years. The chief was an angular man with a shock of bright white hair that had, at one time, been an equally bright red. He was a thirty-four-year veteran of the force who worked his way up from uniform cop to chief the old-school way.

While usually a man of good cheer, tonight the chief was pensive and foul-mouthed. The daughter of one of his best friends had been abducted, and in his city, no less. Not only that, but the mayor, Hizzoner

Ted Olson, and the FBI's local agent in charge, Ed Duffy, were standing just outside their room, monitoring the chief's every move. Neither of them had much love for the chief, nor he for them.

"Where are we at?" the chief demanded.

"We've got what apparently the media's got," Riles said.

"Which is?"

"Zip," Riles started, opening his notebook. "She was taken in the parking lot behind the café. She was thrown into a white van, which we found in River Falls. The kidnappers burned it there. Doesn't look like there was much left behind. We have some crime scene techs going out there. Who knows, they might turn something up."

The chief sighed and ran his hand through his thinning hair. Peters asked the obvious.

"So you don't think you'll get anything?"

"Doubtful," Mac replied. "The River Falls cops didn't know they were dealing with a crime scene right away. Police and fire trampled all over the place and hosed up what evidence there might have been."

"Maybe the FBI can help," Peters replied.

"They're in for sure then?" Rock asked.

"Yup," the chief said. "As you saw, Ed Duffy is in the house."

"Bet that makes you happy," Lich said with a wry smile.

"Well, no, it doesn't. But let's put that all aside tonight shall we," the chief replied. For whatever reason, the two men did not get along with one another. Duffy replaced an old friend of the chief's whose career was unceremoniously brought to a premature end due to some management discrepancies. Duffy came in, aired the management issues, made changes, and did a little more end zone dancing about his predecessor's departure than the chief thought appropriate. On top of that, Duffy was good friends with Mayor Olson. Chief Flanagan and Olson were also on the outs, the mayor tiring of the city's long-serving police chief.

"I'm more worried about Shannon Hisle than fighting a turf war," the chief continued. "The FBI can help."

"Lyman's political friends have been on the horn," Peters added. "And apparently one of the Bureau's best on kidnapping is in town this week to work with local agents. He's coming in on this."

"Who's the guy?" Mac asked.

"A fellow named Burton. John Burton," Peters replied.

"*That guy*!" Riley replied, surprised. "I've heard of *him*."

"Is he the guy who brought that judge's daughter home? The one who was kidnapped by the white supremacists in Montana last summer?" Mac asked.

"He is," Peters replied.

"I remember that," Rock added. "That's *this guy*? He won't need us much."

"He is *that* guy," the chief replied. "But don't worry, you boys are working this. That's the way I want it. That's the way Lyman wants it, and that's the way the FBI will deal with it."

"I saw the mayor hanging around out there," Mac noted. "The four of us aren't exactly his favorites." That all stemmed from the PTA case last winter, not to mention a recent investigation into a cop killing. Rock and Mac, with Riley and Lich in tow, finished a controversial chase and shootout with an African-American suspect in the old Rondo neighborhood. There were complaints of excessive force and the shootout was in the news for weeks. The chief was unyielding in his support of his men, which led to political discomfort for the mayor. And if there was anything the mayor hated, it was political discomfort.

"Hizzoner pushed hard for the FBI's involvement," Peters said. Everyone groaned.

"Nice he has confidence in his department," Mac commented.

"It is what it is," the chief said. "But listen, I want to get Shannon back, so we eighty-six the political bullshit. Do you boys read me on that?"

Everyone nodded.

"How's Lyman doing?" Mac asked.

"About as well as could be expected," the chief answered. "I can't possibly imagine what he's going through."

"He wanted to see you guys when you got here." Peters opened the door. "He's back in his library." Everyone fell in behind Peters, walking down the back hallway and into the library, where they found Lyman sitting at his desk. He was talking with Detective Frank Franklin, better known as Double Frank, as well as a few other dark-suited men that they all recognized from the local FBI field office.

Mac made eye contact with Lyman, who broke away from the group and walked over. Mac gave him a hug.

"Michael, I'm glad you are here," he said. "I just can't believe this is happening."

"I know Lyman, I know," Mac answered quietly. "We'll get her back."

Lyman gripped Mac's shoulders and looked at Lich, then to Riles and Rock as well.

"Gentlemen, it's good to have you working on this."

"We'll do everything we can Lyman, you know that," Riles replied. Everyone else nodded.

"I know you men will; I know you will. Now, tell me where you're at and don't bullshit me. I need to know."

Riles gave Lyman the rundown of what they had and then asked, "And I assume we haven't heard from the kidnappers yet?"

"No," Double Frank replied. "We'll be ready when they call."

Just then there was a commotion in the hallway and a rangy man with a shaved head strode into the room with Ed Duffy in tow. Duffy made the introduction, "Chief, Mr. Hisle, this is Special Agent John Burton."

"Burton," the chief replied, taking his hand. Then Flanagan paused and gave the FBI man a long look. "You look familiar for some reason."

"I worked out of the Minneapolis office way back in the early nineties, Chief," Burton replied. "Our paths crossed on occasion. I wondered if you would remember."

"Good to have you," Flanagan replied. "This is the girl's father, and a friend of mine, Lyman Hisle."

Hisle took Burton's hand. "Word is you're pretty good at this sort of thing," Lyman said.

"I've had some success, Sir. We're going to do everything we can to get your daughter back."

"Well, let me tell you one thing that will help you," the chief said. "You keep my boys over here in the loop," Flanagan waved toward Mac and the others. "They're damn good."

"Wouldn't have it any other way," Burton replied blandly, shaking hands and getting names. When he got to Mac, he held his hand an extra moment, "*McRyan?* Are you a relation of Simon McRyan?" Burton inquired with an unmistakable tone of respect.

"He was my father."

Burton held the handshake and pointed, "He was a hell of a cop son, a hell of a cop. You worked that PTA case with the CIA guys, right?"

"With these three," Mac answered, gesturing to Riley, Rock, and Lich. Burton turned to the chief.

"Damn right I want to work with these guys." There was noticeable approval in the FBI man's voice. Then he looked to Riley, the senior officer.

"What do we know?" Riley gave the run down for what seemed like the tenth time. It didn't sound any better no matter how many times he told it, Mac thought.

"Well, probably not a nut then," Burton said.

"No," Mac replied, "it was a well-orchestrated attack. These guys knew *exactly* what they were doing."

It was dark now, approaching 10:00 PM, but the temperature was still in the mid-seventies. If it weren't for the fact he had just completed a kidnapping, it would have been a lovely night to be out for a drive, Smith thought. Apparently, many Minnesotans agreed. During the summer, Minnesota cabin owners tended to stay up north at their lake places as long as possible before trekking home for another week grinding away at their jobs. As a consequence, even at this late hour, an endless stream of headlights glowed for miles in the distance, coming in the opposite direction on Interstate 94. The mass of traffic heading back into the Twin Cities would be of assistance to him soon enough.

Smith approached the Clearwater exit, which was forty-five miles from the Twin Cities and eleven miles southeast of St. Cloud. He took the exit ramp up, turned right, and drove a quarter mile before turning right into the parking lot of an abandoned fast-food restaurant. The lot was full of weeds, plastic soda bottles, and discarded fast-food bags. He pulled his car up to the single pay phone on the side of the building, the back of the car facing the road.

He stepped out of the car with a duffel bag. At the phone, he reached into the bag and pulled out a plastic bag with ten dollars' worth of quarters, a Dictaphone, and a portable voice changer. He attached the acoustic coupler to the handset and adjusted the selector switch for a low voice. He then reached with his gloved hand for the pay phone and put in enough quarters to cover his call back to the Twin Cities. He dialed the number and put the receiver to his head with his left hand and held the Dictaphone in his right hand.

"Here we go," Burton said, jumping into action as the phone rang. Waving Lyman over, he put an arm around his shoulder, directing him. "Try to keep him on as long as you can," Burton said to Lyman. "Keep him talking and maybe we get a fix on his position. Keep him going a little longer and maybe we can get somebody there. Get your daughter back! That's your job, your mission here. Get her back. Keep him talking."

On the third ring, Lyman picked up, "Lyman Hisle."

The voice came over the intercom, obviously disguised.

"We have your daughter."

"How do I know that? How do I know she's alive?"

There was a muffled sound followed by a click and then the slow, quivering voice that made Lyman cringe.

"Daddy. I am okay. I have not been hurt. Please do as these men say, and I won't be harmed. I love you...."

The tape cut off. There was another muffled sound, and a few seconds later the voice was back. "Satisfied?"

No, I want to speak with her," Lyman answered.

"This is all for now," the voice answered.

"Wait," Lyman pleaded, "I need to tell you something. Shannon is a diabetic."

"Sorry, I've got to go."

"Are you hearing me?" Lyman implored, stringing it out as best he could. "She's a Type I diabetic. She requires daily injections of insulin. If she doesn't get it, she can get very, very sick. She could go into a coma without it; she could die. What good is she to you if she's dead? You have to help her with that."

"Then you better do as we say," the kidnapper replied.

"I won't do that until I speak with her, so I can hear her voice, so I know that she's okay."

"We'll be in touch."

"Wait, wait.... Her insulin! She needs her insulin!" Lyman yelped, but the line was already dead. He looked helplessly to Burton as he slowly set the receiver back into the cradle. The chief went to his friend, putting an arm around him.

Burton looked to the agent working a laptop.

"Anything?"

The agent held his hand up while watching the screen.

"It's coming ... wait.... Bingo! A landline ... payphone, in ... Clearwater."

"Where's that?" Burton asked.

"An hour northwest, up Interstate 94, toward St. Cloud," the chief said, turning back to the group. "I take that exit going north to my cabin."

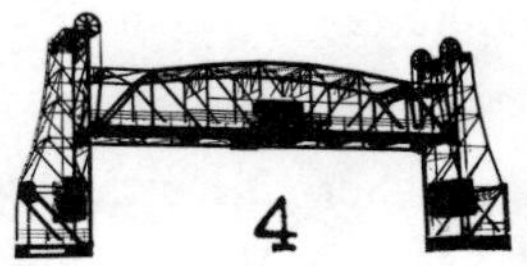

4

"He's got options from here."

The Explorer sped north, engine roaring, the siren and lights moving traffic out of the left lane as the needle on the speedometer passed one hundred. Mac worked the wheel, with Lich scanning a Minnesota map, checking out Clearwater. Riley and Rock were trailing in an unmarked sedan, alternately on the phone with Clearwater Police, the State Patrol, Mac and Lich, as well as Burton and Peters.

Five miles from the exit, Mac said, "You know what was weird about the call?"

"What?" Lich asked.

"They didn't ask for the ransom," Mac replied. "If this is about ransom, why not ask for it right then?"

"They'll call back, I'm sure," Lich replied. "Maybe he figures if he stays on the line too long he'll get pinched."

"Maybe. Maybe. But something doesn't seem right."

"There's nothing right about any of this."

Mac hit the exit ramp, hammered the brakes, and turned hard right. Two state patrol cruisers, a Clearwater squad car, and a Sherburne County Suburban, lights flashing, clustered at a pay phone in the parking lot for an abandoned fast-food-joint. Lich sighed.

"That's what I feared."

"What's that?" Mac asked.

"He's got options from here."

"Options?"

Lich pointed at the map, where Interstate 94 and State Highway 10 bracketed their position. Mac understood immediately.

"He could make the call and go north on County 24 for four miles, which gets him to State Highway 10, or he could go left and back over to 94," Lich said.

"Or just stay south on 24, which will take you toward Annandale and Maple Lake twenty miles to the south," Mac added. "Shit."

"And if he jumps onto 94 heading back to the cities, with the traffic coming home from up north, he just blends in with everyone else," Lich said glumly as he climbed out. Riles and Rock were out of their car, and Riles immediately started in.

"Shit, he could go any number of ways...."

"...out of here," Mac finished.

"We know," Lich said with disgust. "He has options."

The area around the phone had been taped off by the locals. Forensics personnel from the Bureau of Criminal Apprehension (BCA) would arrive shortly and begin processing the scene. The Clearwater police chief, a pot belly man named Billy Miller, introduced himself and then ran it down.

"No surveillance cameras, this old burger stand's been closed for over a year now."

"How about at the convenience store across the road, Chief? Is there any surveillance over there?" Lich asked.

"A trooper went over and asked and looked at their surveillance system. But...."

"You can't see anything across the road and into this parking lot," Mac said, shaking his head.

"Correct," Miller replied.

"Are we checking with all these businesses, gas stations, and restaurants around here?" Riley asked.

"My two guys are on it," Miller answered, "along with a couple of troopers. They've been at it for a half hour, but as far as I know, they haven't come up with anything."

They turned and watched as the BCA folks arrived and began walking around with flashlights, fingerprinting the telephone, bagging everything in sight. The effort was being made.

"Maybe the BCA will turn up something," Rock said unconvincingly.

Miller shook his head, downcast as the rest of them.

"I don't suspect much will be found, and when he rolls out of here...."

"We know," Rock replied, waving to County Road 24. "He's got options."

11:42 PM

Smith dropped the car at the Park & Fly, which was emptier now, and jumped back into the van. Inside the van, he revved the engine and turned the radio to the talk station. The kidnapping of Shannon Hisle was big news, and the talking heads were focused on it. Of course, so were the nuts, all of whom were frothing at the mouth, ranting for all to hear.

"I agree, it was a brazen act in broad daylight," the host responded to a caller.

"Well, with something like that, it's just further evidence that people should be carrying a gun to defend themselves. If this girl had a gun, she could have defended herself."

"Well, as all you listeners know I'm an ardent supporter of the Second Amendment, conceal and carry," the host responded, "but I think that response is perhaps an overreaction...."

Smith smiled at this as he turned left onto Shepard Road, motoring east back to the safe house. A gun wouldn't have mattered for Hisle. Even if she did have one, Dean was on her so fast she never could have used it. But what really made him smile was the environment such coverage created—of people behaving hysterically, stupidly, carrying guns, calling the police to report every little thing, distracting them from the task at hand. It was perfect.

And then he smiled again.

If people were hysterical now, just wait until his next plan went into effect.

5

"Only the paranoid survive."

It was after midnight when Mac pulled back into Lyman's driveway. The crowd had thinned some, but there were plenty of folks hanging around, family, friends, and media, all hoping for a break.

The group made its way back to Lyman's office and found him, the chief, Burton, Duffy, Peters, and the mayor quietly talking. For now, it appeared that the chief, the mayor, and Duffy were all tolerating one another. The chief had to be chafing. They had learned on the way back that the mayor wanted the FBI to take a prominent role and had essentially forced it on the chief. Mac imagined that, when they got in private with no mayor, no Duffy, and no Burton around, the chief would swear a blue streak.

"Nothing, I assume?" the chief said.

"We crapped out," Riles replied.

"No surveillance cameras?" Burton asked.

Everyone just shook their heads.

"Probably wouldn't have mattered," the chief said. "I know the place. It's right on County 24 up there and when he pulls out of the parking lot...."

"He's got options," they all replied in unison.

"Plus, if the abduction is any indication, even if there was surveillance or we got a plate, I'll bet you it was stolen," Mac said. "These guys have thought this through. They knew exactly what they were doing and were gone like that." He snapped his fingers, a little admiration in his voice.

The group hashed over the abduction, River Falls and Clearwater all over again, but a sense of helplessness, at least for the time being, pervaded the room. If there were to be any progress, it would come from Lyman's files, some tip, or a mistake by the kidnappers. Finally, the chief suggested Lyman try to get some rest.

"One thing I want to do first," Lyman said as he reached inside a duffel bag. "I prepared a couple of these black bags while you were gone." He handed one to Mac and one to Riley. "The bag contains a vial of Glucagon, a needle, and a syringe. You would administer this if her sugar is too low."

"Wouldn't she need insulin?" Mac asked.

"She may and I've included a vial of that as well. I've also included a spare glucose meter. If you find her, depending upon when and the last time she took insulin and depending upon what her blood sugar is, she may need either glucagon or insulin. Are you familiar with this Mac?"

"I used one once," Mac said.

"Me, too," Riles added.

"Good. But as refresher for you guys, here is what you do." Hisle showed the group the contents and instructed them in administering the proper dosage.

Mac asked the hard question.

"How long can she go without insulin?"

"It's hard to say," Hisle answered. "She has had some episodes in the past where she went without insulin for just a few days and got very sick. So it depends upon when she last took insulin and I suppose whether she has any with her and they let her take it. If she hasn't been diligent and she doesn't have any with her, she could have issues within a few days. So it just depends on when she last had insulin. Did you find her purse at Cel's?"

"No," Mac answered, "just her cell phone and keys."

"Well, if they have her purse, hopefully she'll have an extra dose or two with her. She should. I've always told her she needs to do that, but she's a college kid. If she has insulin with her and they allow her to take it, she shouldn't have a problem, at least not for a few days. If she doesn't have insulin with her, she doesn't get the proper food, then if this goes for a while, it could be an issue, a big issue."

"What do you mean by a big issue?" Mac pressed.

"If she goes too long without insulin, she can become disoriented and then eventually pass out. If it goes beyond that, she could end up in a coma. That almost happened once a few years ago."

"So if we find her, we give her some insulin or glucagon and that should help get her blood sugar back in line."

"At least until she gets medical attention. She knows what to do if she has insulin and food available."

"Then let's hope they're taking care of her," Burton said. "I expect they will. If there is a demand for ransom, which is what we're hoping for here, they'll take care of her."

"If anything comes up, anything at all, we'll let you know," the chief said, "but for now, my friend, you need to try to get some sleep." The chief added as he walked Lyman out of the library and put him in the custody of his sister, who would take him across the house to his room. Hisle was spent and exhausted. He needed to rest, although sleep would likely prove elusive.

Once sure that Lyman was gone, Lich cleared his throat uncomfortably.

"Are we sure Lyman is in the clear?" Mac shot Lich a look, as did a few others, but he was undeterred.

"I'm sorry, but the question has to be asked."

"And it's been answered," the chief answered sternly. "Lyman's clear."

"Burton and I put him through the paces," Peters added.

"For the record," Lich replied, noting the looks from others, "I didn't think he had anything to do with it. But I thought a prudent investigator should ask the question."

Mac took his chance to change topics.

"So what do you think? Is this all about money?" he asked Burton. There was a hint of doubt in his voice.

"That's certainly a part of it," Burton replied, and added confidently, "And if it is, we'll have a good shot at catching them."

"Because of the drop?" Lich asked.

"Exactly," Burton replied, "Hell, I always pray it's about the money. If it's about the money, the person kidnapped stands a better chance of making it. The other thing is that if it is about the money, that gives us a good chance of catching them because they have to pick up the money. That's when we get 'em."

"What are the odds on the drop?" Peters asked.

"Overall, really good," Burton answered confidently. "Like I said, they have to expose themselves to get the ransom, that's when we can catch them."

"What about doing the money electronically?" Lich asked.

"Nah," Mac answered before Burton could answer, "I'd think it would be easier for the FBI to track that. Especially as good as the government has gotten on that with the war on terror."

"You're mostly correct about that," Burton answered. "Since 9/11, I haven't had anyone try it on me that way, at least on a domestic kidnapping. If you have someone, however, who's really *really* good at the electronic transfer process, and moves it to countries that have been less than helpful, then it could be an issue, although in the end we'd still probably be able to track it down."

"We're talking money here, aren't we being just a little presumptuous. I mean they didn't demand the ransom when they called," Mac stated and then he turned to Burton. "Does that strike you as odd?"

Burton was nonplussed. "A little. But I'm pretty confident they'll get to it. Given how they've operated thus far, I sense were only part way into whatever it is they have planned."

"You're thinking this is only about money though?" Riley pressed.

"Not necessarily," Burton answered. "I suspect there is a personal element to this as well. These guys aren't crazy. What they did was well planned, well thought out. They picked Shannon Hisle for a reason, and that reason may well have something to do with her, or...."

"Or more likely her father," Mac finished. "Lyman has represented a lot of high-profile people and taken on a lot of high-profile cases. Somebody certainly could have it in for him."

"So I've been told," Burton said. "So we need to be looking at his associates, clients, everyone he's come into contact with over the years."

"Man that's a lot of people," Lich said, running a hand over his bald head. "That could be hundreds of people."

"More likely thousands, given clients, friends, political contacts, business contacts," Riles tallied.

"Speaking of clients, that will be the deepest pool we'll fish from, have we started that process?" Burton inquired.

"I've started the process of looking through his client files," Peters said. "I'm not getting too much flack from his law firm. We'll have files to look at first thing in the morning. They're trucking them over to our place."

"Criminal and civil?" Mac asked.

"We should probably focus on his criminal clientele," the chief said.

"What about his civil cases?" Mac asked. "Lyman's done a lot of work there. I don't want to forget those."

"We can and should look at those as well," Burton answered, looking to Peters for confirmation.

Peters nodded.

"Good," Burton replied. "However, I think the chief is right. The criminal files are the better bet, at least to start with."

"Even looking at just the criminal files, it's going to be a long list," Peters pointed out. "And if we find someone in these files worth looking at, it'll be a bear to track them down."

"Indeed," Duffy said. Burton snorted his disagreement.

"Difficult? Yes. But we have all of the FBI's resources at our disposal," he said. He turned to Peters, adding, "What's mine is yours. We'll hook you up with everything we've got, including manpower. Just let me know what you need, and we'll make it happen."

"I appreciate it," Peters said, taking out his cell phone and calling downtown.

"No problem," Burton replied. "Look, technology is our strength. We can find patterns, tap phones, conduct electronic surveillance, run censuses, and create spreadsheets like nobody's business." Nodding to Mac and the boys, he smiled. "You guys are good street cops, not always the Bureau's strong suit. I need to have you guys looking over the data we get, checking the possibilities we find, talking to your folks on the street. A cop is only as good as his informants, and around here, you guys are the ones who have them. Let's share and stay in touch."

"We can do that," Riles agreed.

"Good," Burton answered, rubbing his hands together, on a roll now. "I'm going to have my team in first thing tomorrow, three men and two women. Everything we collect, no matter from where, we feed it to the team and see what we come up with. It's a process that's worked well for us, helped us get people back. Add that to your resources and we have a shot at bringing the girl home in one piece."

"Sounds good," Peters replied. "Where do you want to work out of, your local office?"

"You can run out of your place," Duffy added, "We'll run out of our...."

Burton cut Duffy off, "No. No. No. Ed. We'll run everything from the police department headquarters. If we're split, we're not sharing information and we get dumbass turf wars, people trying to one-up each other. Us Fed types are classic for that. I don't care who cracks this thing. I know that doesn't necessarily sound right to all of you, but I really don't care. So let's work it together; feed your information to my team on the technical side, and you can access anything you need. You feed us what you're hearing on the street, and we'll crack this thing. And getting back to business, when is it again we'll have Hisle's files to work through?"

"First thing in the morning," Peters answered.

"So until it's ready, you boys get some sleep," the chief ordered.

Mac quietly opened the door to the bedroom and went to his side of the bed. He lightly laid his wallet, badge, and watch on the nightstand and looked down at Sally lying under the bed sheet, wearing a red teddy, looking beautiful.

He had met her eight months earlier. Sally Kennedy was the prosecutor on the case where he made his name. Mac was immediately attracted to her long red hair, curvaceous body, perfect bright smile, and passion for everything. Not to mention, she was smart, tough as nails, and a damn fine prosecutor.

Both were recently divorced when they met, and both looking to get back into the dating game. But they knew it right away—they were right for one another. The relationship quickly moved beyond dating, and they were now practically living together. Well, there was no practically about it—there were half-emptied boxes all over the house and far too much furniture. Some of it would have to go into storage—the two of them just hadn't figured out which pieces yet. His mother, a devout Catholic, of course protested the living arrangement prior to his moving in.

"That's living in sin," she had lectured.

"I'm already divorced mom. What could I possibly have to lose in God's eyes at this point?"

"Well at least make her an honest woman then," his mother said.

"Mom, don't *even* go there," Mac had replied. He and Sally hadn't even uttered the word. It was as if there was an unspoken agreement to not discuss marriage. Their divorces left them both scarred and fearful of the "m" word, but not commitment. They loved each other, said so to each other often, and were very happy together. For now, that was enough for both of them.

Sally woke as he put his keys down.

"Tell me. Is it as bad as it seems on the news?"

"Right now, yes," Mac answered and then brought her up to date. "I don't know," he finished. "Something about this is off."

"They didn't make the ransom demand, perhaps?"

"That's exactly it, babe. It's got me wondering," Mac replied, nodding. "Nobody else seems terribly bothered by that, but I thought it was odd. I figured the kidnappers would want to move quickly on that before we had a chance to start digging. Instead they're giving us a chance to start the hunt."

"But the kidnappers said they want money."

"They didn't say that specifically. It sounds like they do, their actions suggest they do, everyone assumes that's the case, but there was not a specific demand made. But if that's what they're after, not asking for it right away is strange in my mind."

"Maybe they're after Shannon," Sally offered. "It could be they want her."

Mac shook his head. "Naw. If that's what they wanted, why call? Just to be sadistic? I don't think so. I don't think harming Shannon for the sake of harming her is part of the game here."

"So they're not crazy."

"Other than kidnapping a woman in broad daylight in the middle of a big city—no."

"It sounds like they've planned it well so far," Sally noted.

"That's for sure. The abduction was ballsy, but it was done with precision and planning."

"They sound like they're good," Sally replied. "And from what you're telling me, the pay phone, on that road, left him...."

"...with options," Mac finished, frustration seeping into his voice. "Damn it. To me, abductions are the worst. You know something bad is coming and you're almost powerless to stop it, no matter how hard you try." He undid his shorts. "I'm going to take a quick shower," he grumbled.

Mac went into the bathroom and started the shower, letting the water heat up. The house was over seventy years old and had a bathroom that, while remodeled, retained its original charm and fixtures. The shower poured water into a long and wide cast-iron bathtub.

Climbing inside the shower, he tilted his head up and let the warm water wash over his head while he had both arms up against the wall of the shower. He needed to unwind. For five minutes he let the shower loosen his muscles, letting his mind clear. Then the shower curtain slid open and Sally stepped into the shower behind him. He turned to say something, but she put her fingers to his mouth and then kissed him lightly.

"I know you. You're all wound up." She reached for the soap. "I'm going to help you relax. Otherwise you're no good to Lyman, and he needs you."

Mac didn't fight it and just let the water run down his body while Sally soaped his back and lightly rubbed his muscles, letting her breasts brush lightly against his back. After a few minutes of washing and rubbing, she spoke.

"What about the FBI? They're in?"

"Yes," Mac replied, not moving. "We're lucky ... I *guess*. Their best kidnapping guy—this guy named John Burton—was coming to town to do some training, so now he's working it."

Sally detected his uncertain tone.

"What's the problem with the FBI guy?" she asked, washing around his right hip.

"I don't know, he was awfully...."

"What?"

"Helpful. Seemed like a good guy."

"And that's bad?" Sally asked, lightly reaching around him, washing lightly down his lower stomach, moving ever lower.

"No, except..." Mac hesitated, Sally's hand having gone very low. He was about to turn to her when she lightly pushed him back into place.

"Juuuust relaaaaax," she murmured, moving the soap to her left hand, "and tell me about the FBI guy."

Mac did as he was told and let her continue washing and relaxing him.

"He said all the right things. 'We're here to help, we'll coordinate with you, access to everything they have, anything you need, we're going to get Hisle's girl back,' so on and so forth."

"Again, that's bad?" Sally replied, coming around in front of him.

Mac smiled—a small wan one.

"The FBI can often be territorial and condescending. They consider the local cops to be good for traffic control, writing parking tickets, breaking up domestics—and maybe, just maybe, a run-of-the-mill homicide. We usually don't have college or law degrees, nor have we gone through the mystical Quantico. We're not the almighty F-B-fuckin'-I."

"You're paranoid, you know that?"

"Only the paranoid survive."

Sally laughed and then continued.

"I've heard that about the FBI before, but they want to make the case just like you do. They want to get Shannon back—maybe not at the emotional level that you do, but they want to get her back just the same."

"You're probably right," he said, leaning down and kissing her on the lips. She returned the kiss, slowly putting her arms up around his neck and pulling him to her. After kissing him deeply, Sally pulled away and looked Mac in the eye as she slowly guided him down onto the bottom of the tub and then followed, straddling his body while kissing him deeply, probing with her soft, moist tongue. Mac pulled his mouth away.

"Is this what you meant by relaxing me?" he whispered.

"Uh huh," Sally replied in a hushed moan. She rose up and let Mac softly suckle on her breasts while she eased him in, the water of the shower cascading down on their bodies. Sally slowly increased her pace, breathing faster and arching her back, her breasts flattening. Mac responded to her need, pulling her hips closer and pushing his thighs up so that her back rested against them. He moved his hips faster and in rhythm with her, causing her moans to become louder. He felt the wet ends of her hair brush against his legs as he brought her close to climax. And then, as she so often did when they made love, she brought her mouth back to his, breathing heavily and moaning lightly as she came, her body trembling, causing him to respond in kind, as he exhaled a breath into her mouth, his lips brushing against hers.

As the water continued to flow down, the two lay in a silent embrace, looking in each other's eyes, quietly catching their breath. After a minute, Sally sat up, and he looked into her deep green eyes.

"I love you, you know that?" he murmured.

"Yeah, I do," she replied softly, leaning back down, and gently kissing him on the lips. "The feeling is quite mutual."

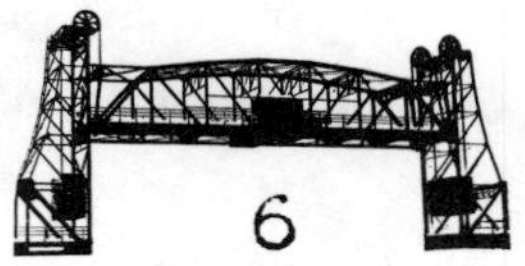

6

"What are we looking for?"

MONDAY, JULY 2ND

7:54 AM

Mac, Lich, Riley, and Rock were joined by a half dozen other detectives milling around in a conference room, mixing coffee, and talking the case. Burton and his crew, along with Duffy, joined them with a quick exchange of pleasantries and introductions.

The map of the area around the café was tacked to the left side of a bulletin board. Pictures of the scene and a sketch of the woman suspected of signaling the kidnappers were pinned up on the right. The St. Paul cops and FBI agents discussed the situation that was less than sixteen hours old. A couple of hours of sleep and contemplation provided no answers, only more questions.

Peters walked in and called everyone together.

"I've got two things," he announced through a yawn. "First, this is a list compiled by Hisle of former clients that he thinks might have the ability to pull this off."

"What's the second thing?" Rock asked.

Peters turned and into the room came men with boxes on dollies.

"We've got boxes and boxes of Hisle's old criminal files coming, stuff from his firm and an off-site storage place. We need to start digging through it all."

"What are we looking for?" someone asked.

"You're the cops, you tell me," Peters replied edgily. He was sleep deprived, all of them were. He stopped, took a deep breath, and said, "Sorry, it's been a long night. What you're looking for, it's a little bit of you-know-it-when-you-see-it. These guys yesterday set up and executed a complicated plan. In looking through the client files, does anyone strike you as having the ability to develop and execute such a plan? It wouldn't necessarily have to be a kidnapping. Lyman's represented jewel thieves, break-in artists, confidence guys, and the leaders of some crews who specialized in high-end crimes. Not to mention all the white-collar criminals he's represented. So, if you run across anyone who has pulled off or was accused of pulling off an elaborate, well-planned crime, let's take a look at them.

"It also could be someone who wasn't a client," someone else noted.

"That's right," Peters said. "This is just one avenue to pursue. We're looking at other angles as well. We're talking to Hisle's family, her roommates, her friends to see if anyone unusual was hanging around, any strange phone calls, angry ex-boyfriends, etc."

"Anything from the café or over in River Falls?" someone asked.

"Not yet," was Peters' response. "BCA and FBI are going through it all, but our sense is, don't hold your breath."

"How about from the Clearwater phone?"

"Ditto," Peters replied.

"These guys know what they're doing and probably have a pretty good idea of what we'll be doing," Mac added. "So we're not just looking for someone who would have something against Lyman. We're looking for someone who has something against Lyman and the mental acuity to pull it off without a trace."

"Mental acuity?" Lich whispered mockingly. "What the fuck's mental acuity?"

"Something you don't have, knuckle-dragger," Mac snickered back, though Lich possessed plenty of it.

"One other thing," Captain Peters added, pointing to four other people who entered the room. "These are lawyers from Hisle's office. They're in a..." the captain struggled for the right words. "... a difficult spot. There are some attorney-client issues related to our reviewing the files. These lawyers will help with that."

"How will they help?" Lich asked.

"By helping us work through the files. They have clearance from the Minnesota Lawyers Professional Responsibility Board for us to access the files. But at the same time, we don't know if anyone in these files is even involved with this. So there needs to be some sensitivity to that."

"So what's going to happen?" Double Frank asked. "They going to read it first and tell us if something's relevant? What we think matters and what they think matters could be entirely different."

Summer Plantagenate, one of Hisle's lawyers, spoke up.

"We're not going to pre-screen for you. You can look at everything. We're more concerned with where the information goes after you review it, especially for people you conclude are not involved. My firm needs to protect those folks, so that's where we could have issues. But you can access everything and we'll go from there."

That answer satisfied everyone. Coats were jettisoned, more coffee was brewed and poured—and boxes were opened. Mac sidled up to Summer, who he'd known since law school, they're time at William Mitchell overlapping. She had recently been named a partner at Lyman's firm and was viewed by many as his protégé. Always immaculately dressed, Summer was a cool customer, an attractive woman with icy blonde hair and a cool demeanor to match. That demeanor caused some to call her "Winter." But at the moment, it wasn't hard to see the anguish on her face. Not only was Lyman like a father to her, she also knew Shannon Hisle well.

"So you guys get to work the other side of a case, huh?" Mac asked.

"Yes, we have to," was her short reply. The attorneys were there to help, but also ethically bound to protect their clients' interests. Letting the police rifle through clients' files created an ethical quandary for any attorney.

"So what do we have here?"

"All of Lyman's criminal files, both from the office and from offsite storage," Summer replied.

"How about his civil stuff?" Mac asked, taking a sip of his coffee. Burton walked up as Summer answered.

"It'll be here soon," Summer answered. "Agent Burton and the chief think this is coming from the criminal side, and I tend to agree with them, but the civil files are coming just the same. We'll get them over here by early afternoon."

Mac nodded, recalling the conversation from the night before, and began to survey the mass of files, running a hand through his hair.

"You've worked for him for awhile. "He asked, "does anyone come to mind that would have the ability to pull this off?"

"I've been wracking my brain on this, but no," she replied, "But some of these files go back long before my time, so there are names I'm not familiar with. I mean, there are files that have old dittos with the yellow and pink carbons."

Mac and Lich flipped the top off a box and started working a file. The folders had notes, photos, statements, news clippings, and listings of evidence. For the next four hours, the group worked through the file folders, reading through cases and names, some of which were familiar to the cops in the room. Detectives made frequent comments on the file notes and the lawyer's written evaluations of the detectives involved in the case. A few inspired snide comments directed at the attorneys in the room.

Possible suspects went into a pile so that current whereabouts could be determined. Detectives, vice cops, uniforms in plain clothes, and local FBI were already out on the streets, interviewing potentials. If something didn't seem right, the cops or agents were to bring the potentials in for further questioning. It was tedious work, reading through case notes, getting a feel for Lyman's clients, their families and witnesses in the case. Problem was, everyone was a potential suspect, whether a client, witness, or victim.

Mac was reading through a file when he ran across the name Bobby Jacobs. The name rang a bell.

"I remember this guy," he said to himself. Bobby Jacobs was the debonair leader of a clever crew that the chief, a detective back then, had busted after a jewelry store heist. It was suspected that Jacobs had been involved in many high-end robberies: a bank, an armored car, and even homes, but the chief had no evidence to tie Jacobs to any of the others. None, that was, until the chief busted a fence, who, in an effort to avoid a long prison stretch, spilled the beans about fencing for the Jacobs crew. Jacobs ended up with a much longer sentence, even though he'd been represented by Lyman. That might be motive.

"Riles?"

"Yeah."

"You remember Bobby Jacobs?"

"Hell yes," Riles said with a smile. "One of the best damn crews I ever saw. Best the chief ever saw. They were damn good"

"He had fourteen years in the can; he'd be out by now wouldn't he?"

"Yeah he would, except...."

"Except what?"

"He's dead."

"No shit?"

"Yeah, he died of cancer a few years ago while still serving the tail end of his sentence out at Stillwater."

"How about the rest of that crew?"

Riles looked skeptical.

"Jacobs was the brains of that operation. The other guys made for a good crew, had good skills and all, but Bobby ran the show. But you know what?" Pat added, "Bobby Jacobs and people like him are what we should be looking at."

Mac kept at it. He was looking through a file covering a builder who defrauded a loan company when Peters burst into the room, white as a ghost, shock on his face.

"What is it?" Riles asked, seeing the fear in Peters's face. "Is it Shannon?"

Peters shook his head. "No. It's worse than that. There's been another abduction."

"Who?" Mac asked, getting out of his chair and grabbing his suit coat.

"Carrie," Peters responded. "Carrie Flanagan."

That stopped everyone in their tracks, the room falling deathly silent.

"Flanagan? Any relation to the chief?" Burton cautiously asked Peters, who nodded slowly, responding in almost a croak.

"It's his daughter."

7

"People see parts but not the whole thing."

The crime scene was Fairview Avenue between Summit and Grand avenues on St. Paul's far west side. Half a dozen squads were already on the scene, concentrated around the entrance to a parking lot of a natural foods store at the northeast corner of Fairview and Grand avenues. Another cluster of cops worked the entrance to an alley on the opposite side of the street. The abduction had taken place in the midst of a commercial area bounded by the natural foods store, a small bank across Fairview, and a couple of restaurants across Grand.

Patrol was holding everyone, asking questions, taking notes, talking on radios. Sirens signaled more units were on the way, flooding the area around the crime scene. The whole of Fairview Avenue between Summit and Grand was already taped off. Any van within the area was being pulled over. A helicopter hovered overhead. The media, on alert since yesterday for any breaking news, was already on the scene, filming the action. With the noon hour just minutes away, they'd be reporting live on the news shows. Dozens of onlookers were gathering around despite the weather, already ninety-two degrees with matching humidity.

Mac and the others climbed out of the Explorer, walked under the crime scene tape and took in the scene. Outside his truck only thirty seconds, Mac could feel the sweat beading on his brow, his sunglasses fighting to keep the glare of the day out. He checked his watch, 11:57 AM, the sun directly overhead now, the heat of the day rising.

A uniform cop named D.B. Skrypek ran up with a notepad.

"Whatcha ya got, Pecker?" Mac asked, using the patrolman's well-worn nickname.

Skrypek pointed to the entrance to the natural foods store. "A black van, panel type, came out of the grocery store parking lot and turned left. A guy—big guy—came out of the alley on the other side of the street behind the bank, scooped up Flanagan, and threw her into the van while it was on the move. The van then peeled off and turned right, headed west on Grand. Sounds like the same thing as yesterday."

Everyone nodded in agreement.

"Do we have a broadcast out on that? Black van, et cetera?" Mac asked, looking around the scene, using his hand to shade his eyes.

"Yes," Skrypek replied.

"How long between their taking her and us getting it out on the air? How long before we were pulling over vans?"

The young patrolman's shoulders slumped.

"The witnesses," he pointed toward a group of four people by his squad car, "seem to think it took us two or three minutes to get here. I asked a few questions and put it out. At best, it's five, more likely six or seven minutes before we got it out."

"How do we know it was Carrie? Are we sure?" Riles asked.

"A guy that Carrie works with at Lamonica's Pizza over there was standing out front and sweeping the sidewalk," Skrypek answered. "He heard a squealing of tires and looked up in time to see a brunette woman who looked like Flanagan get scooped up and thrown into the van. Her shift starts at 11:45 AM, after her class ends over at St. Thomas, just in time for the lunch rush."

Carrie Flanagan was a summer student at the University of St. Thomas, which sat six blocks to the west. The campus was a classic, with old stone buildings and ivy-covered walls set on the north side of Summit Avenue.

"The Lamonica's guy told me Flanagan has an apartment a block further east on Grand," Skrypek continued. She usually walks the five or six blocks over to the school and then walks back this way along Summit, then takes a right on Fairview and comes to the pizza joint. She hasn't showed for her shift, so we're pretty sure it was her."

Before they could discuss matters further, Burton pulled up with his entourage. Riles gave him the rundown.

"What's the connection between Hisle and Flanagan?" Burton asked.

"We don't know," Pat replied. "The chief and Lyman have been involved in a lot of cases over the years. Hell, we've all ... crossed ... paths with ... Lyman ... over the years. Shit. Are we all the targets?"

"Shit," Rock said, suddenly panicked. "My wife...."

"I gotta call Dot," Lich said, reaching for his cell phone.

"Let's get uniforms with spouses and kids," Burton ordered.

"Hold it! Hold it! HOLD IT!" Mac said, putting his hands up. "Calm the heck down and keep your heads, for cripes' sake. They're not taking everyone right this minute. We'll get uniforms on our people and move them. But right now, we need to stay on Carrie. Let's concentrate on these motherfuckers in the here and now."

Everyone gave Mac a peeved look at first, but then quickly calmed, realizing he was right.

"McRyan has a point," Burton said. "Though just to be safe, I'll put a man on arranging protection for your families."

Everyone nodded appreciation. Riley quickly got back to the case.

"Okay, so what do we know now?"

"We've got to work this," Mac said.

"Lyman's a criminal lawyer, and we got the chief," Lich said. "That's the connection, someone the chief busted and Lyman represented. The answer has to be in the criminal files."

"That's the most logical connection, and we're already fishing in that pond," Burton agreed. "That should narrow things down considerably, especially once we start matching up against cases Flanagan's worked. That's where all our resources will go now. We were going to start into civil cases as well but now we need to focus on those criminal files."

"We got to get the chief and Lyman together," Riles added. "Get them talking. If this is connected, which you'd think it has to be, then maybe there's a name that will ring a bell to them."

"We're going to see Flanagan," Burton said, turning back to his black Suburban. "You guys run the scene here. If these were our guys, the chief's apt to be getting a phone call and I want to be there."

"Burton," Riles said, grabbing his arm, walking along with him. "You better have Rockford and I go with you. The chief's going to need friendly faces."

"The other thing is, we need Hisle as well," Burton said.

"Agreed," Riles answered, reaching for his pocket. "I'll call Peters and ask him to bring Hisle in."

"Mac, you and Lich work this," Riles said, the urgency in his voice clear. "You *work* this fuckin' scene."

For the next hour, Mac and Lich worked the witnesses, standing where they stood, going over what they saw in detail, walking through it again and again. Mac went so far as to put the witnesses back in their spots, trying to get a picture for the abduction. He had them close their eyes and describe it, wringing every last detail out of their memories. It was frustrating work—the witnesses all saw parts of things, but nobody saw the *whole* thing.

Carrie's coworker saw a brunette, who he thought was Carrie, get picked up and thrown into the van. He took down the plate. The plate was reported stolen, but didn't match up with a van.

A female pedestrian, who had just crossed Summit seventy-five yards or so back from Flanagan, noted that the guy who threw the girl into the van was large and muscular. He wore a baseball cap, a black long-sleeve shirt, and blue jeans. That was the extent of her description.

An elderly woman had been putting groceries in her car. She noted the squealing of tires and saw the van pull out, slow down in front of the alley, and then pull away and turn right on Grand Avenue. She knew the van was a Chevy Express Cargo, just like her son drove.

A St. Thomas student in a football jersey said that the driver had worn a baseball cap and sunglasses and had black gloves on his hands.

By the time Mac and Lich interviewed everyone, they thought they had a pretty good idea of what had happened. Carrie had been walking down the sidewalk on the west side of Fairview, going south, having left the St. Thomas campus on her way to work. The black van had been parked in the grocery store parking lot on the east side of Fairview, the perfect position to see her coming. The van probably signaled the man in the alley so that he could time it perfectly, coming to the alley opening just as Carrie reached it. When the man in the alley moved, the van pulled out of the grocery store parking lot, turned left, slowed long enough for the man from the alley to throw Flanagan inside, and then took a right on Grand Avenue.

From there it got a little sketchy. Mac looked at his notes. The van drove six blocks west to Cretin Avenue. One witness said he thought that the van turned right on Cretin Avenue, heading toward Interstate 94, a mile or so north. Another thought the van had turned left on Cretin, which takes you south toward Ford Parkway through a much more residential area. When Mac thought about it, he bet it was a right turn to the interstate, the quickest way out of the area.

"Man, it's like yesterday," Lich said. "People see parts but not the whole thing."

"I hear ya," Mac said, shaking his head. "The whole thing happens fast. Before anyone really realizes what happened, these guys are gone like that—" He snapped his fingers.

"In broad daylight no less," Lich said, shaking his head, chewing harder on his unlit cigar.

"In the chief's city, Dick. Not in Minneapolis. Not is some suburb. But in his own *fuckin'* backyard."

"These guys are good," Lich said. "They're really good."

"They scouted this, Dick," Mac agreed. "They knew she worked today. They knew when she would be coming and where she'd be coming from. They timed it perfectly. In fact, I wouldn't be surprised if they didn't have someone watching her over on campus and following her over here, over what, the six or seven blocks from campus."

Lich looked at Mac closely.

"Is anyone pulling surveillance footage on campus?"

Dick was right. Mac whistled to Odegard and Goth, two uniform cops who quickly came over.

"Go over to St. Thomas. Find out what class Flanagan was in. Get with campus security and get their surveillance footage. We think someone might have been giving these guys the eyeball."

The two officers nodded and jogged away.

The two detectives stood with hands on hips for a few minutes, peering around, contemplating what happened and their next move.

Mac took a white hanky out of his pocket and wiped his forehead. He could feel the sweat forming on his body. Lich broke the silence.

"You don't suppose," he asked, "there's something the chief and Lyman don't want us to know, do you?"

"What the fuck?" Mac growled, turning on Lich, getting in his face.

"Easy partner, easy," Lich replied, putting his hands up. "I know how close you are to the chief. But we got two girls missin' here. So somebody ought to ask the hard question. Were the chief and Hisle up to something?"

"No way," Mac replied, shaking his head.

"Well they sure as hell pissed someone off," Lich replied.

"They did, but no way. Not in a million years," Mac answered coolly. He pulled his sunglasses off to look Lich in the eye.

After a minute, Dick backed down and shook his head.

"I don't think so either."

"Then why the fuckin' question?" Mac asked.

"Because your ability to detect bullshit is better than anyone's I've ever seen," Lich replied. "If you're not thinking that, then I feel better, that's all. But Mac," Dick continued, "the question had to be asked and you know it. And I'll tell you another thing: I'm not going to be the last one to ask it. You know King Burton and his pinstriped FBI court will be thinking it. And take a look at the frickin' media. They'll be talking connections, conspiracy theories, and scandals before 5:00 and they'll be doing their own investigating on this, prying into the lives of the chief and Hisle."

Mac nodded quietly, knowing his partner was probably right. He'd have probably asked the question himself but for the fact the chief was involved. But then something else occurred to him.

"You know how I said last night this could be personal? That maybe it wasn't just about money?"

"Yeah."

"Well I'm right. If you just want money, you don't kidnap the chief of police's daughter in his city."

"The chief has money, Mac," Lich answered. "His wife's family. The money from the logging up north. They've got millions."

"Sure, we'll get a ransom demand," Mac said, shaking his head, waving Lich off. "But there's more in play here—a lot more."

A uniform came running up.

"Mac. They got an explosion over near Lake Street behind an old abandoned building. Black Chevy Express Cargo van."

8

"It's like *Groundhog Day.*"

Smith backed the van into the garage and punched the button that closed the garage door. Carrie Flanagan lay still, finally done with her frantic squirming. A pillowcase covered her head and duct tape covered her mouth. Smith opened the sliding door to find Dean, David, and Monica pulling their ski masks back on. He pulled his own back on, then knelt down to Carrie and slid the cover off her head. He spoke softly.

"Carrie, we don't want to hurt you," he said, his hand placed lightly on her stomach. "We're not going to hurt you. We're not going to rape you. That was not why we've gone to all this trouble, okay? I want you to nod your head that you understand."

Flanagan nodded. Smith continued.

"I know you're afraid, but I want you to understand that we're after money. You're simply a means to an end. Once we get what we want, we'll let you go. Okay?"

Flanagan nodded.

"Good, Carrie. If you play ball, things will go better."

She nodded her head one more time. Smith smiled through his black mask.

"We're going to move you inside the house now. You can't break free, so it will be better for you to just be still and let us carry you, all right?"

She nodded again.

The brothers lifted her out of the van, Dean carrying her under the arms and David by the feet. Flanagan was relatively light in their arms, although a little heavier than the petite Hisle. Smith opened the door to the basement bedroom and Shannon Hisle turned her head to see them coming in.

"Carrie, like I said, we have no desire to hurt you," Smith repeated. "Over on the other bed is Shannon Hisle. Do you know who she is?"

Flanagan nodded.

"She has her arms and legs cuffed to the bed, but she hasn't been harmed in any way." Smith looked over to Hisle. "Shannon, you haven't been harmed, have you?"

Hisle shook her head.

Flanagan nodded, but she still had a frantic look in her eyes. Smith wanted her calm.

"We're going to do the same with you. It will be easier if you just let us do it, okay? We're not going to harm you, all right?"

Carrie nodded again, but the eyes were still wide.

The two brothers laid her on the bed. David got on top, sitting on her waist and holding her down while Dean cut away her restraints. He cuffed her arms and then her legs to the bed. Once she was secure, David eased off and moved back while Smith sat on the edge of the bed.

"Carrie, I'm going to remove the tape, okay?"

She nodded.

"Don't scream."

She nodded again.

"Because if you do scream, I will have to hurt you."

Carrie looked over toward Shannon, who nodded back. Carrie looked up at the masked man and nodded her head.

"Okay, this will hurt a little," Smith said as he yanked the tape from her mouth. Flanagan gasped for air, breathing deeply, trying to speak.

"Why...." She gasped. "Why ... why are you doing...."

Smith laid his fingers lightly over her mouth.

"Why? Like I said upstairs, we're after money. Your fathers have a lot of money and we want it. That's all," he said, his voice almost monotone and totally conversational. "This isn't about you; this isn't about harming you. That's not what I want to do. It's not what I intend to do."

"Okay," Flanagan answered weakly.

"Alright then," Smith said and then looked over to Hisle, who was gagged. "Do you need to go to the bathroom?"

Hisle nodded.

Smith looked back to Monica, "Let's get her to the potty. Then get her something to eat and drink."

Monica, ski mask over her face, simply nodded while Dean and David undid the manacles for her arms and legs from the bed. Hisle then laid still while David put a different set of manacles on her feet that allowed her to shuffle out of the room.

Once Hisle was out of the room and the door was closed, Smith turned back to Flanagan.

"Now see. We have no desire to harm you. After we finish what is next, we'll get you to the potty if you need it and some food and water as well."

Flanagan, while still scared, had calmed down.

"Do you know who my father is?" Carrie asked.

Smith smiled through the mouth hole in his ski mask.

"You mean the revered Charlie Flanagan, chief o' police for the city of St. Paul? Oh, we're quite familiar with who your father is." Smith smiled through his mask. "And we are not the least bit concerned about it." He paused and patted her on the thigh. "Now Carrie, if you play ball with us and your daddy follows directions...." He leaned back and clasped his hands across his stomach. "Well, everything will all work out."

"What does that mean?"

"It means, if you do as we ask, your chances of making it out of this are a lot better. If you don't help us out, well ... it certainly could go much worse." Smith paused. "Now that's not what I want, so let's play ball, okay?"

"Do you really think my father will pay you?" Carrie asked in disbelief. "He'll hunt you down with everything he's got."

"Oh, I expect he will," Smith replied calmly, unconcerned. "But in the end, your father will pay us."

"Why?"

"Because you're his little girl. That's all the motivation he'll need."

"It's like *Groundhog Day*," Mac quipped.

The scene was eerily similar to the one from the day before in River Falls. The burned-out van had been found behind a vacant building on Lake Street. The entire area was essentially deserted, the alley lined with abandoned houses and the storefronts empty, except for a small printing company a block to the west. Signs on the front of the vacant and now burned-out building announced a future home for street level retail, with condominiums overtop. It was all part of Minneapolis's efforts to rehab the Lake Street area.

For the past twenty or thirty years the area had been one of crime and drug dealing, with seedy bars interspersed between hit-and-miss storefront businesses. In the 1950s and 1960s, it had been a thriving business area surrounded by large Victorian and Tudor homes.

Minneapolis was in the process of revitalizing the Lake Street strip, rehabilitating historical buildings and sweeping away dilapidated ones. Soon, those efforts would overtake the vacant and crumbling building Mac and Lich were now standing behind.

As on the day before, the van had been parked and then incinerated after the kidnappers left the scene. However, in an area with an already high crime rate, the van was immediately recognized as a crime scene. The Minneapolis cops established a wide perimeter. The FBI and Minneapolis and St. Paul crime techs were working the scene, walking around carefully, photographing, marking, bagging, and collecting anything they could. Another helicopter was flying overhead.

Mac and Lich walked up to the scene and found a diminutive Minneapolis uniform cop that Mac knew named Norman.

"Hey Mac," Norman said.

"Norms, what do you know?"

"Not much really," the Minneapolis cop replied. He pointed toward Lake Street. "Old guy was walking along Lake Street and saw the smoke rising behind this building. He came around back and saw the burning van, walked a block or two to the gas station and called it in."

"Anyone see anything?"

Norman shook his head.

"Not that we've found. Everything on this side of the street is abandoned, awaiting demolition. In fact, the wrecking ball hits this building after the Fourth of July holiday. And of course, some of the normal clientele of this neighborhood are a bit averse to talking to us police."

"Drug trade?" Mac asked.

Norman nodded.

"So you've checked all these houses behind us?"

"Yes. But as you can see, they're empty. If anyone was hanging inside them, they skedaddled before we got here."

"Looks like a second set of tire tracks," Lich said, pointing to the left of the van.

"Agreed," Mac said. "Truck or van of some kind, based on the width of the tracks. We'll get molds of the tire tracks, see what that tells us."

"Let's get one of the pros on it then," Norman said as he waved over one of the crime scene techs.

"Probably a van," Mac said, "if it's our assholes."

"We've got some footprints as well," Lich noted, bending over carefully and pointing with his pen.

"Two that I see," Norman added. "Similar size, big feet—I bet size twelve or thirteen."

"That makes some sense," Mac answered, now standing and looking around. "Witnesses have given us the general description of a big man."

"Great," Lich said, unimpressed. "We have van tracks leaving the scene. Two sets of footprints for bigger dudes. Only if we're extremely lucky do we get any forensics off the van. And, we appear to have no witnesses who saw anything at all. We've got nothing."

Mac simply nodded as his cell phone went off.

"It's Peters," he said to Lich as he looked at the display and then answered. "Hey Cap.... Huh? ... You want us to do *what*?"

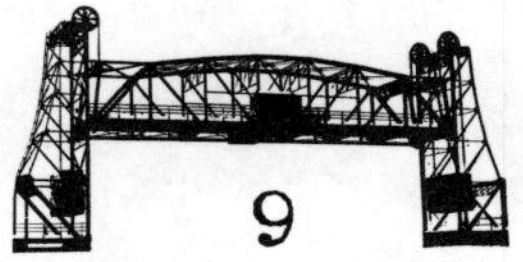

9

"You're a pugnacious shit aren't you?"

Mac exited from Interstate 94 at West Broadway, just north of downtown Minneapolis. The north side of Minneapolis west of the interstate was a rougher part of town. In the 1950s and 1960s, it had been a proud and prosperous working-class area. However, since that time, the area slowly had deteriorated. Pockets of poverty and drug-dealing had slowly eroded the once-bustling businesses and homes. Now, what businesses still remained did so with metal bars over the windows and bulletproof glass around the cash registers. It wasn't uncommon to find bullet marks, drug paraphernalia, and graffiti around the exteriors. Gangs patrolled neighborhoods, drugs were dealt in the open, and the sound of gunfire was not uncommon, particularly at night. Much like the case of Lake Street, the city was trying to help the area. Unlike Lake Street, solutions for the north side had proven far more elusive.

One person who was prospering on the north side was the man Mac and Lich were on their way to see—Fat Charlie Boone. Boone was the north side's most prominent and notorious businessman. Six months ago, Boone's sister's son was killed in a hit-and-run accident. The driver was a wealthy, white businessman, and Boone's nephew was a young black man with some legal trouble in his history. Lyman

Hisle represented the driver and, as he so often did, got him off on a legal technicality, largely due to the bungling of the cops working the accident scene and the county prosecutor working the case. The chief was front-and-center, accepting the blame, explaining how the accident scene was mishandled and the breathalyzer test was improperly administered. Boone loudly claimed that if the victim hadn't been black, the outcome would have been different. It was a rare public display from someone who built a fortune operating in the dark shadows of Minneapolis' north side.

"You buy this Boone business?" Lich asked.

Mac was doubtful.

"Seems kind of obvious don't you think?" He thought a little more. "I mean I know about those rumors for the last few months, Boone wants payback on the department, the county attorney's office, Hisle, all that. I've heard that noise, but it just all seems a little too convenient."

"Yeah, but," Lich answered, "he's wealthy, he's got resources, and he's smart."

A mile west along West Broadway, Mac turned into an aging SuperAmerica gas station. At the station were two plainclothes Minneapolis homicide cops, one bald and the other with a head full of gray Einstein-like hair and a cigarette hanging from his mouth. They were both leaning against an unmarked car and, despite the heat, sipping tall coffees. Pulling up alongside, Lich laughed as he powered down the window.

"Aren't you two fossils lookin' at daisies from the wrong side yet?"

"Diiiiick Liiiiiick," the bald one called out.

"If it ain't the Beeeaaaver Lick," Einstein replied boisterously, loud enough for everyone in a three block radius to hear. Lich was known, loved, and ridiculed all over. Dick exchanged handshakes and profanities with them and then introduced Mac.

"Mac, these two relics are Bud Subject." Lich pointed to the bald one. "And Ed Gerdtz," the gray-haired one.

"Mac, I knew your old man. Hell of a cop, one hell of a cop," Gerdtz replied in a deep, raspy voice, damaged from all the years of pounding coffin nails. They all shook hands, and Gerdtz never stopped laughing, talking, or smoking. You'd have thought they nominated a new pope with all the white smoke that came out Gerdtz's head. It took five minutes to get back on task and into a car to drive to Boone's.

Subject was behind the wheel while Gerdtz turned to them, blowing smoke through his mouth and nose as he spoke.

"Fat Charlie's office, if you want to call it that, is over on the corner of Lowry and Penn. He's got a hardware store and law office over there."

"Law office?" Mac asked.

"Yeah," Gerdtz answered, "one of Charlie's sons—he has eight of them you know—runs his practice out of the basement over there. Get this, though, his kid graduated from Stanford Law School."

"Stanford?" Mac asked in disbelief.

"Hell yes! Did quite well, bright kid. Now he helps the old man run his businesses," Gerdtz answered.

"Stanford law degree and he runs the old man's drug business? I don't get it."

"It's a lot more than a drug business these days," Gerdtz replied, smiling. "Fatso's gone upscale. He has that hardware store, law firm, a funeral home, three restaurants, four laundrymats, and now he's branching into real estate."

"Real estate? A slumlord?" Lich inquired.

"No, downtown real estate, the high-end shit," Gerdtz answered ruefully, shaking his head. "We've heard he's got money in the condo developments that have been exploding down by the river and might even be getting into some of the developments going up around the new Twins ballpark. Charlie's moving up in the world."

"So, let me guess," Mac said. "He hasn't touched drugs, a gun, or the dirty side of things for years. Now he's just the bank."

"That about sums it up," Subject answered, slowing for a stop light. "Charlie's gone legit, and there are way too many layers between him and the street." The veteran cop sighed as he pulled up in front of the Lowry-Penn Hardware Store, a fairly nondescript building with a red brick exterior and large storefront windows displaying a power-washer, lawn mower, power generator, and table saw. Peering inside the windows, one could see rows and rows of shelves deep into the interior.

"Seems like a big hardware store for this area," Lich said.

"Half the building used to be a law office," Gerdtz answered. "I grew up around here, and an attorney named Riley ran a street practice in the left half of the building. He retired in the early '80s, and sold the building. It turned over a few times before Charlie bought the whole kit and caboodle, in '90 or '91 I think."

"So you guys know him," Mac said. "Taking the girls sound like his style?"

Gerdtz turned serious.

"I've got my thoughts on that, Mac, and so does Bud. We were talking about it a lot before you and Dick Lick got to the SA. But I want you to form your own opinion first."

Subject waved them past the front door and around the south side of the building, past a sign that said "Attorney's Entrance in the Rear." They walked around the back and down a narrow set of cracking steps. At the bottom, Gerdtz knocked on the door. A large, black bodyguard dressed in black jeans and a black T-shirt tight over bulging muscles let them in and walked them through a kitchen and the law offices to a large room. There they found the man himself: Fat Charlie Boone.

Mac remembered seeing video footage of Charlie Boone walking into court six months ago, when the fat moniker fit and he was well over 300 pounds. The moniker no longer fit. Fat Charlie was still a large man, well over six feet, but now, like many, he was just a bit overweight. He sat in a high-backed armchair and wore a gold golf shirt open at the collar, tan slacks, and a lavender sport coat along with several gold rings and a gaudy gold watch. He held a cigar between the fingers of his left hand and a drink in his right. A haze filled the room, a prime specimen of early "pimp" styling with two round green felt card tables, a large bar with "Fat Charlie's" stenciled on it in burgundy, and a series of couches and chairs set around a big screen TV. The floor was black-and-white checkered tile, contrasting against the dark-paneled half walls and red shag on the upper half. Two other men, probably Charlie's sons, watched the cops over their own drinks.

"Detectives Subject and Gerdtz," Charlie said in a deep but even voice.

"Charlie," Gerdtz replied evenly. Then, spreading his arms, he boomed out, "What the fuck happened to you? You look like you've wasted away, fat man."

"Had me that gastric bypass bywhatchamacallit." Charlie laughed out loud, standing up and opening his coat, showing the svelte new Fat Charlie and conveniently proving that he wasn't armed. "What do ya think? A new me, eh?"

"New you," Subject said. But his next comment took the air out of the room. "Of course, the business is the same."

"Well, let's talk bidness then," Charlie replied flatly, sitting back down in his chair.

"These boys here are from St. Paul," Gerdtz said.

"I recognize these men," Charlie replied, a little smile on his face. "I've seen them on TV. The young one, I believe, is Michael McKenzie "Mac" McRyan, and the other is detective Richard Lich." He sounded well prepared for the meeting. "Grab a chair," he offered, waving them toward similar high-backed chairs. He held up his glass. "Care for a nip?"

Mac waved him off, as did Lich.

"So, what can I do for you gentlemen?" Boone asked.

"You know why we're here," Mac said.

"About those girls, I suspect. Just saw the report about the chief's daughter on the big screen over there."

"I saw you six months ago. You had some pretty harsh things to say about Hisle, our department, and particularly the chief," Mac said. "I quote: 'Maybe people like Hisle and Flanagan ought to experience the loss of a child. Then they'll know what my sister and I are feeling today.'" Mac sat back in his chair. "Now Hisle and the chief are both missing a child. Sounds a lot like payback. What better way to get it than going after the chief and Hisle?"

"You're right, of course. But I had nothing to do with that."

"Bullshit," Mac retorted, turning on the pit bull tone. "You and your people have never feared taking a body or making one disappear. I've heard about it for years. Maybe your hands aren't dirty, you haven't touched the body directly, haven't pulled the trigger, but you sit in that throne over there, drink your drink, smoke your cigar, and give the orders on who lives or dies."

Lich jumped in as if on cue, the good cop.

"Look, my partner here can be a little harsh."

"Being an asshole is more like it," Fat Charlie added.

"Fuck that," Mac countered angrily, playing the bad cop. "What's taking the chief's and Hisle's daughters to someone like you? It's no different than going after someone trying to move in on your drug real estate here on the north side, like Pinky Miller ten years ago. One day he's king shit over here, the next he's gone, never to be heard from again, and you've got his ten blocks of real estate over by North High School."

"Thanks for the history lesson," Charlie calmly answered. "But again, I have nothing to do with the disappearance of those girls. It's not my style."

"What's not your style?' Mac said sarcastically. "Killing? Taking lives? Abductions? Your name's been attached to all of that stuff over the years. It's the way people like you operate."

"You're a pugnacious shit, aren't you?" A big smile washed over Charlie's face, his perfect white teeth contrasting with his dark black skin.

"You don't know the half of it," Lich said and everyone laughed and the tension eased.

"I like it, no bullshit. We should all operate that way," Charlie said, and he meant it. "But to directly answer your question Detective McRyan, I've got nothing against your chief or Mr. Hisle. I said those things, sure, and I was pissed—I was damn fucking pissed at that department of yours. But Hisle was just doing his job, and from what I know of Flanagan, I doubt he wanted the case to go south like it did." Boone took a sip of his drink and gestured. "Now I'm pissed at the cops who blew the case and the prosecutor who screwed the pooch. And if I were to be going after people, *that's* who I'd go after. Not the people responsible for cleaning up the mess." Boone paused and then leaned over, elbows on knees, looking at Mac. "But detective, I didn't do this, because it's simply not my style."

"I don't know about that," Mac answered. "Maybe you're feeding us a line of shit here, and you got the chief's and Hisle's daughters. Maybe that's the price the chief and Hisle pay for screwing the pooch."

Boone got a serious look on his face. He'd had enough of McRyan. "No. I have a rule, a rule which is not to be violated, *ever*."

"Which is?" Mac asked.

"Never go after a citizen, never put a gun on a citizen, and never hurt a citizen," Charlie responded. "I've never, ever, gone after someone who wasn't in the trade, who wasn't in our line of business."

"And you follow that rule?" Mac asked, skeptical.

"It's the golden rule," Boone answered seriously, pointing at Mac with his cigar. "I ain't gonna bullshit you, Detective. We've been in some nasty stuff over the years. But not once did any of that ever involve someone who wasn't in the trade."

"Cops are in the trade, aren't they?" Mac asked. "I mean, aren't we cops up in your shit all the time? And if cops are in the trade, wouldn't their families be fair game?"

"For some people up here on the north side, maybe, but not me," Boone answered, falling back into his chair. "Gerdtz and Subject, if they're honest, will tell you that I've never, ever, picked a fight with the police. In this line of business, you don't last long doing that shit. You keep your profile low. You buy for a dollar and sell for two is all you ever want to do." Charlie took a sip of his drink and tacked in a different direction, "And one other thing."

"What's that?" Lich asked.

"I've got three daughters of my own, plus eight sons. Family is *everything* to me. I can't imagine what those fathers are going through, but I sympathize with them." He took a puff of his cigar and slowly blew smoke. "Taking those girls?" Charlie shook his head. "If I had a beef with someone, I'd go after them, not their wives or kids. What do they have to do with anything? Nothing. They're just citizens. And I never go after a citizen."

"So why then," Lich asked, "is word out on the street that you've wanted payback on the St. Paul Police, the county attorney's office, and Hisle? What's all that noise about?"

"That's my competition, I suspect."

"Fellow drug dealers?"

"I think it might be someone worse."

"Who's worse?" Lich asked.

"Politicians," Mac answered, smiling.

Fat Charlie guffawed loudly.

"You're perceptive, son. They're some city-hall types who wouldn't mind seeing me discredited. They don't like the idea of my involvement in legitimate business, the real estate market, and the area around the ballpark. My money apparently has a different tint of green."

"Perhaps it wasn't sufficiently laundered," Mac said acerbically.

Ten minutes later, they were driving back to the SuperAmerica. "You guys knew this was a waste of time, didn't you?" Mac asked Gerdtz and Subject.

"We both suspected that to be the case, although we heard the rumors, too," Subject answered.

"So this golden-rule shit is the real deal?"

"Pretty much," Gerdtz said. "While he's never been afraid to drop a body, to the best of our knowledge, he's telling the truth about that golden-rule business. He doesn't involve citizens."

"He sure talked out of school in front of you boys," Lich said. "I mean, he didn't exactly hide from his past."

"No, he didn't," Gerdtz replied. "We've taken our run at him over the years, but now we'll never get him. The county attorney's office doesn't want anything to do with him. They've been embarrassed too many times."

"So what," Mac asked quizzically, "there's like a truce or something with him?"

"Kinda," Gerdtz said. "You said it yourself, he's the bank. There are just too many layers between him and the street. Hell, he's making so much legitimate money now that I wouldn't be surprised if he got out of the drug trade in two or three years. He's gonna be what Michael Corleone always wanted to be."

Subject echoed the thought.

"He's even been helpful on occasion when other people operating in that part of town have violated Fat Charlie's rule. People don't know it, he asked us to keep it quiet, but you guys remember that stray bullet that killed the little girl four years ago?" Everyone nodded. "Fat Charlie clued us in on who to look at. Hell, Boone called me, *me*, the guy who's been in his shit for years, to tell me."

"What did he ask for in return?" Mac asked.

"Not one damn thing," Subject replied. "He's never even mentioned it since."

Mac snorted. Fat Charlie Boone, one contradiction after another, a saint and a hood all at the same time. He exhaled.

"Well he did say he'd call us if he heard of anything."

10

"Where's Ellsworth?"

Smith and Monica left the safe house in a minivan. Ten blocks away, they pulled into an empty school parking lot and affixed an Airport Ride sign to the side window. Five minutes later they were at the Airport Park & Ride lot. Smith was now wearing stylish rimless glasses, dressed business casual in a navy blue sport coat, a blue-and-white striped, button-down collar shirt, tan cuffed slacks, and sharp, burgundy-tasseled loafers. He dropped out of the van, then reached back to hoist a travel bag over his left shoulder and a nylon laptop case over his right. He pulled out the keys, popped the trunk, and put both items inside, looking like one of the mass of business travelers doing the same thing. He gave the van, and Monica, a quick wave and then ducked into the Impala.

The kidnapper exited the lot and quickly mixed in with the Monday rush-hour traffic, driving east out of St. Paul along Interstate 94, listening to the 5:00 PM top-of-the-hour local newscast on the FM talk radio station. A reporter named Tanya Morgan was currently making a live report from the St. Paul Police Department.

"Although the FBI and St. Paul police won't go on the record, confidential sources have indicated that the two kidnappings appear to be connected. The abductions were conducted in similar manners, and the descriptions of the perpetrators are also similar."

The program next cut to a statement from the Local FBI Agent-in-Charge Ed Duffy.

"We are working closely with the St. Paul Police and other jurisdictions to bring these girls home and the kidnappers to justice.

Smith particularly liked the next question from a reporter:

"We're hearing reports of family members of the police and the county attorney's office being assigned police escorts. Is this true?"

It was a no-win for Duffy, and his answer spoke volumes.

"I have no comment at this time."

Smith liked the response. The police were most assuredly escorting people around town for safety, which meant fewer people looking for him. A pleasant development indeed. But if Smith liked that question, he loved the last one.

"Are the kidnappings over, or do you expect there may be another attempt?"

It was a tough question to answer, but to Duffy's credit, he didn't duck it.

"We can't be certain. Everyone needs to be careful until we apprehend the kidnappers. People, particularly women, need to walk in groups. We need citizens to be vigilant and report any suspicious activity. One thing we do know is that the kidnappers tend to lay in wait at places where they know their targets will be. So people should vary their routines. And, if anyone notices any suspicious activity, they should immediately call...."

The FBI man gave the phone numbers, and then the show cut back to the two hosts, who began discussing the kidnappings as if they were experts. While they did, Smith motored south on State Highway 61 and into Hastings, a sleepy town on the far southeastern edge of the Twin Cities metro area. It nestled into a curve of the Mississippi River as it ran east to join the St. Croix on the border with Wisconsin.

In Hastings, he stopped for a quick drive-through bite to eat, a double cheeseburger, fries, and a chocolate milkshake. He enjoyed the warm, humid evening. A light southerly breeze moved the tops of the tall oak and maple trees as he drove south into a green sea of southern Minnesota farm country. The cornfields would definitely be knee-high by the Fourth of July. The radio predicted a continuing heat wave, with highs in the nineties and matching humidity. A heavy thunderstorm was forecast for later in the evening, which would be fine with him as long as they got their work done in time.

As he devoured the burger and fries, Smith drove further south on 61 to the tiny town of Miesville. The town was only four or five blocks long and appeared to be deserted. In reality, all of the town's citizens appeared to be at or heading to the baseball field to see the Miesville Mudhens, the town's legendary Minnesota townball team. Smith passed the park on his left, a throwback to a bygone era, with a large wooden grandstand and an outfield fence made of signs for every business and in every color under the rainbow. At the last block, he turned right and then left behind two enormous silver silos and stopped. He jumped out and put on magnetized temporary license plates. Back in the car, he turned around, pulled back onto 61 and continued south. Just outside of town, the highway expanded to two lanes in each direction, running parallel to the Mississippi River. He reached the quiet town of Red Wing just after 6:30 PM, and he fell in with the local traffic.

Smith drove through the town and past Red Wing's historic St. James Hotel. Past the hotel, he took a left, crossing the bridge over the Mississippi River and into the Wisconsin countryside. In another forty-five minutes he meandered into the small town of Ellsworth, where he arrived at 7:30.

In Ellsworth, he drove down the main drag, getting a feel for the rhythm and pulse of the slow and easy small town. The storefronts were mostly closed, except for a few small restaurants and retail shops, with the odd pedestrian strolling along. Further down, he motored past a set of playfields where kids played baseball and adults relived their youth on the softball fields. He chuckled as he saw a forty-something adult slide into second base, get called out, and jump up and start berating an umpire as if he were playing in the seventh game of the World Series.

Four blocks past the athletic fields, he turned left on a quiet county road heading north out of town. He went three more blocks and found the pay phone in front of the abandoned gas station, across the street from a small, sparsely populated and neglected city park. Smith had found the spot a few weeks earlier on a scouting trip. He pulled up to the phone, which was set at the height of his car window. He then scanned the park across the street, saw what he wanted and smiled. Taking his time, the kidnapper casually pulled on rubber gloves, fitting them tightly. The car idled as he dug into the duffel bag, pulling out the portable voice changer, Dictaphone and roll of quarters, which he spent a minute opening. Checking his watch, he noted the time was 7:42 PM.

After working Fat Charlie, Mac and Lich stopped in at police headquarters and picked up a packet of information on the connections between the chief and Hisle. As Mac drove the Explorer over to the chief's home, Lich scanned the report, fifteen pages long, consisting of the possible suspects, details about the cases and their outcomes, and transcripts of the preliminary interviews.

As the car idled at a stoplight, Lich closed the file. Mac broke the silence. "Anyone on the list fit the mold?"

Lich sighed and shook his head.

"Not in an ideal sense."

"Nobody worth a look at all?"

"Worth a look? Maybe a few. But this is off-the-top-of-their-heads kind of stuff. Hisle's had hundreds, maybe thousands of criminal clients over the years, as we saw with all those files this morning, so we've just started to dig into all of that. And now we have the chief's history to work through. So this is only the most partial of lists at this point."

"One thing we probably do know, however," Mac answered. "The answer lies somewhere in the files. Lyman's *and* the chief's."

"True enough. But between those two, we're going to have a huge shit-pile of people to work through. Chief's been a cop for thirty years and Lyman's practiced law for damn near the same amount of time. Their paths have crossed many a time."

"True that is. But somewhere in all of those cases is our connection."

"I'm sure you're right," Lich answered, but his voice took on a skeptical tone. "But I look at this list here," he held up the three-ring binder, "and there are guys in here that may be worth a look but...."

"Not exactly blowin' your drawers off?"

"Uh huh."

"Is the list just known connections between Lyman and the chief?"

"At this point, yes, just the connections. Cases they both touched or remember touching."

Mac pondered that approach as he pulled up to another stoplight.

"Anything come of the interviews with Hisle's family and friends?" he asked.

"Not that I've heard. The FBI and our guys, Double Frank and your cousin Paddy did the interviews. Nobody noticed anything odd or weird. Shannon Hisle hadn't mentioned anything to her family or roommate. Her roommate, who Hisle's lived with for two years, reported no strange phone calls, men, vehicles, or anything odd. The roommate says Hisle is paranoid. She was mugged last year walking home from school and is particularly sensitive to people following or watching her. So, according to Paddy, and I quote, 'Nobody's seen shit, heard shit, wondered about shit, or noticed shit,' end quote."

"Well, that's the same story with Carrie Flanagan."

"Yeah?" Lich asked.

"Yeah. Riley said a couple of Duffy's boys interviewed her roommate, coworkers, and family. Nobody was aware of any problems or noticed anyone odd hanging around. If Carrie was worried about someone, something, anything like what we're looking for, she hadn't confided in anyone about it." Mac shook his head. "We've got nothing."

"Hell, we've got less than that," was Lich's apt reply.

Mac slowed for another stoplight.

"All of this makes me raise my question again, do you think Hisle or Flanagan have anything to do with…" Lich started.

"No fucking way," Mac replied. "No way, no how."

"How about a family member who has a grudge? You know, families can have their own weird politics, grievances, hidden hatreds. Maybe one of the girls is in the way of some money, inheritance, whatever. Someone should at least look at it is all I'm saying."

"Carrie's the youngest child of the chief, and her brothers absolutely adore her. As for Shannon Hisle, I don't know her well, but I know Hisle has good relationships with his kids. He was something of a single parent since his wife died years ago so he's close with Shannon and the rest of them. I've never heard of any problems." Mac was quiet for thirty seconds. "I know what you're saying Dick. Nobody notices anything. These guys take the girls at vulnerable spots and obviously were aware of their habits, schedules, and so forth. So you get to thinking that maybe someone from the family tips them off or gives them the place. But I just don't buy the family angle. Maybe if it was just Flanagan or just Hisle, I'd be more inclined to think that way, but together? I don't see it coming from the families, conspiring in this way. I suppose it's possible, but it just doesn't feel right."

"You're probably right partner," was Lich's reply. "But somebody should be at least thinking about that angle."

Mac sighed, "We just thought about it and I talked about it with Riley an hour ago."

"You did?" Lich responded, turning in his car seat.

"Yup. You said you like my bullshit detector, and I do too—I trust my gut. But I trust Riles as well, and we walked through it for about ten minutes. We both came to the same conclusion."

"Which is?"

"It's not family. It's personal. It's someone or a group of people the chief and Lyman pissed off somewhere along the way."

"So we just have to find the connection then," Lich replied.

"Only one problem with that."

"Which is?"

"I don't think it will be that easy. The connection is going to be complicated, hard to make, and...."

"And what?"

"I'm not sure we'll be able to make it in time. If it's just Shannon and Carrie and nobody else, we're going to be talking ransom soon and delivery not long after. We don't have a lot of time. I'd guess twenty-four hours, forty-eight at the most."

Mac pulled up to the Flanagan house. The chief lived in the Highland Park neighborhood, an affluent section in the southwest corner of St. Paul. A generally tranquil upper-middle-class area filled with professionals of all kinds, it seemed unaccustomed to the mass of police cars and media trucks parked in front of one of its houses.

The chief's home was a stately two-story colonial revival with a red-brick exterior, white trim, black shutters and a white portico entrance. It was a classic beauty in a neighborhood of Victorian, Georgian, Colonial, and Cape Cod-style houses built at the turn of the twentieth century. The house was larger and finer than what you would expect for a career cop, even for a chief. However, Charlie Flanagan married well, his wife's family having earned a significant fortune in logging in northern Minnesota. In addition to the Highland Park home, the chief had a sprawling cabin on Cross Lake on the Whitefish Chain, prime lake real estate two hours north of the Twin Cities.

As they walked in the front door, Mac immediately noted the massive number of cops, active and retired, ready to help at a moment's notice. The mere number of people present spoke volumes about Charlie Flanagan. In many big cities, there's separation between the chief and the force, but not in St. Paul. The chief started as a beat cop in the city, moved up to detective, chief of detectives, and, ultimately, chief, where he'd been for the last nine years. He was one of them. Charlie Flanagan never morphed into a police politician. He wasn't the police chief; he was the chief of the police. He was a cop and always thought of himself that way. Charlie Flanagan always had the force's back and supported his men without fail, even when it wasn't the most politically prudent thing to do. The most recent example of the chief's support was the recent cop shooting and resulting manhunt. The chief never once wavered in his support of his men, Mac and Rock in particular, despite the media and political pressure. However, the support of his men didn't come without a price—it meant strained relations with the mayor, a politician tiring of trying to keep his chief of police in line.

Peters spotted Mac and Lich's arrival and quickly pulled them aside into a small side room. The update finished with their trip to north Minneapolis.

"So Boone was a washout?"

"Waste of time," Lich answered.

"Okay, I need to tell you boys something, and you're not going to like it," Peters said. "With the chief indisposed at the moment, the mayor's put the FBI, and Burton in particular, in charge of this thing."

"What the fuck?" Mac railed.

"Political hack," Lich raged.

"I agree with you both," Peters answered, holding his hands up. "I agree with you, believe me. The mayor's issue is that he doesn't want us getting out of control. He's falling back on the cop shooting, and the involvement of you, Rock and Riles. You're the chief's boys and he figures you'll tear the city up to find Carrie."

"Goddamn right," Mac growled.

"Well, that's what the mayor's worried about Mac. He wants you corralled."

"How so?"

"If you don't follow Burton's lead on this, you'll be off the case. Frankly, if the mayor had his way, you boys would be off it completely already."

"I'm half surprised we're not," Lich muttered.

"You're not because the chief raised holy fuckin' hell," Peters answered. "And Burton told the mayor he wants you working it, that you guys are too good to waste on the sidelines. He told the mayor you'd work it anyway, so he'd just as soon have you on his side. So the chief has your back and Burton wants you on it. So play nice and we're good here."

"Nice of Burton to do that," Lich said. "Maybe he's not too bad a guy after all."

"So far, so good with him. He's killing all my FBI stereotypes," Mac said in agreement and then changed directions. "How's the chief doing?"

"Let's go see him," Peters answered, waving them to follow. He led them up the open staircase to the second floor and then the chief's home office at the back corner of the house. Formerly a bedroom for one of the Flanagan kids, now grown, the room was converted into a well appointed home office with a large mahogany desk and high-backed leather chairs. The chief stood behind the desk, hands in his pockets, slumped shoulders, staring out the window and Mac felt a lump in his throat and his chest tighten.

Charlie Flanagan was like a father to Mac, and Mac like a son to the chief. The chief was with Mac when Mac's father was killed in a freak hunting accident. Mac was close to his mother and three sisters. But after his father's death, Mac became part of the Flanagan family and the chief was his father figure. He spoke with the chief about things a young man sought guidance from a father about. It was the chief who was at Mac's college and law-school graduations, leading the cheers at college hockey games, providing advice on getting married, buying homes, or investing money. Mac was close to the chief's sons and his daughter, his baby girl Carrie. She was twelve years younger than him, but he looked upon her like a little sister. Mac went to her high school events, attended her graduation, and checked out her boyfriends, making sure they were worthy of his adopted little sister. While Mac liked Lyman and had met Shannon a few times, with Carrie and the chief now involved, it had become all too personal. Mac exhaled, steadied himself, and put on his stone game face. He didn't want the chief to see him as anything other than ready to go.

The office was full. Burton, Duffy, and the mayor quietly chatted in one group, while Riley, Rock, and a few others talked in another. All were waiting for the phone to ring, for the inevitable call to come. Hearing new people entering, the chief turned around. Mac sucked in a breath as the chief slowly approached and gave him a hug, pulled him close and whispered in his ear.

"You do whatever it takes, you understand? *Whatever* it takes."

"Yes, sir," was Mac's quiet reply. There was nothing else to be said. The chief pulled back and looked Mac in the eye, and that was that. Mac felt a cool, analytical wave wash over his body. It was time to go to work, and there would be no stopping until Carrie came home.

When the chief walked back to his desk, the mayor eased over next to McRyan.

"I assume you know who's running this investigation," he said.

Mac stared straight ahead and nodded.

"Good. I don't want any problems," the mayor added and then walked away. Mac glanced to his right and caught Burton's eye. The FBI man approached.

"How you doing?" Burton asked. "I know you and the chief are close."

"I'm fine, ready to go."

"Listen, don't worry about your mayor. I want. No wait. Make that, I need you guys working this. They're coming after cops and the people most important to them," Burton said and then added darkly. "These bastards are going down for that."

Mac nodded his approval.

The phone rang.

The chief went to the phone and exhaled, letting it ring twice before answering.

"Flanagan."

"We have your daughter," a now-familiar disguised voice on the other end replied. Everyone was huddled around a speaker phone, the chief on the regular line. Burton motioned with his hands to try to string out the call.

The chief knew how this would play.

"How do I know you have her? I want to speak with her."

There was a click, and then a nervous and slightly muffled voice played on a recording.

"Daddy. I … I … I'm okay. I haven't … been hurt. Please do as these men say and I won't be harmed. I love you." The tape cut off. There was no question that it was Carrie Flanagan's voice.

The mechanical-sounding voice came back.

"I trust that answers your question."

"Do you have Shannon Hisle as well? Is she still alive?"

"She is. Hisle was the appetizer and your daughter is the main course."

"You son of a bitch, you harm her and I'll..." the chief growled into the phone, but the look on his face was calm, almost placid. He was doing what he could to keep the call going.

"Do as we say, and that won't be a problem."

"What is it that you want? You want money? You want me? You want Hisle? What is it you want, you motherfucker?"

"Money," the voice answered flatly.

"How much? What's it gonna take to get my little girl back? How much to buy you off you goddamn son of a bitch?"

"We'll be in touch." The line went dead.

The chief slammed the receiver into the cradle and violently swept the phone off his desk into the wall, turning his back to everyone. Hisle, the only man in the room who truly knew what he was going through, immediately went to him and put an arm around his shoulder.

Mac turned to the agent working the laptop.

"It's a landline from a payphone in Ellsworth. Ellsworth, Wisconsin."

"Call the Ellsworth cops. Call them now!" Burton ordered. The FBI tech did as instructed. "Where's Ellsworth?"

"It's about forty-five minutes, maybe an hour southeast of here," Mac answered, knowing generally where the town was. He walked over to the desk where Double Frank started unfolding a Minnesota-Wisconsin roadmap, looking for the exact location. Another FBI man was calling the Ellsworth police department. Problem was, they had no idea who they were looking for, what they were driving, anything.

As everyone tried to contact Ellsworth, Mac didn't feel like waiting. He grabbed Lich by the arm.

"We're going down to Ellsworth."

Smith drove north out of Ellsworth and worked his way up to River Falls, where he pulled into an empty elementary school parking lot and removed the false license plates. A half-hour later he returned to the Park & Ride, where Monica was waiting. Ten minutes later the two were back at the safe house.

"Are things ready to go?" Smith asked Dean.

"The girls are ready. They'll be out for eighteen to twenty hours, so we have plenty of time."

"Equipment and materials?"

Dean opened the back door of the van, and Smith inspected the contents.

"As you can see, we're good to go," Dean noted confidently.

"Good," Smith replied. "Let's bring them up and get going out to the farm then. I want to be sure to finish before the storms roll in."

Unlike Clearwater, which was right off the highway, Ellsworth could only be reached by a circuitous route east on Interstate 94 into Wisconsin and then south on State Highway 63. Mac and Lich worked their way to the abandoned gas station, where a patrol car and sedan were parked with two cops casually sitting on the hood, one in uniform, one with a tie, both smoking. They'd kept it low-key, no lights or crime tape. There was no reason to wake everyone up and draw a crowd.

Mac pulled up and he and Lich jumped out. A forensics team pulled in behind them and started unloading, pulling on rubber gloves, and assembling their gear. The cop with the tie and a sweat-soaked shirt jumped off the hood.

"My name's Kleist, chief here in Ellsworth," he said. Kleist was a short, squat man with a nose far too large for his face. "Haven't touched a thing," he reported, wiping his brow with a red handkerchief. "Heck, there hasn't hardly been anyone passing by since we got here."

"What did you find when you got here?" Lich asked.

"Not much," Kleist replied, rubbing a finger hard along the side of his nose. "Phone was on the hook. But," he waved them away from the phone toward a back exit onto the street, which traversed through a patch of bare ground and dirt, "If you look close enough, there appears to be some fresh tire tracks, I'd say car width, maybe a sedan of some type that those guys," the chief pointed to the forensics team, "might be able to do something with."

Mac and Lich peered down to the tracks. They were narrow, fresh and definitely from a car. Lich waved forensics over.

"Let's get pictures, maybe even a mold," he ordered. A forensics tech nodded and started snapping images.

"So they're using vans and cars, eh?" Mac asked.

"Looks like it," Lich answered. "Just another little wrinkle."

Mac nodded.

"He didn't just drive here and stumble onto this place either. He scouted it." Mac motioned to the station. "This isn't a bad spot really. The park looks almost abandoned, just a few homes around with little traffic, foot or car. Make a quick call, hang up, leave, and nobody sees a thing."

They walked back over to Kleist, who'd returned to the hood of his sedan. "Chief, has anyone gone door-knocking?" Lich asked.

The chief thumbed at the other cop.

"He knocked on all the doors before you fellows got here. Only one person was home, and he didn't see anything, said he was watching the

Twins game. I've got another one of my men surveying the perimeter of the park and the nearby streets to see if a pedestrian saw anything."

"I know the answer to this question," Mac said. "I don't suppose there's any surveillance cameras, anything like that around here is there?"

Kleist smiled apologetically and shook his head.

"Nope. Don't have the budget for it or the need really. Big night for us might be a fight at the bar, a little speeding or drunk driving, a domestic."

"So if a guy makes a call here," Mac waved around the area, "and then wanted to leave town, how would he do it?"

Kleist rubbed his nose hard again, and Mac noticed it was redder along the right side. The rubbing must be a frequent nervous tic.

"Oh, a guy would have a couple of ways to go I suppose." The cop pointed northeast, "He could go back up 63 and get onto 94 and head back the way you boys came."

"Or?" Mac asked.

"If a feller wanted a more scenic trip, he'd probably go southeast, out along 63 until it finds 10 over yonder, which would take him west to Prescott." He rubbed the nose again, "or stay south on 63 until he got to Red Wing. In any event, he'd have plenty of…."

"Options," Mac replied, shaking his head. "We know."

The chief was called away by one of his men. Lich didn't miss a beat.

"He said, 'yonder.'"

"'Feller,' too," Mac added. "I love small-town folks" He shut up as Kleist headed back.

"I think I got something you boys might be interested in," he said. An Ellsworth patrol car pulled up with an elderly man in the back seat, along with a golden retriever. The uniform cop got out and let the man and dog out. The dog came right up to Mac.

"Hey there buddy," Mac said, kneeling down to scratch the pooch behind the ears.

"Explain," Kleist said to the uniform cop.

"Henry here," the uniform said, pointing to the old man, dressed in a striped short-sleeved shirt, plaid shorts, and dark socks, "said he was sitting on a park bench across the street about an hour ago, and ... well...." The uniform pointed to the old man. "Tell them, Henry."

"I was sitting on the bench over there." The old man pointed kitty-corner from the gas station to an old bench with "Ellsworth Lions Club" painted on it in fading letters. "I was taking a rest with Reggie here." The old man rubbed the dog's head. "Anyways, I saw this blue sedan pull into that old gas station and park by the pay phone."

"When was this?"

Henry pulled out a tarnished gold pocket watch and flipped the top open.

"Oh 7:30, 7:40 or so. Sometime around then." Mac and Lich exchanged a look.

"What kind of car, Henry?" Mac asked.

"Chevy I think, one of them new ones, what do they call them, Impalas? I've never owned one myself; I'm a Ford man...."

"See a license plate number?" Mac interrupted.

"I know the letters because they were odd. They spelled 'cat,' I think."

"Cat? You mean the letters were C-A-T?"

"That's right," the old man replied, his glasses sliding down his nose as he nodded. "And it was a Minnesota plate, had the blue color and them pine trees."

"I'm going to call it in," Lich said, pulling out his cell phone. Mac continued.

"How about the driver, you get a look at him?"

"Not a good one," the old man said.

"Black or white? Blonde hair or dark hair? McRyan pressed. "Anything like that?"

"White, I think," the old man answered. "I think he had a baseball cap on, but other than that, I didn't really notice anything."

"And you were sitting on the park bench across the street?"

"That's right young man, right over there. We come through here just about every night at this time."

"Let's walk over there, okay? You can bring Reggie along."

"Okey dokey," Henry replied and with his slow gait followed Mac across the street and away from the abandoned gas station. At the bench, Mac stopped.

"Henry, right?"

The old man nodded, "Henry Finkey."

"My name's McRyan, I'm a detective from St. Paul."

"You're a Minnesota boy, eh?" Henry replied, mischief in his voice. "I can't stand them Vikings. You a Vikings fan?"

"I am Henry, I am. They're going to kick the Pack's tail this year," Mac replied, sitting down next to the old man and petting Reggie's snout.

"We'll see about that," Henry answered. "So what's this all about?"

"I can't really tell you why this is important, at least not yet sir," Mac answered.

"Does this have something to do with those girls being kidnapped? I figure that must be it. No other reason for a St. Paul cop to be here in little ol' Ellsworth."

Mac remained neutral.

"Like I said, I can't say. What I need though is for you to walk me through it again, what you saw. Take a minute if you need, close your eyes, whatever, but I need to know everything."

Henry set himself on the park bench, leaned back, and thought for a minute.

"I was out taking my nightly walk with Reggie. We go for a good hour or two walk every night in the summer."

"Okay."

"We usually walk through the park each night, and I like to sit on this bench. This used to be a nice park when I was a kid. I like to just sit and remember good times here."

"So you're on your walk and you come to the park and sit down?" Mac asked, moving him along.

"That's right, son. I let Reggie off his leash, and he was walking around, doing a little business on some trees, when I noticed the car pull in off the street and up to the phone."

"Then what?"

"Well," Henry stroked his chin and squinted. "Well nothing happened for a minute or two, maybe more. He just sat there idling, which I thought was a little odd, I suppose. It caused me to look a little closer I guess. I noticed the car, the plate—you know C-A-T and Minnesota—and then I looked away and back to Reggie. He was getting a little far away, so I called to him. He didn't come right away, so I had to yell after him a couple of times before he minded and came back to me."

"Then what?"

"I put Reggie's leash back on."

"How long did all that take?"

"A minute or two I suppose."

"And the car was still there?"

"Sure was, but now the guy in the car was using the phone. I could see the cord from the phone running into the car."

"How long was he on the phone?"

"Not long. I didn't time it or anything, but it wasn't real long. Then he hung up and pulled on out and he was gone."

"Henry, did you notice anything about the driver? Anything about him?"

Henry closed his eyes for thirty seconds but shook his head.

"I'm sorry, but I just didn't get a look or notice anything, son. I just didn't." The old man looked disappointed.

Mac patted him on the knee.

"Good job, Henry. You've helped us out."

Lich and Kleist came running across the street, Lich smiling.

"We got a hit!" he called.

"Stolen vehicle, right?" Mac asked.

"No," Lich replied, pulling Mac away from Henry. "No report of it being stolen. There's one navy blue Impala with the tag letters of CAT."

"And you're telling me there's a connection," Mac said.

"Yes." Lich said. "Dead on the money."

11

"Something's going on here."

A 2006 Chevy Impala with license tag CAT was a fleet vehicle belonging to Drew Wiskowski Construction in Cottage Grove. The connection was Drew Wiskowski, Sr.

Wiskowski had come to St. Paul thirty years ago from the south side of Chicago, and he brought with him the sort of no-holds-barred approach to business characteristic of that notorious neighborhood. Wiskowski made his fortune in construction, but it wasn't always pretty. There were disputes with competitors, and Wiskowski wasn't shy about using a little force, corruption, and intimidation to get ahead. He had had more than one run-in with the authorities and building inspectors in his early days. However, once he made his pile and could afford his estate on the river down by Hastings, he went low-profile and let his money pile up while quietly building reputable homes and commercial buildings in Minnesota and the rest of the Upper Midwest.

Unfortunately, four years ago the long-dormant Wiskowski name came alive again. This time it was Drew Jr. who turned up in St. Paul running a home-improvement business. He was using the old man's name, but Drew Sr. was not involved in the business; it was owned solely by his son. And the son appeared to be taking a page from the early years of his old man's playbook.

A powerful thunderstorm with straight-line winds rolled through town, damaging roofs and siding and blowing out windows. The storm hit some of St. Paul's Hmong neighborhoods particularly hard. Drew Jr. swooped in and marketed his home-repair business hard in those areas. The damaged houses needed new siding and shingles. Wiskowski lowballed all of the other contractors and consumed all of the business. Many of the Hmong folks didn't speak or understand English well, so Wiskowski said he'd work with their insurance companies directly, handling everything if they'd just sign over the insurance check to his company. The result was predictable. Drew Jr. defrauded the homeowners and did substandard work on their homes, if any work was done at all.

Drew Jr. may have profited, but he underestimated the Hmong community. They went to the police, and the story made its way to the chief, who made it his personal mission to go after Drew Jr. Lyman was originally Drew Junior's lawyer, since he was on retainer with the old man. But Lyman knew right away it was a bad case—the kid was a swindler, and that he wanted no part of it. Lyman found a way out of the case, and Drew Jr.'s defense was eventually handled by a lesser lawyer. The younger Wiskowski ended up with six years in Stillwater state prison.

"That was four years ago," Lich said as Mac sped across the Interstate 94 over the St. Croix River and into Minnesota.

"So he's coming after the chief and Lyman. An eye for an eye then, their daughters for his son. It makes some sense in a warped mind sort of way. How did Junior buy the farm in prison?"

"Apparently," Lich said, "the kid was an operator inside, and went a little too far. Two months ago a fellow inmate on a life sentence shoved a shiv up his rectum, and Drew Jr. bled out."

"Ouch," Mac said grimacing.

"Not my preferred way to go either. Anyway, the old man and his other son went batshit in an interview on the radio,"

"Ahh, I remember hearing about that," Mac replied, swerving through traffic.

"Yeah. He blamed the chief and the police for his kid's death, claiming his kid never did anything wrong. He specifically ripped Lyman a new one because he withdrew from the case, claiming his old friend turned his back on him when he was most in need. He ripped the department because his other son was busted for pot possession after Drew Jr. ended up in the can, and Wiskowski claims it was a frame. So he's got plenty of bile built up for us. And there's one other thing."

"Which is what?"

"Drew Sr. has cancer—terminal," Lich said. "He found out maybe a month ago, and he's going fast."

"So what's he got to lose?" Mac finished. "Take a last shot at the men you think are responsible for the death of your son before you're six feet under."

"Or so the theory would go," Lich said agreeably.

"It's a good theory," Mac answered. "Wiskowski is smart, wealthy enough to hire people willing to help him, he's got the motivation, and he doesn't care what happens to him." He thought about it for another minute and then said gravely. "If he doesn't care, that may not bode well for the girls."

"Agreed," Dick answered. "We gotta move fast on this."

"Then I assume they're bringing the old man in?"

"As we speak. There's a convoy coming up 61 now from Cottage Grove. Riley, Rock, Burton, and Duffy all went down and are bringing Ol' Drew back up right now. We just might beat them there."

The distance lit up brightly with multiple lightning strikes as Mac pulled into the police department parking lot.

"With this storm and Wiskowski coming in, we're going to get thunder, lightning, and fireworks all at the same time," Lich said with amusement.

He couldn't have been more right. As Mac and Lich jumped out of the Explorer, the convoy carrying Wiskowski arrived, four cars strong.

"No, no, no," Mac groaned as the convoy stopped at the steps, right where the newsies were waiting. The media had clearly gotten wind of the Wiskowski connection and descended on the convoy like locusts. "They should have gone in the back."

"This should be interesting," Lich mused. "Let's hold back and let them get in. Besides, you should let Riles and Rock have some media time. We're all sick of seeing your handsome mug on TV anyway."

"Fine by me. I hate the media."

"Riiiiiiight," Lich said rolling his eyes in disbelief.

"Whatever, asshole," Mac answered angrily. He didn't like the media exposure for any number of reasons. He knew he was a damn good cop, smartest in the department, but he was still in his early thirties and mindful that senior cops didn't always like the young hotshot getting all the attention. But for now, he was out of the picture. The horde followed Wiskowski, and it wasn't pretty.

Wiskowski was as sick as Dick had suggested. Drew Sr., with an oxygen tank and IV in his left arm, was slowly walked up the steps by a woman, dressed like a nurse, and a man in an expensive suit, probably his attorney. But with the crush of media pushing in to take pictures and yell out questions, and the cops pushing back in kind, trying to keep them away, something bad was bound to happen—and it did. All the jostling caused the old man to be pushed sideways, and he fell to the steps, yelping in pain as the needle for the IV was yanked out of his arm.

"We better get in there and help," Mac said running toward the crowd, Lich right behind. They got into the group in time to hear Wiskowski scream bloody murder.

"You get this on film. These bastards took my son and now he's dead. They've tried to take my other son away. Now I've got cancer and it still isn't enough for them. When will it be enough for these people? When!?" He hissed as Riles picked the old man up as gently as he could. "I can't be allowed to die with any dignity," he growled in a raspy voice. "I'm going to sue this city. The police in this town are out of control. The mayor, it's his damn fault, letting Flanagan run roughshod over him all the time." Wiskowski railed and then coughed uncontrollably, the cancer sapping his angry energy. But the fight was there, and he looked ready to stir the pot.

"Look what they're doing to me! Before this is done I'm gonna own this damn city. I'm going to own Charlie Flanagan's ass."

With Wiskowski having gone down and now providing some good copy and footage, the media backed off just enough. This allowed Mac, Lich, and several uniforms and plainclothes who'd come from inside to help, to surround the group so the old man could be led into the building.

When the doors closed, the media focused on Mac.

"Detective McRyan, can you confirm that Drew Wiskowski Sr. is the prime suspect in the kidnappings," a petite brunette yelled, sticking a Channel 8 microphone in his face.

"No comment," Mac answered.

"We've heard that Wiskowski was identified through a phone call from somewhere in western Wisconsin, can you confirm?" a round male reporter from Channel 3 asked, sweating profusely.

"No comment."

"Has Wiskowski admitted to taking the girls as revenge for the death of his son?" a willowy blonde from Channel 6 asked, at least aware of the motive angle.

Mac stopped, hesitated, and then repeated, "No comment." However, as he opened the door for Lich and others he looked back out and saw in the distance, leaning against a railing, Channel 12's Heather Foxx, for once not one of the horde accosting them as they walked into the building.

However, if outside was the frying pan, inside the building was the fire—the political fire. Mayor Olson had just witnessed the spectacle, on live TV no less, and was none too pleased to have his name dragged through the muck. Hizzoner was pissed and let everyone hear it as he followed Riley and Rock down the hall.

"Jesus Christ," the mayor yelled. "You couldn't have done this a just little more low-key? You couldn't have handled this in Cottage Grove? You couldn't have perhaps figured out a way to avoid that fuckin' mess outside? Hell, you had that son-of-a-bitch looking sympathetic for Christ's sake."

Riles stopped in his tracks, turned, and stood stone solid, letting the mayor nearly run into him.

"Sorry, Sir," Riles said, his six-foot-three-inch frame towering over the diminutive mayor. "It perhaps could have been handled differently. And you know what? You can chew my ass for it for a week *after* we get the girls back. But if you don't fucking mind, I have a job to do. Or are you going to run the interrogation?"

"I'm not sure you should, Detective," the mayor answered. "Perhaps Wiskowski is right, you're out of control. You're *all* out of control."

Burton stepped between Riley and the mayor before Riley, fists balled, face red with anger, did something as stupid as what he looked ready to do.

"Let's everyone calm down," Burton demanded. Mac and Lich pulled Riley away while the FBI man eased the mayor back from the gathering crowd.

"As for the media fiasco out front," Burton said, shrugging his shoulders, "That's as much my fault as anyone's. I could have anticipated that. But Detective Riley is right, we deal with that later. Right now, we got bigger fish to fry. This guy may well have the girls, and it's these men you think are so out of control that broke this thing for us. Let them do their job for now. We can analyze crowd control later." Burton turned toward Riles and the rest of the crowd and, with his back to the mayor, winked before he led everyone away.

Around a corner and out of earshot of the politician, the FBI man muttered in Mac's ear.

"Your mayor is a fuckin' idiot."

12:30 AM

The interrogation was nothing more than a brawl, with both sides aggressive, uncompromising, gesturing, shouting, and foul-mouthed. Riley and Rock pulled their dual bull-in-the-china-shop routine, while Burton and Duffy jumped in to play the softer edges, trying without success to calm it down. Old man Wiskowski was having none of it. Gaunt, looking like the dying man he was, Drew Sr. was nevertheless animated and pugnacious, the tough Chicagoan coming out strong. While his attorney tried like mad to restrain him, Wiskowski was constantly up and out of his chair, cussing and shouting at the top of his lungs at Riley, or Rockford, or the one-way glass on either side of the room. He waved and pointed, risking another removal of the IV from his arm. It was an altogether ugly, yet somehow morbidly entertaining sight.

"And you were so careful, stealing the vans, burnin' them, and you planned it so well Drew," Riles thundered, leaning down to Wiskowski's face, with both hands on the table. "But then you or your people got sloppy, using your own vehicle, the car."

"Fuck you," Wiskowski yelled back. It was his favored response.

Mac and Lich watched intently through the one-way window, fueling up with coffee. The chief and Lyman were watching from the observation room on the other side.

"He isn't exactly denying involvement," Mac mused, sipping the last of his coffee.

"He isn't exactly admitting it either," Lich answered, putting a stick of gum in his mouth. "The only thing I know for sure is that this interview is going nowhere."

The chief apparently agreed. Barging into the interview room, he grabbed Wiskowski by the collar of his shirt and screamed, inches from his face.

"Where's my daughter, you piece of shit? Where is she? Where is my *daughter*!" It was all Riley and Rock, both as big and strong as bulls, could do to pull the chief off of Wiskowski.

"How do you like it now?" Wiskowski fired back, the fight still raging as another spate of hacking shook him. "How does it feel, you Mick piece of shit? My son died because of you."

"He got what he deserved. He got prison. What happened to him in there isn't on me. That's on you. He was nothing more than a carbon copy of you." The chief spat as Riley and Rock held him back, letting a different interrogation play itself out.

"Well he's dead now. And if there's any justice in this world, you'll soon know how it feels."

"What's that mean? You son of a bitch, you have her. Where is she? Where is my daughter?"

"Go fuck yourself, Flanagan," Wiskowski replied as the Boys escorted the livid chief from the room. But for the first time a smile appeared on his face.

Mac saw it. He'd never taken his eyes off of the old man.

"I wonder what that little smile is all about?"

"What smile," Lich asked. "I didn't see a smile."

"I did, right when Wiskowski said, 'go fuck yourself.' Everyone in the room was trying to push the chief out, so they wouldn't have seen it. But I saw it."

"You think that means he has the girls?"

"I'm starting to think maybe he does. That or he's just enjoying pulling everyone's chain," Mac said. He opened the door and jumped into the hallway to tell Burton.

"It might be worth a shot," he finished.

"It might at that," Burton answered, "And we're not getting anywhere. But let's let things cool just a bit for a few minutes, then we'll go back in."

"That's good. I need to grab something first anyway." Mac said. He went to his cluttered desk and grabbed an oversized maroon coffee mug with a large, gold "M" on it—symbol of the the University of Minnesota—from atop a *Parade of Homes* magazine. Mac had an affinity for looking at houses and real estate, even with the housing market in the tank. He picked it up and looked at the cover, which featured four high-end houses, one of them a Wiskowski-designed home. Mac put down the magazine and went back down to the interview room. He found Burton talking to Riley and Rock, explaining that McRyan was going to take a run at Wiskowski.

"Where's the chief?" Mac asked.

"Up in his office with Hisle and six uniforms to make sure neither of them moves."

"What's with the coffee cup?" Burton asked, pointing to Mac's hand.

"Wiskowski has donated a lot of money to the football program at the U over the years. He has a soft spot for the program."

"Gonna try to create some common ground, are we?"

"The direct approach hasn't worked."

"Going softer?"

"A little indirect perhaps. One other thing. If he's got the girls, he has to be holding them somewhere, right?"

"Yeah, we're looking at his home, businesses, other places right now."

"Have your guys take a look at recent real estate purchases as well," Mac said. "Something out of the ordinary, something that doesn't fit with what the company normally does."

"Like what?"

"I don't know. Just something that doesn't seem right for his business dealings. He builds luxury homes. Is there a purchase somewhere that doesn't fit?"

Burton promptly sent one of his team members off on a computer search.

"Anyone else from Wiskowski's world unaccounted for?" Riley asked.

"We can't find his kid Steve yet," Duffy answered. "We think he might be shacked up somewhere. He's apparently a pussy hound."

"Steven Smith Wiskowski. Lots of money and a fast life," Lich added, flipping through a file on the kid. Steve had his own run-ins with the law in the past over drugs, minor pot possession mostly. "He's not much of a winner either. Word is he went after the reporter who did the TV story on Drew Jr.'s death. Apparently he felt it was exploitive."

"Kind of like Drew Jr. on those Hmong folks," Rock replied. "A whole family of assholes, as far as I'm concerned."

"What's the story on the driver of the car we saw in Ellsworth?" Mac asked, getting back on track.

"Worker named Frank McDonald is the driver. He's down the hall in an interview room," Burton said. "McDonald claims he left a construction site in Menomonie at approximately 7:00 PM. Wiskowski is building homes at a development there." Menomonie was a Wisconsin town, forty-five minutes east of St. Paul off Interstate 94. "He says he closed up one of their models at 7:10 or so and drove back. Says he pulled into Wiskowski Construction over two hours later, at around 9:30 or so."

"So what time was the call from Ellsworth?" Mac asked.

"7:42," Burton answered.

"So he leaves the construction site and makes the call on the way home, right?" McRyan followed.

"Yup," Lich replied, looking at the notes. "Plenty of time to get it done."

"One other thing," Burton added. "McDonald has a record."

"Really," Mac's eyebrows shot up.

"He did time for extortion five years ago down in Chicago, so working with Wiskowski on a kidnapping is not beyond the realm of possibility."

"Or Wiskowski hired him into a good gig when nobody else would, and now his boss calls his marker due," Mac added. "Either way, he looks good for the call."

"He does," Duffy answered. "My guys worked him over. He denies making the call, but he says the timeline is two and a half hours to get home."

"So what's he doing along the way?"

"Said he stopped in Ellsworth."

"Really?" Lich said, surprised.

"And did what?" Mac asked.

"He's got a little woman down there," Duffy answered with a wry smile. "Apparently everyone in Wiskowski's world is a hound. Anyway, she's married, so he goes through town on the way home while the husband's out playing softball and running around with the boys. The husband gets home by midnight on game night, so McDonald goes down, gets a little and gets outta Dodge before daddy comes home."

"And it's a perfect little cover to make the call," Burton added.

"Are we checking his story?"

"We are," Duffy answered. "The Ellsworth cops checked it out. She admits to the affair and that he was there tonight. She says he arrived just before eight, stayed about an hour, finished the job, and left."

"So he makes the call, goes to her house to cover the trip, and then comes home as if nothing happened," Lich said.

"This is looking better by the minute," Mac added as he opened the door into the interview room.

"So what now, I get the junior varsity," Wiskowski said with a smirk as Mac walked into the room and sat down. The old man noticed the cup and looked Mac over again. "You're McRyan aren't you?"

"That's right."

"Nice coffee cup. Hockey player at the U right?"

"Back in the day."

"You played for one of the national title winners."

"I did."

"I prefer football myself. I've donated a lot of money for the new football stadium," Wiskowski said.

"And to your church, don't forget. I know you've been very generous with your church in Cottage Grove," Mac wanted to soften him up.

"I've given some money, yes."

"More than some, Mr. Wiskowski. The new church exists because of your donation."

Wiskowski nodded.

"I for one am pleased folks like you have stepped up to help fund the new stadium," Mac continued quietly. "I look forward to going to an outdoor football game on campus."

"I will not live to see it open."

"But your generosity will live on."

Wiskowski nodded but then spoke again.

"Of course, the way my name is being dragged through the mud today, the U might not be so inclined to have my name remain."

"So why, given those good works, would you take Carrie and Shannon?" Mac was humanizing the girls, not mentioning their last names. "What possible good does that accomplish? All your hard work, all your generosity, all the work to build up your good name and then you do this?" Mac shook his head. "Here's what I'm thinking."

2:54 AM

Mac spoke quietly, going on an hour now with Wiskowski, trying to wear the man down.

"Drew, we've talked a long time now. You have motive, you have the means, and we have your man making a phone call. We have those things locked down." McDonald wasn't admitting to making the call but Wiskowski didn't know that.

"And I've told you that I had…." Wiskowski coughed uncontrollably, doubling over until the coughing fit stopped, and he leaned back in his chair, exhausted. "I've told you for hours now, I have nothing to do with nothing."

"We'll find the girls sooner or later," Mac said, taking another sip of coffee, his cup having been refilled twice now. He'd kept Wiskowski talking for over an hour, walking through what happened to his son, the case, his anger at the chief and Hisle, and at the same time playing to his vanity about his legacy. "We'll find the girls. The thing is, it would be better for you if you told us where they are now."

"Why's that?"

"Because Shannon Hisle is a Type I diabetic. She can get very sick if she doesn't receive insulin. She could die if she doesn't get her medicine." Mac let it hang in the air for a moment. "Do you want that on you? Do you want to go to your grave with that on your conscience? You wanted revenge. Your son was killed in prison. You blame the chief and Lyman Hisle. So you strike back in a way you know that will hurt them. And you've succeeded. Trust me, I know both of those men, and they are hurting. You saw that yourself a few hours ago." Mac paused, and then asked quietly, "But do the girls have to die?"

"I had nothing to do with this," Wiskowski answered. "I can see why you would look at me, I really can. And I don't know what Frank McDonald is doing, but he's done with my company I can assure you. But I have nothing more...." Another coughing fit shook him, the sixth time in the last hour. "I didn't do this." He coughed and wiped his hand across his mouth. "I have nothing to do with this." Wiskowski slumped back into his chair, his head tilting to one side.

As Wiskowski coughed again, an FBI agent stuck his head in and called Burton out.

Mac slumped back into his chair, checking his watch. It was nearly 4:00 AM, and he felt nearly as tired as Wiskowski. The old man's lawyer sensed it as well.

"My client has nothing more to say detectives," the lawyer said. "He's answered your questions time and again. He has nothing to do with the kidnappings. He's weak and tired. He needs to be allowed to go home and rest."

"Sorry counselor, but we obviously think otherwise," Mac answered, although the old man's persistence was causing him to start to wonder if he *was* involved. He wasn't breaking, and he should have by now.

Burton stuck his head back into the room.

"I've got something you need to see," he said, looking at Mac.

Mac and Lich moved back into the hall, joined by Riley, Rock, and Duffy.

"What's up?" Mac asked, yawning.

"You said we should look at recent real estate purchases, right?" Burton asked.

"Yeah, so? Did your people find something?"

"Maybe. Most of the recent purchases are at least six months old, development parcels in the suburbs. They're multiple acres, clearly for residential housing, either high-end houses or townhouses. But there is one that's odd. It's for a single-family home down east of Northfield. It was bought by one of his smaller subsidiary groups, DSW Inc., which is run by Drew and Steve. And it was bought in the last month or so."

"After he found out about the cancer," Mac said.

"That's right," Burton said. "What could be the possible point?"

"Are there other houses around?" Lich asked.

"We did a satellite search of the property," Duffy answered. "It's off by itself. Well in from the county road. There are no other homes nearby."

"Nice country house, perhaps?"

"Doesn't appear to be. Rambler, fairly large, but just a nondescript rambler out in the country."

"How big a piece of land?" Mac asked.

"It was a twenty-acre parcel, maybe a hobby farm, but it's in the middle of nowhere," Duffy replied. "It wouldn't be developed for years, if ever."

"What's Northfield have to say about it?"

"I called out and had them do a drive-by," Duffy answered. "They said a couple of vans are parked in front of the garage. Otherwise, very little going on."

Burton looked to Mac.

"What do you think?"

"Let's ask the old man."

Mac and Burton went back into the interview room. Wiskowski's lawyer looked up.

"I said, we are done."

"I got just one other thing I want to ask about." Mac said.

"What's that?"

"What do you know about this?" Mac slid a sheet of paper in front of Wiskowski and his lawyer. It was the property listing for the Northfield house.

Wiskowski's mouth opened and then his shoulders slumped, like he'd been caught.

"What's out at that house?"

Wiskowski shook his head.

"Maybe that's why McDonald is involved."

"McDonald?" Mac asked, standing now, leaning down to the old man, his voice rising, "McDonald? What's at that house damnit?" He pounded the table, "What's out there?"

Wiskowski looked at the picture.

"Ohh Steve." Drew Sr. put his hands to his face. "I wondered why he bought that place. Why would he do this?" he pleaded to his lawyer, who just shook his head.

"Steve?" Mac asked. "Your son?" They hadn't been able to find Wiskowski's son as of yet. "What's Steve have to do with this?"

Wiskowski pleaded with his lawyer.

"Why would he do this?"

Burton grabbed Mac by the arm.

"We've been looking at the wrong Wiskowski. Let's go."

4:32 AM

Mac and Lich were in the back of an FBI Suburban with Duffy and Burton in front. Two additional Suburbans followed. Just outside the east side of Northfield, the group met up with the Rice County sheriff and three deputies in a parking lot behind a church.

Burton leapt out and was greeted by the sheriff.

"You must be Agent Burton."

"I am."

"George Glenning, Rice County sheriff. The place you're looking for is four miles or so up the road on the right side. House is set well back from the road in a light grove of trees."

"You do a drive-by?"

"Did it myself, fifteen minutes ago. Looks pretty quiet. A few vans are parked in front of the garage, but no activity. Lights off on the main level, although I thought I could detect some light out of the window wells. Someone might be awake in the basement."

"Pretty sleepy, huh?"

"That's my read," Glenning answered. "You have, what, twelve men? Plus my four. That should be plenty of power. How do you want to hit the place?"

"Let's go up nice and easy, without the Suburbans," Burton answered. "If the girls are in there, we don't want to give these guys any warning."

"So we pull up to the end of the driveway and walk in quietly, then."

"Yeah," Burton answered. "From what you're telling me, we'll have a little bit of cover as we approach the house."

"A little. The trees are tall but not terribly thick—cleared out around the bottom. The grass is pretty high, but no brush or anything to hide behind. So you can get to a tree and have some cover, but we'll be exposed when we go for the house."

"Let's do it then."

The Suburbans made the four-mile drive to the house.

"Do you think the girls are really there?" Lich asked, looking at Mac.

"I don't know," Mac answered, checking the clip for his Sig. "But the way Old Man Wiskowski reacted when we showed him the picture of the house, it was as if he put the puzzle together himself. It makes sense. The house is isolated. Steve Wiskowski was torn up about his brother. His dad's going downhill and has been talking about Drew Junior's death. How it's Charlie Flanagan's and Lyman Hisle's fault. The old man is dying in front of him and can't do anything about Flanagan and Hisle, so the kid does. We haven't been able to find the kid. The old man claims he doesn't know where he is." Mac shrugged his shoulders. "This could be it."

"I've heard of crazier things," Lich said, pulling on his vest.

"It at least makes some sense," Mac answered and then added, "We'll know soon enough."

The Suburbans stopped at the driveway, and everyone jumped out. They carefully made their way up to the house, a single-story with white siding and brick halfway up the front. To the right, the driveway swung around to a detached three-stall garage with two vans parked in front. As the group approached the edge of the treeline, there was a noise to the right. A man in blue jeans and a dirty white T-shirt came out the side door to the detached garage, wiping his hands with a rag. The man saw them, dropped the rag, and took off running towards the woods behind the garage.

"We got a runner," a sheriff's deputy yelled and took off after the man.

"You know what that means," Lich said.

"Something's going on here," Mac answered.

The sheriff looked left.

"Now," he said. Two deputies ran up to the front door. Everyone else fell in ten feet behind. One deputy opened the screen door and the other used the big ram. The door blasted open.

"POLICE! FBI!" Burton and Duffy yelled as they burst in and went for the basement stairs. Mac and Lich were right behind went left down the hallway.

"Back right, Mac!" Lich yelled.

"POLICE!" Mac yelled as he burst into the back right bedroom. A man sat up in bed and immediately put his hands up.

"Don't shoot!"

"On the floor! On your knees!" Mac ordered. The man complied quickly. Mac pushed him down onto his stomach. "Hands!" The man again complied. Mac quickly cuffed him and then was up again, following Lich across the hall to check on Riles and Rock, who had their man subdued.

Mac and Lich then cleared the bathroom and closets in each bedroom.

"McRyan, Riley, get down here!" Burton called from the basement.

"Are they down there?" Mac yelled as he bounded down the steps two at a time. "Are they ... here?" Mac's jaw hit the floor as he came to the bottom of the steps. "Are you kidding me? Are you fucking kidding me?" he groaned.

Rows and rows of mature marijuana plants lined up beneath the room's ultraviolet lighting. Its street value was likely in the millions. Steve Wiskowski, kidnapper or not, was definitely a drug supplier.

Burton sighed, "Well at least the DEA will be happy."

12

"The ransom."

TUESDAY, JULY 3RD

Just before 7:00 AM, Mac, Lich, Riles, Rock, and Burton slid into a large booth at the Cleveland Grille. Going to the Grille was like going into a time warp back to the late 1960s or early 1970s. It had old mustard and orange vinyl booths, a speckled tile floor, and very Brady striped wallpaper. It also served the best and most filling breakfast around. Everyone was exhausted and needed to fuel up. The Cleveland would do the trick.

Mac loved the place, the food, and the old atmosphere. Lich loved the place because his girl Dot worked his table. Lich and Dot hooked up at the same time as Mac and Sally last winter during the PTA case. Dot was a treat: a wonderfully warm, salt-and-pepper-haired waitress in her late forties who wore a uniform two sizes too small to show off her ample topside. Lich, of course, loved it. He came in each morning, she doted on him, and he'd pat her on the ass. Mac loved her to death and often wondered whether, if the two got married, if he'd have to call her Dot Lick.

"The usual, Hon?" she asked Mac, setting her right hand on his shoulder.

"You bet." The usual was the CG breakfast burrito, chock full of eggs, sausage, hash browns, peppers, cheese, and salsa. "Get everyone the same," he directed. "Trust me," he said, looking to Burton. "You'll love it. It'll fill you up, and you'll thank me for it later."

While they awaited for their food, they began the postmortem on the raid. No evidence of the girls was found at the Northfield house and alibis were checking out. Wiskowski Sr. was still of interest, but it was dying by the minute. Everyone knew, in their hearts and heads, that he was a dead end.

"I thought it was Wiskowski," Mac groaned, sipping at a large glass of ice water. "I can't believe how wrong I was about him. It all fit, right down to the house out in the country."

"It wasn't just you. We were all wrong," Burton said. "I thought it was Wiskowski, too. I'd have bet my pension on it."

"Someone explain the car in Ellsworth to me then," Riles asked, rubbing his eyes. "Were we wrong on that too?"

"If Wiskowski is not involved in this, but one of his cars ends up involved, is it a setup then?" Lich asked.

"These guys have been so careful. And then to get caught with an actual license plate by some old man sitting on a park bench?" Burton said. "I was surprised they would have screwed up like that."

Dot appeared with five GC Burritos. She added two extra pots of coffee. Hunger took over for a few minutes as everyone inhaled the first few bites of food.

As the initial assault on the burritos slowed, Mac snorted.

"I bet it was a setup. God, the more I think about that car in Ellsworth, the more it seems like it was."

"What has you so sure now?"

"The driver of the car, whoever it was, sat there for a while, perhaps five minutes according to our witness in Ellsworth," Mac answered, leaning back against the back of his booth and crossing his arms.

Burton nodded, picking at his plate.

"Why wait around when you want to make the call quick and be done?"

"Right. Why sit at the phone for five minutes, if not more, *before* making the call, unless...."

"Unless you want to be seen," Riles finished, scratching the deep stubble on the right side of his face. "Cripes, these guys have thought of everything."

"So whoever this guy is," Riles continued, "he sits at the phone until our witness shows up. Once our guy is certain he's been seen, he makes the call and then leaves."

"We find the witness, get the plate, start down the Wiskowski path, and lose all this time," Rock added.

"Well, if it was a setup, they got exactly what they wanted," Lich said.

"Right, we're spending all our time looking at Wiskowski and not in the right place," Burton said, shaking his head. "Shit."

"It certainly would fit these bastards," Mac noted. "They wanted to push us in another direction, even if for just a short period of time. All the while, they continue doing what they're doing and we fall farther behind."

"It makes sense, when you think about how these guys have operated," Burton added.

"Maybe we should have seen it sooner," Mac said, stuffing a fork full of food into his mouth.

"You mean, besides the car angle?" Rock asked, adding some toast to his butter.

"Yeah. Maybe we should have seen it in the motive," Mac said.

"How so?" Burton asked.

"The kidnappers have operated as if ransom is their motivation, with a personal element added in. For Wiskowski, maybe that whole equation doesn't work. He's got more money than he could ever spend, so ransom doesn't make sense, but he's got motive up the wazoo personally. If he wanted revenge for his son, he could've just killed the chief and Lyman. Why go through all this bullshit with phone calls, switching vans, and the whole nine yards? Mac let it hang in the air for a moment. "We didn't see it because we've been working around the clock to find the girls. It was the first thing that looked good to us. A lot of the parts fit—just not all of them. But you know what really scares me?"

"What?" Burton asked.

"What's really *really* scary," Mac replied, "is that they scouted and planned it to the point of finding this McDonald guy and hanging him out to dry as part of this. They have been planning this for a long long time to get that part right."

"I can hardly wait to see what comes next," Lich replied, resignation in his voice. "They're way ahead of us."

Dot showed up and asked if anyone needed anything else. Everyone begged off. Dot set the bill down and Burton grabbed it.

"You don't have to do that," Riles said.

"Naw. I got this. I usually don't get asked out for breakfast by the local police. I appreciate the offer."

"Well, don't let me stand in your way," Lich said with a smile.

"So what about other possibles?" Rock asked.

"We're continuing to work through the files," Burton answered. "We never stopped, but nothing else has popped."

"And the time is passing quickly," Riles noted.

"Indeed," Burton answered. "And I have a feeling we'll hear from the kidnappers again real soon. So at this point, I'm going to start something else."

"Which is?"

"The ransom. That demand is going to come soon, I think, and we need to be ready. To Mac's point on how prepared the kidnappers seem to be, there may not be time to find out who these guys are. We may need to wait for the money drop."

"I don't like just sitting back," Mac said with some annoyance.

"We're not sitting back," Burton answered calmly. "Just working dual angles is all. We need to be prepared. I don't have any intention of stopping the hunt for these guys." The FBI man's answer seemed to satisfy everyone.

"Back at it then," Mac said.

"We need a break," Burton said.

"If the girls don't get a break..." Rock started.

"I hear ya, I hear ya," Burton broke in. "But I've got my guys, and yours, working the files. Until they get something to work, you guys need a few winks, just a couple of hours. Be back downtown by eleven."

"He's right," Riles said, yawning. A couple of hours of sleep seemed like a good idea.

Everyone got up to go. Lich asked Mac to hang back. He wanted a few minutes with Dot. Mac stayed in his booth and sipped at the rest of his coffee. He jumped as a hand touched his shoulder. He looked up to see Heather Foxx staring down at him.

"Good morning, Detective," Heather said. "Can I join you for a moment?"

"Heather, Heather, Heather, you know I can't tell you anything," Mac answered.

"Yeah, yeah," she replied with a dismissive wave, opening a muffin she'd bought at the counter. She mixed cream and sugar into a to-go coffee. She'd had some sleep and looked good in a white linen coat and blouse with a short black skirt. She looked damn good. And she'd behaved herself the night before.

"Let me ask you something," Mac started.

"Shoot."

"How come you weren't up front with the rest of the hyenas last night when Wiskowski was brought in?" Mac asked.

"No comment," Heather replied with a mischievous a smile.

"That's my line," Mac replied, smiling back.

"Really, what are we going to find out shouting questions as you guys walk in?" Heather retorted, sitting up. "My producers love that stuff, but I hate it. I'd always just prefer to talk to people, get a one-on-one interview after I've earned some trust. But just running around like an idiot?" She shook her head. "That ain't for me."

Mac liked that answer. It was the answer of a professional, and Heather Foxx was a good reporter. Maybe she deserved a little break. The Wiskowski raid had yet to hit the media.

"So, where are you at on this Wiskowski thing?" Mac asked.

Heather looked at him quizzically at first, but then her right eyebrow rose just a bit at the hint of an opportunity. "You guys had him in for questioning overnight. I assume that you have something more than just his radio rant a few months ago—maybe something on a car or a truck—but beyond that I have no idea. However, my esteemed colleagues seem to have him convicted already."

"Yeah, we heard that, too," Mac answered. "Reporters should really get their facts straight before they hang a man, don't you think?"

"I take it, it would be wrong to have hung him at this point then?" Heather asked, sensing she was about to get a scoop from the last guy she ever expected to get one from.

"Let's just say that, if you haven't been out in front on this, then you're in a good position." Mac gave her a little bit on the Northfield raid, just enough for her to check around, particularly with the Rice County sheriff.

"In other words, it may be fair to report, if someone were to do that sort of thing, that questions have arisen with regard to Mr. Wiskowski's status as a suspect," Heather said.

"He may not be completely out of the woods yet, but it would be fair to conclude that a few issues have come up that suggest Wiskowski is not involved with the kidnappings," Mac said, smiling.

"Well, I hate to eat and run," Heather said.

"Don't let me stop you," Mac answered. "I'm going to bed."

Smith awoke to the tropical humidity of a Minnesota heat wave wafting through the window. He rolled out of bed and pushed the curtains to the side with the intent of viewing a clear sky, but instead found a grayish haze already hanging thick in the air. It was going to be a steamer.

Smith shook his head. People thought Minnesota was some frozen tundra, and that certainly could be the case in January. But in the summer months, Minnesota temperatures routinely hit the nineties, with periods of insufferable sultry air that could last for days on end. They were in such a stretch now, and there was no foreseeable break in the forecast. The afternoon trip to the river would be refreshing, but there was other business to attend to first.

He looked back to the empty right side of the bed. Monica was already up. Through the crack in the bedroom door he could hear her moving around in the kitchen. He also heard the sound of paper bags being unrolled. The unmistakable smell of a greasy drive-through breakfast drifted through the house. He sat up and threw his legs over the side of the bed, looked at his hands and shook his head. He was wearing rubber gloves, even in bed. He and the rest of the crew were doing everything they could to avoid leaving a trace, so in the safe house, everyone wore gloves. It was an odd way to live, but it was only necessary for a few days. He picked up his watch off the nightstand, slid it over his gloved left hand, and checked the time. It was 8:27 AM.

Out of bed, he stepped across the hall to the safe house's other bedroom and nudged the door open with his left foot. Dean and David lay side by side on the floor on olive green inflatable Coleman mattresses. Smith kicked them awake and then made for the kitchen, where he found Monica laying out a smorgasbord of McDonald's breakfast options. The smell of grease, egg, sausage, and coffee lifted Smith out of his stupor. He walked up to Monica and kissed her on the lips. He sat down at the metal card table and opened a McGriddle. Taking the plastic top off a white Styrofoam cup, he carefully took a sip of the piping-hot coffee. He ripped the tops off of two creamers and poured in the contents, along with a pack of sugar to sweeten the cup.

Monica sat down with a separate bag, pulled out a yogurt parfait, and began mixing the fruit and yogurt.

"What time do you plan on leaving?" she asked as she sprinkled in the nuts.

"I want to get going by nine o'clock or so and get into position as soon as we can—get a feel for the area for awhile before I move."

Dean and David came shuffling down the hall, buttoning their shorts and sliding baseball caps onto their heads. The large men yawned as they surveyed the buffet. They each selected several wrapped items, sat down, and immediately commenced gorging. Smith told them he wanted to be on the road by 9:00. The brothers simply nodded as they stuffed their faces full of egg and sausage.

"While you're gone, I'll clean everything out of here again," Monica said. "I'll meet you in Hudson later."

Forensics.

Smith, Dean, and David were all in the system, so they needed to be careful, thus everyone wore gloves in the house, but that wasn't all.

For each of the past five days, Monica had cleaned the place like it had never been cleaned before. After cleaning each time, she dumped the garbage, linens, and cleaning materials far from the safe house. The next day, she started with new sponges, mops, and buckets. The vacuum cleaner was used twice a day and, when not being used, was stored in one of the vans. They never made meals or drank water out of the faucet. The only thing they used in the house was the toilet, but only the one upstairs and they flushed three times and cleaned it with every use. Monica also cleaned it twice a day on her rounds. If the house was discovered, Smith didn't want to chance that even a single print or hair would be left behind.

"What time do you want to make the call?" David asked Smith.

"I want to make it by 11:30," Smith said. He looked at his watch, "That'll give 'em just over thirty hours to get everything together."

"What time will you make it back to the river?" Monica asked. "I don't want to be too early."

"Two o'clock, maybe 2:30. We'll go check on the campsite, set up the ladder, and make sure everything is still in place, especially after the storms last night."

They ate in silence for a few minutes. When the food was gone and the garbage completely cleared away, Smith grabbed the keys off the counter and Dean asked him.

"They're not on to us at all?"

"Nope."

"You're sure?" David pushed.

"Positive," Smith replied. "We're clean."

13

"Prepared, complicated, and motivated."

Mac rubbed his eyes and checked his watch. It was 8:03 AM when he dropped Lich off. Mac agreed to pick him up in a couple of hours, and he powered up the window to keep the blazing heat out. Sometimes when storms blew through town, as they had the night before, a cool front would come in behind and bring some relief from the heat. This was not one of those times. Mac's dashboard thermometer registered eighty-six degrees. It was going to be a miserable day.

Mac exhaled. There was a complicated plan in motion—a plan that was only partially executed, and they had no idea what was coming next. Furthermore, Mac worried that the kidnappers knew—had to know—that the police and FBI would be applying immense resources in search of the connection. The kidnappers either knew this and didn't care, which Mac doubted was the case, or they believed that the connection would be made, if ever, only after they were long gone, somewhere on the other side of the world, living off the ransom with new identities, never to be found. If the connection was that hard to find, the odds of making it were not in their favor.

Burton was worried about the timeline as well, so he was focusing on the money drop, figuring that might be their best chance. Having the money so close that the kidnappers could taste it might cause a mistake that the FBI and police could pounce on. The FBI man had the experience and the success, but Mac wasn't so confident about catching the kidnappers when it came time to pay the ransom. Burton was good, no doubt, but they were up against someone with all the advantages at this point. And this was not a by-the-numbers case. The kidnappers were keeping them off balance and would be ready for the ransom drop. It wouldn't be simple.

What bothered him the most was what was motivating the kidnappers. There was no reason to pick both Carrie Flanagan and Shannon Hisle other than to get at their fathers. This was as much about revenge or retribution—whatever you wanted to call it—as it was money.

Mac turned left and made his way to Berkley Avenue and halfway down he pulled up in front of Sally's house. He snorted and shook his head. He always thought of it as *her* house, and she kept telling him he needed to think of it as *theirs*. Well, it might be "their" house, but she got the one-car garage, so he parked in the street.

Out of the Explorer, he stretched his arms, moved his head from side to side and yawned, the last day finally catching up with him. As he walked slowly up the driveway he ran everything through his mind again. He sat down on the back stoop and pinched the bridge of his nose. Another thing was beginning to gnaw at him. He didn't feel like he or everyone else was really doing anything, pushing the investigation and beating the bushes, throwing out theories, doing what Lich liked to call "that investigative shit."

Tired as he was, he could feel the time ticking away. He didn't know what the clock was, but he was certain that they were way behind and that the time remaining was short. It was like being down by two touchdowns with less than two minutes to go, and the other team had the ball. Mac went inside and into the kitchen. He grabbed a bottle of water out of the fridge and went back out to the stoop. Taking a pull off the water, he closed his eyes and tried to think about what they had done thus far and what they needed to do. He took out his notebook and started jotting down notes about the case. In the center of a fresh sheet, he wrote down his three concerns, boiled down to three words: prepared, complicated, and motivated.

The door opened behind him and Sally, dressed for work, stepped out onto the stoop. She sat down, kissed him on the lips, and put her hand up the back of his shirt to scratch his back while he continued with his notes.

"Prepared, complicated, and motivated?" Sally asked.

"That's what these guys are?"

He surrounded the three words with notes, thoughts, and names. He was tired, exhausted really, and needed sleep. But his mind was working a little now, churning, moving, and he wanted to get it down on paper, then sleep on it for two hours. He would let it all roll around in his subconscious. Fifteen minutes later, his head hit the pillow with "prepared, complicated, and motivated" percolating in his mind.

14

"In reality, a million dollars isn't that much."

11:47 AM

Smith walked past the bank, through the alley, and across the street into the quiet city park. He was in Duluth, Minnesota, two hours north of the Twin Cities. Sitting at the far southwestern tip of Lake Superior, Duluth was an old port city with a large and deep harbor. At one time, Duluth was a booming shipping town, a pickup point for taconite, iron ore, and agricultural products to be shipped through the Great Lakes and onward to the Atlantic. However, with the decline of northern Minnesota's mining industry, Duluth had suffered both economically and in population, which was now just over 87,000. Back in the 1950s it had been well over 100,000. Still, Duluth was a beautiful town, built into the rocky hillside overlooking the largest of the Great Lakes. The steep cliffs and the roads traversing them vertically made him think of San Francisco, though without the Golden Gate and the trolley cars. As Smith looked back between the buildings, he could see the lake off in the distance, its dark cool blue water meeting the deep cloudless blue horizon, making the lake look like an ocean. The cool water of the lake also moderated the local temperature, making things more comfortable in Duluth than the rest of the state. While the temperature was going to hit the sticky upper nineties in the Twin Cities, Duluth was an easy seventy-four degrees as the noon hour approached.

Smith turned to the task at hand. He'd chosen the park weeks ago. Set in an older neighborhood on the southern end of town, it was pleasantly empty, as it had been when he first visited. Nonetheless, Smith wore a baseball cap pulled down tightly, wraparound sunglasses, and a nondescript outfit of jeans, a plain white T-shirt, orange reflector vest and tan leather work gloves. He carried an orange toolbox containing a variety of tools including screwdrivers, wrenches, and a hammer. To anyone walking by, he would look like a run-of-the-mill city maintenance worker.

The pay phone sat on the wall outside a small, octagonal cinderblock building that served as a warming house for ice skaters in the winter. He checked the door of the building, which was locked. He looked through the metal-grated window to make sure it was empty inside. It was. Scanning the area around the park, he noted only an older woman walking her yip dog on the far side of the park, at least a hundred yards away.

With the park clear, Smith opened his toolbox, took the top tray out and pulled out a roll of quarters and his voice-masking device, which he placed over the phone. He dialed the number for Flanagan. The chief of police picked up on the second ring.

"Flanagan."

"Hello, Chief, and greetings to the many members of the Federal Bureau of Investigation listening in. Good day to you all. Chief, we want five million dollars total for your daughter and for Shannon Hisle. The cash is to be in non-sequential hundred-dollar bills. No dye packs or GPS tracking devices. Keep it simple and comply. You have until 6:00 PM tomorrow. We will call your office phone at that time with instructions for the drop."

"What about our daughters? I'm not giving you anything until I speak with my daughter live on the phone."

"Sorry, Chief but that isn't possible now. If you go to Griffin Stadium at St. Paul Central High School and look under Seat 10, Row 15, Section C, you'll see why. We have a little gift for you that will, I think, motivate you and Mr. Hisle to meet our more than reasonable demands. Good day."

Smith cradled the phone, took off the masking device, and kneeled down to reassemble his tool box, closing the top and fastening the latch. He walked briskly back across the street and through the alley. Dean saw Smith approaching and started the van. Once inside, Smith checked his watch. The walk back to the van took a little over a minute. Dean pulled out onto the street, turned left, and traveled four blocks north. As he waited at a stop light, a Duluth police squad car roared through the intersection, rollers and siren going, heading in the direction of the park.

"Could be something else," Dean said, noting the pensive look on Smith's face.

Smith simply nodded as he contemplated their next move, noting the swiftness of the police response, if that was in fact what it was.

"I want to make sure. Let's take a more leisurely drive back," he said as the van merged onto Interstate 35 south a few minutes later.

Dean nodded and took the bridge east on Highway 2 over St. Louis Bay, crossing over to the city of Superior on the Wisconsin side. The group drove back south toward the Twin Cities on Wisconsin's quiet State Highway 35 instead of Minnesota's popular Interstate 35.

"McRyan," Mac said, answering his cell phone with a yawn.

"Where are you at?" Burton asked.

"Just south of downtown on West Seventh."

"Meet me at Griffin Stadium."

"Griffin Stadium? At St. Paul Central High?" Mac asked quizzically. "What the heck for?"

"Kidnappers left a gift for us. And we have the ransom demand."

Two minutes later, Mac was weaving in traffic again, the siren moving traffic.

"Five million dollars?" Mac said skeptically, turning a hard right onto Lexington Parkway and heading north. "That's light."

"What do you mean light?" Lich asked, confused.

"Split three ways, maybe four, that's not that much money," Mac said. "Four ways, my Cretin High School math tells me that's $1.25 million per." He shook his head. "Odd."

"Maybe to you," Lich said, "But to me, I could make $1.25 million go pretty far. Especially tax-free."

"Yeah, after alimony, you'd have a buck twenty-five left," Mac snickered.

"Smart-ass."

"All kidding aside, think about it. You kidnap the daughters of the chief of police and a high-priced lawyer, and all you ask for is five million for the two?" Mac questioned. "I don't buy it. All that risk for that little reward, relatively speaking. I mean in reality Dick, a million dollars isn't that much. A nice house with some equity, some money in a retirement fund or two, a little inheritance, and you're there. I mean, five million split between three or four people just isn't that much."

"If you say so," Lich replied. "You're the one with the money, so you should know." Mac did have money. He had invested in a coffee business with two high school friends a number of years ago. There were now twenty-seven Grand Brew Coffee Shops with more on the drawing board. While a minority investor, Mac's ten percent investment left him sitting pretty. It was one secret Lich had managed to keep. Mac didn't want everyone on the force to know that he was going to be—in fact already was—wealthy.

Lich changed topics.

"God, the air conditioner feels good," he said, wiping the sweat beads from his bald head. Sweat had already filtered through his fresh red Hawaiian shirt. He looked like Norm Peterson on a *Cheers* episode. "And not a cloud in the sky. We're gonna bake today."

"Grab the white beach cap in the back seat," Mac replied. "It'll help keep your head cooler." Not to mention that the last thing Lich needed was a sunburned head.

"God, it feels like this is all I've done for the last twenty-four hours," Lich said, reaching in back. "Run around."

"That's what the kidnappers want," Mac said, decelerating hard as he approached a left turn onto Marshall Avenue, with St. Paul Central High School on his left. Mac turned in front of the school, drove past the front door and smoothly turned right into a parking lot behind the football field. Two squad cars were there already, as well as a Tahoe from Forensics. The uniform cops had crime scene tape up, creating a perimeter. A guard waved the Explorer through a break in the tape.

As Mac hopped out of the Explorer and looked back, Riley, Burton, and the others pulled in. He noticed a few media types already loitering against the tape, including Heather Foxx, who was still looking good in that white sleeveless blouse. Her tastefully short, black skirt hugged her hips and revealed her tan legs. Heather looked happy. The Wiskowski tip put her well into first place in the morning media game.

"Mac?" He turned to see his second cousin Tip, a patrol cop, pointing to the football bleachers. "Up in the stands."

Mac, Lich, and the rest hustled through the tunnel in the middle of the grandstand and then up the bleachers to the spot just in front of the press box, where a tech was taking photos, dusting for prints, and evaluating the package. Wrapped in clear plastic, it hung underneath a wood bleacher like a bat in a cave. Mac walked down the row just below where everyone was hovering. He crouched down, took off his sunglasses, and looked underneath. "What do you see?" Burton asked.

"Laptop," Mac answered, noting the red and blue inputs on the back. The laptop was held to the seat by duct tape, which looked to be covering Velcro straps

"Any prints?" Burton asked the crime tech.

"Nada. It's clean," was the curt reply from the tech.

"Not even on the tape or the plastic?" Lich asked. The tech just shook his head. The kidnappers weren't leaving them anything to work with.

"Are we canvassing?" Riles asked, wiping sweat off his upper lip with the back of his hand.

"I've got bodies coming, yours and ours," Burton replied. "We'll blanket the neighborhood, see what turns up."

Mac snorted and shook his head.

"Got to do it I know, but it's a big fuckin' waste of time," he said.

"Never know, someone could have seen something," Burton said.

"You really think so? These guys haven't left us anything up to this point," Mac replied in disgust.

Burton exhaled and shook his head.

"No, but like you said, gotta do it."

"What about the laptop?" Lich asked. "Want to look here or downtown?"

"Downtown," Burton replied. "I want my people taking a look at it. I'm guessing we have video."

15

"How are they going to breathe?"

Channel 12 broke into its early afternoon soap opera for a special report. The tanned, toothy, and well-coiffed anchor Paul Phillips walked the lead in.

"We're cutting into our regular programming to bring you breaking news about the kidnappings of Carrie Flanagan, daughter of St. Paul Police Chief Charlie Flanagan, and Shannon Hisle, daughter of prominent St. Paul attorney Lyman Hisle. Right now we're going to Channel 12's Heather Foxx in St. Paul, who's been tracking this story for us. Heather."

"Paul, we're at the St. Paul Police Department headquarters, where the FBI and police have just arrived with a laptop computer found under the stands in Griffin Stadium at St. Paul Central High School," Heather said perfectly to the camera. She loved doing this on the fly, the rush of excitement, pulling it off without a hitch. Reports like this got you a network or cable gig, she thought, when you were quick on your feet, looking good, totally under control, regardless of the adrenaline pumping through your veins. "And, in another Channel 12 exclusive, we've learned that the police have received a ransom demand for the two girls."

"Do we know what the ransom demand is, Heather?" Phillips piped in.

"At this point, no, Paul," Heather answered. "We've been unable to learn the amount."

"Did the FBI and police learn of the ransom demand from the laptop, Heather?"

"No, Paul. The ransom demand was received by phone. At that time the authorities were apparently directed to the laptop at Central High."

"Do we know what is on the laptop."

"No, we don't. It is my understanding that the police were bringing it back here to analyze it."

"Heather," Phillips asked, tacking in a different direction. "What about the police and FBI takedown in Northfield that you reported on earlier? Any further developments?"

"The police have released Drew Wiskowsi, although his son Steve is now in custody. However, it appears that neither of them are involved in the kidnappings of Shannon Hisle and Carrie Flanagan," Foxx answered.

"Well," the anchor smiled, showing unnaturally white teeth, "it has indeed been a busy day for the FBI and police."

"Indeed it has, Paul," Heather replied seriously. "They continue to ask for the public's help, particularly with regard to the vans and the descriptions we have of the kidnappers." The pretty reporter provided the now-familiar general description of large men, likely dark hair, operating in the delivery or panel vans common throughout town. Foxx finished by providing the phone numbers to contact the police and FBI and then signed off.

"Reporting from the St. Paul Police Department, this is Heather Foxx, Channel 12 News." She held the pose for a moment, and then her cameraman waved her off.

"Nice report," he said.

"Thanks, but cripes it's hot," she replied, wiping a film of perspiration off her forehead.

A Channel Six van pulled up, and reporter Scott Crossman climbed out of the van in a navy blue, button-down collar shirt and blue tie. His dress shirt was sticking to his body, and sweat rings showed around his pits and collar. He wasn't going on camera any time soon.

"Christ, Heather, who's your fucking source for this stuff?" Crossman was pissed, but there was admiration in his voice.

The detectives and agents filed into the conference room and set the laptop on the conference table. The chief and Lyman wanted in, but Burton, with the help of Peters and Riley convinced them to wait outside while the group took the first look. The mayor, for reasons Mac couldn't quite figure out, joined them. An FBI tech with rubber gloves and a lab coat, flipped the top open to the laptop. He spent the next few minutes checking the laptop keys for prints. Not surprisingly, there were none. While the techs worked, the rest watched Heather Foxx's report.

"She has a good source," Burton said.

"She usually does. She bats her eyes or loosens a button or two on that blouse of hers, and some puppy-eyed cop spills the beans," was Mac's wry reply.

"Speakin' from experience, Detective?" the mayor asked, his tone just a little accusatory.

"If that ain't the pot calling the kettle black," Mac replied, not looking up from the laptop. He heard the mayor snort behind him.

"You *will* live dangerously," Lich warned in a quiet, albeit amused voice as he leaned over Mac's shoulder.

"So what do we *really* have here?" the FBI tech said as he powered up the computer. The laptop was a Compaq and looked new.

"Can we track where the laptop came from?" Riley asked, looking at Mac.

"I should think so," Mac replied, and then looked at the FBI tech, a little edge in his voice. "Can you?"

"Sure, we just need to take this serial number," the agent answered, pointing underneath the computer, "and get with Compaq." He jotted down the serial number and gave it to another agent. "It'll take a little time to track it down," he said to the group at large.

"Pray they bought it with a credit card," Riley replied.

"I doubt we'll be that lucky." Mac replied.

"Might get something," Riley said pointedly. "We gotta have hope," he added through clenched teeth, staring a hole through Mac.

Mac read the sign: watch the negativity and stay cool. The chief was in the hallway, and he didn't need to see his boys with their heads down. Sooner or later, the kidnappers would make a mistake and *then* the Boys would capitalize, but only if they kept their minds open to the possibility. Mac exhaled, nodded lightly, and spoke more calmly.

"We might, we might. If we can figure out when the laptop was bought and where," he added. "Maybe we can get something. They wouldn't pay with a credit card, or at least one in their real names or names we could trace. But..."

"But what?" Riles asked.

"If they bought at a Best Buy, Target, Costco, Wal-Mart, someplace like that," Mac added, "We could figure out which register it was bought at and what time. Maybe we could get surveillance camera footage from the checkout."

"Think we can catch one of the men on the surveillance video?" Duffy asked.

"Or the woman," Lich added. "Let's not forget about her."

"Depends. They might have had someone purchase it for them. But let's check and see. Do you guys have access to that facial-recognition software?" Mac asked.

"If need be," a member of Burton's crew answered.

"Get on that," Burton said, "Let's track that computer down."

"So what's on the computer?" Lich asked, pushing to get back on task.

"Let's take a look," the FBI tech replied. He powered up the laptop, waiting for the screen to come to life. When it did, there was a video icon on the screen. The tech double clicked on the icon, and a video program opened up.

The video began soundlessly with a view out the windshield of a vehicle, either a truck or a van, driving down a rough dirt road with knee-high grass and weeds between the tire tracks. There was taller grass, bushes, and scraggly trees in the background. The picture vibrated as the vehicle jostled into potholes or rocks.

The time in upper right corner showed 9:09 PM, the date July 2, the night before. It was dusk.

After a minute of elapsed time, the dirt road wound its way toward a straight line of tall trees. The road then turned left to run parallel with the thick tree line. The area was vacant with no activity.

At 9:15 by the video clock, the vehicle abruptly turned right onto an overgrown path, its long grass matted down by what must have been only a couple of previous trips. The vehicle pulled up to a tree with orange tape tied around its massive trunk.

The video went dark, and someone groaned in dismay.

The picture came back to life ten seconds later, the time now reading 9:23.

Laying motionless on the floor of the van was Carrie Flanagan on the left and Shannon Hisle on the right. Shovels and PVC piping surrounded them. Black ties bound the girls' wrists and ankles. Both were blindfolded and gagged. They did not appear harmed or beaten, simply sweaty and disheveled. Hisle, still dressed in her café golf shirt and khaki shorts, looked pale. Flanagan still wore her jean shorts and a smudged white tank top.

A too-familiar voice finally broke the deathly quiet of the conference room.

"The girls are alive," it said. The camera zoomed in on Flanagan and then Hisle for long enough to show that the girls' chests were moving. "They have been drugged. They will probably awaken around the time you are watching this video."

Mac looked at his watch: 1:22 PM.

"Now let's go see where they will wake up," the voice continued, and the camera panned to the right to a black-clad man wearing a gloves and a ski mask. He pulled a piece of PVC piping out from the right side of the van. The camera followed him as he turned his back on the camera and walked away, off to the right of the screen.

The video went dark.

It came alive again, the time now 9:47 PM.

"This is where the girls will be when they wake up." The girls were lying motionless in a sturdy reinforced plywood box, side-by-side, their arms and feet no longer bound.

"What's that box, maybe two feet high, four across, and six feet long?" Mac asked quietly.

"Looks about right," Burton answered softly.

The camera zoomed, showing that what looked like a Dictaphone and a flashlight lying between the girls.

"You'll note the absence of food and water," the voice said, as if reading everyone's mind.

"Ah shit," Rock uttered quietly.

"Motherfuckers," Mac muttered, knowing where this was going.

The camera pulled back to show the box lying in a large hole, four to five feet deep. Portable lights provided just enough illumination to film, but not enough to identify the location. The video showed the arms of two men laying a piece of reinforced plywood over the box, then using electric screwdrivers to set it in place. There was no hole in the top for ventilation.

"How are they going to breathe?" Rock asked.

"The PVC piping," Mac answered as he pointed to the lower right side of the screen. "If you look, there are holes on the right side of the box."

The video went dark.

It came back to life, five minutes later, now 10:01 PM.

As Mac had suggested, one of the men was securing the PVC piping to the right side of the wood box. The camera pulled straight back to show that the pipes were four to five feet long, and would probably stick just above ground once the dirt was shoveled back into the hole. The voice came back, briefly.

"The girls have two pipes for air to breathe."

The video once again went dark.

Ten seconds later, it came back to life, 10:27 PM.

The last of the dirt was being shoveled into the hole. The pipe stood inches above the ground. The camera pulled back to show that the area was a small clearing in the midst of thick woods. Logic dictated it couldn't be far from the edge of the tree line, but there was no way to tell. The voice came back one last time.

"Mr. Hisle, I bet you're wondering about your daughter's diabetes. That Type 1 is nasty stuff. Your daughter will just have to hang on. So if you and the chief want the girls back alive, you follow our next set of instructions to the letter."

The video went dead.

The room was silent for a minute.

“Motherfuckers,” Rock railed, pounding the table, rattling the laptop, coffee cups, and water bottles. He wasn’t alone—several officers found something to hit, or at least some space to pace, to try to regain their composure. But Mac, Riles, and Burton stood still, deep in thought. Burton had his arms crossed, stroking his chin with his right hand. Mac grabbed a notepad and scribbled his thoughts down, working the gum in his mouth hard. Riles took a look over Mac’s shoulder and nodded.

“We gotta ... gotta ... find these guys,” Lich ground out, running his hand over his bald head. “We don’t have much time.”

“We need to go over this video with a fine tooth comb, find anything and everything,” Mac said. “I know a guy. We need to get this to....”

“We’ve got that covered,” Burton interrupted. “This is the FBI’s bailiwick. Technology is our deal.”

“Yeah, but wait a minute...” Mac persisted. “I know a guy....”

Burton steamrolled him and took control of the room.

“Duffy,” he said, pointing to the laptop, “let’s get our video people on this, every second of that video. I want them going over it, picking it apart, find something that we can use.”

“I’ll make it happen,” Duffy answered.

“Wait,” Mac pleaded, but Riley grabbed his elbow.

“Keep your powder dry for now and let Burton do his thing,” Riles whispered into his ear, “this is the FBI’s show. Let them play it out.” Riley gave him a look that recommended patience.

“We don’t have the luxury of time,” Mac retorted under his breath.

“See what Burton does,” Riley replied, equally quiet. “Let’s see if he’s as good as they say he is.”

“And thinks he is,” Mac replied, with just a touch of skepticism. Riley returned a knowing smirk. “I like the guy,” Mac added in a whisper, "but I only see him reacting to events. We need to push this thing."

"We need to stay at the table. The mayor's here for a reason. He's just waiting for us to fall out of line."

"What about that pipe for air from the..." Lich asked the room, struggling for what to call it.

"Grave. It's a fucking grave," Mac said, finishing the thought out loud, drawing looks from the room. "And that's how they want us, the chief, Lyman, all of us to think of it. If we don't find these guys, that's where those girls will die."

"They're not going to die," Burton replied with fervor. "We're going to find them."

"How?" Rock asked.

"First," Burton answered, "We're going over that videotape. If there is something there, we'll find it. Something in the van, an identifying characteristic or mark on one of the kidnappers, I'll bet that there's something there. The road and land they're on, we need to see if there's any identifying landmarks or features on it. We just have to break it down and look."

Mac joined in.

"We need to, at a minimum, get this out to local sheriffs and chiefs within an hour of the cities. The girls are buried somewhere rural, but they can't be *that* far from town. They need to be somewhat close, so maybe, just maybe, some county mountie will recognize something."

"Why don't you think they're farther away?" Riles asked.

"They want isolation for sure, they have to have it to bury the girls and not draw any attention with those lights. That takes time and privacy. But they can't be working two or three hours away. That's not convenient enough. They'd want to stay close," Mac shook his head. "They're not up in Brainerd and then driving two, three hours down here to plant laptop computers under football bleachers. They're centered somewhere around here and then driving from the Twin Cities, or somewhere nearby, up to Clearwater or down to Ellsworth. They're not that far away."

"McRyan, the last phone call was from Duluth," Duffy noted. "They made it from a city park. They could be prowling around up there. That creates an awfully wide net."

"Fine then. Let's send the thing out to the whole state as well as western Wisconsin," Mac said. "But I doubt they have the girls up in Duluth or any place that far from the Twin Cities. They're in closer somewhere."

"Then why go to Duluth?" Duffy pressed.

"Because now they're not on as tight of a timeline. They're not calling us until 6:00 PM tomorrow night. So they have time to go a little farther away, gain that extra layer of safety. And at the same time, they get the chance to make us think they're that far away. They want us expending resources casting that wide of a net, spreading ourselves that thin. But I just don't think they're that far away. They're closer than that. They have to be."

"Still an awfully big area ... essentially the fifteen-county area," Lich said, looking at the map pinned to the bulletin board. "And we don't know this for sure."

"No, we don't," Mac replied. "But it feels right, makes sense, and gives us something to work with, a lot of eyes to give us a look. Who knows? Maybe some sheriff's deputy, forest ranger, or cop gets a look at that video and says, 'hey six years ago I responded to an emergency call down that road.'"

"I don't know," Duffy said, with apprehension in his voice. "What if this thing leaks? I mean, this is pretty unsettling video. It'll create a media firestorm if it gets out. I'd rather control this." Mac got the feeling that FBI control of the investigation was of more concern to him than the girls or the kidnappers.

"Agreed," the mayor added.

"Are you two fucking kidding me?" Mac growled. "Media firestorm's worth it if someone finds that spot."

"I don't want to create a panic, Detective," the mayor asserted. "We put this video out there, there's a chance we'll create hysteria. Hell we've got calls coming in by the dozens from people worried that every van that drives by carries a kidnapper."

"So what? You don't want help from citizens?"

"No, I do," the mayor answered. "But I got calls today where we've got three different panel vans stopped along Grand Avenue by you guys because somebody called in a tip with two or three big men in a van."

Mac looked incredulous. "Heaven forbid we disrupt traffic on Grand Avenue trying to find these guys. My gosh," he mocked, "a voter might call City Hall to complain and you might have to do some work."

An agitated Duffy interceded. "All the mayor is saying, Detective, is that people are on edge and panicky. If this gets out, that only adds to it. We don't want a panic. Hell, I've heard people on the radio talking about the need to carry a gun to defend themselves."

"Great, just great. That's all we need," the mayor complained, "someone to up and shoot some family guy driving along in a van because it matches the descriptions all over the news."

Mac wouldn't have it.

"Jesus Christ, whose side are you two on?"

"Hey," Duffy yelled.

"I resent the implication..." the mayor started.

Mac thundered on.

"I could give a flying fuck about your, frankly, ridiculous concerns," Mac said pointing at Duffy and then to the mayor, "or how inconvenient its release could be politically." The biggest crime story in the country was taking place in St. Paul, and Mac suspected the mayor didn't like the glare.

"Now just a minute..." the mayor started.

"All I care about—all anyone in this room should care about—is finding those girls," Mac shouted, slamming his fist on the conference table. "Everything else, *everything*, politics, who's running this investigation, whose backside might be exposed, all of that shit is secondary. For Christ sake, I'm only talking about releasing the video to law enforcement, not to the general public. Although, the more I think about it, the more I think we ought to do that as well. By getting this out, we increase our odds of finding the girls. The risk is worth the reward."

"You'd like to release it to the whole public?" the mayor asked, stunned.

Mac, seeming equally stunned, replied, "Hell yes. At least the first part, where they're driving on the road, path, through the field, sure, you bet. Have the media run it every half hour. Who knows what we'll find. There's nothing problematic in that. The rest of it, we hold back and only have law enforcement review it."

"Christ, we'll have calls coming in by the truck load and a huge panic. Especially if the whole video gets out," the mayor pressed. "And I bet it will."

"Since when does the mayor's office tell us how to investigate?" Mac asked, up and out of his chair, pointing while Rock reached for his arm to pull him back. "It's fucking fundamental to do this. We need to get as many eyes on this as possible, not as few. This is not something to cover up. It's the difference between police work and politics."

"*That's enough*," the mayor bellowed. "If you can't keep your cool, Detective, you can go grab a barstool at that pub of yours."

"Got all the answers don't ya," Duffy added derisively.

Mac kicked a chair out of the way and moved toward Duffy, his fists balled, but Lich and Rock jumped in front of him and pushed him back to his chair.

"You're no good to the chief if you're not in this room," Lich said quietly through clenched teeth. "So dial it the hell back."

Riles jumped in, casual.

"I wouldn't worry about it, Mayor," the veteran detective said, shaking his head. "We're talking about the chief's daughter. There isn't a cop out there who would compromise this and release the whole video. McRyan's right, we should get the whole thing to other law enforcement agencies and the front end out to the public."

The mayor looked at Duffy, who then looked over to Burton, who'd remained passive through the whole blow up, taking it all in.

"What do you think?" Duffy asked Burton.

"Like I said," Riles added one last time, staring straight at Burton, "I don't think it'll be a problem."

Burton stood quietly for a moment, scratching his chin with his right index finger. After a moment, he nodded and spoke.

"I think McRyan is right. We should get the video out. It can only help. And we get it out to *both* the public and law enforcement. Mac, one part that maybe I disagree with is does law enforcement need to see the part where the girls are going into the ground? What can other cops tell us about that?"

Mac shrugged, "Probably not much."

"I think that's right," Burton answered. "We get the first part out to the public and police and see if anyone recognizes the road, area, or any landmarks."

"Thanks," Riley said. Mac nodded his approval from his chair, and tension drained from the rest of the Boys.

"I'll get it started," Peters said, and then he turned to another. "Paddy, get a copy and then let's get this e-mailed to all the police and sheriff's departments. I'll start making some calls."

"Done," Paddy said.

"What else?" Riles asked.

"I gotta work on Plan B," Burton answered.

"Which is what?"

"Talk to Flanagan and Hisle. We have to let them know what's going on and prepare the ransom," Burton answered. "If we don't find these guys, we're going to have to make a money drop."

16

"Hello, girls."

The first sensation was thirst. Her mouth felt dry as she slowly moved her tongue over her lips, then smacked her lips together and exhaled lightly. She felt groggy and lethargic as she moved her left arm out from under her head and felt the skin of her right bicep scrape along the wood and dirt. Taking in a deep breath, she smelled dirt and wood, new wood, like the plywood she'd smelled two weeks ago up at her folks' cabin when they were building a gazebo. Was she still asleep and dreaming? The smell wasn't right. Why would she smell that? Where the heck was she?

She opened her eyes to pitch blackness. She blinked her eyes and strained to focus, but no light seeped in through windowshades or under a door.

Carrie Flanagan lifted her head up and banged the right side hard, just above her ear, against something above her.

"Ow!" she exclaimed as she brought her head back down. The feeling of pain was quickly overtaken by panic. She flipped off her left side and onto her back, and her right hand felt another body.

"Jesus!" she yelped as she jumped back, hitting her head and back against the hard wood.

The other body didn't move.

"Hello," Carrie whispered but there was no movement. She reached over with her right arm, looking for the other body, when her hand hit something round and metallic. She grabbed it. It was a flashlight. Carrie turned it on.

"Oh my God! Oh my God! Oh my God!"

Carrie ran her hands along the top of the box and the left side.

"Oh my God! Oh my God! Oh my God!"

Shannon Hisle slowly awoke. Carrie reached for her arm.

"Shannon, wake up! Wake up!"

When Shannon's eyes fully opened, her screams matched those of Carrie's a few seconds earlier.

"Carrie! Carrie! Oh my God, where are we! What have they done to us? What have they done to us?"

Both girls frantically felt around the box with their hands and feet, pushed at the top, kicked at the end of wood box.

After a few minutes of frantic pushing, kicking, and screaming, the girls settled some. Both women were breathing hard, sweating, still wildly looking around, disbelieving where they were.

Where they were was a wood box. It was maybe two feet high, four feet across and six feet along.

And it was solid. They weren't going anywhere.

They were buried alive.

The girls lay on their sides facing one another.

"What have they done to us? What are we going to do?" Shannon asked weakly, sniffling, tears streaming down her face.

"I don't know," Carrie answered, using the back of her left hand to wipe away her own tears.

It was time to take stock.

Carrie used the flashlight to search the box.

"What are you looking for?" Shannon asked.

"Air, how are we getting air?" Carrie replied. She found what looked to be the answer. "It's behind me, two holes with vents over them." She turned her back on Shannon and flashed the light on the nearest vent. "We're getting air, so I guess that's good news."

Shannon put her mouth to the opening.

"Help, can anyone hear me?"

Carrie put her ear to the grate to see if she could hear any response. She repeatedly yelled and then listened for a couple of minutes. There was no response.

She scanned the top of the box and upon inspection understood at least one reason why they couldn't push the top off.

"Look at that."

"What?"

"The screws. Or at least those little silver tips sticking through the wood. The top of this thing is screwed on. No wonder we couldn't budge it."

She used the flashlight and scanned the box again. Down by Shannon's feet, in the corner, there was a small black object. Carrie reached with her left leg, caught the object with her toe and dragged it back so that she could reach it with her hands.

It was a Dictaphone.

Carrie slid the button up. There was a whirring, then crackling sound, followed by the voice she heard when lying on the bed.

"Hello girls. First, if you haven't done so already, you will want to turn on the flashlight. But economize its use; you may be in the box for a while."

Carrie reached to the flashlight to shut it off.

"Leave the light on for now," Shannon said. "I like being able to see."

"Okay," Carrie answered and then started the Dictaphone again.

"A little information about your new home," the voice said. *"It is five feet underground. You are in a reinforced plywood box from which you have no hope of escaping, so it would be unwise for you to waste your time and energy doing so. Also, you are in an isolated spot, so yelling is pointless."*

Carrie stopped the tape.

"I guess you can save your breath," Shannon said. "They've probably got us buried in the middle of nowhere."

Carrie nodded and started the Dictaphone again.

"So how long have you been down there, you're wondering? We gave you a sedative. It knocked you out for what I expect would be eighteen hours, give or take. By the time you're hearing this tape it will be mid-afternoon on July third."

Carrie showed Shannon her watch, confirming that it was 2:10.

"How long will you be in your current abode, you ask? If all goes according to plan, you will be out of that box by tomorrow evening, maybe even in time to see some fireworks. I do apologize for your current accommodations. While I'm sure they are most uncomfortable and frightening for you, they were nevertheless necessary to provide proper motivation for your fathers. This is also why there is no food or water inside. If your fathers follow our instructions to the letter, you'll be back with them soon enough. If not?" the voice paused.

"Let's just say that there will be no getting out."

17

"Any problems getting down?"

Dean pulled the van into the parking lot of the diner across the street from the Bayside Marina in Hudson. Smith climbed out and looked back.

"We should be up there in about forty-five minutes," he said.

"See you there," David replied.

Smith slid the door closed and walked away a changed man. Gone were the work clothes of two hours ago. Now, the kidnapper was a skipper in boating wear with flip-flops, a Brewers baseball cap, flowery Speedo swim trunks, a white cotton golf shirt open at the collar, and black mirrored wraparound sunglasses. He hoisted a black nylon carry-on bag over his shoulder as he walked across the street and through rows of luxury cars and high-end SUVs in the marina parking lot. Beyond the parking lot, he came to the massive, ten-foot-wide, graying wood pier jutting out into the dark waters of the St. Croix River.

The Bayside Marina had four rows of boat slips. His destination was the last row of slips to the north, a guest slip on the outside at the far end of the dock. In the guest slip floated their white thirty-two-foot offshore express cruiser. They'd stolen the boat from a marina along the river in Davenport, Iowa, six weeks earlier. After they applied a new customized paint job of blue and red stripes, they launched the boat in Lake City and spent a great day boating up the river and to the slip in Hudson.

Monica was onboard already. She came up from the cabin dressed in white jean shorts over her one-piece black Speedo swimsuit, accessorized with wide black sunglasses and a white Nike tennis cap. Without saying a word, she tossed the boat keys to Smith.

Smith put the key in the ignition and smiled as the boat roared to life. Monica cast off the ropes, first for the bow and then the stern. Once she was back on board, Smith slowly backed out of the slip and, when the bow was clear, turned right and headed for the river.

He loved the water. Smith had grown up on the water in Garrison, Minnesota, a small town located two hours due north of the Twin Cities. It sat on the west side of Lake Mille Lacs, one of the largest of the state's ten thousand lakes. His dad ran a charter fishing service on the lake. From age sixteen through his college summers, Smith had driven his dad's boats and became an accomplished skipper. Though he'd spent fifteen years in prison, the skill that came back to him quickest was operating a boat. He'd felt the excitement of a young child when they launched the boat in Lake Pepin down at Lake City. He couldn't wait to get on the water and drive the boat, feel the rocking of the waves, the sun beating on and weathering his face, the cool splashes of water spraying him as they took on the large waves of Lake Pepin, working their way up the mighty Mississippi and then turning north at the mouth of the St. Croix River in Hastings. When Smith was in prison, lying on his bed with his eyes closed and mind cleared, he remembered boating, rolling over the waves of Lake Mille Lacs or through the chop of the St. Croix on a weekend, just what he was doing the day before the arrest.

Smith slowly navigated the minefield of speedboats and houseboats in the small bay separating Hudson and the marina from the St. Croix River proper. Once through the bay, he turned to the right and passed under a rusting steel train bridge and suddenly he was out into the wide section of the St. Croix that ran from Hudson to Stillwater, five miles north on the Minnesota side. In open water, with space to maneuver, Smith pushed the throttle down and opened up the boat, slicing through the waves like a snowplow through fresh snow. Monica approached with a bottle of water for him. He took a sip and smiled.

"You love this, don't you?" Monica said.

"There's nothing better," he replied, taking another drink. "After we're done with this, you and I are going to get a boat like this and spend a lot of time on it."

Monica smiled and leaned up to kiss him on the lips. "I can't wait."

Five minutes north of Hudson, Smith steered to the west side of the river and then sped past a massive window plant in Bayport. Such a waste of beautiful river shoreline, Smith thought. The industrial plant's two-hundred-foot-high smokestack and chain-link fencing mixed oddly with the gorgeous foliage and exposed rock of the shoreline and river bluff. However, while the use of the land was a waste, it would prove beneficial for him.

A short and narrow channel ran just to the north of the plant. While the window plant may have used the channel at one time, it was now largely abandoned. It would be of use tomorrow.

He'd already looked at the channel from land, walked the abandoned dock they would briefly use tomorrow, and even observed the odd fishing boat on the channel. Looking over charts at the local library, he'd learned that the channel was ten to fifteen feet deep if you stayed in the middle as it wound its way to the old dock. But until now, he hadn't seen it from the water. From the river, the opening was plenty wide, he thought upon inspection. He could see how he would have to maneuver the boat out of the channel. And, while he couldn't see the dock from the river, he knew it was there.

Satisfied with his short recon mission, he turned away from the channel and slowly accelerated back out into the open waters of the river. In another five minutes he was approaching Stillwater.

As Smith passed the town, with its parks, restaurants, and marinas, he approached Stillwater's defining feature, the lift bridge. Built in 1931, the bridge spanned one thousand feet across the St. Croix River, carrying a two-lane highway connecting Minnesota to Wisconsin on fixed arched steel trusses over concrete slabs. On the half-hour, a middle section with towers and cables lifted to allow larger boats to pass through.

Smith took a sip from his water bottle as the boat passed underneath the bridge and moved further north, Stillwater falling away behind them. The river gradually narrowed and shallowed, requiring a slower pace and more attentive navigation. Smith eased back on the throttle, falling in a hundred yards behind a flat-bottomed houseboat, probably better known as a party barge. Several people lounged on the upper deck, sunning themselves and drinking cocktails. He followed the houseboat until it made a gentle right toward one of the long, narrow, sandy islands that occasionally split the river. This island, the second they'd come upon, was filling with boats and tents, people preparing for the revelry of tomorrow's holiday.

Past the second island, the boat traffic diminished significantly. As the river curved to the left around a high rock escarpment jutting out into the river, the railroad bridge came into view. Sitting two hundred feet above the river, cutting an impressive figure against the deep blue sky, the bridge spanned the expanse of the river from Wisconsin to Minnesota. The bridge served as a marker for Smith's destination. As they approached the bridge, the river cut through a deep canyon. At the base of the steep walls on either side of the river lay isolated sand bars and beaches, one of which was Smith's destination.

Slowly, Smith steered the boat to the Wisconsin side, toward a small patch of beach in a narrow channel set well back from the main body of the river. For years, this had been his favorite spot on the river. The last time he boated before the arrest, before prison, was an overnight camping trip in this very spot with his wife and daughter—their last family outing together.

Carefully, Smith navigated to the end of the small channel, not wanting to beach the deep V-hulled boat on the zig-zagging sandbars hidden just beneath the dark water's surface. Two hundred yards out from the shore, he swung the boat far out to the left and then, after another hundred feet or so, slowly veered back right. Fifty yards away, he looked to his depth finder, waiting for and then finding the deeper water, an odd drop-off to fifteen feet, which allowed him to turn left and go straight toward the shoreline. The whole maneuver took five minutes. He beached the boat fifteen yards short, the front two thirds of the boat resting on the soft sand but the rear third in deeper water that would allow him to back off the sandbar with a single reverse thrust of the motors.

Dean and David emerged from the woods and walked out into the water. Monica jumped onto the bow and tossed two ropes with stakes on the ends to her brothers.

"Any problems getting down here?" Smith asked David.

"Nope, took a few minutes, just to make sure it was solid, but once we did that," David smiled, "it was a piece of cake."

"Well show me," Smith ordered. "After that, I want to head back to St. Paul."

18

"That's worth a look then."

The video hit the men hard, with Hisle's bottom lip trembling when he saw Shannon lying in the box just before the cover was put on. The chief's eyes closed and his head dropped when the video showed the box buried, only their air pipes showing.

After watching the video, both men had hard questions for Burton. He had few answers.

"We have to get the ransom ready."

"Does that mean the investigation is over?" the chief asked. "That we're going to sit around and wait for the next call?"

"No. We're not stopping." Burton explained releasing parts of the video to law enforcement and the public. "We may get a break with the video's release, and we're still working through files and might catch a break there as well. We're not stopping. But…."

"It is what it is," the chief said."

Burton nodded.

"Chief, we need to be ready."

Before the chief left with Burton, he pulled his boys aside. He was gaunt and ghost-white, as if his summer tan had faded in less than one day's time. Dark circles had formed under his eyes, and salt and pepper stubble aged his face. His body seemed frail, looking like a listing coat rack for his clothes. But the intensity was there in his eyes, and his deep gravelly voice was commanding as always.

"I've heard the story from the FBI, but not from my people. Tell me, no bullshit."

Mac didn't bullshit him. "The FBI isn't lying. We're nowhere."

Riley added details, but the result was the same. The chief shook his head and pinched the bridge of his nose as he looked down to the floor. "I can't lose my baby girl," their leader said quietly. He looked each of his boys in the eye. "You need to find her. I don't care what it takes or what you have to do. You find her." He pushed his hand through his disheveled white hair and slowly walked out of the room.

"Ideas?" Riles said into the silence.

Lich said what they were all thinking: "We need a break."

"And," Rock growled, "the bastards haven't given us one yet."

"Look," Mac said emphatically, "*We,* meaning *us,* need to make something happen instead of waiting around. Burton's working the ransom angle now. That gives us some room to work our own gig outside of what the FBI's running."

"The mayor won't like that," Lich said in a warning tone.

"Burton's been pretty decent. I don't like sticking a knife in his back," Rock added.

"Fuck the mayor," Mac railed. "I'm done waiting for that spineless gasbag. As for Burton, I have no desire to cut him out. If something turns up, we can go to Burton and bring him in."

"Agreed," Riles said. "But Mac, you can't be talking to the mayor that way, no matter how big a political half-wit he is. You'll be working third shift in the jail before you know it."

Mac didn't particularly care at the moment, but knew Riles was right. "I hear ya," he said, sighing, and then added, "but like I said, with the G-men working the ransom and the mayor licking Burton's boots, maybe we start making some moves of our own."

"What moves? How? Where? With what?" Lich said, tearing the top off a pack of Big Red. "You have to have a place to start."

"Then let's start with the video," Mac answered. "I'll go through that with Dick." He nodded at Riley. "You and Rock check on the laptop, where was it bought. Someone was supposed to be looking into it, but with all the commotion, who knows? Those are the things we can look at now. After that, the four of us should get out of here for a bit. If we're going to start operating, I don't want to discuss it around here." Everyone nodded agreement, and Riley and Rockford left to run the numbers on the laptop left by the kidnappers.

Mac went back into the conference room and sat down with a department-issued laptop and watched the video again. Lich stood to one side and Paddy was on the other. Mac played the video back and forth, freezing and rewinding in the hopes of picking something, anything, out. He paid particular attention to the view out the front of the vehicle, searching for any buildings, a chimney, snowmobile signs, anything that might give them a lead on the girl's location.

St. Paul cops and FBI agents joined them, quietly watching, praying, willing a clue out of the video. All they wanted was a little shred to give them a lead, something to track, a way to find the girls. After a half hour of running it to the end several times, Mac sat back in his chair, sighed, and asked, "Anyone recognize anything? See anything? Have any ideas?" Silence or barely audible no's were all he heard. All he'd accomplished was to burn the video into the hard drive of his brain.

As everyone started to drift away, Mac pulled out his cell phone, walked to a corner of the room and, with his back to everyone, dialed Jupiter. Jupiter Jones was a friend from his university days. Named after the main character from the children's Alfred Hitchcock and The Three Investigators series, Jupiter was a computer and video genius. He had already made one fortune and was working on another with a computer video business. He occasionally worked freelance with the department, as he had with Mac's big case last winter, and also with the Minnesota Bureau of Criminal Apprehension. He answered on the first ring.

"Jones."

"It's Mac. I need your help, and I need it now."

"The kidnappings?"

"Uh-huh."

"Anything for you and the chief, you know that."

"We have a video I need you to look at. I'm going to have my nephew, a uniform cop named Shawn McRyan, drop it off. I need you to break this thing down and see if you can wring anything out of it that we can use to identify these guys. Even the tiniest thing would help." Mac explained what he was looking for and how fast he needed it. "We got shit and we're on a tight clock."

"How tight?"

"Less than thirty hours tight."

Jupe whistled on the other end. "I'll be at my house in twenty minutes."

"Thanks Jupe." Mac flipped his cell phone closed. He grabbed a spare DVD and copied the video to it. He took it out and waved Shawn over, writing down an address. "This goes to Jupiter Jones and nobody else—and I mean *nobody* else. Understand?"

"It's done," Shawn answered. He grabbed his partner and left the conference room.

Mac stood up and stretched, realizing that he'd been paying such close attention to the video that he hadn't noticed just how many men were milling around the room, doing nothing. With the call from the kidnappers about the ransom and video, it was as if the investigation had come to a standstill. Detectives and Bureau agents continued to work through Hisle and the chief's files down the hall, but nothing was coming of it. A few people were being kept under surveillance, but based on what he'd heard about them, they were nothing more than dead ends and easy overtime. Burton was working on the ransom, but nobody was in charge of the room. Everyone was just sitting around, waiting for the next call from the kidnappers. Riley and Rock walked back in.

"We've tracked the computer down to a Best Buy in Milwaukee," Riles said. "It was purchased a month ago, with cash."

"What a surprise," Lich answered with disgust.

"But maybe we get something off the surveillance camera," Mac rejoined hopefully. "We just need a piece, a good picture, something to work off. All we need is a solid I.D. and we'd be off and running."

"We'll see," Riles said. "The FBI field office sent someone over there to see if there is any surveillance video, anything we might be able to use. If there's anything they'll send it right up."

"Let's get out of here," Mac said quietly. "There are way too many people hanging around, plus the mayor and Duffy, and I don't trust either of them right about now. How about a booth at Lucy's?"

Smith smiled and thought of his brief few hours on the river. It felt great. In another week he would be on a boat somewhere, enjoying the sun, cracking open a beer, perhaps a Red Stripe, with Monica lounging on a chair next to him. The fifteen years of prison would seem so far away at that point. Money, a boat, some water, revenge against Flanagan, it couldn't get any better. After a minute, he put those pleasant thoughts away. There was much work left to be done, and he needed to keep his head in the game.

Dean, riding in the passenger seat, switched the radio station over to the talk station. It was wall-to-wall kidnapping coverage. The mantra continued—the authorities didn't have any leads.

"The FBI and police have to feel like the clock is ticking down on this thing now," Dean said, taking a sip from a Coke. He pulled his baseball cap down low over his sunglasses-covered eyes and pulled his gloves on tight.

"Which is what we want," Smith replied, doing the same. The lead kidnapper turned left onto the safe house's street. He pulled past the driveway, stopped, and then began to back the van into the driveway while Dean hit the opener.

Pat Hall shifted in his bed, the large cast on his broken left femur making it difficult for him to get comfortable. An electrician, he had broken the leg five days ago on a job site, falling off a ladder while running wire. Now he was out on workers' comp and forced to spend the day watching really bad TV. No wonder people worked during the day, rather than being subjected to sappy soap operas, Dr. this and Dr. that, nine versions of *People's Court* with Judge Judy, Rudy, or Hootie. Even the sports on during the day were brutal things like paintball and Jet Ski racing. While both would be fun to do, they were about as much fun to watch as undergoing a root canal without Novocain.

On top of all that, the air conditioning in his house was out. He was totally immobilized, watching awful TV, in insufferable July heat. He had sweated through his white muscle T-shirt, and beads of sweat were interspersed with the thin strands of seaweed that were all that remained of his once-full head of brown hair. A hard-working fan in the corner merely circulated the heat and humidity. Thankfully, he was on the main level of his house, and his bedroom was on the north side, under a canopy of elm trees, which kept his room just a smidge cooler. A little breeze to ruffle the curtains of the window would be nice, but there hadn't been one all day.

The one saving grace was the lovely Heather Foxx. Hall made sure the TV was never far from Channel 12. A remote was a beautiful thing. His TV was telling him now that a Channel 12 Newsbreak was on the way.

"This is Paul Phillips with a Channel 12 Newsbreak. With the latest on the St. Paul kidnappings, we go to Heather Foxx at the St. Paul Department of Public Safety. Heather, what's the latest?"

"Paul, as we learned earlier, the FBI and police have received a ransom demand, although we don't yet have the amount."

"What about the laptop recovered earlier?"

"It contained a video. The police have released a portion of that video, Paul, which we'll play now." Foxx waited for the video to start. "What you're seeing is a portion of the footage the kidnappers left on the laptop. As you can see, it shows a vehicle driving through an isolated rural area. The police are asking all citizens to review the footage and contact the authorities at the number on the screen if they recognize anything about the area the kidnappers are driving through."

When the video finished, Phillips jumped back in.

"We will be playing this video every half-hour. Additionally, we will also have it available shortly on the Channel 12 Web site."

"The police are continuing to man the tip line, Paul," Heather reported. "In addition to reviewing this video footage, the authorities are urging people to be on the lookout for at least three men, using vans, and again, not minivans but larger vans; panel- or cargo-style vans."

Hall adjusted again and as he did he looked out his window to the left as the van backed into the rental house across the street. The house had been vacant for the past six months with a For Rent sign in the front yard. The sign disappeared a few weeks ago, maybe longer, Hall thought. He just noticed it missing one day when he came home from work. He'd seen very little activity at the house, other than vans of different colors coming and going for the last couple of days. It was, the more he thought about it, kind of odd behavior.

Never one to cause trouble, Hall was not the type to call in on his neighbors. But the behavior was just off enough that it was worth a phone call. If nothing else, it would provide a potentially entertaining diversion from the heat and boredom.

Lucy's was a sandwich joint located in the Payne and Arcade area on St. Paul's working-class east side. A true hole-in-the-wall, the restaurant was a welcome change from the sterile chain sandwich places going in all over town. At Lucy's, if you were smart, you ordered the Juicy Lucy, which was a hot hoagie sandwich piled high with a mountain of pastrami, completely smothered in melted American cheese, and served on a fresh-baked bun. The sandwich came with homemade pickles and kettle chips so greasy the sheikhs from OPEC were seeking drilling rights. The whole concoction was served on an oversized red-and-white checkered tray.

Lucy was short for Lucius, a robust black man who'd eaten a few too many of his own sandwiches. Big Lucius worked the register and made the occasional sandwich if his son working the back got too busy. Lucius bullshitted Mac, who twirled a toothpick from side to side in his mouth, awaiting his sandwich order.

Mac looked at his watch while Lucius chewed the fat. It was 4:15 PM. The day was ticking away far too fast.

"You and the boys in a hurry there, Mac?" Lucius asked. Lich, Riley, and Rock were in a booth in the back of the sandwich shop, out of public view.

"Not so much that, Lucius. It's just this case, the time is tickin' away."

"Well, let me check on that food for you boys," Lucius said and then turned to yell at his son in the back. "Where the hell are those Juicy Lucys, boy?"

As Mac waited for his order, he felt a light tap on his back. He turned to find Heather Foxx smiling at him.

"Heather Foxx, we meet again."

"Thanks for the tip this morning," she whispered. "I appreciate it."

"Don't get used to it."

"Why did you give it to me?" Heather asked, curious. "Typically, you're loath to help us out."

"I helped you because you didn't swarm us last night like the rest of your media friends," Mac said.

"That's good to know," the reporter replied. "In any event, maybe I can return the favor at some point." She pushed a strand of her brown hair back behind her left ear.

Mac snorted, his inherent distrust of reporters showing through. "It's not too often you guys do us any favors."

Paddy McRyan took his bottle of water out of the vending machine. Generally, he was morally opposed to paying money for water, but with the heat, a soda just didn't sound or even feel like it would taste remotely refreshing. Besides, once he polished off the contents, he'd just refill it out of the water fountain. As he took a sip, he saw Bonnie Schmidt, a uniform cop working the tip line, sprinting toward him. "What's up?" he asked.

"We're getting tons of stuff on the tip line, most of which is garbage, but this sounded interesting," Schmidt said, handing him a note. Paddy took a look at it and walked into the conference room to Burton.

"This might be worth a look."

"What do we have?" Burton asked, as Duffy, Peters, and the mayor approached. The rest of Burton's team and cops in the room pulled in behind them.

"A guy in a neighborhood off of West Seventh, down by the old brewery, claims that for the last couple of days there have been vans, our kind of vans, coming and going from a house across the street."

"So?" Burton asked, mixing a cup of coffee.

"Well, the house is a rental and nobody was at the house for months until a couple of days ago. Now vans are coming and going. Again, our kinds of vans."

"Let's go take a look then," Burton replied, looking at his watch: 4:25 PM. "Where's McRyan and the rest of those guys?"

"They went to get a bite to eat at Juicy Lucy's," Paddy answered.

"That's over on the east side, right? Payne and Arcade?"

Paddy nodded. Burton pulled out his cell phone and dialed.

"Mac? Burton. I need you to check something out."

"*Get out! House blown!*" the text message read.

Smith flipped the cell phone closed, looked at his watch—4:28 PM—and then to Dean. "We've gotta bail," he said.

"What's going on?" Dean said, seeing Smith's ashen face.

"I don't know for sure, but we're blown," Smith said, running for the back door. "The police have the safe house. They're on their way."

"H ... h ... how?" Dean stammered. "How?"

"I don't know," Smith answered, in the garage now, at the far van. "I don't even know what the police have. All I know is, I got the text message and the house is blown." He jumped into a van. "Stay on your cell. I'm going left and you go right. I'm going to go south on 35E, you go north and take it from there."

The garage door opened and Smith pulled out and turned hard left, tires squealing. Dean followed and turned right.

19

"Gloves."

Mac parked behind the detached garage in the alley behind a well-kept blue rambler with white trim. The owner of the home, and the man who called in, was Patrick Hall. Others would be joining the party shortly, but for now Burton was holding them back several blocks, letting Mac and the rest in first to get the lay of the land. Riley and Mac called from the Explorer, and Hall picked up on the second ring. The homeowner was in bed with a broken leg, but directed them to a spare key underneath the bottom of his "piece-of-shit" air conditioner.

Riles found the key in a little black magnetized key box. The detectives let themselves in the back door and entered the kitchen. They noticed the heat immediately.

"Now I know why he called the AC a piece of shit," Riley noted.

Mac called out to announce their presence, and they heard an "in here" from the front of the house. There they found Hall, lying in bed, a cast encasing the entire length of his left leg. To say the man looked uncomfortable was an understatement.

"Man, you have got to get your air conditioning fixed," Mac said, noting both Hall's sweaty appearance and the impact of the heat on his own body after just a few minutes in the house.

"I hear ya," the man answered. "I really need a new one, but with me laid up and all, we're trying to watch what we spend."

"Try Craig's List. You could get a window unit for cheap at least."

Riles got down to business. "So what's the deal with this house across the street?"

"Like I said to the gal on that tip line, these guys have been around, oh, I'd say the last four or five days, I guess. My wife said they started showing up the day I got hurt. I broke this leg of mine five days ago and got back home three days ago. I haven't been out of the bed much since."

"So you've been watching these guys across the street then?" Mac asked, casually pulling the curtain back to sneak a peek out the window.

"I wouldn't say watching," Hall said, shaking his head, "I'd say I've *noticed* them coming and going in vans is all."

"How often?" Riles asked, walking over to the other side of the window. The house was across the street and to the right, a single-story home similar to Hall's in a neighborhood of similar homes. It was gray, with faded burgundy trim and shutters and a high wood privacy fence around the backyard.

"Hard to say really," Hall answered, "other than often enough that I noticed them coming and going is all."

Mac turned to Hall and away from the window, "You said you've noticed them. What have you noticed?"

"Such as?" Hall asked.

"Men? Women? Height? Weight? What did they look like?"

"I never really got a good look at anyone," Hall replied.

"How come?" Mac asked, confused.

"I figured you guys were going to ask that," the man replied, wiping his forehead with a towel and taking a drink of water. "These guys were coming with vans, backing them into the garage and closing the door. Or, they'd open the door and leave. Nobody ever walked around outside that I can recall. At least not that I ever saw."

"You never saw them at all?"

"Not really."

"Detective McRyan asked whether they were men or women?" Riles asked.

"Men, I'd say."

"Did you ever notice what were they wearing?" Mac inquired.

"Baseball caps for the most part. Dark shirts usually. Sunglasses and...."

Hall paused and Mac looked back at him. "And what?"

The man closed his eyes for a minute. "There was something else now that I think of it. I saw, or I remember seeing, once or twice, and I just thought it was odd since it's been so hot." Hall sat still, his head back against the pillow, closing his eyes. After a few seconds, a smile spread across his face, "Gloves. They wore gloves."

"Gloves?" Riles asked.

"Yeah, when they drove the vans, they had gloves on. You know black leather gloves, like you might wear in the winter."

Mac and Riles exchanged a quick look. He was maybe onto something. The kidnappers had yet to leave a print behind, and black leather gloves this time of year were unusual. Plus, two other witnesses to the abductions mentioned gloves in their descriptions. Some people liked to wear gloves when they drove, but not many.

"Was it one guy wearing gloves or more than one?" Mac asked.

"Not totally sure. I mean, I couldn't tell one from the other. I do know that I noticed gloves more than once."

"So these guys wore dark shirts, hats, and gloves. Anything else?" Mac pressed.

"Not really. At least nothing I recall right now."

"Just vans?" Riles asked, tacking a different direction.

"Yeah, for the most part. I might have seen a car once, parked in the driveway overnight, but other than that, pretty much just vans."

Mac looked back from the window. "What kind of vans?"

"Those panel kinds of vans."

"Get any license plates?"

"No," Hall answered, shaking his head.

"How about just what states the plates were from?"

Hall shook his head again.

"Always the same vans?" Mac asked, pushing.

Hall thought about that one for a moment. "You know, now that you mention it, I don't think so. There were different ones, colors, makes, models. Not a bunch, but it wasn't always the same two either. There was some variety to them."

Mac sat down in a chair in the corner of the room and started jotting down some notes. Riles continued.

"You mentioned a car. What kind of car?"

"White. I think it was a Taurus," Hall thought a little more. "Yeah a Ford Taurus."

"Get a license number?"

"No," Hall answered. "I didn't really think anything of it except for those Heather Foxx reports on Channel 12. She was talking about vans being used in those kidnappings, and I noticed these guys coming and going."

"How about now?" Mac asked. "Are they there now?"

"I don't think so," Hall replied, shaking his head. "They've been gone a bit."

"How long?" Riley asked.

"Oh, maybe half-hour, a little more. They left around the time I called in. My wife told me they left anyway. I didn't see it when they did. My wife said she'd just seen them leave when she came into the bathroom and helped me off the potty."

Mac looked Mr. Hall over. He was a working man, an electrician, in his mid- to upper fifties. The house was neat and orderly, nothing suggested the guy was a kook or anything. The yard around the home was neat, with flower beds and well-trimmed hedges. There were pictures of family around and what appeared to be a grandchild or two. All in all, Hall seemed on the level.

"You need anything?" Mac asked Hall.

"I could use a fresh glass of water," he replied. "It's a little hard for me to get to the kitchen at the moment."

"I imagine it is," Mac said smiling. "We'll be right back." Mac led Riles toward the kitchen.

"So what do you think?" Riles asked as Mac opened the freezer and grabbed ice cubes.

"I think this guy is on the level. Could be our guys," Mac said.

"Maybe," Riles added. "Vans, different ones, and wearing…."

"Gloves," Mac finished for him, turning on the tap water. "Witnesses mentioned that yesterday. These guys have been careful all along. We never found any prints off those vans, partly because they blew them up, but also, I bet, because they were wearing gloves. And according to Hall, these guys are wearing gloves. It's starting to add up."

"You don't suppose the girls are over there do you? Buried in the backyard?" Riles asked.

"No. I mean we go check there in a minute, but unless that video tape was a huge ruse, no, they're somewhere else."

"If these are our guys then, why use this house?"

Mac walked into the living room and peeked through the curtains. "Safe house, maybe. An hour ago we were talking about how they were centrally located, running up to Clearwater one night, Ellsworth the next, then to Duluth. They'd need a central spot to operate from. Maybe this is it." Mac let the curtains fall closed and walked the fresh glass of water to the bedroom for Hall. Once Hall was taken care of, Mac came back to Riley. "Let's walk across the street."

Mac and Riles exited Hall's house out the back door. Riles quickly walked back to the Explorer, instructing Lich and Rock to slowly pull around the house and to the street, just in case they needed backup.

Mac put his sunglasses on and untucked his shirt so that it covered his Sig. Riles, given his girth, already wore his out. The two detectives walked down the alley at a leisurely pace, turned left, and walked to the street corner. Checking traffic, the two men quickly jogged across the street and then walked north along the sidewalk to the house. They walked up to the front door and knocked. There was no response. Riley tried the doorbell, but again, no response. He pulled the storm door open and peered inside one of the three thin vertical windows in the burgundy front door.

"See anything?" Mac asked.

"Not really. Odd, though."

"What's that?"

"No furniture. The place looks empty. The only thing I can see is part of a card table and some folding chairs."

Mac stepped back and looked at the front picture window. The drapes were pulled shut. The same was true of the rest of the house as he walked around, climbing over the privacy fence to get into the backyard. All the windows were covered with shades or drapes. Mac climbed back over the fence along the south side, where Riles was waiting.

"You notice how the basement windows are painted black?" Pat asked.

"Yeah," Mac replied. "Nobody is supposed to be able to see inside."

"So are these our guys?" Riles said, "Or are we so desperate for a break that we're seeing what we want to see?"

"Only one way to find out," Mac replied. "We have to get inside."

Riles flipped open his phone and dialed. "Burton? Riley. We need a search warrant."

20

"Hit me with it."

Smith checked the rearview mirror non-stop since he had left the safe house. The further the Twin Cities faded away behind him, and the more rolling green fields of soybeans and corn he passed, the more at ease he felt. Nobody had followed he was sure of that now, having doubled back twice and finding no one behind. The police scanner in the passenger seat remained quiet. Perhaps the text message had given them enough time to get some distance from the house before the police connected the dots.

He had known that, sooner or later, something would go amiss. It was why they'd taken all the precautions, multiple vehicles, using a safe house, burying the girls out of town, prepping the boat and campsite. They were flexible, untethered to any one place or path. If need be, they could adjust on the fly, as they were doing now.

The police would search the house, but he wasn't sweating it too badly. As long as Monica did her job earlier—and he trusted she did—there would be little for the police to find and certainly no way to trace them.

Smith exited the interstate and traveled east on a county road toward the college town of Northfield, home of St. Olaf College and prestigious Carleton College. Smith fell in with early evening traffic of the town. The gas gauge on the van was low, so he pulled into a service station.

Smith pre-paid for the gas with cash and then went back to the pump. He took inventory of his situation as he filled the tank. The first order of business was to check on Dean. He pulled out his cell phone and dialed.

Dean answered on the third ring. He was well north of Minneapolis, pulling into the small town of East Bethel. Best Dean could tell, he didn't have anybody on his tail. He'd changed roads frequently, doubled back twice as directed, and had yet to find a common vehicle or vehicles following him. He felt he was clean.

Smith pulled the gas nozzle out and placed it back in the pump.

"Besides, what are the police going to be looking for?" Dean said. "Plain white vans? There are hundreds of these in the Cities and thousands all around. We're fine."

"Just the same," Smith replied, "Find a place to dump the van. I'd prefer someplace it won't be found, like a lake or something."

Next, Smith dialed Monica. She already was on the move, driving toward East Bethel to rendezvous with her brother.

Smith contemplated his options and emptied his pockets. He had the keys for the Chevy at the Park & Ride. The police were looking for plain white vans. Who knows, the police might start pulling them over at random. While it was a little bit of a risk, he decided to drive back into the city and dump the van for the Impala at the Park & Ride. Then he would drive up to the northern suburbs for the evening's meeting.

Carrie's watch told her it was 6:05, which she assumed was PM. In the dim light of their flashlight, the two girls had assessed their situation. A search of the box revealed nothing other than the flashlight and the

Dictaphone. They tried together to again push the roof on their box, hoping against hope that their captors had lied about burying it. The top didn't budge.

For lack of a better option, they listened to the tape again and again, listening for anything that could help them: a slip of the tongue, information to help them get out. It was a pipe dream. There was nothing.

"We're stuck, plain and simple," Carrie said, now lying flat on her back with her eyes closed, trying to breathe slowly.

"I'm not feeling well," Shannon replied with a little sniffle.

"Me neither."

"No, you don't understand," Shannon answered. "I'm diabetic. I haven't had insulin for awhile."

"How long?" Carrie asked.

"I haven't had any since Saturday night after dinner. I usually take it when I eat. I was out super late on Saturday night with some friends. I overslept on Sunday so when I got up, I grabbed some quick breakfast but I forgot to take my insulin. I usually bring my insulin with me, but I was running late Sunday and I accidentally left it at home. Then after work I was going to run home quick and take some. But before I could do that...."

"You were taken," Carrie finished for her.

"Yes. And I didn't have any with me in my purse, so I didn't get to take any while we were at that house."

"So what happens to you if you don't get the insulin?" Carrie asked.

Shannon sniffled again. "Depends how long I go without. My doctor has said I have a sensitive system. There are few times in the past where I want a few days without insulin and I got really sick. I tend to get disoriented and once I passed out. If I go long enough, I could lapse into a coma."

"Has that ever happened before? The lapsing into a coma part?"

"Almost. One time, a few years ago, I got frustrated with the whole Type I deal. My boyfriend broke up with me, and I thought the reason he did was because I was always having to take insulin. All my friends were leading a normal life, and my boyfriend was leading a normal life, and here I was stopping to take insulin three to four times per day."

"Was that really the reason he broke up with you?"

"Later on I asked him and he said no. He met someone else," Shannon answered. "But at the time, I thought that had something to do with it so I said 'screw it' I wasn't going to take the insulin any more."

"So what happened?"

"I went a couple of days without. I became disoriented and didn't really realize what was going on. Eventually, I fell asleep on the couch with nobody around. My roommates came home and they couldn't wake me. They rushed me to the emergency room. I ended up in the intensive care unit. Thankfully, the doctors were able to revive me, but it was a close call. I could have easily died if they hadn't found me. I've gone a couple of days now. I'm worried what's going to happen to me. I could die in here before they find us."

"Shannon, that's not going to happen," Carrie replied, summoning all the confidence she could muster into her voice. She grabbed Shannon's hand.

"I wish I had your confidence," Hisle replied, her eyes welling with tears.

Carrie squeezed Shannon's hand. "Don't you worry, Honey. I know who's looking for us."

"Who?"

"Our fathers for one. Those are two men who can make things happen."

"They've got to be going crazy about now," Shannon answered. "How can they possibly find us?"

"I don't expect my dad or yours would," Carrie answered. "But my dad's boys on the other hand...."

"His boys?"

"Yeah. Mac McRyan, Pat Riley, Big Bobby Rockford, and Lich. I know them. They are relentless. They will do anything to find us, and they will not stop until they do. They will not let anyone stand in their way. We've just gotta have a little faith, Sister. They'll find us."

Plain-clothes cops had already spread out down the street, knocking on doors and asking questions, as well as distracting neighbors. Mac and Lich climbed over the fence into the backyard again, this time moving to the back door to the garage. Down on a knee, Mac went to work picking the lock on the ancient doorknob. He fiddled with it a minute, and then he heard a little click and felt the lock pop open. Mac opened the door, and he and Lich quickly moved inside the garage and closed the door.

"Let's clear the house quick," Mac said, his Sig in his right hand.

Lich nodded as he pulled his Smith. Neither of them expected to find anyone, but this needed to be done. Mac pushed into the house, and he and Lich quickly moved throughout the first floor and then quickly down to the basement. There was nobody inside.

Mac grabbed the radio of his belt as he walked back up the stairs from the basement. "The house is clear. Come on in."

Lich yelled from the front of the house, and Mac hit the garage door opener. As it opened, the white police surveillance van backed into the driveway. The back door of the van opened, and four forensics techs, two each from the department and the FBI, exited the van. With everyone out, the van pulled out and rolled down the block as the garage door closed. Mac slipped on rubber gloves while everyone else got their equipment together.

With everyone ready, Mac opened the door and led them into the one-story house. The group stood in the eating area, which was separated from the dark wood cupboards and mustard yellow Formica of the 1970s kitchen by a waist-high counter. The card table that Riley had seen was the only furniture in their immediate view. Mac pointed to an FBI and St. Paul tech, "I'll work up here with you two."

"And I'll take you other two downstairs," Lich added.

Now that the house was clear, Mac took his time walking and looking around. His first stop was the living room to his left, which was devoid of furniture, its beige shag carpet the only contrast against the stark white walls. The only thing worthy of notice was the fresh vacuum tracks in the carpet. Leaving the living room, Mac walked down a hallway to the two bedrooms and full bath. The larger of the two bedrooms contained only a queen-size mattress and box spring, but no bed frame or headboard. There were no sheets on the bed. The closet was empty, not even a solitary hanger on the rod. Again, there were fresh vacuum tracks throughout the room.

Across the hall, the other bedroom was tiny, maybe ten by ten, also empty and freshly vacuumed.

"Empty?" a tech asked, walking up behind Mac.

"Yeah, nothing. Freshly vacuumed is about all that I see of note."

"Being careful?"

"If they were using this house, yes. They have been careful every step of the way," Mac replied with a sigh. "But it's a long way from vacuum tracks to saying they were here. It could be that a cleaning company has been in and out for all we know. That might explain the vacuum tracks."

"I'll process the room and maybe we'll find out," the tech said.

Mac stepped out of the bedroom and checked on the other tech working the bathroom, which was a narrow deal with a tub and shower on the left and the vanity and toilet on the right. "You got anything?"

"No," was the terse reply. "I think someone was in here recently, if only because the smell of disinfectant is so strong. This room has been cleaned to within an inch of its life, and today I'd say." The tech pointed to the vanity. "There's just the slightest film around the drain of the sink. I'd guess it was cleaner. I took a sample."

"How about the shower? Maybe the drain?" Mac asked, stepping past the tech and pulling back an orange shower curtain. It clashed badly with the pink tile of the shower and vanity top. "All we need is one hair, and we'd have something to go on."

The tech shook her head. "I hear you, Detective, but the shower is spotless. There's nothing in the drain. I checked already. I half wonder if it was even used."

Mac stepped out of the bathroom and moved back into the kitchen, checking the cabinets and under the sink. All he found was peeling shelf and drawer paper. No silverware, plates, pans, or glasses. The kitchen was empty of any utensils or other common accoutrements.

Next he moved to the two-stall garage. It was vacant except for a green, wheeled garbage can. He flipped the top open. It was completely empty, nary a scrap of paper inside. Looking around he noted nothing in the garage. No shovels, rakes, brooms, tools, garbage bags, anything one would typically find in a man-cave. The cement floor was nearly spotless, other than a light coating of dust and some light tire marks, truck width apart, vans perhaps. There were no cleaning supplies, no mops, buckets, rags or vacuum cleaner, and no dirty towels or refuse. The place seemed almost sterile.

Back in the kitchen, Mac stood with his hands on his hips, looking around. This could be the place, but if it was, the kidnappers had again left nothing behind. It could just as easily be that the house was being cleaned or readied for tenants, not occupied, although Hall seemed pretty certain that people had moved in. They were trying to track down the home's owner. Maybe he'd be able to shed some light on it all.

"*Mac!* Come down here," Lich bellowed from the basement.

Mac bounded down two steps at a time. At the bottom he turned right, down the dark wood-paneled and linoleum-floored hallway that wrapped around the steps to a back bedroom on the left. Inside the bedroom he found Lich and the two techs standing between two twin beds. The beds had silver-barred head- and footboards, along with mattresses and box springs, but no sheets or blankets. The beds sat on a gray cement floor. As with the rooms upstairs, this smelled faintly of disinfectant.

Lich waved Mac over to the bed on the left and pointed to the end posts. "See the scrapes here?" Lich said, pointing at the right post of the headboard and then to the left side. "Then, on the other side, the same thing. Then down on the footboard, the side posts, same thing."

"Yet," Mac said, waving to the head- and footboards, "the rest of the rails are pristine, unscratched."

"Right," Lich said, then turned to the other bed. "And we have exactly the same thing over here. You know what I think?" Dick asked, a twinkle in his eye.

"Hit me with it," Mac said.

Lich moved to the end of the bed on the right. "Girls are on the beds, arms cuffed to the posts for the headboard and either cuffed or manacled to the footboard," he said, pointing with his pen at the headboard and then back down to the footboard.

"And the scratches are from the cuffs moving up and down on the posts, the girls struggling to get free," Mac added.

"*Right*," Lich said, nodding.

"The girls were here, man," Mac said, with conviction now. "I can feel it. Upstairs, the house has been cleaned top to bottom. The techs are processing it, but they're finding nothing. These guys are so careful, they even remove the cleaning supplies and the trash. All of that stuff is gone." Mac spoke with a modicum of admiration. "They're ready even when we get a break."

"My gut tells me your gut is right," Lich said in agreement.

"I'm right," Mac said, walking out of the bedroom, down the hall and back to the family room at the bottom of the steps. "They used this," Mac said, waving his arms around, "as a safe house. They take Shannon on Sunday, drive out to River Falls, dump the one van, transfer into the other, drive back here and chain her to the bed in the basement. Then they can take an hour, run up to Clearwater to place the call, and then come back nice and easy-like. Whole thing takes maybe three to four hours."

"They stay here overnight," Lich said, picking up on the thread. "So they're close to St. Thomas and are in position to take Carrie the next day."

"And then," Mac said, pacing now, his left hand grabbing the back of his neck while he gestured with his right hand, "They bring Carrie back here after they dump the van over in south Minneapolis."

"Precisely," Lich said.

Mac laughed.

"What?"

"You said, 'precisely.'"

"Fuck you." Lich went back to the task at hand. "Monday night, one of the kidnappers drives over to Ellsworth to make the call and then drives back."

"Then they take the girls and put them underground, but it's someplace that isn't *that* far from here," Mac said. "So while we're running around down in Ellsworth and dragging Drew Wiskowski in for questioning, they're putting together that videotape."

"Which they put under the stands at the football field sometime overnight," Lich added. "After which they come back here."

"Exactly," Mac said. "The house gives them a good central staging area, so they can be close to town and operate, yet they're not too far from wherever the girls are buried."

"I shouldn't smile," Lich said, smiling. "But we're on it, man. This is something. We just have to lay in wait."

"*If* they come back," Mac said, doubt creeping onto his face. "This place has been cleaned, *is* clean," he said as he climbed the basement steps. "What if they're not planning on coming back? The ransom call comes tomorrow at six. What if we've missed them?"

"Only one way to find out," Lich said following.

"I know. We've got to sit on it," Mac answered.

21

“What do you mean ‘ripped out?’”

7:45 PM

The small monkey wrench thrown into the day’s plans was having an unintended but pleasant effect. After exchanging vehicles with Dean in Cambridge, a small town nearly an hour north of the Twin Cities, Smith and Monica had started driving back into town when she spoke.

“There’s a little motel.”

“Looks like they have a vacancy,” Smith added, turning right off of Highway 65 and into the dirt parking lot of the 65-Hi Suites. They had several hours to kill before a midnight meeting. There were ten rooms at the motel and five cars in the parking lot: just enough that they wouldn’t be memorable to the motel clerk, and just few enough that there was minimal risk they would be remembered by a guest.

His first two weeks out of prison, Smith stayed in Chicago and went on a binge, hooking up with a different woman every night. Some nights it was a woman he picked up in some bar. A divorcee, a woman looking for a fling, he wasn’t real particular. If he couldn’t find a woman at a bar, a hooker in a cheap hotel room would do. The quality didn’t really matter. He was working off fifteen years of pent-up sexual frustration, so any woman did it for him.

After Chicago, he moved to the Twin Cities and joined up with Dean, David, and their sister Monica to start the planning. He was immediately attracted to her. Monica was in her mid-forties, but the years were being very kind to her. Twice divorced, Monica was a petite woman with creamy skin, short, jet-black hair in a stylish cut, deep green eyes, a tiny, slightly upturned nose, and full ruby lips. And she was smart as a whip. A CPA, she worked the books for a number of years for area jewelers. That was where, three years ago, she had crossed paths with Lyman Hisle. He didn't know her, but she knew him.

Monica was in a jewelry store on Ford Parkway, balancing the books, when Hisle walked into the store, dressed in a two-thousand-dollar French suit and two-hundred-dollar Italian shoes. He spent ten thousand dollars in fifteen minutes without blinking an eye, money that Hisle had made off of people like her father.

Anger raged within her as Lyman Hisle whipped out his American Express card and spent the money as if it were nothing, as if he were buying groceries or a DVD. From that point forward, she never let the rage go. As far as she was concerned, Lyman Hisle had killed her father. He didn't pull the trigger, her father did that. But Hisle drove him to do it. For ten years she'd suppressed the anger, shoving it to the back of her mind. She'd been able to cope with the damage Hisle's work did to her father, the drinking, the pills, the loss of all the money, and finally the suicide. But seeing Hisle, seeing him spend all that money so cavalierly, brought it all back.

She was looking for the same kind of payback Smith was looking for. As the planning for the kidnappings began, she and Smith spent many hours together, scouting sites and observing targets. Their passion for revenge ignited the same within them, as though the two feelings fed off of one another. Within a month they were sleeping together. In another month, Smith and Monica knew they would escape together when everything was over. He was in love with her, and she said the feeling was mutual. Monica was married twice and divorced twice. Both times she had married unworthy men, weak men, men she couldn't trust. Her brothers told her that Smith was none of those things. He was strong. He'd been a man in prison. He was a man they could trust, a man who wanted what they wanted and possessed what they didn't: the ability and the connection to pull it off.

Now it was 8:27 PM, and they were lying in a musty motel room with an air conditioner working overtime to cool the room. They lay naked on the bed, her head just under his chin, the sheets and blankets on the floor and the sweat from the sex cooling on their bodies. Smith reached over and grabbed the remote for the TV. He turned to Channel 6, which was running a special bottom-of-the-hour report about the kidnappings. For the first time, Smith saw the videotape played by the media.

"I didn't think they would release that to the public," Monica said.

"I'm not sure I did either."

"Are you worried about that?"

"Not particularly. The video snippets are short. The land is mostly private. I'm sure they're hoping that somebody will recognize the road or some marking in the background. I don't see that happening."

"Maybe we shouldn't have put so much into the video."

"You might be right," Smith answered mildly. "I wanted to build the anxiety for Flanagan and Hisle before we showed the girls going under. I wanted them to see the process, let the pressure and suspense build. I wanted them fully motivated to pay. In the end, perhaps less would have been more."

They listened to the rest of the report.

"Nothing about the house," Monica said. "Perhaps the coast is clear."

"Maybe," Smith answered, lightly scratching her upper back. "The media has been on most breaks in the case, but they're not on this one.

Either the police have done a good job of keeping this one quiet, or they don't think we were at the house."

"What do you think is the case?" she asked, running her fingers through his chest hair.

"You cleaned the house well?"

"Yes. It's clean."

"They might think we were there. But they're not finding anything, which means they're no closer to finding us. And besides, we're not going back," he said, cupping her breast in his hand and stopping her questions with a kiss.

Jupiter Jones grabbed a Red Bull out of his Sub-Zero refrigerator and a bag of chips out of the walk-in pantry. He loaded up his coffee maker for a night's worth of fuel. Frequent jolts of energy would be needed for what looked to be an all-nighter. The video of the kidnappers burying the girls alive had his utmost attention. If the video didn't hit you, you weren't human. He couldn't imagine the impact on the chief or Lyman Hisle.

He tied his Hefner robe shut over his shorts, slid his feet into his flip-flops, and went back to his home computer lab. The FBI techs—who were good–very good—had gone over the video all afternoon and found nothing that seemed helpful beyond identifying the van as a Chevy Astro, 2001 edition, based on elements of the dashboard design. Jupiter didn't believe there was nothing else there. There was always, *always*, something to be found, something that could help. To do that required patience, a keen eye for detail and, most importantly, top-of-the-line equipment—all of which he had. His equipment was better than anything law enforcement had. Mac had called Jupiter in on more than one occasion as a secret weapon. Mac often said that Jupiter should be in one of those "Break in Case of Emergency" cases. Jupiter thought Mac was right.

Having watched the video a number of times, Jupiter had a feel for it now, knowing what it showed and how it flowed. Nothing jumped out at him initially, but then again, if something like that were there, the FBI or police would have found it. No, what he was looking for wouldn't be obvious, if not flat-out hidden. But it was there somewhere. You just had to know how to find it, or get lucky enough, and then extract it.

He needed to break the video down frame-by-frame. Jupe took a sip from his Red Bull, grabbed a handful of chips and started at the beginning: the van driving through the field.

Mac wiped sweat off his forehead as he sat on a dining room chair, looking out the front window of the Hall house and across the street at the rambler. The crime scene techs found nothing inside the house: no prints, no hairs, no odd fibers, no nothing. The house was clean. Or, as Mac bitterly stated, "It's a safe house for these bastards because it's clean."

It took three hours, but Burton and the FBI found the owner, Gavin Harvey, who was out on his boat on Lake Minnetonka. Arriving dressed in a bright orange swimsuit and unbuttoned blue and white Hawaiian shirt, not to mention half in the bag, Harvey turned over a manila folder with a thin set of rental documents for the house.

The renter was Ramona Jones. No picture identification was in the file. Simply a one-page, two-month rental agreement and a notation of $2,000 cash paid up-front. It was nothing unusual, according to Harvey. This was one of his lesser rental properties, and he was contemplating selling because he couldn't regularly rent it. When Jones came along with $2,000 cash and a two-month rental request, it was "a no brainer," Harvey said, "Otherwise the joint sits empty."

Harvey's description of the woman wasn't helpful either. "Small, petite, she was attractive, had long blonde hair, nearly down to her ass. I took a little run at her, if you know what I mean," Harvey said, smiling crookedly and winking at Mac. "But she blew me off."

"I can't imagine why," Lich cracked.

"Where was she from?" Mac asked, suppressing a chuckle.

"I don't know, beyond what's on the rental sheet," Harvey said, the booze on his breath causing Mac to wince and take a step back. Good thing this guy had a lackey driving him.

The rental sheet revealed a nonexistent address in Duluth. Harvey said that he had spoken to Jones once over the phone, met her once in person to have her sign the lease, collected the money, and gave her the keys. Harvey hadn't stopped by since.

The FBI was running down women named Ramona Jones fitting the general description provided by Harvey, but nobody was holding their breath. Like everything else in this case, it would probably be a dead end.

Neighbors were questioned, but nothing useful was coming of it. People had seen vans, but they couldn't give consistent answers as to colors, makes, models, or plates. Men were seen, but nobody seemed to know how many or what they looked like beyond being big. Nobody spoke to the men or ever saw their faces. They were seen pulling in and out of the garage, black-clad torsos with hats and sunglasses on. Otherwise, they were never seen and never did anything to draw attention.

Burton, Duffy, and Peters were also convinced that the kidnappers were using the house. Now, if only they would come back. Mac ran the facts continuously through his head as he watched the house and the neighborhood. The neighborhood was eerily quiet. The heat was keeping people inside. A normal July 3rd night would have people out walking their dogs, taking a run, enjoying the small window of summer weather in Minnesota. Instead it was quiet.

Stifling a yawn, Mac turned away from the window to see the massive Rock sitting in an undersized armchair, reading, of all things, *Better Homes and Gardens*. Rock wasn't exactly the kind of guy who cared about curtains or tulips or anything of the like. He was bored. So was Lich, who was failing miserably in his attempt to complete a crossword puzzle in the *Star Tribune*. The kicker was Riles, a man who absolutely hated pop culture, reading a *People* magazine. Pat far preferred watching the Discovery and History channels or reading a *Newsweek* or *Time*.

Mac had to laugh. Riley, all six feet, three inches of him, wearing a faded blue Minnesota Twins cap, a dark blue golf shirt, and khakis, sat on the right side of a small couch. On the other side sat the short, squat Lich, wearing white tennis shoes, lightly soiled off-white pants, a red Hawaiian shirt with white collar, and a white beach hat he'd fished out of Mac's backseat earlier. It was the Skipper and Gilligan.

Mac slyly caught Riles' attention before he said to Lich, "Hey little buddy," in his best Skipper voice. Riles, right on cue, hit Dick on the head with his blue hat. Rock howled in laughter.

"Fuck you all," Lich growled, rubbing his head. For no reason at all everyone started talking about their favorite *Gilligan's Island* episode. Rock argued for five minutes, mostly tongue-in-cheek, that the show was racist. "I didn't see no brothas on that show. Why not? That Sherwood Schwartz dude was racist."

"Oh, right," Mac answered, rolling his eyes. "There were lots of African Americans who were going on charter boat rides in Hawaii back in the mid-sixties."

"Fuck that," Rock answered. "They just didn't want a good lookin' black dude like Jim Brown, Fred Williamson, or Richard Roundtree scoring with Ginger or Mary Ann."

"You know what I don't get? Why weren't the skipper, professor, or Gilligan drillin' Ginger or Mary Ann to begin with," Lich said, his mind always wandering in a certain direction. "I mean, you know Thurston was putting the Howell the III to Lovey."

"Oh God," Mac howled, doubling over with laughter, "I think I'm going to be sick."

"Okay. Which one, Ginger or Mary Ann?" Rock asked smiling.

"Mary Ann!" Mac and Riles replied in unison.

"Agreed," Rock said. What about you, Dick Lick?" Rock asked.

"Ginger. Definitely Ginger. She could suck a golf ball through a straw," Lich said, smiling, sticking his tongue out in his best impression of Morris from *Slap Shot.*

Mac got up out of his chair, still clutching his stomach, and went to check on Hall. Mrs. Hall, whom they had yet to meet, was out shopping although she was due back any minute. In the meantime, Mac and the others would check on Mr. Hall from time to time. When Mac walked in he was lying in his bed, watching the Twins game.

"Can I get you anything?" Mac asked. Hall was sweating through yet another shirt.

"A refill on my water," Hall answered. "I have to take some medication."

Mac arrived in the kitchen just as Mrs. Hall came through the back door with two bags of groceries.

"You must be Mrs. Hall," Mac said as he introduced himself and pulled out his shield. Mac explained what he and the others were doing.

"How is Pat doing?" she asked.

"He needed some water for his medication."

"I can get that," she said.

"That's fine," Mac answered. "You put your stuff away. I can run it in for him."

Riles walked in, putting his cell phone back in his pocket. "That was Peters. We've got relief coming in a bit. We get until 0600 to get some rest. They'll call us if anything comes up."

Mac nodded, grabbing some ice cubes out of the freezer. "I'm starting to think these guys have bolted."

"They might have, but what else do we have at this point?"

Riles was right. What else *did* they have? Or, why weren't they looking for something else? Mac wondered. All they'd done in the last two days was react to whatever the kidnappers were doing. To Mac, it still seemed like they weren't pushing the investigation. Rather it was being pushed at them. Three words surfaced again in his mind: complicated, prepared, and motivated.

Mac walked back to Hall's room with Riley in tow. As he placed the glass on the nightstand he heard a vehicle slowing outside. Mac turned to the window to see a minivan pulling into a neighbor's house, but not to the house they were watching.

"Nothing, eh?" Mr. Hall asked, taking a sip.

"Nada," Mac answered. "How are the Twins doing?"

"They're up four. Mauer is three-for-three," Hall said, then added with a little pride, "That St. Paul kid is hitting over three-forty again."

"He's got a shot at another batting title," Riles said, straightening his Twins cap on his head.

Mrs. Hall walked into the room to check on her husband. Riles and Mac stood watching the game for a moment and both clapped as Mauer flared a single to left field, now four-for-four in the game.

"He's unbelievable," Riles said of Mauer.

"That he is," Mac replied as he went back to the window and pulled back the curtains.

"They haven't come back, have they?" Mr. Hall asked disappointedly.

"No," Mac answered, looking out the window.

"You think they're the guys?"

Mac looked back and nodded slightly.

"Too bad I didn't pay a little more attention when they ripped out of here earlier," Mrs. Hall said. "Maybe I could have seen something that would have helped."

"Ripped out?" Mac asked, turning back to Mrs. Hall.

"What do you mean ripped out?" Riles added.

"I might have missed them when they left," Mrs. Hall answered, "except that they squealed the tires pulling out. I probably wouldn't have noticed if the air conditioner was working. But with the windows open, I heard the tires and saw them go."

Mac pulled out his notepad, checking his notes from earlier. "Mr. Hall, you said they left just after you called it in right?"

"That's right."

"How long after you called?"

"Five minutes at the most, I'd say," Mrs. Hall answered for her husband. "Pat was on the potty when it happened."

"They ripped out of here?" Mac asked. "Like they were in a hurry?"

"It sure seemed like it."

"They ever do that before?" Riles asked. "Or was that a first?"

"Not that I recall," Mrs. Hall answered. She thought about it some more. "They were usually pretty quiet." Hall thought a few seconds more and then shook her head. "No, that was the first time I recall them leaving so fast. What about you, Pat? Did you ever see them leave like that?"

"Not that I recall."

"And again, this was *after* you called," Mac pressed. "You're *sure* it was after?"

"That's right," Mrs. Hall answered.

Mac and Riles shared a look. They left the Halls and went back to the kitchen.

"Do you think...." Riles started.

"...that they were tipped off," Mac finished as he led Riles back to the living room. "I think it's entirely possible."

In the living room, Lich and Rock were peering out the front window.

"I think we might have missed something," Mac said in a hushed but excited tone.

They all looked at him. "Like what?" Rock asked.

Mac related what Mrs. Hall had just told them. "We got the call from Burton, what? At about four thirty?" Mac asked, looking at his notebook.

Riles nodded. "Yeah."

"At about the same time we're getting that call, these guys, according to Mrs. Hall, bolt as well. They ripped out of here."

"They ever do that before," Rock asked.

"No," Mac and Riles answered in unison.

Lich's face paled. He pinched the bridge of his nose and grimaced. "Fuck, Mac," he said heavily.

Pat ran his hand hard through his thick mane of black hair. "They ripped out of here, boys. Mrs. Hall said that she almost missed them because they ripped out of here."

"At roughly the same time we're getting the call, which is five to ten minutes after the call from Mr. Hall originally came in," Mac answered, pointing at Rock with his notepad. "Isn't that awfully convenient? That they left the house like *that* at about the same time as I got the call? And we've been sitting here how long, and nobody's been back?"

"Could be a coincidence," Rock answered. "They could be back any minute for all we know."

Riles looked at Mac, who said, "I doubt it. We can keep sitting on this house. But they're not coming back."

"Oh shit," Lich said, rubbing his face with both hands.

"Motherfuckers," Rock muttered. "They've got someone inside."

"We've got the rest of the night off," Mac said. "We need to figure out what we're going to do."

"Who can we trust?" Lich asked.

"Peters," Riles answered.

"Double Frank, I'd say," Rock added.

"And any McRyan," Mac said. "And Sally—we could use her help. But beyond that?" He shook his head. "We gotta keep this close."

"We got lots of people hanging around," Riles said. "Within the department and then all those FBI people. God," he sighed, running his hand over his face. "It could be anyone."

"Not to mention Hisle's law firm," Lich added. "Lyman's a good guy, but who knows?"

"I'd start with the department," Mac said matter-of-factly. That stunned everyone. Mac had more institutional love than anyone else.

"Why not the fuckin' FBI?" barked Rock.

"Easy, Rock," Mac answered, holding up his hands. "It could be them, too. But, if you're with the Bureau, how could you know for sure you'd be on the case?"

"Whereas people in the department..." Lich started.

"Could be certain, or at least more certain, that they would be involved," Rock finished. "I see Mac's point."

"We need to move carefully, boys. *Very* carefully," Riles said. "Ideas?"

"Let's go to the Pub," Mac answered. "Just us and Peters. We'll get Sally over there, too. We gotta start making some moves of our own."

22

"You're a drop dead gorgeous woman, with a fantastic body, a great mind, and impeccable timing."

10:45 PM

Mac pulled in behind the bar and noted that it was a slow night for the other family business: McRyan's Pub, a true St. Paul institution. The pub sat on West Seventh Street, just on the outskirts of downtown and one block from the Xcel Energy Center, home of the NHL's Minnesota Wild. It was the favored watering hole of hockey fans and the St. Paul Police alike, not to mention the single largest employer of ex-cops in the city.

As the window over the front door indicated, the Pub was established in 1907. Opened by Mac's great-grandpa Patrick, the pub had a colorful history of serving drinks before, during, and after Prohibition. During Prohibition, they had been served in the now-infamous Patrick's Room. Located in the basement, Patrick's Room lay behind a hidden door disguised as a built-in wooden buffet, the type you would find in any older St. Paul home. A latch inside the middle drawer of the buffet pushed the door into a large party room. During Prohibition, the police, politicians, citizens, and even notorious criminals like John Dillinger sat together, knocking back illegal drinks and having a good time.

Today, the inside of Patrick's Room was adorned with black and white photos of that bygone era, while a plaque outside described the room's infamous history. These days, the hidden room was used for private parties, meetings, and the occasional cop poker game.

Mac walked in the back door and stepped left into the main level of the Pub. A classic old-fashioned bar—a massive stretch of mahogany with a brass rail—ate up half of the length and breadth of the room. Behind the bar were the typical bottles and taps and a long mirror with "McRyan's Pub" stenciled across it, along with the Minnesota Wild logo, a badge, and a shamrock. On most nights, this part of the bar was full of cops having a bump after a shift, happy to have made it through another tour, swapping war stories and telling lies. Tonight there were a few hanging around, but things were eerily quiet, voices in a hushed murmur. Nobody was in a happy, celebratory, or terribly talkative mood.

Mac made conversation for a few minutes with the bartender, a retired patrol cop, until Uncle Shamus walked in. Shamus, a retired St. Paul detective, was the Pub's current proprietor.

"Michael," Shamus said, coming over to give his nephew a big bear hug. "Boyo, let's get you something to drink and go down to Patrick's. I've got food on the way, whatever you and the boys need."

"Thanks, Shamus," Mac replied, looking longingly at the beer taps. He was dying to have one—a Grain Belt Premium or a Schells, his current favorites. Instead he had the bartender mix him a tall Arnie Palmer, which, while not a beer, would be cold and refreshing nonetheless.

Shamus led Mac down the stairs and past a small game room, which was currently occupied by two regulars playing pool. Turning right, Shamus opened the middle drawer of the buffet and popped the latch to Patrick's Room. Inside, Mac found a table set up with chips and salsa and a gray tub that was full of Diet Cokes, Sprites, and bottled waters.

"I'll have some warm food brought in," Shamus said, grabbing a phone to call the kitchen. "When will everyone else be coming?"

"Within the hour," Mac replied as he opened two dark wood-paneled doors, revealing a whiteboard. "I could eat right now, though."

"BLTs?" Shamus asked, familiar with his nephew's favorites. Mac nodded. Shamus dialed up to the kitchen and placed the order. "They're on their way," he said as he hung up. "So tell me, boyo. Where you at?"

Mac gave Shamus the rundown on the last two days, leaving out his suspicions about someone working the case from the inside.

"You ain't got shit, do ya, boyo?" Shamus asked.

Mac shook his head with disgust.

Shamus patted him on the back. "Well, it ain't over yet," he said. "You never know what's gonna break a case, my boy. But let me tell ya, I've had the old hands in here by the dozens today. You need any help, you let me know. We'll call in the brigade." Shamus headed upstairs to check on the food.

One of the reasons Mac wanted to come to Patrick's Room was the chance to be away from Burton, Duffy, the mayor, and everyone else and think and talk things out. Patrick's Room was used for bar training and business meetings. Consequently, Shamus had outfitted it with all one needed for such things, including an overhead projector, drop-down movie screen, whiteboard, along with tables and chairs.

A psychologist friend said Mac was a visual learner, which meant he needed to see it, feel it, touch it, and write it down. While Mac was inclined to think it was a bunch of quack psychoanalysis, he had to admit that there was a bit of truth in it. He needed to see things laid out to understand the patterns and connections, to comprehend the whole picture. He loved puzzles, laying out the pieces and trying to make them all fit. It was time to mind-map—to lay out the pieces of this case and see what larger picture they formed. He took out his notebook and grabbed a black marker and started jotting down notes on the whiteboard. Along the top of the board he wrote:

Complicated – Prepared – Motivated.

For the next half hour he jotted down what the investigation had thus far.

Kidnappers: Probably three men? Big, over 6 feet. Hats, sunglasses, gloves. Vans, no consistent makes or models and always stolen. The one running the show has thought of everything. Seems to know what we'll do.

Woman: Black hair, forties, smallish, purchased laptop, was the eyes inside at Cel's and at St. Thomas University. Rented the safe house? Landlord said she was attractive, but with blonde hair. Wig? Same woman? Were there two women?

Vans: Last five days, panel-type, different makes. Gloves on drivers' hands.

Hisle and Flanagan cases: No connections (at least yet) on criminal cases between Flanagan and Hisle.

Mac thought about that lack of a good connection. Wiskowski was a setup. The rest they'd looked into were weak at best. That still bothered him, which brought him back to something he'd said earlier.

Investigative Focus: Pick a good candidate, even if not obviously connected to both men.

He scratched his head at the last note. That sounded good in theory, but it would take time to work through all of the names again and they had less than twenty hours. He left that for the time being and moved on to today's clues: the laptop and safe house.

Laptop: Purchased by woman? Was it the same woman as at Cel's? Store video was inconclusive. No match from facial recognition software. Woman had dark hair, wore a baseball cap and sunglasses. Computer purchased with cash, no credit card trail.

Safe house: House now abandoned? Clean. No evidence other than paint scratches on bed in basement. No forensic evidence. Feels right.

The door opened and his cousin Kelly walked in with a BLT and another Arnie Palmer. She gave Mac a little hug and a few words of encouragement before heading back out. Mac took a bite out of the sandwich and moved back to the whiteboard.

Ransom: $5 million. It should be more. What's that mean? Is it important? The chief and Hisle could easily come up with more.

Video: Jupiter working it. FBI found nothing. Video shows isolated area—abandoned farm? Land the kidnappers own or owned?

Mac called Jupe, who had nothing to report yet. He said he would call as soon as something popped up. Figuring Jupe needed a second set of eyes, Mac called his cousin Shawn out of bed to go over and help. After the call, he went back to the whiteboard to deal with their newest concern.

Inside Job: Phone call and kidnappers "rip out" within five minutes. Did someone tip them off? Timing suggests it, but who? Inside department? FBI? Hisle's law firm? Most likely in the department.

Mac pinched the bridge of his nose. They needed to figure out who knew about the call. Paddy and Double Frank were there at the time. In fact, Paddy told the room about it. He jotted down a note to call Paddy and Double Frank and have them make a list.

Then he turned his attention to the girls. He drew a map of the state of Minnesota and Wisconsin, marking River Falls, Clearwater, Lake Street in Minneapolis, Ellsworth, Duluth, and the safe house in St. Paul. He thought that the girls were within an hour of the Twin Cities at most. If that were the case, Duluth didn't fit; it was at least two hours away. Was Duluth used to throw them off? Make them search a wider area? That was possible.

Where are the Girls? Phone calls from Clearwater, Ellsworth, and Duluth. Buried underground. Must be rural, private, wooded area that public doesn't use. Within an hour of the Cities.

Phone calls: Clearwater, Ellsworth, Duluth. Voice disguised. Speaker was blasé, clipped, except one thing. "Hisle was the appetizer and your daughter is the main course." Is one of the girls more important than the other? Is the chief or Hisle more important?

Mac looked over as the door opened and Sally strolled in. She was carrying a duffel bag. Mac realized that he was beyond scruffy, his hair messed and his clothes dirty, sweaty, and smelly. His girlfriend looked like a million bucks, khaki shorts revealing her shapely, tanned legs, a white, v-neck sleeveless shirt tight to her wonderful breasts, and fiery red hair up in a bouncy ponytail. She greeted him with a big hug and a long, warm kiss.

"I've missed you," she said, looking into his eyes.

"Likewise," he answered, giving Sally another kiss and holding her for a few minutes. He instantly felt better. "What's in the bag?"

Sally opened it and handed him a change of clothes, a truly welcome sight. As he went behind the wet bar to clean up, Sally took a look at the whiteboard.

"Inside job?" Sally asked, astonished. Mac explained as he turned on the tap water and waited for it to warm. "Damn, you're probably right," she said, shaking her head as Mac splashed water over his face. "What will you do to the person if you find them?"

"Baby, you don't want to know," Mac answered as he toweled off his face. "So tell me about your day for a minute, get my mind off mine."

"Mine was uneventful, but for a friend of mine, holy frickin' cow," Sally said, a big smile crossing her face. "Do you remember Homer Snodgrass from law school?"

"Homer the homo right?"

"He wasn't gay!" Sally protested.

"He was a gunner though," Mac answered. "He asked way too many questions in class and always thought he had all the answers. Hell, all he was ever doing was quoting from the Emanuels study guides."

"That might be true."

"Homer Snodgrass," Mac chuckled. "I could never understand how parents with the last name of Snodgrass would name their kid Homer."

"Someone named Lich gave their son the name of Richard."

"Good point," Mac answered, zipping up his pants.

"Anyway, Homer's making millions as a class-action lawyer these days."

"Figures."

"Now *his* day was eventful."

"Why's that?"

"Do you remember hearing about that portable heater class action a couple of weeks ago?"

"Vaguely. Wasn't it something about a flaw in the design causing fires, something like that? Jury awarded something like $20 million?"

"Exactly," Sally said. "That was Homer. Anyway, it was a bet-the-company case. The company lost, and the owner paid—or tried to pay—Homer a visit today over in Minneapolis."

"That couldn't be good," Mac said, pulling a fresh white-and-blue stripped Adidas golf shirt over his head.

"No, it wasn't," Sally replied. "This guy shows up in a trench coat, which on a day like today with the heat, should have been a sign of trouble in and of itself. In any event, he barged past the front desk at the firm. He's stalking the halls, looking for Homer, and when he sees him," her eyes lit up, "he starts chasing Homer with an axe—not a hatchet, but a big red fireman's axe. Can you believe it, with an axe?"

"No way," Mac said, laughing out loud, a disbelieving smile on his face. "What the hell happened then?"

"Oh shit," she replied smiling, enjoying the chance to tell the story. "I guess Homer starts running, although where do you go on the forty-fourth floor of the American Financial Tower? But he starts running, goes down a flight of steps, trying to get away from this guy, who's running after him like a crazed lunatic, waving this axe, yelling 'I'm gonna kill you. I'm gonna kill you.' People ducking for cover everywhere—it was a zoo."

"So did the police get there?"

"No, it was the security guards. American Financial has pretty serious security in the building, since they occupy most of the floors. They finally caught up and subdued the guy."

Just then, Riles, Rock, Lich, and Peters burst in, all of them freshly washed and changed. Lich asked what was so funny. Sally told the Homer Snodgrass story again as Mac turned his attention back to the whiteboard, twisting the black dry erase marker through his fingers like a baton.

"The rental cops from downstairs earned their keep today," Sally finished.

"Went nuts over his company, huh?" Riles said, grabbing a sandwich off the table.

"Yeah. He's in a rubber room now, I'd suspect," Sally said, popping open the top of a Diet Coke and pouring the contents into a red plastic cup filled with ice. "Homer says these people in class-action suits get pretty pissed off at him. This isn't the first time he's had death threats, for cripes' sake." Mac stared at the notation on the board:

Hisle and Flanagan cases: No connections (at least yet) on criminal cases between Flanagan and Hisle.

He dramatically underlined "criminal" and suddenly the pieces fell together into a new picture. "It's the civil cases. I bet it's the damned *civil* cases," Mac exclaimed loudly.

"What?" Sally asked.

"You know what, Kennedy? You're a drop-dead gorgeous woman with a fantastic body, a great mind, and impeccable timing," Mac said, giving her a big wet kiss on the lips.

Sally looked at him, stunned.

"What the hell's got into you?" Peters asked as the others stared.

"A guy went after a lawyer with an *axe* because he lost his company in a class-action suit, right?"

"Yeah, so?"

"She also said this guy has received death threats—more than once."

"Again, so?"

"Lyman Hisle is one of the most successful class-action and discrimination lawyers around. We all think of the criminal stuff because that's where *we* deal with him. But he's made millions upon millions on those class-action and discrimination cases and we haven't been looking at those cases."

"Why not?" Rock asked.

"Because Burton and the chief thought the criminal cases were the most likely connection when we had just the Hisle kidnapping. Then, when they took Carrie Flanagan, everyone naturally assumed that it had to be the criminal cases again, because it involved a criminal lawyer and a cop. But what if Lyman's civil world crossed with the chief somehow? Somebody who lost a ton of money to Lyman, and where there's a connection to the chief."

"Or with multiple kidnappers? Maybe one hand is washing the other," Lich added. "Someone pissed at Lyman joins up with someone pissed at the chief, or visa versa."

"How would that happen?" Peters asked. "Who knows?" Mac said. "But maybe it has. We haven't found the connection on the criminal cases. So we have to take a look at it from the civil side."

"How many cases or people we talking here?" Riles asked, aware of the ticking clock.

"Hundreds, maybe thousands, given how prolific Lyman is," Sally said. "It could be a defendant in a case he won, could be a plaintiff in a case he lost."

"Probably a defendant," Mac said. "And it fits with these guys." He smiled, looking at his three words. "They've been prepared. It's complicated, and this is why. Because it's a connection between a case the chief worked and some civil matter of Lyman's." He paused, and then added with a little admiration in his voice, "Man, that's a nice little twist on their part when you think about it."

"Which fits with two of your words up there," Riles said. "Now all we need is the 'motivated.' We need to figure out what's motivating these guys."

"I wonder if they tipped their hand on that," Mac said.

"How so?" Lich asked.

Mac underlined the quote. "It's what the kidnapper said when he called the chief. He said: 'Hisle was the appetizer and *your* daughter was the *main course*.'"

"And you think?" Peters asked.

"That the guy running the show is after the chief. The man running the show is someone the chief busted, or a family member of someone he busted, something along those lines."

"And Hisle?" Sally asked.

"The price this guy is paying for the help."

"But does that really get us any closer?" Lich said.

"Not yet," Mac conceded. "But if we figure out the who, then we'll probably be able to determine what is motivating them. So we still have to run the chief's entire list against Lyman's civil cases, but it gives us another piece, another way of looking at this. But I'm betting the brains of this little operation are on the chief's side of the ledger.

The help is from Lyman. But we've gotta dig into all of that and we've got to do it now."

"I'll call Burton," Peters said.

"NO!" everyone cried in unison.

"Why the hell not?"

"Someone's workin' the inside on this," Mac answered quietly and without emotion.

Peters stared at him as the rest of the room fell silent, a disbelieving look overtaking his face. "You better tell me what you got," their captain said quietly.

Mac and Riley told him about the timeline, the call from Hall and the vans' sudden departure. It was thin, they all knew that, but it seemed right. Peters sighed.

"So we can't trust anyone?"

"Beyond the people in this room and a few others, Paddy or Double Frank at least, no," Riles said.

"We need to do this ourselves," Mac added.

"That won't make the mayor happy," Rock warned.

"Screw the mayor," Mac said. "Besides, he is one of the people we can't trust."

"And Burton?" Rock asked.

"He's a good man, from what we've seen. If we start getting somewhere we can bring him in. But for now, we need to keep this close."

"So what do you propose we do?" Peters asked.

"We need to set up shop over at Lyman's offices and away from everyone else. We need to be able to hook into that database we've been building at the Department of Public Safety, and we're going to need someone technical to make that all happen."

"Hisle have anyone like that?" Lich asked.

"I doubt it," Sally answered. "Law office the size of Lyman's will have someone who runs their document management systems, but I doubt it's someone who has higher-end computer skills. And it sounds like you need something slightly illegal here."

"How about your buddy Jupiter?" Peters asked.

"I've already got him doing something else," Mac answered. He explained what Jupiter was looking for in the video.

"How about someone from the department?" Rock said.

"There's one person who is pretty good," Mac said. "That IT guy, Scheifelbein. I think we can trust him. But we're going to need him to tap into that database and cover our tracks on that end, so he needs to stay put. We need to get someone from the outside."

"Then who the fuck do we get?" Rock asked harshly. "You don't just pick up someone like that off the street." He looked at his watch, "At eleven twenty-four at night I might add."

Mac smiled. He loved it when his mind got going. He could be a devious motherfucker when he did. "How about a convict?"

Riles snorted, shook his head, and smiled. "Hagen? You want to get Hagen don't you?"

Mac simply nodded.

23

"Where the hell are you going?"

11:35 PM

The money was pretty much set to go and Burton breathed a sigh of relief that the safe house had come up dry. By this time tomorrow it would all be over.

He looked outside for the media, some of whom were still hanging around. Those who were left hovered near the main entrance to the Department of Public Safety building. Burton slipped out the side and found his rental, a silver Ford Taurus, one of the world's most popular fleet cars. He threw his leather briefcase and black suit coat into the backseat, dropped his lukewarm Diet Pepsi into the cup holder, and lowered himself into the driver's seat. He slowly drove around the edge of the parking lot, avoiding attention, especially from the media. At the parking lot exit, he pulled out and steered his way over to Interstate 35E. With downtown St. Paul and his room at the Crowne Plaza to his immediate left, he instead turned right and took the entrance ramp north on the interstate. Traffic was light at this hour, and he easily settled into the flow, staying in the right lane and hovering around the sixty-mile-per-hour speed limit as he traveled north out of St. Paul.

He loosened his tie and tuned the radio to the talk station. Word was out about the ransom, and speculation ran rampant. Oddly, there was nothing about the safe house on the news. Of course, the crime scene people struck out, finding nothing. The lease information for the house was a dead end. Now he had St. Paul's best cops, the chief's Boys no less, sitting on a house their targets never intended to return to.

Perfect.

Burton wasn't doing this for the money. His payoff on this wasn't much. He would get $200,000 from Smith in six months, just after his planned retirement from the Bureau. No, he was paying a debt.

Seventeen years ago, when Smith was pinched by Charlie Flanagan, Burton was his partner, making sure the local FBI office in Minneapolis wasn't paying attention while Smith underreported his drug seizures. They split the money off of Smith's drug sales fifty-fifty. While Smith retired his gambling debts, Burton put the money away, thousands of miles away, down in the Caymans and over in Zurich, letting it quietly mature over time. That money, smartly invested and reinvested, was now over two million dollars, a nice little nest egg nobody knew about, not even his ex-wife. The $200,000 from Smith would simply be walking-around cash.

The St. Paul police and the Bureau had suspected Smith had a partner when they took him down, but Smith never put Burton's name in play. He took all the weight. When Smith was being sodomized in jail, when the Bureau visited him, talking about how they could make his life easier if he just told them who he worked with, he didn't give in, didn't fold, and didn't turn in his partner. Burton knew all this, tracking his partner's incarceration, always worried he might break. He never did.

Meanwhile, Burton moved to kidnapping and found his true calling within the Bureau. When he brought home the daughter of one of New York's wealthiest businessmen, taking down the kidnappers in a spectacular chase through the subway tunnels, his name and reputation were cemented. He published a book, traveled the country speaking about his cases, and now performed training for the Bureau. Retiring at the end of the year, he could expect to greatly enhance his wealth on the speaking circuit. Several prestigious colleges had inquired of his interest in teaching. His life was set.

Then, four months ago Smith showed up on his doorstep. Burton owed him and there was no argument. His life was what it was because Smith never turned him in. Smith took all the heat, and Burton ended up with all the glory.

Burton spent days and nights thinking of ways out of helping Smith. He offered up part of his nest egg. Smith wasn't interested. Burton offered to put him in touch with people who would put him to work, let him earn a respectable living, start a new life, a comfortable life, a decent life. Smith wasn't interested in any of that. He wanted one thing: he wanted Charlie Flanagan, and he didn't just want to hurt him, he wanted to gut him. And Burton owed him. And if Burton refused, Smith would kill him.

If he could just get through the next day, help Smith get what he wanted and get his crew theirs; he'd be free and clear. Smith would be gone. Burton could retire a happy and wealthy man. If Charlie Flanagan, Lyman Hisle, and their daughters had to pay the ultimate price for that—well, it was him or them. If that was the way it had to be, he'd just have to live with it.

The upcoming road sign told him three miles to his exit in Forest Lake.

Heather Foxx passed the Forest Lake exit.

A half-hour ago she had been slumped in the back seat of her rental car, slipping on her Nikes, exhausted from a long-day in ninety-five-degree heat, and hoping to get a few hours of sleep, when the Taurus approached, driving cautiously around the perimeter of the parking lot. Looking up through the strands of hair falling across her eyes, Foxx saw that the driver was John Burton, the mysterious FBI man running the investigation, but unwilling to speak with the media. Rumor was he had a room down at the Crowne Plaza. With all of the other vultures hanging around, there was no way to approach him, let alone get any time with him. But, looking to her left, she saw that the rest of the media types were oblivious to his escape. Heather thought this might be her chance. She started her car and followed.

If she could catch him at the hotel, maybe she could talk with him one-on-one—get a hint at what tomorrow might hold. But instead of driving into downtown, Burton took the entrance ramp on I-35E north out of downtown.

"Where the hell are you going?" Heather said out loud, pulling in a good two hundred yards behind him. She was suddenly thankful that her little sports car was in the shop and she'd been forced to use a nondescript rental. Perhaps Burton had double-crossed everyone and was staying at one of the nice business hotels that were strategically located along the I-694 strip, a Residence Inn or Country Inn Suites perhaps. But he continued on I-35E past I-694 and was now well out of downtown and passing the last of the White Bear Lake exits, cruising into the countryside north of the Twin Cities.

"This is damn peculiar," she muttered as Burton kept driving on, now twenty miles out of downtown and continuing north as Interstate 35W and 35E merged to form Interstate 35 to Duluth. Heather contemplated giving up, but Burton hit his right turn blinker and took the Forest Lake exit. At the top of the exit ramp, the FBI man turned right and drove a mile east into downtown Forest Lake, pulling into the parking lot of the Ranger Bar. A bright white marquee on the front indicated that the Ranger—a play on the nickname of the local high school— was open until 2:00 AM. From the looks of the cars in the parking lot, it was apparent that the party was going plenty strong inside. Tomorrow was the Fourth of July, and a lot of people in the Forest Lake area were getting a head start.

Burton had turned into the lot on the north side of the bar. Foxx drove past the front and pulled into the lot on the south side and then cruised around to the back of the bar and out onto the street running along the backside so that she could look at the back of Burton's car. She parked along the curb and slumped down to watch. The FBI man stayed in his car, contorting his body around—she saw his arms waving over his head as his shirt came off. Five minutes later, he was out of the sedan, dressed in jean shorts, a dark T-shirt, baseball cap, wire-rimmed glasses, and flip-flops.

Foxx took one look in the rearview mirror and realized she would be noticed without some alterations. Popping the trunk, she grabbed her duffel bag and quickly jumped back into the car and inventoried the contents. She'd gone to her fitness club early the day before, so there was an extra clean tank top, a hair binder, and a white Adidas tennis cap. She changed shirts and put on the baseball cap, sliding her pony tail out the back, but it wasn't quite enough. There was also a sky blue Reebok nylon sweat top in the bag. It was a little gamy as she zipped it up, but that was okay—it might keep people, meaning men, away. The last thing she did was take out her disposable contact lenses and toss them out the window, sliding on her dark-rimmed glasses instead. She was as unrecognizable as she could make herself. Grabbing her purse, she walked into the bar.

Forest Lake sat on the far northeastern edge of the Twin Cities, so it was considered a suburb, but it had a country feel. The Ranger created a melting pot for the clash of those suburban and rural cultures. One look at the massive throng revealed a great mixture of the denim-and-belt-buckle, NASCAR-hat crowd and the Tommy-Bahama types.

As Heather entered from the back, she found a large bar beneath dark-paneled walls covered with framed sports jerseys and newspaper clippings, souvenirs of the Twins '87 and '91 World Series victories and recent Minnesota Gopher hockey national championships. In the dim lighting, she noted pool tables and dartboards in a segregated area to her immediate right. Straight ahead, a short hallway led to the main bar area where booths and tables surrounded a long, four-sided mahogany bar. In the far right corner, karaoke was going strong with an *American Idol* wannabe belting out Eddie Money's "*Shakin*'" —badly.

Heather picked her way around two sides of the main bar before spotting Burton, who was sitting in a booth, talking to another man. She grabbed an open bar stool, three from the corner nearest to Burton, and sat down.

The bartender appeared instantly, a good-looking, six-foot, black-haired early twenty-something in a tight black Ranger T-shirt, which showed his chiseled upper body. "What can I get ya', darlin'?" he said with a bright white smile.

Darlin'? He was cheesy for sure, but definitely cute. "You know what a Vodka Sonic is?"

"Sure darlin'. Vodka, club soda, splash of tonic, and a lemon. We call it a Jolly Roger around here."

"That's what I want."

"Vodka Sonic for the pretty lady it is," the bartender replied, strolling off to mix the drink.

Heather alternately looked at a table tent menu with nightly specials and toward Burton, still deep in conversation with the other man, who was perhaps a little shorter. The man had short black hair, slightly graying at the temples. His profile revealed a large nose with a knot two-thirds of the way up, where it had been broken before. Both men had a beer in front of them, one-third finished, along with a bowl of popcorn. They leaned in close as they talked, their hands crossed in front of them.

"So where is the investigation at?" Smith asked, taking a pull off of his Budweiser.

"We're good," Burton answered, hat pulled down low. He ignored his Miller High Life and cautiously peered around the jam-packed bar, trying to determine if anyone was watching or looking in their direction. He wasn't comfortable meeting in this environment, but Smith insisted and he was the one pulling the strings. "The discovery of the house today actually worked to your advantage."

"How so?" Smith asked with raised eyebrows.

"Besides the obvious, which is that we didn't find anything to identify you, it means that the best St. Paul has to offer are sitting on the house right now. It's the only break the case has had, so they're lying in wait, hoping you'll come back."

"Which means they're wasting their time and not looking for us," Smith answered, smiling, taking another hit off the beer. He was so happy, he was thinking of ordering another.

"And that's a good thing," Burton said. "These guys aren't bad, particularly this McRyan character."

"Now that name's familiar," Smith answered. "Why do I know that name?"

"Let me tell you why," Burton took a sip of his beer. "You were still in the can at the time, but last winter the St. Paul police took down a crew of ex-CIA guys running security at Peterson Technical Applications, you know, PTA, in St. Paul. This McRyan was the main guy in all that, figured it out, broke the case wide open, and chased the guy behind it through downtown. He put him down in the RiverCentre Parking Ramp."

"I saw a TV report on that," Smith answered. "Shootout in downtown. Arms sales and stuff like that."

"That's it," Burton replied, taking a couple of kernels of popcorn out of the basket. "Anyway, this kid's a pretty good cop. He's fourth generation. I knew his old man, a detective named Simon McRyan."

"*That's* why I remember the name," Smith said, nodding his head.

"As well you should," Burton added. "Simon was a hell of a cop, one of the best local cops I ever saw. His son is a chip off the old block for sure, scary smart and just tenacious as hell."

"Tenacious?"

Burton related the argument about releasing the video to local authorities and the mayor and Duffy's objections. "He didn't back down one bit. He's essentially calling the mayor, his boss I might add, an idiot and political hack in front of a room of cops and agents. He was one hundred percent right and wouldn't back down until he got his way."

"What lets him get away with that?" Smith asked, stunned.

"I'm not totally sure. If I had to guess, at least part of it is his DNA. Word is he's never, ever, backed down from anything. On that arms sales thing, he was repeatedly told to leave it alone, but didn't. Hell, he wouldn't, and he brought that thing home. If he thinks he's right, he won't stop."

"He'll end up on the street if he keeps doing that."

"Perhaps, but I don't think he worries about it. He's got money."

"How? He's just a cop."

"It's not widely known, even within his department, but he invested ten grand about five or six years ago with two old high school friends in a coffee business, the Grand Brew. You've seen them around town haven't you?"

Smith nodded.

"Well, that little enterprise is up to nearly thirty shops, with more on the way, and McRyan has a piece of that action, gets a check every so often. When that little business goes public or gets bought by a bigger corporation a few years from now, he'll be a multi-millionaire. It gives him a certain freedom to say what he thinks and do what he wants. He doesn't have to worry about whether he can make the mortgage payment."

"Tenacious and he's going to be rich, which is good for him. But what makes him like the old man? What makes him someone we should be worrying about? I mean he can't be that old? What, early thirties?"

"Thirty-three to be exact." Burton snorted and shook his head, "You haven't seen him in action. Let me tell you a little about him." The agent pulled out a paper-clipped set of papers out of his pocket. "I got myself a look at his personnel file. Honors graduate of the University of Minnesota and William Mitchell College of Law, second in his class. His college entrance exams and LSAT to get into law school were off the charts. The guy is brilliant."

"Why did he become a cop, then?"

"He's fourth generation. Two of his best friends growing up were two cousins, Peter and Thomas McRyan. Apparently, the three were tight and all planned on becoming cops. But Mac has the college grades, marries a smart and pretty girl, and they both head off to law school, graduate with high honors, and line up the six-figure jobs after graduation."

"Still doesn't answer my question. Why the cop bit?"

"Two weeks after he takes the bar exam, his two cousins die in the line of duty, and he feels the calling of the family business. That was eight years ago. He trashed a legal career where he'd probably have made a big pile of money and blew his marriage because the wife didn't like him being a cop, all to take up the family business. I guess he felt obligated."

"So in eight years, he's the best St. Paul has? I bet the veterans *love* that."

"It's an interesting dynamic for sure, but from what I've seen the vets roll with it pretty well. You can tell they all know he's the smartest one in the room. Plus he's a McRyan, a name that means something around here. These guys—Riley, this big guy Rockford, and fat Lich—all try keeping him just enough in line to stay employed, but then run interference for him so he can do his thing."

"Sharp cop, then," Smith acknowledged.

"Damn straight," Burton answered, taking a pull from his beer. "He knew the safe house was the safe house five minutes after he got there. Long before they got into the house to look around."

"What told him that?"

"Gut. Instinct. He just knew it was the place. He said he could *feel* it. Cops like that scare the shit out of me. They see what you don't want them to see." Burton took a last pull from his High Life. "I feel much better knowing I got McRyan sitting still." Burton finished the popcorn, picking out one piece at a time and popping them into his mouth. "So tell me about the plan for tomorrow."

"The call will come in at 6:00 PM...."

Heather nursed her drink, a small amount of the diluted, yet refreshing liquid remaining amongst the melting ice cubes and squeezed lemon. She looked at her watch, 1:22 AM, and the bar was still going strong. The crowd was whoopin' it up, including the woman strangling a cat in the corner, or maybe she was just singing karaoke.

Burton was still in the booth and had been talking for over a half hour with the other man. Heather had only seen his profile, except for now. The man looked her direction just briefly and then turned away and back to Burton. The conversation had been equal at first, but now the other man was doing most of the talking, counting off on his fingers while Burton nodded along, only occasionally speaking.

"You want another drink darlin'?" The cute bartender was back.

Heather learned that his name was Skeet, which couldn't possibly be his real name. She contemplated the offer, the first drink having tasted so good. "Sure. Easy on the vodka though."

"Anything for you darlin'," Skeet answered, giving her his big cheesy smile and a wink as he started to mix the drink in front of her. Heather smiled inwardly and chatted with the bartender while he poured. This guy was working her, and he thought he was closing the deal, which was the funny part. Skeet put the drink in front of her, smiled again and moved away, beckoned by a loud crowd demanding Kamikazes on the other side of the bar.

The reporter took a small sip of her fresh drink and casually turned her gaze over to the right. Both men were gone.

24

"Did you ever see *Forrest Gump*?"

WEDNESDAY, THE FOURTH OF JULY

1:28 AM

Mac, Lich, Peters, and Sally waited at the security guard station of the World Trade Center Tower in downtown St. Paul. Lich chit-chatted the men working the desk, who were retired suburban cops. The three men discussed pensions, benefits, and divorces; as it turned out, all of them had one. Dick got on a roll, causing hoots and howls with stories about getting cleaned out by his ex-wives. Mac's partner was looking at possible retirement, at least early retirement, in a few years and frequently worked his numbers, figuring what he would have to live on. Dick would have to work long past age sixty-five, whether it be at a security desk or taking up Shamus' long-standing offer to tend bar at the Pub.

All of the men looked up as Summer Plantagenate pushed through the interior glass doors. Stressed and tired, with bags under her eyes, the tall, thin lawyer arrived with her long blonde hair pulled back in a tight ponytail, wearing a zip-up gray nylon sweatshirt, white jogging shorts, and running shoes. The last two days had been hard on Lyman's protégé, and she answered on the first ring when Mac called. Unable to sleep, she welcomed the chance to do anything to help. Summer led them to a bank of elevators for floors twenty-eight through thirty-seven.

Hisle & Brown occupied the entire thirty-seventh floor. The firm resided in ornate offices, their dark-paneled walls appointed with fine paintings and impressive statues. In the spacious lobby, a waterfall separated the reception desk from the leather chairs and sofas of the waiting area. The offices proved a powerful aphrodisiac when enticing clients or lawyers to join the firm.

Summer led them through the lobby, past the reception desk and into a large interior room. It was a training room, with a bank of six computers set along one wall, a mahogany conference table surrounded by high-backed black leather chairs in the center, and floor-to-ceiling bookshelves along the other wall, stocked with reference materials, legal reports, and treatises. On one end wall, cherry cabinet doors opened to reveal a large plasma-screen television on the left and a whiteboard to the right.

"We can set up shop in here," Summer said. "We can use all these computers to access our system and the conference table to look through the paper files."

"Are your other people on the way in?" Peters asked.

"Yes. I've got three of our civil lawyers, a paralegal, and two secretaries on the way—all people who've been here for years. They all love Lyman and would do anything for him."

"Good, we'll need them all, and Sally can help, too. The guy we're going to have run the computer part of this should be here any time," Mac answered and then looked to Peters. "You better get Scheifelbein back over to HQ."

"I'm on it," Peters answered, pulling out his cell phone and walking out of the room. Lich followed as his cell phone started chiming.

"Why do you need a computer guy here?" Summer asked, grabbing Mac's arm. "Can't you just have a guy run it from your place?"

"Problem is," Mac said, looking around the room quickly and then back to Summer, "we think someone might be working this from the inside." Mac explained their theory, Sally nodding along. Plantagenate was stunned.

"They could have ... been ... gaming this thing from the get go." She put her hand over her mouth, astonished.

"That's right," he answered. "This just developed in the last couple of hours. We're not looking to shut the Feds out. We just don't want to take any chances. That's why we wanted to run it out of here until we know something more concrete."

Summer nodded. "Do we tell the rest of my people coming in?"

"Let's not if we don't have to," Mac cautioned. "I want to keep this part of it quiet for now."

Two lawyers and a secretary walked into the room. Summer broke off from Mac and Sally to give them the rundown. The three immediately went to the computers and started them up, and Summer waved Sally over, showing her what to do. The idea was to pull every name they could find from the civil side of Lyman's practice. When Hagen arrived, he'd run that information against the database of information at the Department of Public Safety.

Mac went to the whiteboard, flipped open his notebook, and started copying out the thoughts he had at the Pub. He excluded his speculations on the inside job, keeping that close for now. With it all back up on the whiteboard, he scanned once more for the big picture. *Lyman and Chief, long list of cases*. How long? Mac turned to Plantagenate.

"Can you access all of Lyman's civil cases here at the office?"

"Everything in the last five years or so," Summer replied. "The rest is off-site."

Mac sighed. Nothing was ever easy. "Where? Where is the off-site?"

"North St. Paul, up off of Highway 36, place called Old Files," one of the other lawyers answered.

"We need people up there as well. Get them there with cell phones, laptops, Dictaphones, the works," Mac said. "We're on a tight clock here." Summer started dialing.

Lich came back into the room with an odd look on his face. "We gotta go somewhere."

Riles and Rock stood with the warden at the front entrance to the Ramsey County Correctional Facility, otherwise known as the County Workhouse. The short and heavyset warden of the facility, a man named Ferm, worked his second Marlboro. He talked about the first-place Twins, the weather, and the circus that often was the Fourth of July event in his hometown of Stillwater.

"Shit, with all the boats on the river tomorrow night, there's sure to be trouble."

"How many boats?" Rock asked as he sucked on a cigar he'd bummed off Lich, skillfully blowing smoke out through the gap in his front teeth.

"In Stillwater, around the bridge," Ferm replied, "hundreds for the fireworks. Not to mention it'll just be busy as hell up and down the whole thing all day. My wife and I love the river." Ferm blew smoke and then shook his head, "but we never go out on the Fourth. The only place it'll be quiet is up north, near the old railroad bridge and even then, with the fireworks in Stillwater, not to mention those who people just shoot off normally, it'll be a raucous night. I just hope nobody gets hurt."

Just then, the diminutive Hagen came through the doors with a pair of guards. He saw Riley and Rock and smiled. "I should have known it was you two fuckers."

"Ooooo, it's the hardened convict," Rock said, smiling, pulling cuffs out of his pocket and dangling them in Hagen's face before slapping them on the man's wrists. The cuffs secured, Rock eased him into the backseat of their Crown Victoria.

Riley shook Ferm's hand and got behind the wheel, pulled away and drove back west on I-94 toward downtown St. Paul. Once on the highway, Rock reached into the back and undid the cuffs. The cuffs were just for show anyway. Hagen was an unlikely flight risk.

Arrested last winter as part of the bust on PTA, Hagen, a computer whiz, was seduced by the money offered by the company to run their network and computer systems. The company, and in particular the vice president of security, a man named Webb Alt, noted Hagen's computer skills and put him to work on operations that monitored company employees. Before he knew it, Hagen was working for former CIA operatives who had no trouble dropping bodies to protect a covert arms sales operation. When Mac and Company came down on PTA, Hagen was found in a basement bunker in the PTA building, running the computer operations for Alt's crew. In an effort to shave years off his sentence, Hagen worked with the police and federal authorities to piece together the PTA operations and track down missing PTA personnel.

He was no hardened criminal. Small in size and about as far from intimidating as you could get, Hagen had been dragged into the whole thing without much choice. He could have been sentenced to years of prison time, but Flanagan, Mac, and the rest took a shine to him as he helped tie up loose ends on PTA. Sally successfully worked to get his sentence reduced and also have it served in the County Workhouse.

Hagen had another six months to go on his one-year sentence. Two times already, Riles and Rock had sprung him to do a little work for the police department. This was on top of all the computer work he did at the workhouse. It would cost the county millions to pay contractors for what Hagen was providing them in return for three hots and a cot. Now they were calling on him again.

"So what is it this time?" Hagen asked flippantly, rubbing his wrists.

Rock turned and gave him a serious look. "The chief's daughter has been kidnapped."

Hagen's smile vanished.

"We need your help with that."

"Whatever you need," Hagen answered. "*Whatever* you need."

3:04 AM

Mac pulled his Explorer up in front of Fat Charlie's place in North Minneapolis. The Fat Man had been cryptic with Lich, merely saying he needed to see them about some information that might prove helpful. Three large African-American men were waiting for them, all with their arms crossed and heads shaved, each sporting sunglasses and a skin-tight black muscle shirt—all in all, an impressive "gun show." Fat Charlie needed good security in his game, and these guys looked the part. Mac gave them a quick scan and noted no weapons. The guns wouldn't be far away, however, perhaps stored in the wheel wells of the Tahoe also parked out front. The one in the middle, slightly taller than the other, two spoke up in a deep yet poetically smooth voice. "Charlie sent us up to watch your ride while you're inside."

"Thanks," Mac said. "Around the back again?"

The man nodded.

As they walked around the back, Lich couldn't help himself, quipping, "What's with the shades at three fuckin' AM? Shit, it's darker than their skin out here. That's just," Lich grappled for the right word and missed, "silly."

Mac smiled. "Silly? Maybe. But I tell you what, you go tell that dude, all six-plus-feet, two-forty of him, that he looks silly. Christ. His upper arms are the size of my *thighs*. See what he does with you."

"Ahh, I'd just pump a little of my Smith into him," Lich said, touching his hip.

Mac snorted. "Anything out of your Smith would just bounce off those guns of his."

Down the back steps, the door was already open and one of Charlie's sons, attired in a white dress shirt and blue silk tie, was waiting for them. *Deja vu* set in as he walked them back into the barroom, where they found the same haze of cigar smoke and Charlie sitting in the same chair.

Dressed in a more subdued gray suit with a black and white striped tie, Charlie sat with a cigar in his right hand and a drink in his left, a bottle of Wild Turkey and a bucket of ice sitting on the table in front of him. His sons sat on either side of him. On the couch to the left of Charlie sat what looked like a homeless man dressed in dirty, worn jeans, a soiled white T-shirt, and a black stocking cap. The man was eating a towering ham sandwich off a plate full of chips and cole slaw.

Mac took a chair in front of Charlie, and Lich stood behind him, both hands on the back of the chair. Mac could feel the time running down, so he skipped the pleasantries. "You said you had something for us?"

"And good evening to you, Detective," Charlie replied, a little put off by the curt start.

Lich jumped in, always ready to soften Mac's attitude. "Look, Charlie, we just don't have a lot of time for chit-chat," he said mildly. "We need to get right to it."

"Pretty tough the last couple of days, huh?"

Mac nodded and exhaled slowly. "Although, we might be on something now that will help us and we need to get back to it. So...."

"We best get to it then," Charlie said, nodding and pointing to his right. "This is the guy you need to talk to. Meet Ron." The homeless guy acknowledged them with a nod.

"This guy?" Mac asked skeptically.

"Yes," the drug lord replied. "I know he don't look like much, but looks can be deceiving. Trust me. He provides an important service for me."

"Which is?" Lich asked.

"He watches my competition."

Mac understood immediately. "He looks like a junkie." And then turning to Ron, "But I take it you're not?"

"Correct, Detective," Ron replied, looking up from his plate of food. He wiped the corners of his mouth neatly with a napkin. "I'm incognito," he said in a matter-of-fact voice, sounding nothing like a strung-out street raver.

"That's great Ron," Mac answered. "But why do I need to talk to you?"

"Before he speaks," Charlie interjected, "we're just talking here, right?" The drug lord wanted to help, but he didn't care to be pinched either.

"I work St. Paul. I don't care what you're doing in Minneapolis," Mac replied. "So what do you have?"

"This last week, I've been watching our competitors down along Lake Street," Ron said. "There are a couple of good crews down along there, and I'm evaluating them."

"So?" Lich said, rolling his hand.

"I was sitting in a vacant house a block north of Lake Street around noon on Monday, getting out of the sun and eating some lunch, when

I saw a van pull up across the alley behind an abandoned building. It pulled up right alongside another van."

Mac turned his chair toward Ron. Lich pulled up a chair of his own, taking out a notebook. "What happened next?" Mac asked.

Ron grabbed Lich's notepad and pen and drew a diagram. "I was just casually looking out the window—I was at a bit of a distance away from the vans, which were across the alley and to my right at maybe a forty-five degree angle." Ron drew a line from his perch in the vacant house to the vans across the alley. "But something about the movement looked a little odd to me, so I went to the window."

"What then?" Mac pushed, leaving his chair and taking a knee at the coffee table, looking at Ron's diagram.

"I saw two men get out of the van on the left and get into the front seats of the van on the right."

"What did they look like?" Lich asked.

"Big guys, easily over six feet. Big arms, shoulders, pretty defined," Ron said, running his hands over his pecs and arms. "They'd done some weightlifting, I'd say, based on the way they carried themselves."

"What did they look like?"

"Hard to say," Ron said. "They wore baseball caps and sunglasses. I'd say black hair. They had darker complexions, maybe what looked like dark razor stubble."

"That's two men. Did you see anyone else?" Mac asked, looking up from the diagram.

"I didn't."

"Charlie's told you what's going on, right?" Mac asked. "You know about the kidnappings we're working?"

"Yes."

"So did you see these men transfer a girl between the vans?"

Ron shook his head. "I saw them moving something between the vans, but I couldn't make out what it was. It happened very fast, and the vans were kind of angled away from me," he said, pointing to the diagram. "I could tell they transferred something between the vans, something that took two people. But I couldn't see what and, at that time, I didn't know about the kidnappings, so I didn't really have any context for it."

"Are the two men the only people you saw?"

"Yes and no. There was someone who jumped from the one van to the other, but other than seeing the blur of him jumping, I didn't see anything else. I only really saw the two I described to you."

Mac shared a look with Lich. Ron was on the level. "Anything else?" Mac asked.

"Yeah," Ron answered. "There was one other thing about the big guys."

"Which is what?" Mac asked.

"Did you ever see *Forrest Gump*?"

"The movie?" Mac asked, puzzled. "'Stupid is as stupid does.' 'Life's like a box of chocolates.'"

Ron nodded.

"Sure, what about it?"

"Remember the part where Forrest finds out he has a son? Then he goes and sits down in front of the television with the little boy? The way they're sitting exactly the same, tilting their heads to the left at the same time as they watch TV. You realize they're father and son. Brothers do the same type of things."

"So you're saying...."

"If I didn't know better, I think they might have been brothers."

"Brothers?" Mac asked, interested.

"Yeah. The way they walked, the way the swung their arms, along with height and physical appearance. It was very much alike, very similar. And then, the kicker was that before they both got into the van, they each crooked or rolled their neck to the left, like a nervous tic."

"Let me get this straight," Lich said skeptically, "you got all this watching them for a couple of seconds?"

"I know I saw them for just a few seconds," Ron answered, nodding, "but the neck roll, the gait, you know it just ... registered with me that they looked like brothers."

"You think just brothers?" Mac asked, buying what Ron was selling. "How about this ... could they be twins?"

Ron closed his eyes and stroked his bearded chin, trying to remember. "Maybe. It's possible, I mean there were definite similarities between the two based on how they looked and walked. They were the same size. Complexion was the same." He looked away for a few seconds and then nodded his head, "I think it's entirely possible, but again, that's based on just a few quick seconds."

"So what happened after you saw them get into the van?"

"They pulled out and turned to their right, my left, went down the alley, and that's the last I saw of them."

"What did you do next?"

"I went back to eating my sandwich and then...."

"The van blew," Lich said.

"That's right," Ron said, mimicking the explosion with his hands. "Then I heard sirens, so I bailed."

"You what?"

"I bailed."

"You fuckin' bailed?" Mac was incredulous. "You see this and you fuckin' bail?"

"There's a reason for that," Charlie interjected. "He has orders from me to avoid contact with the police at all costs."

"Why?"

"It's why I didn't want Gerdtz and Subject here," he answered. "Ron scouts for us. He's unknown to my competition as well as the police. I want to keep it that way," Charlie said. "I don't want the authorities thinking I'm looking at moving into that area. I don't want the police thinking I'm eying people up for a hit, because I'm not."

"So why scout it?" Lich asked.

"I'm not interested in new territory. I am keenly interested in how they operate, what their strength is, what the quality of their shit is," Charlie responded. "Minneapolis is rehabilitating Lake Street and the surrounding neighborhoods, pouring in tons of money, public and private. I mean, take a look at what they did to the old Sears building. It's magnificent. Hell, I've got some money in the businesses going up. But with all that investment, the city will not stand for open drug-dealing down there. Those crews are eventually going to get pushed out. They gotta go somewhere, and every time turf gets shut down around the city, the guys who lose the turf come up to the north side and try to set up shop. I want to know what my people might be facing."

"In other words, you want to know in advance who might need to be popped, eh?" Lich said bluntly. "I mean, we're just talkin' here, right?"

The drug lord shrugged his shoulders. "You don't have to kill someone to make them go away," Charlie said. "I prefer my people talk business without stickin' a gun in someone's face. I get a read on someone before they come up here, then my people will know what's coming and how best to handle it. You end up with less trouble this way. There's crews that have come up here, moved into my area, and after a little talk, have gone to work for me. There were others that," Charlie shrugged, "didn't make the cut."

Mac nodded and gestured to the scout. "And Ron here let's you know what you'll be up against."

"That's right," Ron said. He sat back in his chair, crossing one leg over the other and lighting a cigar, talking as if Charlie's place was his private office. "I spend a week or two roaming around, making some buys, sizing up the crews, evaluating how they operate, and getting a sense of how they'll tool up if they moved up here."

"I get all that," Mac answered. "But still, you see those two vans, one blow up and these kidnappings are all over the news and yet you don't...."

"I didn't know about the kidnappings," Ron answered. "Not until tonight."

"How is *that* possible?" Lich asked. "It's been all over the news."

"When I go undercover, I go undercover," Ron replied, shrugging his shoulders. "I'm walking around twenty-four seven doing the junkie thing. I watch these crews until late into the night, sleep in a vacant house, under a bridge or overpass, looking all the part of a junkie. I'm not watching the news, reading a paper, monitoring the Internet. A junkie doesn't do that, so I don't. I'm a junkie when I'm scouting, the only difference being I don't use what I buy."

"No cell phone?" Lich asked.

"Nope," Mac answered before Ron, knowing the answer. "Police could be listening to cell phones."

"Correct," Charlie added. "Cell phones and the drug business do not mix."

"So how is it then," Mac asked. "That Ron comes to us now?"

"I put word out after our meeting the other night for our people to keep their eyes open. Word went out face-to-face. It's old fashioned I know, but safe. My guys are out driving around, talking to our crews and spreading the word that way. Because of that, word didn't get to Ron until after dark tonight. And when it did, he immediately said he needed to see me. Once he told me what he's just told you, I made the call."

Mac looked at his watch, now 4:10 AM, and yawned. The hours were catching up to him. He looked back at Ron, relaxing back in the chair, smoking his cigar. If it weren't for the clothes, you'd think the only thing missing was a snifter of brandy.

"So Ron, where'd you go to school?"

Ron smiled. "I suppose I blew my cover, huh? I was in the Army out of high school. After I got out, I used the GI Bill to pay for college. I was a business major at Minnesota State–Mankato. After I graduated, I went to work for Charlie in his real estate business."

"How'd you end up as a scout then?"

"I had the Army background, and Charlie asked me to put it to use. It's a little dangerous, mind you, but kind of fun as well. Lets me feel like I'm working recon again."

"You don't have a problem with the drug trade?" Mac asked, interested.

"Maybe a little, but I get an adrenaline rush from doing it," Ron said, and then smiled. "Plus, I get hazard pay for this, which is more that I get paid for real estate work."

25

"I wonder what that is?"

Mac yawned and then put the cup of coffee to his mouth. He stared at the whiteboard, jotting down notes or questions every so often. He added the information they got from Fat Charlie's in red.

Two men, large, over six feet, dark hair, and muscular. Brothers? Perhaps twins?

If they were twin brothers, that might make it a little easier. He ordered Hagen to figure that little nugget into his search criteria.

He glanced at his watch, 5:02 AM. A quick glance out an east-facing window showed just a small cord of the sun peeking over the horizon.

The whiteboard was getting full. He had more pieces to work with now, although he still wasn't sure what the puzzle really looked like. It was like you needed an answer key. Perhaps somewhere in all the paper and electronic data, they would find it.

"What are you thinking?" Sally asked, putting her arm lightly on his lower back.

"That if we can find just one solid piece, the dominos will fall. We just need one little thing," he said optimistically. "One good name or little connection between names and it will all come together."

Of course, any optimism he felt dissipated when he turned around. The more they dug into the civil files of Lyman's firm, the harder it all became. The sheer volume of what they were looking at would have been daunting if they had a week, let alone twelve hours. Class-action cases involved thousands of names, and that was just the plaintiffs. Then there were all of the witnesses, family members, and experts on Lyman's side of the cases, not to mention the defendants, experts, and executives on the defense side. Then there were the sexual harassment, discrimination, and personal-injury type cases, with thousands more names involved. And it wasn't enough just to have a name. This was Minnesota. By its very nature, any class-action case involved multiple Johnsons, Petersons, Andersons, Swansons, or Ericksons. Consequently, you needed date of birth, address or addresses, occupations, social security numbers, and any other piece of information to specifically identify and ultimately find these people. To harvest the names, the attorneys, paralegals, and secretaries were going through the computer and paper files one by one. In the paper files alone, it required scanning the correspondence and pleadings, not to mention trying to speed-read two-hundred-page deposition transcripts for people not mentioned elsewhere in the correspondence or pleadings files. There was no analysis taking place. They were simply pulling names and entering them into a database that Hagen had created. If something popped on a name, they would then go deep into the file.

Hagen was talking to Scheifelbein at police headquarters, his head crooked sideways, cradling the phone as his fingers pounded at lightning speed across the keyboard. Scheifelbein was tapping into the various FBI Systems. Mac walked over to take a look, and Hagen pulled the phone away from his ear.

"Barry's getting me access to the database you already have, plus Social Security, IRS, INS, NCIC, and even state and federal penal systems."

"Don't get any ideas," Mac said crossly, more worried about the appearance of a felon accessing social security numbers than of Hagen actually trying anything.

Hagen shot him a dirty look back. "I'm out of the can in six months. I'm not gonna fuck that up." He turned back to the task at hand. "In about an hour, I'll have this thing running so we can run every name we get through the system. If these guys have a connection to anyone on the chief's list, we'll find it." The computer magician turned back to his monitor and frantically typed while simultaneously carrying on a conversation with Schiefelbein. Hagen looked like a pig in shit as he worked away, a cigarette burning in an ashtray and three coffee cups littering his work area.

Mac walked back to the whiteboard. The phone call was coming at 6:00 PM so they had a little more than twelve hours. He worked the board over, making notations, drawing arrows between items, jotting down questions and theories, circling, checking and underlining items. As he ran out of space, he used sticky notes, attaching them to the sides and then adding an easel for more space.

He put the markers down on the board's tray and stood for ten minutes, his eyes fixed on the whiteboard, soaking in all the information and letting it marinate in his mind. Sooner or later it would all come into focus, or at least he kept telling himself that. If it didn't, they would have to rely on Burton's plan when it came time to pay the ransom.

He was deep in thought when a voice bellowed from the hallway. "Mac!"

He turned to see Summer Plantagenate rushing into the room, pointing her cell phone at him, an agitated look on her face.

"What's up?" he asked.

"It's the off-site storage," the willowy blonde replied. "We're having some issues with access."

"What?" Mac replied exasperated. "Why? I mean, don't you have a pass code or something? Aren't those places on a key-code entry system?"

"We do and it is. The issue is that the security guy working won't let anymore than one person to get back to the files," Summer answered, shaking her head. "At that rate...."

"... We'll be screwed," Mac finished.

"Can we get a hold of the owner, a supervisor, something like that?"

"During normal business hours perhaps, but we're not yet to normal work hours and on top of that it's a holiday."

"How about getting a home number?"

"Our people asked. The guard wasn't helpful."

"Where the heck is this place?"

"Highway 36 up in North St. Paul. Our people are up there waiting, wondering what to do."

"Tell them to stay there. I'll take care of it," Mac replied, grabbing his holster off the conference table.

"How?"

"I'll figure it out when I get there. It might involve my gun." He stormed out of the conference room and flipped open his cell phone.

Smith was up at the crack of dawn, placing a call to Burton, who reported that there was nothing new from overnight. The police were still parked at the safe house, but otherwise, all was quiet.

He looked back at the tent, thinking he probably should still be sleeping, since the day was going to be long. But it wasn't possible. He'd waited fifteen years for this day. So he left Monica to sleep. Dean and David were asleep in a separate tent, fifty feet away.

He grabbed three logs and put them in a tepee formation, crunched up some newspaper and started a camp fire. Reaching inside a knapsack, he pulled out a small stainless steel coffee pot, coffee, and bottled water. He loaded it up and set it on the fire. The coffee and water slowly started to percolate.

Sitting in a blue canvas lawn chair, Smith took in the humid Fourth of July morning, the sun rising up behind him, lighting the trees and cliffs on the west side of the river. Along the far side of the river, two men trolled in a fishing boat, up early hoping to hook a lunker.

The campsite was on a small patch of sandy, low-lying shore, surrounded by a thick forest of trees and brush. Cliffs and steep bluffs rose at alternating heights well above the beach as far as you could see in either direction. The boat sat moored in the water, the bow fifty feet out from shore with two anchors securing it. The body of the St. Croix River flowed two hundred yards in the distance.

Dean and David would take the boat later in the morning and move down to the slip in Hudson. Smith and Monica would be on the road by 9:00 AM and into St. Paul by noon. The action would start at 6:00 PM. Hopefully it would be over by 10:00 PM. By sunrise tomorrow, they'd be driving east through Ontario on their way to Nova Scotia and, from there, they were on a boat heading for the Caribbean.

The coffee was ready, and Smith poured himself a cup. Rustling to his left told him that David was up, and the smell of coffee drew the big man over. He poured a quick cup and took a sip.

"That hits the spot."

"Couldn't sleep?" Smith asked.

"I slept enough." David took another drink. "Any word from Burton?"

"I called him just a bit ago. Things are quiet. Police are sitting on the safe house, but there's nothing new going on in their investigation. It's in a holding pattern."

Jupiter Jones yawned as he walked back into the room, a hot cup of coffee in one hand and a full coffee pot in the other. He sat back down and stared at the large computer monitor. Shawn McRyan had crashed out on the sofa for a couple of hours, but he was starting to stir now thanks to the aroma of fresh coffee.

Throughout the night, Jupe watched the video from the kidnappers over and over, looking for anything that might give them a read on the kidnappers or where the girls were buried. His perceptive eyes had failed him thus far.

Right now he was running the video in slow motion through the section of the film with the girls and materials being removed from the back of the van. At this point, he was breaking the video down by the second. Taking the full screen, he split it into quarters and then enlarged each quarter, looking for the tiniest detail.

Shawn stumbled to the coffee, pouring a cup. He yawned and scratched the back of his head. "Nothing I take it?"

"Bupkus." Jupe maneuvered the mouse and started in the upper left corner, enlarging it and scanning it. Now the plan was that if something drew his interest, he would break down the quarter into four more quarters and so on and so on. If need be, he could take a frame, run it through a different piece of software and enlarge an object that looked like a speck of dust on the regular monitor.

Jupiter scanned the enlarged quarter, running the video forward a second at a time. Shawn pulled a chair back up next to him and watched as well. The two viewed the upper left-hand corner for five minutes, but nothing jumped out at them.

"Let's go to the upper right," Jupe said, clicking and hitting play. The video displayed the back of the head of one of the kidnappers, who was wearing what looked like a wool ski mask. The kidnapper was leaning down to pick up a piece of PVC piping, then turning to his right, with his back to the camera, he took the piece out of the van.

"Hmmm," Jupe murmured. He ran it back and forth, frame by frame, again and again and then stopped. "Look at that."

"What?" Shawn asked.

"Look, as he turns right with the pipe," Jupe said. "He turns to his right and takes it out of the van."

"Yeah, and?"

Jones rewound a couple of frames, then pushed play again. The kidnapper leaned down, picked up the pipe, and turned right. The pipe passed the rear window. "Right there," Jupe pointed. "Look at that reflection in the rear window. Something is sticking out of the top of the pipe. It's only there for an instant but I think we might have a receipt." He ran the video back a few frames and started it again.

"I think you're right," Shawn said as he looked closer at the screen. "It's a little fuzzy, and it looks like maybe only part is sticking out of it."

"Yeah it's fuzzy, but I have just the thing that will allow us to get more out of this," Jupe answered, moving the mouse around again, this time opening up a new program.

Mac pulled up to Old Files to find four people and a North St. Paul squad car parked and waiting. Two cops leaned against the cruiser. Mac jumped out and introduced himself to the patrolmen, a younger one named Ball and an older one named Woodcock.

"Have you been inside yet?" Mac asked.

"No. We were waiting on you," Ball answered.

"It's my understanding that this guy is being inflexible. I also don't have a search warrant. I may need you to back me when I get in this guy's grill."

"This relates to the Flanagan thing?" Woodcock asked.

"It does."

"Our chief said we extend whatever assistance you need. We'll back your play, whatever it is."

"Let's go then."

The group walked inside to find the security guard waiting at the front desk. Mac showed his shield. "We need to get more people back to the storage area."

"This is North St. Paul, not St. Paul," the guard answered with attitude. "You don't have jurisdiction here."

"Fine. As you can see, these two officers here are North St. Paul Police."

"We'd like you to give access to Detective McRyan and the rest of his crew here. They need access regarding an important investigation."

"Does he have a search warrant?"

"He does not," Woodcock replied. "Nevertheless, he and the rest of these folks need to get back there."

"Can't do it," the guard replied. "Against the rules. Only one person can be back there at a time. You get a search warrant and I'll comply."

Mac blew up.

"Listen, shithead. We don't have time for that. I and these other people will be going back there whether you like it our not. You stand in my way, you're going to end up in handcuffs."

The guard looked to the North St. Paul officers. "Are you going to let him get away with this?"

"Yes," Woodcock answered plainly. "I'd suggest you let the man pass."

Mac walked by the front desk, waving the others to follow, which they did.

"Where are we going, by the way?" Mac asked, now that he was past the front desk.

"The storage rooms you need are fifty-eight through sixty in the way back," an attorney named Neumann replied.

"There are three rooms?"

"Yeah

"Cripes," Mac groaned.

"What can I say," Neumann said, shrugging his shoulders. "Lyman's had a lot of work over the years."

The storage rooms themselves were ten feet wide, fifteen or so feet deep. Each room contained a wall of white boxes. Lyman Hisle had practiced law for over thirty years, and at least the first twenty to twenty-five years of practice records waited here.

Mac looked at the four people from Hisle's firm and suddenly felt like Chief Brody in *Jaws*. Except that, instead of saying, "You're going to need a bigger boat," he was thinking, "We're going to need a bigger crew." He looked to Neumann. "How many more people can you get down here?"

"Let me call Summer. I bet she'll be able to get us more people," he replied.

"Do that," Mac answered and then opened his own cell phone and dialed. It was early, but the voice he was looking for answered on the second ring. "Shamus, I need you to get as many old hands as possible over to Old Files on Highway 36."

"More cops?" Neumann asked Mac, a concerned look on his face.

"Retired ones."

"I don't know about that," the lawyer started. "There's privileged information in there...."

Mac cut him off. "There's no time to argue about this. They're not going to do anything other than help. They're retired detectives. They'll know what's important."

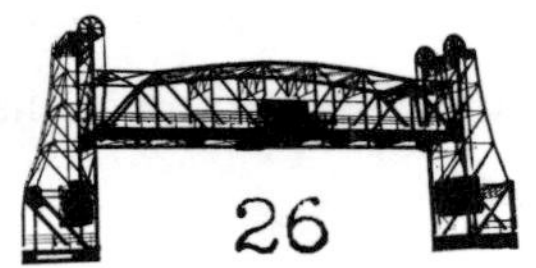

26

"We've got eight hours."

Carrie awoke and lifted her head, only to hit the roof of the box. Reality immediately set back in. She turned on the flashlight and shined it on her watch: 8:03 AM. They'd been in the box for somewhere in the neighborhood of thirty-six hours now. No water or food for all that time, if not more, and Carrie could feel the weakness in her body, the dryness in her mouth as she moved her tongue around, trying to moisten things. She turned the light to Shannon, who started to stir. Shannon looked weak and groggy. Carrie shook her arm to bring her back.

"Shannon, wake up honey."

Shannon didn't move right away. Carrie shook her arm harder.

"Shannon, wake up! Wake up honey!"

Shannon slowly started to awaken. "Where are we?" she said weakly.

Carrie turned on the flashlight and shined it around the box. Shannon was groggy, but her eyes opened wider and looked around and started to realize and remember where she was at. She rubbed her eyes.

"Wake up, Sunshine."

Shannon managed a weak smile and whispered. "Nice try."

"Hey, I always try to operate as if the glass is half-full," Carrie answered, rubbing Shannon's arms.

"Then you must be the most optimistic person to walk the earth," Shannon retorted, more awake now.

"We're still alive," Carrie proclaimed. "And as long as we're alive, we've got hope."

"They better come soon then," Shannon responded.

Carrie held the light closer to Hisle. "Getting worse?"

Shannon nodded as she pulled her legs up to her chest. "I don't know how long I can go on like this."

Carrie knew that Shannon needed to stay awake. "Tell me about your diabetes."

"What do you want to know?" Shannon asked weakly.

"Tell me everything you can. We've got time to pass. Nobody in my family has ever had diabetes. I think I had one friend who had it, but it didn't seem like too big of a deal. My sense is that you have a worse kind."

"I probably do," Hisle replied. "There are two types of diabetes, type 1 and 2."

"Is one worse than the other?"

"Yes. Type 2 is the most common form, and most people who have diabetes have it."

"If you have type 2, what happens?"

"With type 2, your body produces some insulin, but either it isn't enough or the body doesn't recognize the insulin and doesn't use it right. Over time, if the body doesn't have enough insulin or doesn't use insulin properly, then glucose...."

"Sugar?"

"Right. When the body doesn't use the insulin properly, glucose can't get into the body's cells and instead builds up in the blood. If that happens for long enough, the cells won't function properly. Over time, if not taken care of, a person will get dehydrated and fatigued, and you can be more prone to infection. This could take weeks or months before those problems will manifest themselves. Sometimes people go a long time without even knowing they have that kind of diabetes."

"That's probably what my friend had then," Carrie said.

"Probably," Shannon answered, but then got quiet, "That's not the kind I have."

"You have type 1 then?"

Shannon nodded.

"What's makes type 1 worse?"

"With type 1, my immune system has destroyed my insulin-producing cells in my pancreas so that my body doesn't have the insulin hormone. That means glucose won't move into my cells and instead, it builds up in my blood and I get high blood glucose."

"So you need to inject insulin then, right?"

"Yes. I need to take insulin. Like I mentioned before, I take, or I should take, insulin every time I eat."

"How long have you had type 1?"

"About five years. Generally, I'm really good about taking my insulin, but there are times where I've forgotten to bring it with me and of course the time I didn't take it intentionally for a few days and got really sick. I've been thinking of going on an insulin pump but I didn't like the idea of having this little machine attached to my body all day. However, right now I'm really wishing I'd gone to the pump."

"If your body starts to get out of whack what will happen?"

"My body will start to break down. Eventually, I'll get confused and start to shake. I'll probably have issues breathing, rapid breathing."

"And maybe lose consciousness?"

"At some point," Shannon said, her voice down to a whisper, "if it gets really bad, I could go into a coma."

"Anything I can do to help?"

"Let's just try to keep talking. The longer I can stay conscious, the better."

The review of documents at the off-site storage was slow and plodding. It wasn't that people weren't trying or they didn't have enough people. They were and they did as Shamus brought the cavalry. It was simply a slow process. While there was a portable Wi-Fi point set up, the work took a lot of manual labor just to get the information into a place where it could be used. The group had to work through the archived files, pulling out the red-ropes, digging through pleadings, correspondence, memorandums, and depositions to find names and other key data. It was a massive and manic excavation of information.

Once the group mined the data out of the files, the information was placed, via laptop and over the Internet, into a program that Hagen had quickly created over at Hisle's office. The program was cross-referenced into the police and FBI databases that had been created for purposes of cross-referencing Hisle and Flanagan's work on criminal matters. Hagen was now cross-referencing the information the group was finding with those FBI and police databases. Scheifelbein was doing his best to mask it at HQ and to keep the Feds from noticing.

Mac immediately recognized how difficult the process would be. He immediately arranged for the Wi-Fi hookup and organized the operation as best he could. He had people work in teams, matching an attorney from Lyman's firm with groups of the retired cops. The groups worked through the documents, the lawyers explaining where the parties, families, and witnesses could be found in the various legal documents. The cops would read through the information and determine what to enter into Hagen's program.

Riley called Mac from Lyman's office to report that nothing had turned up as of yet, not even a nibble. He was sounding skeptical. "I don't know Mac, we're not finding anything. How much you got left?"

"We've just started out here," Mac answered. "We're maybe fifteen to twenty percent into the files. It'll take a while to get through it. There are hundreds of boxes in these three storage units. I mean, if you have a better idea I'm all ears."

Riles sighed. "I don't. It's just that the clock is ticking."

"I hear ya," Mac answered as he looked out a window. The sun was now bright in the sky, and a look at his watch told him it was 9:56 AM. "We've got eight hours. Something will pop." He didn't know if that was confidence or hope, but he didn't have a choice. They had started down this path, and they had to see it through. "What's going on at HQ?"

"Nothing like what we're doing," Riles answered. "Burton seems focused on the ransom and preparing for the phone call. Although...."

"What?"

"He did ask Peters about what we were doing."

"What did the captain say?"

"He covered. Said we were on the safe house still. Peters thought it might be a good idea for us to make an appearance."

"I hate to break away from this."

"It's what cell phones are for. Burton has called a meeting for eleven thirty. Peters said we should be there. We keep doing what we're doing, but...."

"We keep people from wondering where we are."

While Shawn McRyan watched anxiously, Jupiter Jones opened a computer program he had developed to get as much out of pictures as possible. He set it to enhance the best frame of the reflection in the van's rear window. The program worked slowly, but soon a new window popped up on the screen.

"Is it done?" Shawn asked.

"Let's look." Jupiter scrolled over the part of the picture with the reflection. The enhancement revealed a white receipt. On the screen, the label ran lower right to upper left and you could make out three letters reflected backward in the glass.

"So we have an *H,* then a small *a* and *n,*" Shawn said.

"And part of another letter," Jupe added, pointing to a straight vertical line. "What has a straight line, lower case letters?"

Shawn grabbed a scratch pad, quickly writing down the alphabet, "We got *b, h, k, l,* or *t.*"

"What about *d*?"

"I don't think so," Shawn replied shaking his head and pointing to the screen at the gap between the *n* and the next letter. "The gap between the *n* and the next letter isn't wide enough for a *d,* so it has to be one of the other letters."

"Okay, so we have the PVC pipe, which is manufactured by Ampipe," Jupiter said. "Now we have part of a receipt that's likely from the store where they bought it."

"Maybe," Shawn said. "They could have taken this out of the scrap heap for all we know."

"I doubt," Jupe answered. "The pipe looks newer. There aren't scratches and the white color is bright, not yellowed or dirty. And we have a receipt sticking out of it. That wouldn't be the case if you pulled it out of the scrapheap."

"You could be right," Shawn remarked, putting his face closer to the screen.

"Well, one way to find out is to see if we can get a hold of someone at this manufacturer and see who sells this stuff in Minnesota," Jupiter answered, printing off a copy of the picture. "I've taken it this far. We need Mac or someone else to get us to that manufacturer."

Shawn sighed. "And today is a holiday."

27

"If I didn't know any better I'd say he's up to something."

11:03 AM

Heather Foxx looked in her compact mirror, finishing a last bit of work on her eyelashes in the cool air conditioning of her television truck. She turned and looked through the windshield. Things were starting to percolate around the police department. In these times of a twenty-four-hour news cycle, the story had gone national quickly, especially since it was the Fourth of July. All the heavy hitters were hanging around—FOX, CNN, MSNBC, and the networks. Rather than simply doing puff pieces about parades and fireworks, there was hard news to cover.

Given the potential exposure, Heather went back to her compact to check her makeup again. She wanted things perfect. You never knew who might be watching. As she applied just a touch more lipstick, her thoughts turned back to last night. What had Burton been doing? It could have been an old friend, a late night beer and a chance to reconnect, but that didn't feel right. The conversation hadn't seemed confrontational, but it didn't appear overly friendly either, not like two old buddies sharing a beer and swapping stories. It looked like a colder conversation, a business one. Could it be someone involved with the investigation? Perhaps, but then why meet up in Forest Lake? Why not at the hotel or somewhere closer in town? Why drive thirty miles out to a far-flung suburb? It was odd.

And what exactly should she be doing with this information? She hadn't shared it with anyone. What was there to share, after all? John Burton had a conversation in a bar with another man: alert the media.

She could ask Burton about it, although he'd proven a difficult person to reach, keeping himself in the background and allowing the local FBI office and St. Paul Police to be front-and-center. She'd thought of approaching him in the bar. It wouldn't be the first time she'd done something like that. For some reason, though, she held back. Intuition, instinct, whatever it was, told her not to do it. The whole event was strange, but without any context, it didn't seem to mean much. But it did give her an idea.

She pulled out her phone and dialed Gail Carlson, a veteran reporter who used to work the investigative beat, but now worked general reporting. She was at the station today, but not covering anything.

"Carlson."

"Foxx. I need a favor."

"What's that?"

"Monitor the police band up in the Forest Lake area today."

"Forest Lake, honey? Not exactly a hotbed of criminal activity."

"I know, I know. But all the same, monitor the jurisdictions up there, Forest Lake, Chisago, maybe Wyoming."

"What am I listening for?"

Heather explained. She wanted Carlson listening for anything about the Bureau or St. Paul Police poking around the area.

"Heather, what do you got?" Carlson asked, suspiciously.

"Just a hunch."

Heather's cameraman stuck his head inside the truck. "The scuttlebutt says there's going to be a big powwow here soon: FBI, police, and so forth, and then a press briefing at noon."

"We best get out there then," Heather replied, quickly signing off with Carlson. She stepped outside into the blazing heat, already ninety-three degrees. She decided that her suit coat was a no-go and jettisoned it. Besides the collar of her white, v-neck silk blouse plunged just enough to give a tiny hint of cleavage, which she knew would draw the attention she wanted.

"What do you think they'll be talking about in there?" the cameraman asked.

"Word is there's a call coming later today on the ransom. I haven't been able to find out if there is a set time, or if they're just sitting around waiting for it," Foxx answered as they joined the gathering horde of media at the front of the police department. "There doesn't seem to be much going on from an investigative standpoint."

"You think that's unusual?"

"I'm not a cop, but I do think so," Foxx answered. She watched as Mac McRyan pulled into the lot in his Explorer. His partner wasn't with him, which was a bit unusual. "I can't imagine Mac McRyan sitting around and waiting," she said. "That's not his style."

McRyan, rather than parking to the side, trying to avoid the media, approached the front of the building. This was rather peculiar as well, Heather thought. Despite his friendly little news tip on Wiskowski yesterday, McRyan loathed television reporters. He generally did everything he could to avoid them. Today he looked relaxed, almost cheerful. As he passed her he gave her a "Hiya, Heather," and smiled. As he walked through the media crowd he was pleasant in saying, "No comment" and "I'm sure the department or Bureau will have something to say shortly."

"Now that's odd," Heather remarked out loud as the doors closed behind McRyan.

"What?" the cameraman asked.

"McRyan just now."

"What about him?"

"He was friendly, casual, relaxed—as if he *wanted* to be on camera. Heck, he gave me a wink, a smile and a hello. That *never* happens."

"Heather," the cameraman answered, smiling, "*come on*. Any man smiling at you, even Mac McRyan, is not unusual."

"Yeah, yeah, yeah," she answered, waving him off, but then looked him in the eye. "But *it is* for Mac McRyan. He thinks most of us are parasites."

The cameraman shrugged. "Okay. I'll bite. What does it mean then?"

Heather bit her lip and thought for a minute. "Friendly, casual, relaxed," she said, tapping her index finger on her lips. "If I didn't know any better I'd say he's up to something."

Mac stepped inside the building and stopped, letting the refreshing blast of the air conditioning wash over him. He found Riley, Rock, and Lich drinking coffee and waiting, and they all slipped into an interview room and closed the door.

"Anything from down at the firm?" Mac asked.

"Nothing helpful yet," Riles answered, and then smiled. "But Hagen has them all working their asses off."

"And," Lich added, "whatever he's doing works, I think. He's got this program running, and whenever a name matches between the chief's list and Lyman's clients, it lets you know. At this point, what its finding is common last names like Johnson, Anderson, Peterson or Swanson. Now, a lot of them are eliminated because first names don't ultimately match, or maybe a middle name eliminates them. In a couple of cases where there has been some sort of match, we've taken a look and eliminated them quickly. They weren't even worth a phone call or interview. It was obvious there was nothing there."

"So," Mac said, "if there's a connection to be found...."

"This program Hagen has running *should* find it."

Peters knocked on the door and then entered. "Anything?"

"Not yet," they replied in unison.

"Well, come with me. Burton's about ready to start the show."

They all started to file out, but Mac stopped them. "Scan the room," he said quietly. "If we're right, and somebody is working this from the inside, that person is likely in the room. I don't know what to look for, but look."

Everyone nodded and they walked down the hall and into the overflowing meeting room. Burton saw them walk in and immediately approached.

"Have you been back on the safe house?" he asked, looking at Mac and then to the others.

"Yup," Mac answered neutrally. "They haven't come back yet, obviously, but we think it's still worth watching."

Burton looked to the others, who nodded.

"All right then. Stay on it, at least for this afternoon. However, if they don't come back to the house, we will need you guys when the ransom call comes in."

The group agreed. Burton headed up to the front of the room. Mac and the others found space along a side wall and stood as Burton began to speak. Conspicuously seated at the front of the room, the chief and Lyman watched as Burton called the room to order. The chief in particular looked to Mac, giving a small nod that Mac returned.

Burton began with a recap of where the investigation stood, which was really nowhere, other than the safe house, which was looking deader by the minute.

"We have a crew sitting on the house right now. I've spoken with Detectives Riley and McRyan, and they are of the opinion that the house should remain under surveillance. I concur, and so we will continue to monitor that situation."

"Has anything come of the video release?" a voice asked.

"No," Burton replied. "I'm a little surprised frankly. It's been played every half-hour since yesterday, and we've gotten nothing."

"How about anything from the video itself? Anything to help us?"

"Again, we've found nothing," Burton replied. "Unfortunately, we haven't been able to pull anything off it that is useful." Burton transitioned to the ransom. "As you know, the ransom demand is for five million." Burton explained the details of the demand.

"Do we know when the ransom call is coming?" another cop asked.

"Six o'clock PM," Burton replied. "We expect that we'll receive drop instructions at that time. We'll need to move quickly."

"How's the drop going to be completed?" Double Frank asked.

"We don't know," Burton answered honestly. "We're getting a call at 6:00, and it'll be the kidnappers' show at that point."

"So what are *we* doing?" Mac asked. He wanted to be free for the afternoon, but at the same time, wanted to assess the preparedness of Burton and the bureau.

"Good question," Riles said in his ear.

"Let there be no doubt, we'll be ready," Burton said. "We don't know what they're going to do, that's true, but we will have massive resources at our disposal when it comes time to pay the ransom. They've demanded five million in cash. That's a lot of money, and it doesn't come in a small package. It's sizable. It will fill two large duffel bags. In other words, we should be able to track it. We have plenty of bodies. We'll have birds in the air. We'll put a tracker in the money bag. As you've noted a couple of times, Detective McRyan, the kidnappers are sharp, well prepared, and precise in their planning. That suggests to me that we're looking at a money drop. They will have to expose themselves to get the money, and that's when we'll have our chance to pounce."

"Just like that, huh?" Double Frank snorted skeptically.

"It's never just like that," Burton replied evenly. "All I'm saying is that if something doesn't break between now and then, our best chance to get them is when they go for the money. That's when they'll come out of hiding. They have to."

"We don't know when or where the drop will be?" Mac asked. "And let's be honest, we don't know for sure there will be a drop, you're just getting a phone call at six, right?" Burton nodded, and Mac noted the chief's piercing gaze as he spoke. "They could throw you a curve."

"I'm sure they'll try to. All I can say is we'll be as ready as we can be, Mac," Burton replied, nonplussed by the hard questioning. "I understand the concerns of everyone in this room. I share them. I'd like to know more, a lot more, about whom and what we're up against. But we are where we are."

"What about the girls?" someone asked.

"We don't know for sure," Burton replied. "This is a kidnapping, and we have a ransom demand. We catch the kidnappers at the drop, and we'll find out where the girls are."

"You hope," a voice from the group said.

"I think I'm right. These guys won't want a murder rap. They'll look to start cutting years and making deals. If we handle the drop right, if we get them there, then we stand a chance to get the girls."

Mac wasn't so confident, but didn't want to say so with the chief present. In his mind, there was more than a payday in play. Burton was planning as though it was just about the money, as if it was a simple exchange of dollars for the girls and that didn't feel right. If it was just about money, the ransom demand would be for more. This was about more than money. It was about retribution, and the chief, Lyman, and everyone else was about to be led right into something a lot uglier than a payoff.

28

"What connects him with Hisle?"

12:03 PM

Shamus McRyan knelt down to tie closed a white box labeled *Hammond et al. v. Easy Flow Systems,* a class-action case, and reached for the next box. Shamus was in a row of files that covered the early to mid-1990s.

"This search lead to anything yet?" inquired Percy Wallace, a rotund, black retired detective who was one of Shamus's golfing buddies. Percy was supposed to be working the first tee as a starter at Highland National Golf Club. Instead, Shamus recruited him down to the storage garage.

"Not yet," Shamus answered.

"Man, how many boxes we been through?"

"I stopped counting after twenty, and that was a while ago," Shamus replied.

"So, what do we have here?" Percy asked, pushing the sleeves up on his golf pullover.

"Looks like *Erickson v. TOM Trucking,* 1994," Shamus grunted as he moved the box and opened it up. Wallace grabbed a red-rope folder marked "Pleadings Vol. 1" and started scanning for information.

Shamus grabbed another red-rope that contained deposition transcripts along with the correspondence file, which he flipped open to read the summary of the case. He found that reading the small summaries helped him understand the information he was looking at. The one-paragraph summary on a now-faded green piece of paper indicated that *Erickson v. TOM Trucking* was a sexual harassment case brought by a Barb Erickson and three other women against the owner of the trucking company, Thomas Oliver Mueller, hence TOM Trucking. A notation at the bottom of the summary noted the file was closed in 1994 after Lyman obtained a verdict of $3.4 million. Shamus smirked. Just another cool million for Lyman Hisle.

Wallace noticed Shamus reading the summary and asked, "What's that sheet say?"

"Sexual harassment," Shamus answered. "Appears the owner of the company liked to fondle the hired help."

Just then Henry Brown, the Brown in Hisle & Brown, walked up. Summer had called him in to help supervise. He noted the name on the case and said, "I remember that one. I couldn't believe that verdict."

"Why's that?" Wallace asked, looking up from the pleadings.

"Mediocre facts," Brown answered. "Lyman offered to settle the case for a couple hundred thousand early on, but Mueller refused."

"So they ended up at trial, then?" Shamus asked.

"Yeah, and Lyman did an absolute number on Mueller at trial. The jury came back and nailed him but good. I think the verdict eventually put Mueller out of business. His insurance didn't cover harassment, and he had to pay the verdict out of his back pocket. For a little trucking company, $3.4 million is hard to swallow," Brown said. He moved on to check on the next group.

Shamus grabbed the deposition transcript for Thomas Mueller and found the personal information for Mueller and his family. He looked to a young attorney from Hisle's office named Ramler who'd come to help and was sitting at a laptop.

"Dougie, you ready?"

"Yes sir," Ramler answered, his fingers at the ready.

"Good. I've got a Thomas Oliver Mueller...."

Peters ushered Mac and the Boys into a small, windowless interview room. After a minute, the chief joined them. He was sleep-deprived and ill-looking, with large dark bags under his eyes. But his bright blue eyes were alert as ever, and he cut to the chase.

"What are you boys up to?" he asked.

"What do you mean?" Mac replied.

The chief looked at Mac squarely. "I know you," he said, and then pointed at the rest of the group. "I know all of you. Burton's setting up for the ransom and has everyone waiting it out. They've run all the criminal connections between Lyman and me and crapped out, he says. The only possible lead is this safe house that we got a tip on yesterday. He says *you* guys have been sitting on that house for seventeen hours or something like that. You four? Sitting on a house for seventeen hours? I don't buy it. That's not your style, just sittin' around and waitin'. So while we were in there, I was watching you," he pointed at Mac. "I was watching *all* of you. Mac's standing there, checkin' his watch every two minutes. The rest of you are all looking around the room as if you're looking for someone or something. And your body language says you're not buying what Burton is sellin'. So what are you up to?"

Mac didn't want to burden the chief further—the man was under enough stress as it was. But the jig was up. Mac glanced over to Peters, who nodded.

"We haven't been laying back, Chief."

"But whatever it is you boys are up to, nobody else in that room has a clue, do they?" the chief asked.

"They do not."

"Why not? And I better not find out that this is some sort of fuckin' pissin' match."

"It's not," Mac answered and then put all the cards on the table. "We're worried the kidnappers have someone on the inside."

"What?" the chief replied, stunned. "How did you reach that conclusion? How do you know this? Who is it? Is it one of our people, the FBI, who?"

"We don't know," Riley answered. "But all of us think someone is a source for these assholes."

The chief was flabbergasted. He paced around the room, pinching the bridge of his nose and then sighed. "Tell me what you boys are thinking."

"You better start from the beginning, Mac," Peters suggested.

Mac started, "Chief, these guys have been ahead of us from the start." He laid out what they knew about the two kidnappings, the woman working the inside, the calculated dropping and blowing of the vans, the setting-up of Drew Wiskowski, and the fact that the criminal-case connections between the chief and Lyman weren't panning out. "These guys left next to nothing behind," Mac said. "Then, at the safe house, after we searched it, we were sitting on it, watching from across the street."

"That's when things might have changed, Chief," Riles added.

"How so?"

"Pat and I were talking the owner of the house and his wife, and we start talking about when the kidnappers left the safe house."

"So?"

"It was within minutes of his call. And then we talked about how the vans left in a hurry. Mrs. Hall said, and I quote, 'they ripped out of there.'"

"That triggered all sorts of alarm bells," Riley added. "We started thinking that maybe they got a tip."

"That's a pretty big stretch," the chief replied, skeptical. "And you didn't find anything in the house did you? No forensic evidence, right?"

"Not necessarily," Lich answered, explaining the chipped paint on the basement beds. "It's thin, but we think it was a safe house, the place these guys were operating out of."

"And forensics is telling us that the house was cleaned at least twice in the days before we went in."

"Still, how can you know they were tipped off?"

"Other than the timing of when they left and how, we don't," Mac answered honestly. "My gut tells me something wasn't right about it. And if they weren't tipped off, why not come back?"

The chief nodded at that.

Mac continued, "We know that's a little thin, but ... I don't know. It's a gut feeling."

"So what have you been doing to look into that?"

"Before I get to that, there's one other thing that occurred to us last night," Mac added. "We looked at all the connections for Lyman's criminal cases to you, but one thing we weren't looking at was Lyman's civil cases." He quickly related the story about the attorney getting chased with an axe in Minneapolis the day before. "We've looked at the obvious connections on the criminal side, so now we're looking at Lyman's civil cases. If someone is pissed enough to go after an attorney with an axe, why not do what the kidnappers are doing here?"

"So what are you doing?"

"We have people down at Lyman's office and at an off-site storage unit looking through the civil cases, the harassment, discrimination, and class-action stuff."

"There are thousands of names," Riles added. "Plus Hagen...."

Hagen lorded over his computer, monitoring the program, swiveling back and forth in his chair, twirling a pen through his fingers when his monitor beeped at him with a hit. He sat up and clicked on the search result, which showed connections between a Smith Brown on the chief's list and a David Mueller, the son of Thomas Oliver Mueller, a defendant in one of Hisle's sexual harassment cases.

Sally noticed Hagen peering closely at the computer and walked over. "What do you have?"

"Connection of some kind," Hagen answered, running his cursor over the screen, clicking on and reading various links. "Smith Brown, who was..." Hagen looked away from the computer to a binder-clipped packet of papers, flipping through it until he found Smith's name, "... a DEA agent that Chief Flanagan put in prison fifteen or sixteen years ago, and a David Mueller, who occupied the neighboring cell at Leavenworth Federal Penitentiary."

"Who's Mueller?"

The computer whiz scrolled down the screen and whistled, "Son of Thomas Oliver Mueller, who Hisle sued back in the early '90s. It must have been a good case, because Hisle got himself a $3.4 million verdict."

"Where are these guys now?"

Hagen clicked through several programs and brought up the federal prison system records, accessing the records for Leavenworth. After a minute he found the records, and they both whistled. "Brown finished his sentence six months ago, and Mueller has been out for nine months."

"What are their current addresses?" Sally asked, pulling up a chair and grabbing a notepad.

"Brown has one in Chicago, and Mueller," Hagen clicked on a different link, "Mueller has an address in Osseo." Osseo was a small northwestern suburb of Minneapolis. "Is this worth a look?" Hagen asked, turning his gaze to Sally, who was furiously jotting notes down on a legal pad.

"Keep digging and I'll ask Mac," she said as she took out her cell phone.

"You have Hagen in this?" the chief asked. "How'd you swing that?"

Riles shrugged. "Warden at the workhouse is a friend of mine. All I had to mention was this involved you, and it wasn't a problem. Anyway, Hagen's got this computer program set up and is cross-referencing your list with Lyman's. So if there's a connection to be made, he'll find it."

Mac's cell phone went off and he looked at the caller ID. "It's Sally," he said as he stepped into the hallway to take the call.

"So how many people are in on this?" the chief asked.

Riles chuckled. "Mac had Shamus call the cavalry. He recruited a whole boatload of retired guys to this off-site storage place. They're out there, going through boxes of Hisle's old files. They're using laptops and putting what they find into this program that Hagen created. Apparently, the program is constantly searching the records for a match."

"What's he searching?"

"Social Security, IRS, INS, NCIC, federal and state prison systems, maybe more. Whatever we could access here, Hagen is accessing from the firm."

"Here's where you might have to provide some cover, Chief," Peters added. "Our guy Scheifelbein has been providing Hagen access to this information and masking the access, hiding it from everyone else, so he might need a little chief-like protection if and when this comes to light."

"Done," the chief replied.

Peters nodded. Then Mac burst back into the room and looked to the chief. "Do you recall a guy you put away named Smith Brown?"

The chief looked down in thought for a moment and then looked up. "Yeah. DEA agent. That's years ago, fifteen or twenty. He was holding back bricks of coke from busts here and putting it on the street. He had some gambling debts or something like that. I pinched a bookie, who fed me Brown for a reduction in his sentence, as I recall. It was at one of those times when drug enforcement was big with the first Bush administration and the U.S. attorney wanted to make a statement."

"And you were heavily involved, right?"

"I busted him. You know how I feel about dirty cops."

"So what do they have?" Lich asked. "What connects him with Hisle?"

"He was in a cell next to a guy named David Mueller, who was also in the pen for a federal drug charge," Mac answered, reading from his notepad. "David Mueller was the son of Thomas Mueller. Thomas Mueller owned a trucking company that Lyman sued for sexual harassment. Lyman hit the jackpot with a $3.4 million verdict from a jury."

"That'll piss a guy off," Lich said.

"Well, Thomas Mueller can't be pissed anymore," Mac said. "He committed suicide within a year or two of the verdict. The case killed his business. His wife left him, and his two sons were in prison for drug dealing, apparently trying to make money to help the old man save the trucking company. There's a newspaper article Sally found from up in Chisago Lakes, where Mueller lived. The article quoted his daughter

Monica as saying between his sons being in jail, the loss of the business, and losing his wife, he simply couldn't go on. And there's one other thing."

"Which is?" Flanagan asked.

"Mueller had *two* sons, both, it turns out, in Leavenworth. The other Mueller is named Dean. And there's one other thing about the brothers. They're...."

"Twins," Lich finished. "They're not just brothers, but twins, aren't they?"

"Identical, in fact," Mac answered. "They're both six-three and about two hundred forty pounds, with dark hair, according to their prison records."

"Damn," Lich said. "Fuckin' Fat Charlie actually came through for us," he said, shaking his head.

"So, we have Brown, who the chief put in, and Mueller's father, who Lyman put out of business and who then committed suicide. Mueller and Brown spend years in prison together and probably get to talking about how they both ended up in jail. Brown talks about the chief becoming chief. Mueller sees Lyman getting rich off of cases like the one that did in his father. The two of them probably start talking about payback, revenge. They were in the can together for what? Twelve years?" Mac said. "That's a lot of time to talk about payback, to plan it and to get the courage up to seek it. Then they get out about the same time and put this all together." Everyone nodded. Perverse as it was, the connection made sense.

"This could be it," Riles said. "Brown was a DEA agent. He's probably a pretty bright guy."

"He was, as I recall," the chief added.

"So he's running it. He's the voice on the phone," Rock said. "He's the one calling the shots."

"The one who said Shannon was the appetizer and Carrie was the main course," Mac noted. "It fits. Brown's the brains of the operation."

"And the Mueller brothers are the brawn," Riles added. "They fit the general descriptions we had on both kidnappings. Big guys, dark hair, and so forth."

"That looked like brothers," Lich added, "just as Fat Charlie's guy told us."

Everyone nodded, running it through their minds.

"Where are these guys now?" Flanagan asked, breaking the momentary silence.

"I've got Sally looking into that," Mac answered. "Dean and David currently share an Osseo address, and Smith apparently has an address in Chicago. Sally is calling CPD to have someone check on him, see if he's around."

"He's not," Peters said, pointing at Mac. "He's here. These are our guys."

"I bet they are," Riles added, and then pivoted. "What do you think, Mac? Do we let others know? We might need their help."

Mac thought for a moment, his arms crossed. "Not quite yet. If we're right and someone is feeding Brown information, we don't want to tip them off. We don't know where the girls...." Mac stopped, aware of having spoken about the girls as if the chief wasn't in the room. "Sorry, Chief."

The chief didn't flinch, "It is what it is, boyo."

"We don't know where these guys are, or where they have the girls. If they do have someone on the inside, and we come out with this, the kidnappers get tipped off and the girls could pay the price."

"Agreed," the chief said. "You don't have much time. We're getting a phone call at six. You've got..." everyone looked at their watches, 12:15 PM, "less than six hours."

29

"This is where it gets interesting."

Smith Brown sat in a desk chair in a fifth-floor hotel room, looking east through binoculars down Kellogg Boulevard on the south side of the Xcel Energy Center in downtown St. Paul. He checked his watch: 12:28 PM. There wasn't a cloud in the sky. The heat radiated off the pavement as the temperature continued its inexorable climb to triple digits. He was happy to be inside.

On a national holiday, there was little activity around the brick and curved glass of America's finest hockey arena, which sat kitty-corner from his perch. A digital marquee on the corner of West Seventh and Kellogg announced upcoming events, which in the summer were generally concerts. Bruce Springsteen and the E Street Band were coming to town the last week in July.

Smith glanced to his right, looking south down the ever-expanding restaurant-and-bar-district that was West Seventh Street. There was little car traffic and less on foot. It was one of the traits that made St. Paul unique. The downtown area was generally quiet when the working folks weren't around. Of course, a Minnesota Wild game or event at the arena across the street changed all that, bringing 20,000 people downtown. However, if there wasn't a specific event, activity moved to the other neighborhoods around the city. Given that it was a holiday, the foot and car traffic was even less than its normal negligible amount.

He turned his gaze back to the east to see Monica coming into view, dressed attractively in white tennis shorts and a low-cut, dusty-rose tank top. She was walking toward the hotel along the sidewalk of Kellogg Boulevard, a black nylon computer case hanging over her shoulder. As she crossed the street and stepped under the canopy of the hotel entrance, Smith scanned the area outside, making sure nobody followed or watched her. Satisfied that she was free and clear, he moved away from the window. A minute later he heard the key card slide into the reader, and Monica entered the room.

"Everything go okay?" he asked as he dropped some ice into a hotel glass and poured himself a Diet Coke.

"No problem. It's pretty empty in there."

"You tested the camera?"

"Yes," she answered, putting the shoulder bag onto the bed. "It worked fine. We'll be able to monitor what they're doing."

"Excellent."

"What's next?" she asked as she opened a bottle of water.

"We sit and wait for awhile, try to relax," Smith answered, turning on the TV. "At five thirty I'll drive the minivan over to Eagle Street and wait."

"Dean and David get the easy duty, don't they?"

"At least for now," Smith replied. "David saved my life in prison. If things go awry, he and Dean can walk away, as can you."

"Have you changed your mind about the girls?"

"No," Smith replied.

"You know how Dean and David feel."

"I do," Smith replied looking out the window. "They don't think the girls should pay." He turned back toward Monica. "The thing is, if everything goes according to plan, nobody will ever know who we are.

Or if they do eventually figure it out, it will be too late. We'll be long gone. If we let them know where the girls are, that increases the risk that we'll be found before we're safely away. If we give them the girls, the police very likely *will* discover who we are, probably before we've made the necessary changes to our looks."

"I know, I know," Monica answered, looking down and picking at the carpet with her toes. "Thing is," she started quietly, "the girls are guilty of nothing other than having the fathers they have."

"And what about my daughter?" Smith asked, anger rising in his voice. "What was she guilty of besides having me as her father? She died because of Charlie Flanagan. I'm in prison, and my wife can't get insurance. She can't get treatment for my little girl. When the state finally comes through, my little girl's on her deathbed and it's too late. That's all on Charlie Flanagan." Smith turned back toward the window, away from her. "He needs to feel what I felt. He needs to feel what it's like to lose a daughter. He's going to feel that before he dies."

Mac and the others burst into the conference room to find Hagen's fingers dancing frantically over the keyboard and a printer spitting out reams of paper. "What do we know?" Mac asked, walking up to Sally.

"It doesn't look like Brown is in Chicago," Sally said. "I had CPD go to the last known address. It doesn't exist."

"What do you mean it doesn't exist? The address doesn't exist? It's a fake?" Rock growled.

"Yeah. Brown served his full sentence and was a free man, free to go wherever he wanted," Sally answered. "It would appear that in his six months out he has chosen to fall off the grid."

"And this is the guy who was in prison with David Mueller?" Rock asked, looking at a picture of Smith taken six months before he was released. Six feet tall, Brown had black hair graying at his temples. He had brown eyes and a knot at the bridge of his already large nose.

"Yes," Sally replied. "For twelve years. We looked at Brown's records for Leavenworth. It appears he had trouble on his arrival."

"He's probably lucky to be alive," Lich said. Cops have issues in prison.

"That's where David Mueller comes in," Sally added, flipping to a different page. "He saved Brown's life. Apparently David was pretty good with his fists. He, and his brother Dean, who I'll get to in a minute, were in the Golden Gloves back in the day. Anyway, David seems to have used those skills to save Brown, or at least that's what we're seeing as we read between the lines on some stuff from Leavenworth. Apparently, David, and later Dean, took it upon themselves to apply a couple of beatings, to send a message and that probably allowed Brown to make it out alive."

"So he's loyal to them," Rock said. "And I suppose vice versa."

"What about the Muellers?" Mac asked, looking at pictures taken prior to their release from Leavenworth. The brothers were definitely twins, thick necks, black hair, unibrows, but all-in-all decent-looking boys. The only noticeable differences were their eyes and noses. Dean's eyes were spread a little farther apart from his nose. David had an unnaturally crooked nose, probably broken from boxing.

"This is where it gets interesting. The brothers have an Osseo address, an apartment complex a block off of the main street," Sally gave him a sheet with directions and the address. "I spoke with the Osseo police chief. He says give him a holler at that number," she handed a yellow sticky note to Mac. "He and another officer will meet you at a gas station a few blocks away."

"Okay, but you said 'interesting' a minute ago, what else?" Mac pushed impatiently, reading from the sheet. "What's so interesting?"

"The Mueller boys have an older sister named Monica Reynolds—her married name."

"Tell me the older sister looks like our missing woman," Riles said, hopeful.

"Here's a picture we got from the DMV for her license," Sally responded. "Tell me what you think." Her tone said she thought it a match.

The group gathered around the table to look at the artist sketch of the woman from Cel's Café next to the blown-up DMV photo. They also had security camera stills from Milwaukee and St. Thomas University for comparison. The hair color was right, as were the lips and nose and the eyes. The hair of the woman at the café didn't match, but again, the eyes, nose, and lips looked about right. Mac spoke for everyone. "It could be her, there's certainly a similarity."

"Where is Monica Reynolds at these days?" Rock asked.

"Again, interesting," Sally said, as Summer Plantagenate handed her another set of papers, as smoothly as if the two were going through exhibits at a jury trial. "Up until two months ago, she owned a house over on the east side of St. Paul by Lake Phalen. She sold it for $225,000 and left a P.O. box as a forwarding address. It doesn't appear she has established another home."

"At least not one I can find," Hagen added, looking up from his computer. "I'm still searching."

"The money from the sale ended up in a checking account at Wells Fargo," Sally said, "an account that she closed shortly thereafter, we can't find any evidence she's opened another one somewhere."

"So she's floating out there with a nice chunk of walking-around-money to finance whatever it is these guys might be up to," Mac said. "This is adding up."

"It is," Sally said.

"So we've got a solid connection between the chief and Lyman in Brown and the Muellers. We have physical descriptions that are consistent. They've got motive. Brown gives them the intellect to pull this off," Riles summarized.

"And Brown and Monica at least seem to have pulled a disappearing act," Mac said.

"So what's next?" Sally asked. "What do you think?"

"We check out this last known address," Mac answered. "Lich and I will do that."

"What do you want Rock and I to do?" Riles asked.

"Stay here and work this for now," Mac replied. "We need to look into family for the Muellers and Brown. Do they have family around and where? If they do, we need to be talking to them. We should have someone run Monica's photo over to the café, see what people over there think. Also, run these four against the department personnel files. Maybe we find the mole that way. And one other thing."

"What's that?"

"Someone should be around when the ransom call comes in," Mac said. "I've got a bad feeling about that. Brown and the Muellers have been ahead of us every step of the way. There's no reason to think they aren't now."

"Especially if they have someone on the inside," Sally said.

"Exactly," Mac answered, pointing at Sally. "But now maybe, just maybe, we're evening out the odds here. We finally know who we're up against. Now we just need to find them before this all shakes out."

Mac and Lich turned to leave when Jupiter and Shawn McRyan came into the room. Jupe was holding up a DVD and color pictures.

"Tell me you found something?" Mac said.

"Maybe," Jupiter said, briefly explaining the pictures pulled off the video. "If we can figure out where the PVC piping was purchased, maybe it's another way to get a line on these guys."

"Do that," Mac ordered and then turned to Sally. "Let's get on the horn to this company, figure out a way to find out who's selling this pipe in Minnesota."

"I'll give it a shot," Sally replied skeptically. "The Fourth of July keeps getting in the way. It'll be tough to track somebody down."

"Sally," Hagen interjected. "While you're trying the legal way, why don't you give me what you have there," he said pointing at the picture. "I might be able to find another way."

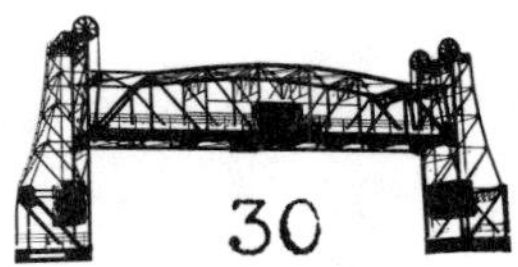

30

"This will serve as my last will and testament."

After talking for a couple of hours, even having a few laughs along the way, conversation between Carrie and Shannon had faded. It was a pattern. Neither of them slept for long or stayed awake and alert for more than a couple of hours. Sleeping, if you could, was the best of the two options. If you were awake, especially if the other was sleeping, you just lay there thinking about where you were. Carrie was also trying to sleep lightly so that she could monitor Shannon's condition. She was beginning to get worried about her and how long she could last.

Following their last conversation, Carrie had slept for a little while, but she was awake now and her mind had started racing again. What else would your mind do when you were buried alive? Flanagan thanked God repeatedly she wasn't claustrophobic. What she needed was something to do, something to occupy her mind.

Carrie picked up the Dictaphone, contemplating its use. What if the kidnappers wouldn't let anyone know where they were buried? She figured since they were buried alive, they were intended to be found. But what if that wasn't the case? What if they weren't found in time? Carrie sighed, and tears welled in her eyes for the first time in hours. What a way to go.

Her thoughts turned again to her family, to her parents, brothers, sisters, even her boyfriend. She never had the chance to say good-bye. She took another look at the Dictaphone. There was plenty of space left on the tape—the message from the kidnappers had been short and to the point.

She remembered watching *M*A*S*H* with her dad. He loved that show and could recite from memory the dialogue from entire episodes. She chuckled at how many times her dad would say, for no reason, "Nope, its oak." Or if Mom cooked a bad meal, he would get that mischievous smile and quote Hawkeye Pierce behind her back, "I don't know how our cook got off at Nuremburg." Her father loved the episodes with Trapper and Henry Blake, the early years of the show. But right now she remembered an episode from the later years, when the show got preachy. It was where Hawkeye was sent to an aid station at the front. Between triaging injured soldiers and ducking bombs exploding all around, he sat and wrote his will on a yellow legal pad, bequeathing gifts to everyone in the 4077.

Carrie was in the same situation for real. She could die. She wanted to say something to the people she cared most about, even if they never got to hear it. Twirling the Dictaphone around in her fingers near her face, she contemplated what to say. She closed her eyes. "I still can't believe this is happening," she uttered quietly, tears still pooled in her eyes. She'd hoped this was just an awful dream that she would awaken from, but it wasn't and she hadn't.

Flanagan opened her eyes and pushed the record button on the Dictaphone, "This is Carrie Marie Flanagan. I am the daughter of St. Paul Police Chief Charles Flanagan." She stopped the tape and sniffled, getting her emotions in check before she continued. She didn't want her family to hear the terror in her voice.

"I was kidnapped on Monday, July 2nd. I'm buried in this box with Shannon Hisle. Shannon is the daughter of Lyman Hisle, a St. Paul lawyer, a friend of my father's. Shannon was kidnapped the day before on July 1st." Carrie stopped again and rested the Dictaphone on her chest, breathing harder.

"Today is the Fourth of July and it's...." she checked her watch, "2:15 PM. We have been in this box for over forty hours now. If we're not found soon, we will both die." She heaved a big sigh and swallowed, a dry swallow, little moisture left in her mouth. She whetted her lips as best she could and pushed up on the record button.

"This will serve as my last will and testament."

She closed her eyes again and wiped the tears from her cheeks, still having a hard time believing she'd uttered those words. You were supposed to do something like this sitting across a large mahogany table from a lawyer, not buried underground, speaking into a Dictaphone that might never be found. But, as her father often liked to say, "it is what it is" and she was where she was. She contemplated what to say next. Carrie thought about the three older brothers who had looked after her all these years, protecting her, and in some, no, make that in many cases, chasing interested boys away, much to her chagrin.

Now her protectors would be feeling helpless, unable to help and guard her. Carrie didn't want them to worry about it. She wanted them to remember the good times, what great brothers they were, how much she looked up to them, adored them and loved them. One of her favorite possessions was the three pictures next to her bed, from her high school graduation: a picture of her with each of her brothers. A proud night for the family, the last of the Flanagan kids graduating from high school. She treasured those pictures.

Carrie pushed the record button. "To my brothers, I bequeath...." She stopped. To her right, she sensed Hisle moving, but it was unnatural. Hisle wasn't adjusting her body, trying to get comfortable. She was starting to shake and reflexively pulling her legs into her chest. Shannon had warned this might happen when her blood sugar started getting really high and she didn't have enough insulin in her body. Flanagan rolled onto her right side, slid over, and lightly shook Hisle.

"Shannon. Are you okay?" she asked in normal tone. Hisle didn't respond. "Shannon! Shannon! Wake up! Wake up!" Carrie said urgently, shaking her shoulder harder.

Hisle started to stir.

"Shannon." Carrie rubbed her arms and shoulders. "Stay with me."

Shannon was shaking uncontrollably.

"Shannon, are you okay? You're shaking."

"I ... don't..." she stuttered. She didn't finish the thought.

"Shannon, are you with me?"

"I'm not su ... su ... sure how much longer I can last."

Carrie could tell that Shannon was breathing fast. She grabbed Shannon's wrist and checked her pulse. Her heart was racing and there was almost a sweat fruity smell to her breath.

"Hang in there with me, Honey. Hang in there," Carrie said, hugging Shannon, rubbing her arms and legs, trying to keep her comfortable and conscious. The lack of insulin had slowly been weakening Shannon. However, now, nearly four days without insulin, Carrie could tell that Shannon's body was now rapidly succumbing to the lack of it. She put the flashlight to her watch: 2:18 PM.

"You'll be okay, Shannon. They'll be here soon. They'll be here soon." Carrie hoped that was the case. She was scared that Shannon didn't have much longer.

31

"Now we're cooking with gas."

3:08 PM

Mac ran the scenario round and round in his head as he and Lich drove north on County Road 81 into the northwestern suburb of Osseo. They were onto it now, finally. Smith and the Muellers were behind this. The motives were perverted, but if Mac could not understand them, he could at least see where they were coming from.

For Brown, it was the chief.

Charlie Flanagan hated dirty cops more than almost anything. In Brown's case, he caught the DEA agent putting coke back onto the street to pay off gambling debts. It might have only been a one-time thing, but Brown was guilty and admitted it to Detective Flanagan. Peters had told Mac that Brown had pleaded—flat-out begged—the chief to let it go. Brown was in counseling for his gambling and hadn't placed a bet in ten months. Faced with the wrath of his bookie and his bookie's muscle, he'd stolen the coke to retire the debt. Brown told Flanagan he'd leave the Bureau and law enforcement if he let it go. Brown also had a seriously ill daughter and was worried about what would happen to her.

Smith Brown simply didn't know Charlie Flanagan. If you were dirty, you had to pay the price. Peters recalled Flanagan ruminating about what to do with Brown at the time, saying, "It would be one thing if he stole a couple of watches, a fur coat, maybe a TV from the evidence room, something like that. I wouldn't condone it, but I could at least understand it. I could let *that* kind of thing slide. But stealing drugs, *coke,* and putting it back on our streets and all that comes with that? *That* I can't look past."

As Peters said, "You know the chief. It was a principle thing."

Mac didn't know what to think of it. He understood the chief's position. But he doubted the chief thought Brown would end up with fifteen years in Leavenworth Federal Pen either. Life had to have been miserable in there, and the information they were finding said that was indeed the case. Fifteen years in prison is a long time to think. Especially after they also learned Brown's daughter died after he went in, at least in part because his wife and child lost medical insurance. That only added fuel to the fire.

"He blames the chief for all of that, I'm sure," Peters said. "I suppose I see how he gets there, but he's wrong."

"Smith might be wrong about the chief's choices, Captain," Mac answered. "But at the moment, he's sitting with two aces in the hole."

For the Muellers, it was Lyman Hisle, the man who killed their father.

The whole conspiracy was simple and made sense once you had the pieces. All of which made Mac more concerned about the ransom.

"This ransom call is about more than money," Mac told his captain. "There's a trap door here that we're not seeing, and the chief and Lyman are going to fall right through it."

"What's the trap door?" Peters asked.

"I don't know," Mac answered. "But the ransom will not be some simple money drop. You're not going to be dropping it into a garbage can somewhere. These guys want blood. The chief and Lyman are going to be involved in the drop somehow, and we need to stay close."

Mac hung up his phone and retreated into his thoughts as they passed the Osseo city limits sign. Mac hadn't been to Osseo for years. As a kid he came up this way to play hockey a couple of times every winter at the Osseo Arena, a rink that looked like a big beige utility shed and felt like the inside of a freezer. It had the hardest and fastest ice around. Back in those days, the town sat by itself among fields, looking like the small farm town you now had to drive out much farther to find. Today, Osseo was a little piece of small-town America completely surrounded by the suburbs of Maple Grove and Brooklyn Park, complete with three-car-garage mini-mansions, big-box retailers, chain restaurants, Lexuses, BMWs, and exploding populations.

Mac turned right off of the highway and onto tree-lined Central Avenue, the town's main drag. Osseo didn't seem a natural choice for the Muellers, who were born and raised in Chisago Lakes, an equally small bedroom community fifty miles northeast of St. Paul. But it started to make some sense when Sally told him that they'd been working for a nearby lumberyard, based on wage records.

"Of course," Sally said, "the Mueller brothers had checking accounts, but they were cleaned out a few weeks ago."

Mac pulled up to a patrol car in the parking lot of the gas station along the main drag. Two uniform cops, one much older than the other, casually leaned against the front bumper of their cruiser, which was parked under the shady canopy of a small group of maple trees. The older of the two, whom Mac assumed was the chief, was smoking. Mac powered down his window and stuck his hand out to shake. "Detective McRyan from St. Paul."

"I'm Police Chief Pete Mitchell," the older cop replied as he took Mac's hand. "This here is one of my patrol guys. His name's Bennett."

Mac thumbed toward the passenger side, "This is Detective Lich. How do you want to do this, Chief?"

"I called the landlord," Mitchell said, taking a drag on his Marlboro and blowing smoke out the side of his mouth. "He says the guys you're looking for haven't been around for a week or two, at least as far as he can tell."

"We still should take a look."

"I figured you'd want to. The landlord will let us in," Mitchell said, stamping out his cigarette and waving them to follow.

The apartment was two blocks away in a rundown 1950s-style apartment building with a water-stained dark beige stucco exterior with brown-trimmed windows. The landlord was sitting on the steps, having a smoke of his own, when they pulled up. The man, dressed in dark brown pants and a white, short-sleeved collar shirt, looked to be in his sixties. His last strands of hair stretched in a brutal comb-over from one ear over to the other. Without saying a word, he turned and led the group up the steps to the second floor and a rear apartment. The landlord knocked on the door, waited fifteen seconds, knocked again, waited, and then slid in the key.

"Like I told Ole' Pistol Pete here," he said in a gravely, smoke-damaged voice, "they haven't been around for a week or two."

Mac and Lich entered to find an apartment evidencing a Spartan existence. To their right was a tiny galley kitchen, straight ahead was a living room, and to the left was a hallway to two small bedrooms and a full bath. The living room had an avocado-colored couch and harvest-gold-upholstered loveseat perched in front of an old twenty-seven-inch TV that sat on side-by-side milk crates. Down the hallway, there were mattresses on the floor of each bedroom, but no sheets or blankets remained. An old clock radio sat unplugged on the floor in one bedroom. The closets were empty. In the bathroom, there was a half roll of toilet paper but nothing more. In the kitchen, the refrigerator was empty except for a nearly empty carton of spoiled milk, three eggs, and a half stick of butter. Mac sifted through the cupboards and drawers, finding only a single pay stub for Zorn Lumber.

"This place is empty," Lich said, standing in the living room with his hands on his hips.

"Abandoned, I'd say," Mac added.

"When's the rent paid up through?" Lich asked the landlord.

"Through June," he answered. "They haven't paid for July yet, and I was startin' to wonder about it."

"I doubt you're going to get July's rent," Mac said. He showed the landlord pictures of the Mueller brothers. "Were these the guys renting the place?"

The landlord nodded, "That's them, all right."

Mac dug out pictures of Monica and Brown. "You ever see either of these folks hanging around?"

The landlord scratched the back of his head and peered at the pictures for a moment. "Her, yes," he said. "You couldn't miss her. She was a pretty thing. I'm not sure about the guy though. They didn't have many visitors that I can recall, although people come and go all the time." He held the picture in his hands for another minute, giving it a good look. "I just can't say for sure if he was ever around."

Mac turned to the chief, holding up the pay stub. "Is Zorn Lumber the lumberyard we passed out on County 81 as we drove into town?"

"It is. Ol' Ray Zorn runs the place. You want to talk to him?"

"We need to."

"I thought you might. I called Ray and told him we might be stopping by. He lives five blocks from here."

Jupiter sat next to Hagen as the convict computer genius's fingers set speed records flying over the keys. Sally was striking out with the pipe company, which was located in Des Moines. There just wasn't a way to get hold of someone on the holiday. If the FBI and their resources could be trusted, they might have been able to throw some weight around. However, Mac and Riles both said they didn't want to do that unless they were left with no choice.

Hagen said they had a choice.

He rolled his eyes when Sally asked him if he could crack into the company's system. Hacking was a skill one never really lost, he said, "like riding a bike." Peters had already promised protection if anyone caught him.

It had taken him about twenty minutes, but now he was into the company's electronic shipping records for the kind of pipe shown in the video. "So where do they ship the pipe to?" Hagen asked, staring at the computer screen with a perplexed look on his face.

"You're in, right? Jupiter quizzed. "But can you find the information you need?"

"I've never been much of an end-user. I'll find what we need, but...."

"It'll take you some time," Jones filled in. "I have a little expertise in this area. May I?"

"Be my guest," Hagen replied, scooting over.

Jupiter wasn't a hacker. He was originally a programmer who had since moved to video. He liked to use technology as a tool to develop information, whether it was business intelligence software, where he had made his initial fortune, or in video, where he was making his next one. Hagen, on the other hand, knew programming and he liked to use technology as a tool as well, but more like a sword to access the information of others—that was where the thrill, and utility, lay for him. It was a different mindset. But Hagen had used his sword, and now, Jupe thought, it was time for the toolbox.

"While I was looking over your shoulder I thought I saw a previous page where I could..." Jones's voice trailed off as he exited the shipping records and moused through menus He clicked on an icon for a program named *CustomerChoice*. "Here we go," he said. "This is business intelligence software. This is the kind of stuff I used to make. It should let me search for what we need."

Now Hagen was the interested one as Jupiter set up a search, entered the kind of pipe, the letter H in the company name profile, Minnesota and Wisconsin in the state field, and then clicked *search*. The program quickly turned out thirty-nine hits. "Now we're cooking with gas," Jupiter said. "I'm going to see if we can't narrow this down a little more."

Ray Zorn lived on a quiet corner in a blue two-story with a white picket fence. Zorn was sitting with his wife at a picnic table under the shade of a large maple tree. He was dressed in an old, yellow Munsingwear golf shirt, Bermuda shorts, and dark socks, along with a John Deere ball cap. Prepared for company, a white tray with a pitcher of lemonade and six glasses rested on the table.

"Hiya, Chief," Zorn welcomed, waving the group over.

"Ray." Mitchell introduced Mac and Lich, who both declined refreshment.

Mac wasted no time, "Mr. Zorn, David and Dean Mueller worked for you?"

"Yes they did."

"They still work for you?"

"I don't think they do."

"'Don't think?'" Lich queried.

"Well, they stopped showing up a few weeks ago and I haven't heard from them since. So if those boys ever show up, it'll only be for me to tell 'em not to come back. Must say, though, I'm kind of disappointed in those boys."

"Why's that?"

"I knew their father. Tom Mueller was a friend of mine years ago. Those boys came to me, just out of prison, looking for work. I had my doubts, but I liked their father and thought I'd give them a chance." Zorn went on to explain that they had been good workers who showed up on time, did whatever he asked, were respectful, caused no problems. "I was surprised when they just stopped showing up. Figured, if they got a better offer somewhere, they'd do me the courtesy of tellin' me, ya know?"

"Did they ever have any visitors when they worked for you?"

"Just their sister. She showed up once, maybe a week or two before the boys up and scooted on me."

Mac paused, then asked, "Did the Muellers ever purchase any lumber from you?"

"I don't right know," Zorn replied. "Employees can purchase from us at a pretty good discount, and they may well have done so. I can check if you need."

"We do," Mac said. "You said their sister stopped by. Would that be this woman?" He placed a picture of Monica on the picnic table.

"That's her," Zorn said. "Pretty girl, I always thought."

"Have you ever seen this man?" Mac asked, sliding a picture of Smith across the table.

Zorn stared at the picture, as did Mitchell. Mitchell spoke first.

"These boys showed me this picture a few minutes ago and it didn't hit me, but now for some reason it does. I think I've seen that guy before. Doesn't he look familiar to you, Ray?"

Zorn wrinkled his nose and looked at the picture closer. "You know, I think you're right there, Pete. He looks familiar. It's the nose I think. That big knot up there on the bridge is what I remember."

"Where did we see him?"

Zorn stared at the photo for a moment more, and then his eyes lit up, "We saw him at the Derby."

"The Derby? What's the Derby?" Lich asked.

"Restaurant out on County 81," Chief Mitchell replied. "A dingy old greasy-spoon you passed on the left as you drove into town. It's an old highway joint, few booths and a counter. Ray and I like to eat lunch there a time or two a week."

"Pete's right," Zorn added. "We saw this feller in there. He was in a booth, the back booth I think, with the Mueller boys." He shook his head. "Good memory, Pete."

"When was this?"

"Not long ago," Miller said. "Few, maybe three weeks ago."

"Now that you mention it," Zorn added. "Probably a few days before the boys up and bailed on me."

Mac and Lich shared a look. "That pretty much locks it up," Lich said.

"These boys have something to do with that kidnapping in St. Paul?" Miller asked.

Mac nodded.

"Anything else we can do to help?"

"It would help to find out if the Muellers bought any lumber from you."

"Why would that matter?" Zorn asked, concerned. "I don't think we did anything wrong."

"You didn't Mr. Zorn, you didn't. But trust me," Lich replied, "it matters for us to know. It just does."

"So that gets us down to three stores with the right letters," Hagen said.

"Hanlin's in Brainerd, Hankley's in Grantsburg, up in Wisconsin, or Hanburg's in Wyoming," Jupiter replied.

"Damn holiday," Sally said. "It'll be a nightmare to try to get hold of these people." She shook her head.

"Call Mac," Riles said. "See what he thinks. Sooner or later we need to bring more resources into this."

"Here we go," Zorn said as he held up a sheet of paper. They had all crowded into his office at the lumber yard. "Employee purchase form right here. Three weeks ago. They bought heavy plywood, two-by-fours and wood screws."

"How about PVC piping?" Mac asked.

"Nope. Just the wood and the screws. We don't sell PVC pipe."

"But they bought it all about the time Smith met with those boys at the diner," Lich added.

Mac nodded, but he was getting anxious. He looked at his watch, which now said 4:10 PM. Time was running out and, while they were confirming the players, it wasn't getting them any closer.

"We know who it is now," Lich said, pulling Mac to a corner. "We know it's Brown and the Muellers."

"Which is great, we've figured out who's behind it. But where are the girls? We're no closer to answering that."

"Maybe we tell Burton, a few select others, see if we can spread the word quietly."

Mac ran that around in his head, thinking about what Dick said, thinking it might be time to broaden their little group in the know. "Maybe…" he started, when his cell phone rang. It was Sally, reporting that Jupiter and Hagen had narrowed the source of the pipe. "Okay, so I have Hanlin's in Brainerd, Hankley's in Grantsburg, or Hanburg's in

Wyoming, just north of Forest Lake up Interstate 35," Mac repeated as he wrote down all of the stores on his notepad.

"What's with Hanburg's?" Zorn asked, overhearing Mac.

Mac pulled the phone away from his ear. He figured anything he said in front of Zorn or Miller was fine. He gave them a quick rundown on the girls being buried alive. Zorn looked sick, probably thinking that wood purchased from his business had been used for that purpose. "There's PVC piping these guys used. You don't sell that here. We think it came from one of those three stores."

"Two things," Zorn said, a dead serious, pissed-off look on his face. The small-town friendly demeanor was long gone. "I know Freddy Hanburg out in Wyoming. He owns that store. He'd be sick about this. I'll call him for you right now."

"And I'll call the Wyoming chief," Mitchell added.

"You said there were two things," Mac said. "What's the other?"

"The Mueller kids are from Chisago Lakes. That's ten miles up the road from Wyoming. You don't have much time left from what you boys are telling me. If I were you boys, I'd look there first."

32

"Hey! I know her."

5:10 PM

Fifty minutes until the ransom call. Wyoming was thirty-five miles east from Osseo. With the light holiday traffic, Mac made the drive in a little over twenty minutes, his portable roller pushing what traffic there was over to the slow lane. Hanburg's Hardware sat on the main drag of Wyoming, a quarter mile east of I-35.

"We're getting our fill of small towns these last couple of days," Lich said as Mac skidded to a stop in front of the hardware store. The Chisago County sheriff and Wyoming police chief were waiting in front, along with a man in his mid-fifties, sporting a large beer belly and a flowered shirt that looked like a tent. He had the look of a walrus, with a bushy mustache and two-day old razor stubble.

Mac and Lich jumped out, showed their credentials, and quickly exchanged introductions. "Ray Zorn told you what we we're here for?" Mac asked Hanburg.

"He did," Hanburg answered over his shoulder as he opened the front door to the store. "I'll do anything I can to help you boys." Hanburg's was an old-school hardware store. Inside the door was an island checkout area with registers on either side. To the right was a more open area for lawn mowers, tillers, and snowblowers. The back of the store was a maze of metal shelves. It reminded Mac, oddly, of the hardware store at Fat Charlie's place in North Minneapolis.

"Can you take a look at these photos? Tell us if any of these people were in your store recently?" Mac asked as they walked to Hanburg's office in the back.

Hanburg took a look, but shook his head. "I couldn't tell ya. But I've made calls to all my guys, and they're on their way here. Maybe they can be more helpful to you."

"When will they be here?" Lich asked impatiently. "We're on a tight clock."

"I know you are," Hanburg replied. "I told them to hurry, not optional if they wanted to remain employed. They're good fellas who work for me. They're hustlin' in. It's tough you know, it's...."

"... a holiday," Mac interrupted, frustrated. "That's been an issue all day."

Hanburg sat in his metal desk chair, pulled up to the computer, and started working the keyboard and mouse. "You boys got a picture of the piping? There are different kinds. I want to look for the right ones."

Mac pulled three still photos out of his folder and handed them over.

Hanburg looked at the sticker. "That looks like one we sell. Let me run a search here. What do you think, back a month or two?"

"At the most," Mac answered, walking around behind Hanburg and sitting on a corner of the desk. Within a minute, the store owner had a report up on his screen. It showed purchases of the PVC pipe over the past two months, providing dates, amounts purchased, and payment methods. There were more than fifty purchases, many of them bulk sales to local building and plumbing contractors.

"How many are in cash?" Mac asked.

Hanburg narrowed the search more. "I've got five that paid in cash."

With Mac and Lich now on the PVC pipe, Sally, Jupiter, and Hagen searched for any connection between Smith or the Muellers and anyone from a list of cops provided by Double Frank and Paddy the day before.

"We're not finding anything," Jupiter admitted.

"Not even a sniff," Hagen added.

"Let's take a look at the FBI people working the case," Sally said.

"You want me searching FBI personnel files?" Hagen asked, concern in his voice. Jupiter flipped up an eyebrow as well.

Sally didn't hesitate. "Do it."

Carrie kept talking, about anything and everything, her family, friends, boyfriend, job, hopes, aspirations, school, everything. She talked about her whole life, as if she wanted to relive it one last time, which she knew she might be doing. Talking about it let her make a mental escape, if only temporarily. It put her mind in a place outside the box, a place where there was light and sun, and she could move wherever and however she wanted to.

Shannon wasn't carrying along with the conversation.

She was barely conscious.

Carrie held her tight, trying to keep her awake. She talked to her, rubbed her arms and legs, doing anything she could to keep Shannon conscious and comfortable. Carrie was trying to buy as much time as possible, praying somebody would get to them soon.

Over the last hour, Carrie had kept talking, about TV shows, her favorite music, and even about politics, a first for her, just to show how few topics were left to comment on. Then she started talking about

Jessica Alba. "I mean, that girl is so beautiful. I can't imagine what she does to keep her body looking that good, can you?"

Shannon didn't respond.

Carrie shook her shoulder, "Shannon, doesn't Jessica Alba have a great body?"

Shannon mumbled incoherently.

"Shannon! Shannon! Wake up, honey! Wake up!" Carrie babbled on for a few minutes before she realized it was no use. Shannon had warned that this could happen. Her body was shutting down. Time was running out.

Gail Carlson pulled into the gas station across the street from Hanburg's Hardware. She'd heard the call come through on the Wyoming police band, a call for the chief, asking him to meet two St. Paul police detectives at Hanburg's. Carlson called Foxx on her way out the door, telling her that her hunch may have paid off.

The veteran reporter jumped into her black Jeep Cherokee and raced from Minneapolis up to Wyoming, a half hour to the north. Now she slumped down in her driver's seat, looking up at her rearview mirror, watching the police cars and a black Ford Explorer parked in front of the store. She pulled out her cell phone and dialed Foxx.

"Where you at, Gail?" Foxx asked without preamble.

"Across the street from Hanburg's Hardware. I'm looking at two patrol cars and a black Ford Explorer."

"I'll bet that's Mac McRyan, that's what he drives." Foxx exclaimed, with just a touch of glee in her voice. "Can you see anything else?"

"No, but people are starting to arrive, so they must be on to something. So what are they on to?" Carlson asked. "You want to let me in on it?"

Foxx related her experiences from the night before.

"So something's going on up here," Carlson said agreeably.

"Yeah, I just don't know what."

The employees of Hanburg's Hardware started filing in. Mac and Lich were talking to them back in Hanburg's office, showing the photos. It was going nowhere. Nobody recognized any of the pictures. There were some comments about people being vaguely familiar, but nobody said, "yeah, I've seen Dean or David or Monica Reynolds or Smith Brown in here recently."

"Fuck me," Mac said, leaning over the desk.

"What next?" Lich said. "We've got what?" He looked at his watch. "Twenty-five minutes until the call?"

Mac looked at the floor, "We put out the description. Brown and the Muellers are probably hanging around for the money drop. Maybe we pick them up that way." He said it without much conviction. Mac didn't believe it was going to be that simple.

"That's what I was thinking," Lich replied. "At least give it to *our* people. People we know we can trust. We still keep it close to the vest, but at the same time, we've got eyes out looking."

"Do it," Mac replied. "Call Riles. We should start driving back that direction anyway."

Lich pulled out his cell phone and started dialing and walked down a back hallway, away from Mac.

"No go, huh?" Hanburg asked sympathetically.

"Long-shot to begin with," Mac replied, exhaling loudly as he collapsed into a folding chair. He felt like they were close. If only they had more time, they might have pulled this off.

"Hey! I know her," a voice belted out from the front of the store.

"Who said that? Who said that?" Mac said, flying out of Hanburg's office into the front of the store.

"I did," said a short, heavyset man who was a dead ringer for Larry the Cable Guy. "My name's Todd Crawford."

"How do you recognize her?"

"That's Monica Mueller, and those are her brothers Dean and David. I went to high school with them back in the day."

"That's great Todd," Mac answered. "But were any of them in here recently?"

Todd nodded. "Monica was about two, maybe three or so weeks ago."

"How do you know it was her?"

"Oh it was her. I went to high school with her. I was a couple of years behind, but everyone knew who Monica was. She was a looker back then. She still is now, for that matter."

"Did she recognize you?"

"I doubt it," Crawford responded with a laugh. "She didn't have much time for my kind back in high school."

"Which was what?"

"Burnout, smokin' in the back forty," Crawford said, and then added, smiling, "Of course, Detective, that was back then. Now I'm a fine, upstanding family man."

Mac ignored the jocularity and asked, "Recall what she bought?"

Crawford nodded, "Sure. Pipe—PVC pipe, I think—and a long extension ladder. Odd things for a woman to buy, generally—it's probably why I noticed her to begin with. It was a Saturday. It was real busy here in the store, people everywhere. I was working my register on one side of the counter and she went to the one on the other side. She's a smaller gal, and she was carrying this big piece of PVC pipe, and she asked for somebody to get the extension ladder for her, so that's what drew my attention at first."

"How'd you recognize her? Was it obviously her?" Mac wanted to make sure Crawford was on the level.

Crawford shook his head. "Not at first. She had on a visor and sunglasses, so I didn't recognize her right away. But she took her sunglasses off, put them up on top of the visor, you know, like golfers do?"

Mac knew what he meant. He did it himself when he played, usually when he putted.

"It was her. No doubt about it."

"You're sure she bought the pipe?"

"Yeah. I remember carrying it to her van. We had to strap the ladder on top and we put the pipe in the back."

Crawford seemed sure of himself. He wasn't bullshitting. But it still wasn't getting Mac anywhere. So Monica bought the pipe; that confirmed that and nothing more. The Mueller boys bought the lumber. Again, they knew who they were up against, but they weren't any closer to finding them or the girls. Mac exhaled and thought a little more about the pipe and ladder. How far away would they drive with the pipe and ladder strapped to the roof? Probably not too far, he surmised. Mac took a shot in the dark. "I don't suppose you have any idea of where she was going with it, do you?"

Crawford shrugged, "I assumed to her aunt's place."

"Aunt's place? What aunt?"

"Yeah, her aunt, or at least I think it's her aunt. Maybe a second aunt. Some relative of hers had a farm place, or at least a big piece of land, over by Marine on St. Croix. I figured they was makin' repairs. The place is kinda run down."

"What's the aunt's name?"

"Anita something? Anita, Anita..." Crawford stroked his chin. "God, it's Anita something." Crawford grabbed a phone and dialed a number. "Mom. What was the last name of Anita, you know, the relative of the Muellers." There was a pause. "Yeah, that's the one Mom. What was her name? Russell? Anita Russell. Thanks, Mom."

Mac's mind was already moving. "Dick, get up here," he yelled as he dialed his cell phone. Sally answered right away. "There's an aunt or something of the Mueller's. Her name is Anita Russell. She has a farm over by Marine on St. Croix. Start looking."

Lich came into the room. "What?"

Mac filled him in and then said to the Chisago sheriff, "Marine on St. Croix is back down in Washington County, right?" Washington County was the next county south.

The sheriff nodded.

"Can you call your opposite number and tell him to call me? And do it so that it isn't broadcast?"

"Where you gonna be?" The sheriff asked as he pulled a cell phone out of his pocket.

"We're driving over that direction," Mac replied.

"Mac, these guys have been awful careful," Lich said. "You really think they would bury the girls on family property?"

"I don't know," Mac answered, "But it's worth a look." His cell phone went off, Sally again.

"What do you got?"

"This access to the FBI system is something," Sally said. "Anita Russell must be a more distant relative or something, because we didn't find her earlier. Anyway, she has a place maybe a mile or two north of Marine on St. Croix. It's on eighty acres." She gave him the address and general directions from Wyoming. "Here's an interesting thing about the property." Sally added.

"What's that?"

"It backs up to William O'Brien State Park."

"That *is* interesting. See what else you can find out about it," he directed and then hung up. He looked at his watch—5:45 PM—and stormed out the front door, saying, "We gotta hustle and right now." Lich chased him.

"Mac?" Lich asked, "What are you thinking? Clue me in, eh?"

"Anita Russell has eighty acres over by Marine on St. Croix. The land backs up to William O'Brien State Park. I'm thinking it's worth a look."

"A look for what?"

"The girls."

33

"Watch your back."

5:44 PM

Riley and Rock walked into the conference room. The shades were pulled and the television turned off. Cups of cold coffee and half-eaten donuts littered the table. Burton, Duffy, and an FBI technician wearing a headset stood around a phone and laptop computer at the far end of the conference table. Peters, the chief, and Lyman milled around the other end. The room was quiet as they waited for the call. Sitting unattended in the middle of the conference table were two large nylon bags, one black and one navy, with five million dollars split evenly between them.

Riles and Rock immediately went to the chief, who, under cover of a hug, asked Riley, "Anything?" The chief and now Lyman both knew about Brown and the Muellers. It had gone no further.

"Mac's working it, Chief," Riles replied, equally quiet, having just got off the phone with McRyan.

"*What's* he working?"

"Something up around Marine on St. Croix," Riles answered cryptically, his voice just a whisper.

"What's up there?" Lyman pressed quietly, his lips barely moving. "I'm familiar with the area. I could make a phone call or two."

"The Muellers have land up there," Rock answered, turning his back. The FBI men at the other end of the room had started looking down toward the conversation. "Mac and Lich can't get back in time, so they're going to check it out, that's all."

"It's a long shot," Riles whispered, unwrapping a piece of Big Red gum and shoving it into his mouth. "But you know Mac," he added.

The chief nodded. If Mac had a hunch, good luck getting him off it until he was satisfied, no matter what anyone else said.

Burton broke away from the group and walked down to the men from St. Paul. "We're set here," he said, and then looked to Riley. "Where's McRyan and his partner?"

"They're in the neighborhood," Riley answered neutrally. "He tends to draw attention when he's around, so he wants to be on the street when the call comes in."

Burton nodded and then looked at his watch. "Should be any minute now."

"Tracking in the bags?" Rock asked Burton.

"Sewn into the fabric. Very small. Can't be seen or felt. Wherever it goes, we'll be able to follow."

Rock walked over to the window, moved the drapes back, and noted the mass of media coalescing out front. There might have been two hundred people milling about. "How do we get out of here without the media being all over this?" Rock asked. "They're hovering like flies out there. Riles and I were practically strip searched on the way in. And it seems like more people are coming by the minute."

Duffy nodded. "We've got three sets of plain white vehicles ready to go in the parking ramp, which the media can't get to. When the call comes, and we have to leave, three sets leave. If, after we leave, the main vehicle still picks up a tail, we'll take care of it before we get to wherever we're going."

"Any idea where we're going?" Riley asked.

"No," Duffy replied, taking a sip from his Styrofoam coffee cup.

Dean pulled into the parking lot of a small beige-and-brown-brick strip mall along Highway 95 in Lakeland, one of many small towns that dotted the Minnesota side of the St. Croix River, south of Interstate 94. The strip mall held a hair salon, an insurance agency, an accounting office, a law practice, and a pay phone. A flat canopy hung over the sidewalk in front of the businesses. Given the holiday, the parking lot was empty. There were no surveillance cameras, sparse traffic on the highway, and zero foot traffic. The nearest houses were on the other side of the highway, at least a couple hundred yards away.

Dressed in flip-flops and a ball cap, Dean looked like any of a thousand men on a warm holiday. The only unusual part of his ensemble was a red nylon shoulder bag, out of which he pulled a pair of black leather gloves. Taking a quick glance around, he slid on the gloves and pulled out the portable voice changer and two quarters. He also took out a three-by-five-inch index card. Dropping the quarters into the phone, Dean looked down at the card and dialed.

The conference room was silent, other than the sound of pacing shoes scuffing against the carpet. Burton and Duffy leaned over the phone, both hands on the table. The call would be recorded, and they would trace it, although nobody expected the kidnappers to stay on the line for any appreciable length of time. Everyone's eyes were on the second hand on the wall clock. When the red hand hit twelve, the phone rang. The chief picked up on the second ring.

"Flanagan."

"You and Hisle at the corner of Washington and West Fifth in ten minutes. With the ransom. No police. We'll be watching."

"What about ... the ... girls," the chief's voice trailed off. The kidnapper had already hung up.

Burton moved immediately. "Let's hustle," he said, leading everyone out of the conference room. "We'll wire these two in the truck." As the group approached the elevators, Peters pulled Rock and Riley aside.

"This is no good," Riles said through gritted teeth. "They're going to wire the chief and Lyman in the truck? This smells. Mac's right, this isn't a simple money drop. They're going to put the chief and Hisle on the move."

Peters nodded. "I want you two mobile. Keep a perimeter and stay on this radio frequency. We know who's behind this, so if you see this Brown or the Muellers, move on them," their captain ordered.

Riles's cell phone rang.

Heather Foxx noted the three separate convoys of trucks pulling out and immediately recognized what she was seeing. "They're running different groups out of here so we don't follow," she said to her cameraman as the trucks and cars streaked out in different directions. She looked back to the side entrance she'd seen McRyan and his friends use in recent days. Detectives Riley and Rockford burst through the doors and ran down the steps. Heather took a look at the news truck and her rental car. "Jump in the rental car," she told the cameraman, fishing out the keys.

"We're supposed to stay here," the cameraman said.

Foxx's instincts told her to get on the move. "Trust me. There's nothing to do here but wait for the police to feed us a statement, and everyone gets the same thing. On the other hand," the reporter said, gesturing toward the detectives, "Riley and Rockford, those are two of the chief's boys. If we follow them, we might actually see something worth reporting."

"Less than ten minutes?" Mac yelled into the phone as he accelerated down the county road to meet up with the Washington County sheriff. "Where?"

"Where?" Lich demanded, doubling up. "Where are they going to?"

Mac put his hand over the phone. "Corner of Washington and West Fifth, that's the northwest corner of Rice Park," and then to Riley, "What then? ... Nothing? They just wait? You know what they're going to do? They're going to run the chief and Lyman around, Riles. They're going to try and lose you ... yeah ... sounds like you're on it? Good. Yeah, I'll have the phone with me." Mac hung up. "I knew it," Mac railed to Lich. "It's not a simple ransom drop. They're going to put the chief and Lyman on the run." He felt no satisfaction at being right.

"FBI will have assets all over the place, Mac," Lich said. "They'll be tough to shake. Especially in the middle of downtown."

"On a normal day, yeah," Mac replied. "But it's the Fourth of fuckin' July, and it's hotter than hell. Downtown is a graveyard. There'll be nobody, and I mean *nobody*, around Rice Park at that time of day. If we've got people following closely, they'll stick out like 50-Cent at a Faith Hill concert."

"Fine," Lich's replied, "But it'll also be hard to lose them, with so few people around. There isn't anyone for them to blend with."

"Maybe, but they've been ready for everything thus far. They'll be ready for that." Mac sighed. Dick's point was valid, but he didn't agree. The sinking feeling in the pit of his stomach told him all he needed to know. The whole thing felt wrong. "The chief and Lyman are the real target, the money's just so they can get away in style."

The Explorer's speedometer read eighty-five, and the flasher pushed cars off to the shoulder as Mac burned south on the county road.

"They should be up just around the bend," Lich said.

As Mac slowed to sixty-five and drove around a small bend in the road, two Washington County Suburbans came into view, waiting on the right shoulder a half mile ahead. Mac pulled in behind them. A paunchy man with a bushy black mustache was already out, walking up to Lich on the passenger side.

"I'm George Head, sheriff out here. The Russell place is up on the left side, another two miles."

"Anyone do a drive-by?"

Head nodded. "I had a couple of my guys drive by five minutes ago. They said it looked awfully quiet."

"Just the same," Mac said. "We need to go check it out."

"You're sure they're the guys?"

"They're behind it," Lich answered. "No question at this point."

"Let's not dick around then," Head said bluntly. "We're just gonna blow right up the driveway and crash the place. You fellas got vests?"

Lich pointed to the back seat.

"Put 'em on."

The sheriff hustled back to his Suburban while Mac and Lich pulled on and secured their vests. Once set, Mac gave a quick honk and they all pulled out, accelerating down the road. The house, a sad place with chipped and fading yellow paint and a slightly sagging green-shingled roof, was set back two hundred yards from the road in a thin grove of maple and poplar trees. A large, rusted, light-blue pole barn sat behind the house. The yard was unkempt, the lawn overgrown and weed-filled. The Washington County Suburbans sped up the long dirt driveway and skidded to a stop at the front porch. Mac stopped hard behind them and everyone was out.

The sheriff yelled, "Go!" Two men went up the porch and hammered down the front door, while Mac, Lich, and a deputy ran around to the back, weapons drawn on the back door. They heard the men working the house, with several "Clears" called out. Within thirty seconds, a deputy pushed out the back door and shook his head. Nobody was home.

Mac and Lich moved inside. A quick inspection of the house revealed no furniture or working power. The only sign of a recent presence was a familiar-looking card table and four chairs in the kitchen.

"They've been here." Mac said. "The table. The chairs. They're clean, new, recently used and the same as we found at that house in St. Paul."

Mac was out the back door and jogged to the large pole barn. The front and back doors were open. It was empty other than a few cement blocks, scraps of wood, two sawhorses, and four new garden shovels and a new spade leaning against the wall. Mac walked to the shovels, the metal still shiny. He looked to his left. At the far end a deputy was kneeling down, picking at the dirt with a pen.

"What do you have?" Mac asked, hustling up to him.

"Sawdust," the deputy replied. "It's just kind of spread here in the dirt, and it's spread around here." The deputy saw the look on Mac's face. "Is this important?"

"Yes," Lich replied as he walked up. "Mac, did you see the new shovels and sawhorses over along the wall there?"

"Yes," Mac answered as he jogged out the back door of the pole barn, his hand over his eyes as he scanned the property.

Sheriff Head walked up to them. "House is clear. I assume you noted the chairs and table in the kitchen."

Mac nodded, but kept the search on. "How big is this piece of property again?"

"Eighty acres," Head replied, following Mac as he started to walk back toward the driveway. "It runs out the back, east to the property line for the state park. What are you looking at?"

Mac walked quickly past the sheriff's Suburbans and his Explorer to where a jagged road ran back toward the state park. Mac kneeled down where the road ventured into taller grass. There appeared to be fresh or at least recent tire tracks. "I think someone's driven through here recently."

He stood up and looked up at a thick forest in the distance, perhaps a half mile or a little more away. The road—practically a trail through the taller grass—meandered like a stream in the direction of the trees. Mac closed his eyes, tilted his head back, and thought back to the kidnappers' video, the view out the windshield that showed high grass, weeds, and a rough road up to a heavily wooded area. Then later they're in the woods, thick woods, burying the girls.

He opened his eyes, looking again into the distance. The land looked right. As Mac looked around, he couldn't see another house or building anywhere in the distance. He knew O'Brien State Park. The area that was frequented by the general public was along the St. Croix River, not on the land backing up to the farm.

"Sheriff, how far to the state park line?"

"Like I said, it's an eighty-acre plot," Head replied, pointing straight out. "It goes back, I don't know, maybe another quarter of a mile, maybe a little more to the property line."

"Is there a fence or boundary for the state park?"

"No," Head replied, shaking his head. "There are some green posts every so often that mark it, but there isn't a fence or anything."

Mac turned to the sheriff. "There are a bunch of new shovels in the pole barn. Grab them!" he yelped back over his shoulder, running to the Explorer.

"Mac!" Lich yelled, running behind him. "Where are you going?"

"You drive," Mac ordered, handing the keys to Lich. "Follow the trail."

"You think the girls are out there?"

"No," he answered. "I know it."

As the van took I-35E south into downtown St. Paul, an FBI tech taped body mikes to the chests of the chief and Lyman. "Just speak normally," Burton said. "These are very sensitive microphones. They'll pick up any conversation you have, even if you whisper."

Lyman and the chief both nodded, tucking their shirts back into their pants.

"Downtown's pretty quiet today. Won't be anyone around," the chief said. "It'll be hard for you to be close."

"We've got you wired, and we've got the tracker in the bags," Duffy said.

"We won't be far, and your boys will be around and they know the streets," Burton said calmly. "Just concentrate on getting your girls back, and we'll worry about the rest."

The chief sat down next to Peters and asked in a whisper, "What do you think?"

"Watch your back," Peters replied quietly.

"Two blocks," the driver yelled.

Burton and Duffy each handed bags to the chief and Lyman.

Foxx pulled up to the curb just short of the corner of Main Street and West Fifth Street. She was parked a block back from Riley and Rockford, who'd taken a left on West Fifth Street and parked their white Chevy

S-10 along the side, just short of the end of the street. The reporter could see Rockford, who had a set of binoculars up to his eyes.

"What are they watching?" the cameraman asked, filming across Heather from the passenger side.

"Well find out soon enough," Heather answered.

The truck pulled up to the corner, and the chief and Lyman jumped out. Without a word, Burton slid the door closed. The truck pulled away down Washington Street and turned right on Kellogg Boulevard, heading out of sight.

Lyman and the chief walked up onto the corner. The chief scanned Rice Park, a park shaded by mature trees. The park took up the entire block, with benches lining walkways running diagonally from the outside of the block to the large marble fountain in the middle. The park was empty.

"What next?" Lyman asked.

Just then a ringing sound came from the garbage can sitting on the corner.

"That," Flanagan answered as he looked down into and than reached into the can, pulling out a duffel bag. A cell phone with a traditional telephone ring tone was inside. The chief answered.

"Flanagan."

Paddy McRyan stood in the empty St. Paul Grill restaurant, inside the St. Paul Hotel, peering out the large picture window that looked out across Market Street and into Rice Park. He'd watched the chief grab a bag out of the garbage can, pull the cell phone out, and start walking toward the water fountain in the center of the park. "Captain, they're getting into the fountain, they're going underwater," Paddy said as calmly as he could, knowing what would happen to the body mikes.

"Copy that," Peters replied into Paddy's earpiece. And then, his captain confirmed his worst fears. "We've lost audio contact."

"We need to keep an eyeball," Paddy said urgently into his radio, moving to his right to improve his viewing angle.

"Copy that," Peters answered, taking charge. "What are they doing now?"

"They're out of the fountain." Paddy put his binoculars to his eyes, focusing the view. "The chief is on a cell phone. Do we have audio back?"

"Negative. We are not getting that feed."

Paddy watched as Hisle and the chief kneeled down to the ground, just out of his view. He couldn't see what they were doing. After a minute, they slung the nylon bags over their shoulders. "They're on the move, south, hold on…." The detective moved to his left, to the far edge of the picture window. "The chief and Hisle are walking out of Rice Park, south, back along Washington Street over to Kellogg."

"Are you sure?" Peters asked. "The tracking devices in the bags show them stationary."

That explained why they had knelt down. "They transferred the ransom into different bags. They are now out of my line of sight."

"I'm on the west side of the Xcel Center," Riles said into a radio. "They'll have to come out onto Kellogg Boulevard, and we have a good viewpoint."

"Copy that," Burton replied. "But keep your distance. Hang on … I'm looking at the map…."

"We'll hold along West Seventh and Kellogg," Riley responded. "We should have an eyeball if they walk our way."

"Do that, but hold to the corner," Burton ordered.

Rock pulled his truck up to the corner of West Seventh and Kellogg, holding in the left hand turn lane, his hazard lights on in case anyone pulled up from behind. Riley was looking east as Kellogg gently curved way like a half-moon. Flanagan and Hisle came into view, walking across the street to the sidewalk on the south side of Kellogg. They turned west, walking toward Riles and Rock. Three hundred yards away, a half-dozen people waited at a bus stop in front of the pedestrian tunnel entrance to the RiverCentre Parking ramp, an underground ramp built into the bluff over the Mississippi River. You could enter the ramp with your car from Kellogg Boulevard on top or from Eagle Street, which ran eighty feet below Kellogg at the bottom of the bluff.

"We have them in view. They are walking in our direction." Riley reported into the radio.

"They're stopping," Rock added. "They're stopping."

"Be advised, the chief and Hisle have approached a group of people waiting at a bus stop at the RiverCentre parking ramp," Riles said. "Are they going to put them on a bus?" he asked Rock.

"Looks like it," Rock answered. Just then a bus approached from the south on West Seventh. It had its turn signal to take a right.

"We have a MTC Bus, an articulated bus, approaching our position from West Seventh. It's turning east on Kellogg." Riles gave the bus number and read the digital board over the windshield. "Be advised. The digital board on the bus says it is going to the Taste of Minnesota." The Taste of Minnesota was a large food and music festival taking place on Harriet Island on the south side of the Mississippi River, opposite downtown. The culmination of the Taste was the big Fourth of July Fireworks show. There were thousands of people on the island taking in the concerts and food.

"Those buses must be thirty, maybe forty feet long," Rock said.

"If not longer," Riles responded and then to Burton he said, "They're going to run the chief and Lyman through the crowds at the Taste and try to lose us."

Burton's voice came over the radio. "We're flooding the Taste of Minnesota. I want units converging on that location now."

"That'll help," Rock said, relieved.

"About fuckin' time we got after it," Riles added.

The bus pulled up to the stop. The chief and Hisle were out of their view now, hidden behind the bus.

"Do I turn?" Rock asked, anxious.

"Hold here," Riles responded coolly. "We have temporarily lost visual," he reported. "We are blocked by the bus." They didn't have enough assets in the area at the right spots. "If they get on, we'll follow."

"Copy that," Burton answered.

Twenty seconds later, the bus's brake lights went off and it pulled east down Kellogg Boulevard. There was nobody remaining at the bus stop.

"Be advised, Flanagan and Hisle are on the bus," Riley reported.

Rock turned left and followed.

Lich accelerated along the path, which had started to smooth out. The sheriff and his deputies followed behind them. The tall grass was halfway up the doors on the Explorer at points as the trail snaked its way towards the tree line. A green metal stake appeared to their left, just as the sheriff said.

"That's the property line for the park," Mac explained. The trees were getting ever closer.

The tire tracks turned in a slow arc to the left until they ran parallel with the tree-line, now two hundred yards to the right.

"God, I wish I had the laptop with me," Mac muttered as he closed his eyes again, pulling up the video in his memory bank. He recalled the van turning to run parallel to the tree line and then abruptly turning right, into the high grass, directly to the woods. Opening his eyes, he saw it, fifty feet ahead, a right turn into the high grass. "Turn right."

"I got it, partner. I remember this from yesterday," Lich said, slowing the Explorer and turning right to follow the fresh tire tracks. "These aren't too old Mac. A day or two at the most."

Mac nodded. The adrenaline was rushing through him now as Lich closed in on the edge of the trees. "Where is it?" Mac said. "Where is it?" He peered at the line of trees, looking for it.

"What? What are you lookin' for?"

"That!" Mac pointed at a tree with orange tape tied around it. "That orange tie. That was on the video. They're here. They're here." He grabbed a flashlight out of the glove compartment and jumped out of the truck before it had even stopped and ran frantically along the tree line, looking for the next sign. Where had they gone in? Mac worked his way down the edge of the tree line to the right of the orange tape. That felt like the right way. The box was wide. It would have been natural to slide it out of the van and walk straight back. The opening needed to be wider to allow them to operate in the dense trees.

He found it forty feet back from where they were parked, an opening with a jagged path that angled further into the trees. Crouching down, he saw matted-down grass and brush. The trees along the path showed broken branches and scraped bark. The area had been trampled through and recently.

"In here," Mac said, following the trampled path into the woods, Lich was right behind, with the sheriff and his men trailing with shovels. "We're looking for a white PVC pipe," Mac yelled back. "At most, it'll be sticking up three or four inches out of the ground."

Mac moved another fifty feet ahead and stopped, wiping the perspiration from his brow. He could feel his hair soaking with sweat and his shirt clinging to his body. There were fresh tracks in the ground straight ahead of him; another set branched to the right off of a larger tree. Lich tracked to the right, while Mac moved straight ahead, deeper into the woods. The mosquitoes hovered in vicious swarms. Within fifteen feet of the split they walked into a clearing, maybe twenty by twenty feet. A thick layer of loose branches and leaves covered the forest floor. Mac panned right to left with his flashlight, and the light bounced off of something unnaturally white beneath a camouflaging layer of twigs and branches.

"There! There it is!" Mac yelled, running and then sliding down to his knees, ripping the debris away from the open pipe.

"CARRIE! CARRIE! CARRIE FLANAGAN! SHANNON HISLE! WE'RE HERE! WE'RE HERE!" Mac yelled down the pipe. He waved frantically to the deputies. "Get those shovels over here! We've found them! We found them!" He bent down again, mouth to the pipe, shouting, "CARRIE! SHANNON! WE'RE HERE! WE'RE HERE!"

Carrie held Shannon in her arms. Shannon's breathing had become more labored, and she had shown no signs of consciousness for the last few minutes. It was just after six now. Carrie didn't think she had any tears left, but she started to cry one more time.

Sobbing, she almost didn't hear it. Then she thought her mind was playing tricks on her. It was there and then it was gone. But then it was there again, muffled, coming from the air pipe, but it was unmistakable. "Carrie! Shannon! Hang on!"

She scrambled over to the vent and yelled as loud as she could. "HELP! HELP! WE'RE DOWN HERE, WE'RE DOWN HERE! HELP US! HELP US!"

"I think I heard something," Mac said, holding up his hand. Everyone froze. He heard the voice, faint beneath the earth. "I hear them! They're down there! They're down there! DIG!"

The deputies dug haphazardly, throwing dirt everywhere. "How far down are they?" the sheriff asked.

"Four feet, maybe five." Mac replied. "In a large wood box, two feet high, four feet wide, six feet long, running to the left of the pipe."

Four deputies were working furiously in the loose soil. Mac stood up and Lich gave him a big hug, lifting him off the ground. "You son of a bitch. You unbelievable son of bitch."

Mac paused to re-gather his wits. "Sheriff, we're going to need air ambulance out here. Shannon Hisle is a type 1 diabetic. She's been without insulin for at least two days, probably more. She's going to be in rough shape. Get an ER doc on that chopper, and I want you to call North Memorial, not Regions in St. Paul."

"Why not?"

"It's a long story, but someone is working this from the inside. So if we fly into St. Paul, that could end up bad for the chief and Hisle. You need to do this quietly, Sheriff—keep it off the airwaves."

"I understand," the sheriff replied, reaching for a cell phone instead of a radio.

"One other thing," Mac said. "In the center console of my Explorer is a black bag. It has a syringe and insulin in it, bring that back."

The sheriff nodded and jogged as quickly as he could out of the woods, Lich in tow.

"Dick, call Riles," Mac yelled after them.

"Where are these guys going?" Heather Foxx's cameraman said as they followed the pickup truck over the Wabasha Bridge and the Mississippi River below.

"I think toward the Taste of Minnesota—Harriet Island. The chief and Hisle must be on that bus," Foxx answered. "This could be really good. Shoot some footage."

"What's up with the ransom?" Mac asked Lich as he hung up his cell phone.

"The chief and Hisle are on a bus heading to the Taste of Minnesota. Riles thinks they're going to try to run the chief and Hisle through the crowd and either do a drop of the money or try to lose the chief and Lyman."

"Are they tracking them?"

"Only with an eyeball," Lich replied. "They hooked up body mikes and tracking in the bags, but now both are compromised."

"How?" Mac asked, and Lich explained.

"We have the girls. Let's just move in." Mac griped. "We'll get Brown and the Muellers later."

"That's what I said," Dick answered. "But Riley wants that fucking mole, and he figures the best way to get him is to catch Brown and the Muellers at the Taste of Minnesota. Burton doesn't know about the girls, but he senses the danger to the chief and Lyman as well. He's locking Harriet Island down. He's got two choppers overhead. He's flooding the area with agents and cops, the whole nine yards."

Thump.

Mac turned his head.

The deputy pushed the shovel down again.

Thump. Thump.

It was the unmistakable sound of a shovel hitting wood.

"Clear the top! Find the sides! Find the sides!" Mac yelled frantically. A deputy quickly found one side and Mac jumped down into the pit, kneeled down and noted the screws, one every six inches along the side. He climbed back out and looked to another deputy standing to the side. "The top is screwed into this thing. We're going to need crowbars, tire irons, anything to help pry the top off. Go!"

The deputy ran out while another returned with an update. "North Memorial's chopper is in route, ER doc on board. ETA is less than fifteen minutes."

The deputies worked frantically to dig out the sides of the box enough so they could have leverage to pry up the top of the box. It took a couple of minutes of digging and clearing. The deputy returned with four crowbars and two tire irons.

Mac and Lich jumped down into the pit to the right side of the box. The remaining deputies surrounded the box. Everyone jammed the crowbars and tire irons in, prying in between the top and side pieces, pushing down with all their strength to pry the top off. At first the screws wouldn't give, but under continuous pressure, the screws started to come loose, groaning loudly, and the top came off with an ear-shattering pop and was pushed to the left.

Everyone froze.

Carrie Flanagan lay on the right and Shannon Hisle the left. Flanagan looked up and shaded her eyes with her left hand. Her hair was matted, and there were dirty tear streaks down her cheeks. Hisle was curled up in a fetal position, unmoving.

Mac jumped into the box, between the girls, and helped Carrie up. Two of the sheriff's deputies lifted her out. Mac knelt down to Shannon, checking her pulse and listening to her chest. She was breathing. Her breathes were rapid, and Mac noted her breath smelled almost fruity.

"Carrie, how long has she been like this?"

"I don't kn ... kn ... know for sure," Carrie chattered. "She's been fading in and out for the last couple of hours."

"What's her status?" the sheriff asked.

"She's unconscious. Her pulse is rapid and so is her breathing," Mac replied as he lifted Shannon and handed her up out of the box. He climbed out and took her limp body from the deputies, carrying her as the group made its way out of the woods. Once clear of the trees Mac gently laid Hisle down next to the trucks, lightly slapping her face.

"Shannon! Shannon! God damn it, you hang on, do you hear me?"

Her head lay against the deputy's lap.

The sheriff dropped down a first aid kit next to them. Mac checked her pulse while Lich opened up the box and grabbed the blood pressure monitor.

"I've got her pulse at 120," Mac said.

"Blood pressure is low," Lich reported. "Eighty-one over forty-five."

"The black bag!" Mac said. "Get me the Glucose Meter."

Dick handed it to Mac and he tested Shannon.

"What's it say?" Lich asked.

"The glucose is high, way high. She needs insulin."

Lich reached inside the black bag and handed Mac a needle and small bottle of insulin. Mac pulled the cover off the needle and stuck it into the top of the bottle, drawing out ten units of regular insulin, just as Lyman had instructed. He rolled Shannon onto her side and plunged the needle into her lower abdomen, injecting the drug into her system.

"Will that snap her out of it?" the sheriff asked.

"I don't know," Mac answered. "The girl's father told us that if she was in this condition when we found her, this is what she would need. After a minute he stood up, leaving the deputy to monitor Hisle's pulse.

He walked over to Carrie, who sat on the bumper of the Explorer with a bottle of water in her hands. Her face was blank, nearly lifeless.

"I told Shannon you'd find us," Carrie said weakly as Mac sat down next to her. "I told her you'd find us," she repeated as she started to cry again. Mac put his arm around her shoulder and held her.

"Wait a second," the deputy said, his hand on Shannon's wrist and his eyes on his watch, "I think we're getting a little better here."

Hisle's eyes fluttered and her breathing regulated. Mac kneeled down and put his right hand to her face. "That's it Shannon, come back to us."

"W ... w ... water," she said weakly. A deputy quickly handed down a bottle, and Mac put it to her lips, letting her take some small sips.

Mac looked up. Lich smiled broadly as the sound of a chopper rose in the distance. The sheriff moved away and shot up a flare. Within a minute, the helicopter was touching down, the *whoosh* of the blades matting down the tall grass. The ER doc, in his hospital blues, was out of the chopper and on Shannon in an instant, checking her eyes and pulse. McRyan gave him the status report.

"You gave her insulin?" the Doc asked.

"Her glucose was high," Mac answered. "So she needed insulin. We gave her ten units."

"Good," the doctor answered as he checked Shannon's glucose again. "The ten units looks like it was a good start. He reached into his own box of supplies and pulled out another bottle of insulin and administered another ten units. He then set up an IV. The paramedics put her on a stretcher and transported her over to the chopper. The doctor stood up and came to Carrie, "How are you doing, young lady?"

"I think better," Mac answered when the young woman said nothing. "She seems okay, physically at least." They all knew that her injuries would be mental.

The doctor looked Carrie in the eye and said, "How about you come with us, okay?"

Carrie looked at Mac, who smiled and nodded. "You go. I'll see you at the hospital later."

Gail Carlson sat on the county road, a quarter mile away from the farmhouse. It had been nearly a half hour since the police went up to the house. She'd driven down the road a little further, inching closer, but neither the Suburbans nor McRyan's Explorer were around the farmhouse now. She heard it first, and then saw a North Memorial helicopter, flying low and fast from the south and passing right over the farmhouse. It passed out of her sight, but almost immediately the sound of its rotors changed to one she knew from experience meant that it was landing. Carlson figured it meant one thing. She pulled out her cell phone and dialed Heather Foxx.

"I think McRyan might have found the girls."

"Where?"

Carlson related her current position in Marine on St. Croix. "So where are you at right now?"

"Following two other cops. We just pulled up to the Taste of Minnesota. The cops are all over a bus that Flanagan and Hisle jumped onto."

"So do you want to go with the story? That they found the girls?"

Foxx heard the question, but was looking at Pat Riley and Bobby Rockford racing back to the pickup and blowing out of the parking lot, siren blaring. Something was amiss. "Not yet Gail. Something's not right here."

Lich smiled around a fresh cigar in his mouth as he handed one to Mac. "God damn it Mac, we found them. Man did you pull a rabbit out of the hat with this one!"

Mac smiled, reaching out to take the cigar, but he paused when he saw the time on his watch. "We're not quite done yet, my friend," he said. "Six twenty-one: they should be at the Taste of Minnesota any minute."

Mac's cell phone chirped. It was Riley. "Do you have the chief? What? Wait. Slow down. Say that again. How in the hell can that happen?"

"What? What's wrong?" Lich asked, his smile gone.

Mac looked at him with a stunned expression. "The chief and Lyman weren't on the bus."

34

"So we play dumb for now?"

Smith followed well back of the minivan driven by Flanagan and Hisle on Shepard Road. The street ducked under the Robert Street Bridge and became Warner Road, with the Mississippi River running parallel on the immediate right. Smith, as well as Flanagan and Hisle, were free and clear of the FBI and police.

As Hisle and Flanagan had waited with the crowd at the bus stop, there was virtually no way for anyone following them to see them as the bus pulled up. Smith and Monica had scouted the location for a month, watching from various positions and angles, anticipating what the police would do. They had discussed contingencies with Burton and ways that he could control the situation from his end.

The Fourth of July holiday was the key. The arena, convention center, and the skyway that connected the arena to the parking garage would have provided surveillance stations on a normal day. But the skyway and the convention center were closed for the holiday. The only unobstructed view of the bus stop was at the Holiday Inn, where Monica had in fact been watching a white pickup truck parked in the left hand turn lane on West Seventh. The pickup had to be the cops, sitting pat in the turn lane with the hazard lights on through several green lights. Of course, the passenger using binoculars was a dead giveaway as well. Had the truck turned left at just the right time, maybe, just maybe, the police would have seen Flanagan and Hisle slip back ten feet and down into the RiverCentre ramp while everyone else climbed onto the bus.

Once Flanagan and Hisle were inside the parking ramp, they went down one level to a waiting blue minivan. One minute later, while the police were tailing the bus, the police chief and the lawyer were exiting onto Eagle Street, far below Kellogg Avenue and the bus stop.

When they exited the ramp, Smith, and only Smith, was waiting on the side of southbound Eagle. He watched Hisle and Flanagan approach in his rearview mirror. A dashboard camera in the minivan provided David, who was waiting on the boat, with a live video feed of Hisle and Flanagan as they drove the van. David in turn provided updates to Smith as he followed. The police scanner sat in his passenger seat. It had been quiet, with no sign that the police had yet realized they'd lost them. That wouldn't last long.

Smith picked up the handheld radio and spoke to the van. "You're doing well, Chief," Smith said. "Stay on Warner until we get to 10."

"Who are you?" Flanagan asked a few minutes later, as the van approached the intersection with County 10. "Tell me who the hell you are!"

"I can't do that yet, Chief," Smith answered calmly, two hundred yards behind the van. "When I'm satisfied, then we'll talk about the girls."

"We'll talk?" Flanagan growled with angst in his voice. "Who the hell are you?"

"Patience, Chief. I want to see you as much as you want to see me," Smith answered. He savored the thought of finally confronting Flanagan, of finally feeling the satisfaction for which he'd waited for years. But there was business to attend to first. "Turn left on 10. We're going to Burns Park. There's a red van waiting for you in the parking lot, and the key for it is in the glove box."

The two men did as instructed. Smith pulled past them, driving another five hundred yards before making a U-turn.

He wanted this last change of vehicles. The police would go back to the parking ramp soon enough, and surveillance footage would give them the blue minivan and the plate number. Changing into the red van would put them in the wind.

"Motherfucker," Flanagan said bitterly as he tossed the handheld radio onto the dashboard.

"We know who they are, or at least who this Brown is. You arrested him all those years ago," Lyman said from the passenger seat. "Why not just tell them? Why not just talk to them like that?"

"Because then they'll know we're onto them, that we know who they are," the chief replied. "If we do that, they might assume we know *where* they are, that we're closing in. If we do that, they could kill the girls."

"So we play dumb for now?"

"We give my boys as much time as possible."

35

"I know you found the girls."

"What the hell happened?" Mac asked, still sitting in his Explorer outside the woods.

"Sleight of hand," Riles explained. "They picked a good spot. We didn't, hell, couldn't have an eyeball on them, believe me." Pat sighed, and Mac could hear the frustration in his voice. "They just picked a good spot. We thought they were on the bus. It's ten minutes, and the bus gets over to the Taste of Minnesota. It had one stop just before it went over the river on the Robert Street Bridge and nobody got off, only on. Then when it got to the Taste of Minnesota and emptied, the chief and Hisle weren't there. They never got on that damn bus in the first place."

Mac closed his eyes. Such a simple thing—never having them get on the bus. It was brilliant, really.

"Where are you now?"

"We're driving back to HQ. We have a surveillance video from the garage attendant that we'll have the techs take a closer look at."

"What do you see on it?"

"The chief and Lyman leaving in a blue Dodge Sport minivan about a minute after the bus pulled away from the bus stop. We've got a plate and a broadcast out. We're pulling over any and all blue Dodge Sport minivans. Nothing as of yet, but we're pulling *everything* over."

Mac pinched the bridge of his nose. They had made a trade. They had the girls, but the chief and Lyman were out of reach. While they had a plate for the van, the window of time they had to find the chief and Hisle before they changed vehicles would be small, if not already closed. "Pat, Brown, and the Muellers had to know you'd be tailing the bus, and that when the chief and Lyman weren't on it, that you would double back to the bus stop. They have to know the surveillance footage from the parking ramp will give you the plate for the van."

"They'll be ready, won't they," Riles said. It was an answer, not a question.

"They've been ready for everything else," Mac answered. "There'll be a switch at some out-of-the-way place. I'll bet a month's pay you'll find it abandoned somewhere."

Riles sighed and then said, "No bet."

Then there was the mole. Mac hadn't spent much time thinking about that for the past couple of hours. But now they needed to pursue that angle full-bore, and they had little to go on.

"Who's the mole?" Mac asked.

"Hell if I know. You have any theories on who it might be?" Riles fired back. "I mean, beyond someone in the department with a connection to Brown or the Muellers?"

"How about the FBI? How about Duffy?" Mac asked, already grasping at straws.

"Or the mayor," Lich added. "I wouldn't put anything past him. Not the way he's operated the last couple of days."

"No way," Riles answered. "I know Duffy and the chief don't exchange Christmas cards, but I find it hard to believe he would do this. What's the upside in that? And the mayor isn't smart enough to pull this off. And besides, what evidence do we have?"

"Nothing, other than they were both around yesterday when the call from Stewart Avenue came in," Mac answered.

"As were thirty or forty other people. What? Are we going to haul them all in?" Riles said skeptically.

"You have any better ideas?"

Riles got quiet on the other end. "I don't. I gotta talk to Peters about it. What are you doing?"

"We're lying in wait out here for now," Mac answered. "Who knows, Brown and the Muellers could show. Where's Peters?"

"He's already back at HQ with Burton and his crew, working the broadcast on the van. It's the only lead we got."

"Get back there and talk to Peters, see what he thinks. The clock is ticking, and we need to make a move." Mac hung up, but his phone beeped at him. Sally.

Heather Foxx had trailed Rockford and Riley for two hours. She had watched as Riley, Rockford, Peters, and the FBI had taped up the parking garage as a crime scene, everyone tight-lipped and grim. Now they seemed to be heading back to police headquarters. It certainly looked like they'd lost Hisle and Flanagan. She thought about the call from Carlson. The medical chopper was in and out fast, but she still had no confirmation that the girls had been found. The police weren't talking about it at all. Gail Carlson was the only media on the scene at North Memorial, which was in lock down mode. None of the stations had that story yet.

If the girls had been found, it didn't seem to make anyone happy. It was as if McRyan wasn't letting everyone, or anyone for that matter, in on the rescue. She doubted he'd be keeping that from Riley and Rockford. Those two were McRyan's guys, along with Lich. But then why was McRyan driving from St. Paul, to Osseo, to Wyoming and now Marine on St. Croix? Perhaps the kidnappers had called in the location of the girls. But if that were the case, she probably would have heard something. It was time to find out what the hell was going on.

"I'll be back," she told the cameraman as they parked two rows behind Rockford's truck in the police parking lot.

"You don't want me to come with?"

"No, and don't shoot anything either. This will be off the record."

Heather hopped out of the car and walked toward Riley and Rockford. She'd never really spoken to the veteran detectives, other than to say hello. As she approached, Riley was pacing back and forth, talking on a cell phone and Rockford was leaning against the truck. Rock saw Heather first, said something to Riley who turned around. She caught his eye as he hung up the phone. It was time to take a chance.

"I know you found the girls," she blurted.

Riley and Rock tried to remain neutral, but Rock twitched, just enough to tell Heather she was right. "I know you found them, detectives," she said. No notepad, no camera, just her making a statement. "I had someone monitoring the police bands up around Forest Lake and heard about the call at Hanburg's Hardware. I've had a reporter following McRyan since. She saw a medical chopper come in over some farm up by Marine on St. Croix. It wasn't there long, and McRyan was running around with Washington County sheriff's deputies."

"Heather, you're right, but you can't report that right now," Riles pleaded. "Hell, only a few of us know about it. Not even the FBI knows yet."

"Why not?"

Riley ignored the question. "How long you been watching us?"

"Last couple of hours, followed you down to the Taste of Minnesota and then back up here."

"So what do you think happened?" Rock asked with an edge.

"I assume something went awry with the ransom."

"Worse," Riles replied, pausing and then running his hand through his thick black hair. The big detective exhaled. "It's much worse. The chief and Hisle are missing. They're out of pocket, and we don't have a clue as to where they are. If you go with the girls being found, the chief and Lyman are as good as dead."

It was Heather's turn to go silent. There was more than just a story at stake here. She could scoop everyone else. Nobody knew the girls were alive. The story would be huge for her and her career. But if she went with the story, Riley was probably right. Flanagan and Hisle would be dead. She quickly decided to do the right thing, but worked it to her advantage, "I'll hold it, but…"

"You want something back in return?"

"An exclusive with McRyan about how the girls were found."

"Done," Riley answered. He and Rock turned to walk inside.

That wasn't a bad deal, the inside story. The networks weren't going to be getting that. "I had the report of McRyan driving up and around Forest Lake today, so I figured something was up," Heather said to them as they walked away. "You said the FBI doesn't know. I figured they did since that Burton guy was up there last night."

Riley and Rock both turned around, surprised looks on their faces. "Burton was up in Forest Lake?" Riley asked.

"Yeah. Last night, after midnight, up at a place called the Ranger. Do you know it?"

"It's the local hangout in Forest Lake," Riley answered, striding back to her. "What was Burton doing up there?"

Heather could tell that something about Burton's little jaunt was important. "He met up with a man. They talked in a booth for a while and then they both left. I'm not much for surveillance work, as I missed both of them leaving the place."

"What did the man Burton met look like?" Riley asked. "Height, weight, age, appearance? What did this fuckin' man look like?"

"Forty-five to fifty, I'd guess. Black hair, graying at the temples, big nose, and he wore glasses. I'd say he was maybe five-ten to six feet tall. That's a guess based on Burton's height. They sat eye to eye in the booth, so I assume similar height and weight."

Riley was suddenly agitated. "Heather, you're sure?"

Foxx nodded.

"Rock, grab the folder out of the truck."

"I have everyone here, running the names of the local FBI agents and Burton's people through Lyman's files and the department records," Sally reported to Mac. She flipped through binder-clipped sheets of paper. "Scheifelbein has been running Brown and Mueller against the personnel records for the department for the last hour or so. We haven't found anything on anyone except...."

"Except who? Duffy? The mayor?" Mac asked, his cell phone on speaker so Lich could hear.

"John Burton."

"What?" Mac asked in total disbelief. Lich was on alert as well. "You can't be serious?"

"Yes. Burton was stationed out of the local FBI office here in the early nineties," Sally said, reading from Hagen's computer screen.

"What else?"

"He left in August 1992, went to Washington, and moved to missing persons."

"Moved from what?"

"While he was here, he worked the usual assortment of cases, some missing persons, bank robbery, and drug enforcement."

"Drug enforcement?"

"Yeah, he worked with the DEA, and that's where the connection comes in. It's cryptic, but on a couple of occasions Brown's name shows up with Burton's on some drug cases. But then Burton transferred back out to D.C. in August 1992."

"When did Brown do this drug deal that put him in the joint?"

"Looks like February or March 1992. He had his gambling issues. The record indicates he lost big on a 1992 Super Bowl bet. At that point, he started moving the drugs to cover it."

"That's the Super Bowl that was at the Metrodome," Mac said, scratching his head. "He must have bet heavy on the Buffalo Bills and they got smoked by the Redskins."

Mac rubbed his bottom lip with his index finger. Burton was in town in February and March of 1992, working drug cases. Both men worked for federal law enforcement out of the Twin Cities at that time. It wouldn't be that unusual for them to cross paths. Besides, what motivation could Burton possibly have for helping Brown? Even better, what leverage could Brown possibly have to make Burton put his career and life in jeopardy?

"Take a look at Brown's file again. When did he go to trial and get sentenced?"

Sally looked to Hagen, who found the record and opened it. Sally put her finger to the screen and read down. "Brown went to trial in December of 1992 and was sentenced to fifteen years, which started immediately. He was released this past December."

Mac thought for a minute, "Sally, what does the FBI file say with regard to Brown's case?"

Sally looked to Hagen and Jupiter, who were opening FBI files, going way beyond what little authority they had, but none of them blinked an eye. After a minute, Hagen said, "Here it is."

"Hang on Mac. I'm scrolling through it." It took Sally a few minutes to read through the case summary. As she read the last paragraph she muttered, "Oh my God."

"What?" Mac asked, hearing her.

"Mac, listen to this, I'm reading from a final report on Brown's case. 'Brown sold cocaine with a street value of slightly over $300,000, yet his gambling debts were only $150,000 and there are no financial records for Agent Brown and his spouse that account for the other $150,000. Agent Brown claims to have sold it at a low price, so as to move it quickly and quietly and pay off his debt to his bookmaker. It is possible that Brown took the other half of the money and placed it into a bank account. We have been unable to unearth any records that would support such a transaction. Instead, it is suspected that others may have been involved with Agent Brown. Agent Brown has denied this, despite repeated questioning and offers of a reduced sentence in return for the identification of any accomplices. At this time, there is no evidence pointing to any specific accomplices. In light of this, we consider this matter closed unless Agent Brown chooses to cooperate.' Mac what if...."

"Burton was the accomplice," Mac finished for her. It was a stretch, a big one, but it was also plausible. "It's a big leap, but I can see it. Brown gets out, wants payback, and look who the FBI's top kidnapping gun is? His old partner in crime, John Burton. So either Burton helps him because he's his old friend or Brown holds it over his head, threatening to expose him if he doesn't. However it goes down, he's had Burton working this thing from the inside, and that motherfucker walks the chief and Lyman right into his hands. It's possible."

"Maybe, Mac," Sally said. "We're just inferring here. There is nothing in the records that we have that shows that Burton was even under suspicion. Burton's file does not mention the Brown case at all."

"Nevertheless, Burton worked here at the time, and on drug cases. The timeline works."

"But how can you know?" Sally said. "This isn't much to go on."

"See if he's been in town lately," Mac answered. "I'm calling Riley."

Rock pulled the pictures out of the manila folder, handing them to Foxx. "Is this the guy you saw last night?"

Heather looked through the photos and stopped on one with a left-profile shot of an older man. She leaned back against Rockford's truck, closed her eyes, and thought back to the night before. The nose looked right, and the graying hair at the temples. The jawline, the nose, it all looked right. "That's the guy. Who is he?"

"Heather, your deal just got better. A lot better," Riles said, but he wasn't smiling. "But you have to sit on the story now. That guy is named Smith Brown. We're pretty sure he is the man behind the kidnappings."

It was Foxx's turn to be stunned. "Oh my ... my ... God," Heather stammered, putting her hands to her throat. "If I'd only said something before now...."

Rock waved her off. "No way you could have known, sister."

"And Burton's been sabotaging the investigation from the inside," Heather breathed.

"Looks like it. You've done good, real good, Heather. We appreciate it, we really do." Riles reached for his cell phone, which was already ringing. "It's as if the motherfucker reads my mind or something."

"What?" Rock said.

"It's Mac," Riles replied, hitting the answer button. "Listen Mac...."

"It might be Burton, Riles. It's really a stretch, but I can manufacture a scenario in which that motherfucker has been playing us all along."

"God, how do you do that?"

"Do what?"

"Figure this out, especially from where you are?"

Mac explained Sally's investigation. "I know its weak, but…."

"It's not weak. As a matter of fact it's dead on the nuts," Riles said, his turn to spring a surprise on Mac. He told him about Foxx's trip the night before.

"Holy shit," Mac said. His phone beeped. It was Sally. "Pat hang on," he said and switched lines. "What do you got?"

"Burton's been to town three times in the last four months," Sally exclaimed. "His last trip in was three weeks ago. Five days—he came on a Wednesday and flew out on a Sunday night." It was at about the time Smith and Monica showed up in Osseo to meet with Dean and David. It was all coming together. "Great work, babe," he said and switched back to Riles to report the new information.

"It's him Mac. He's the source," Riles said. "He has to be.

"That's enough for us to move," Mac said. "Tell Heather we owe her."

"She knows. I've struck a deal with her, and you're the bargain, Mac."

"No problem. But listen, we don't have much time," Mac said. His voice went cold. "You two know what needs to be done."

"With fuckin' pleasure," Riles answered, looking over at Rock, who was punching his fist into the palm of his hand. "With fuckin' pleasure."

36

"Right during the rockets' red glare."

"Take the Highway 95 exit and drive north toward Stillwater," Smith ordered, still five hundred yards behind. He'd driven them around the Twin Cities for the last hour and a half, tailing them all the way. Monica had been even further back in a different vehicle, watching Smith's back and looking for anyone tailing him. When it was apparent that the police were nowhere to be found, Monica went ahead to the boat. At 7:56, noting the sun's decline in the west, Smith started them on the final drive east on Interstate 94.

Now it was 8:21 PM, and the red minivan wove its way through the small town of Bayport, the St. Croix River occasionally visible to the east down city streets. The van passed a bank and then a retirement home on the left, clearing the town proper. The road ahead was clear. "Past the entrance to the window plant, take a right down the dirt road."

Flanagan, who was driving, did as he was ordered, turning right and driving slowly down the dirt road. "Stop at the dock. Do not get out of the van." The van pulled to a stop at the dock.

Smith pulled up twenty feet behind the red minivan. Monica was already out of her car and approaching the front of the minivan, pointing a small 9mm. Dean stood at the end of the dock while David approached the van. The brothers wore blue nylon sweat tops with the zippers opened, revealing holstered .45s. Monica stopped five feet short of the driver's side door and threw two sets of disposable handcuffs into the car. "Put those around your wrists." Both men did as they were ordered and held their hands up to show compliance. "Get out," Monica ordered.

Flanagan and Hisle did as they were told, awkwardly reaching down to open the van doors with their bound hands and stepping out of the van. David pushed Hisle around the front. Smith finally made his appearance, getting out of his van and approaching Hisle and Flanagan from behind, a .45 in his hand. "Hello, Chief."

Flanagan turned and recognized Brown immediately, "Smith Brown."

"You know this man?" Hisle asked quietly, glancing sideways at the chief for effect.

"He does, Mr. Hisle," Smith answered in a mocking tone. "He needlessly put me in jail sixteen years ago."

"Needless my ass," Flanagan retorted, never taking his eyes off Brown. "You got what you deserved." The chief looked over to Hisle. "He was ex-DEA, a cop, and he was dirty. That's why I remember him. He was dipping his bill in the company stash and putting it back on the street."

"Once," Smith said, the anger flashing in his eyes. "I did it once. I did it to take care of debts."

"Gambling debts. And you did it one time that we knew about," was Flanagan's acid reply.

"You sanctimonious son of a bitch," Smith growled, punching Flanagan in the stomach and sending him groaning and coughing to the ground. "I did it once. One fucking time! You could have looked the other way. I said I'd resign, walk away from the job." Smith stood over the chief. "I had a wife, a sick daughter. If you'd looked the other way, I wouldn't have done fifteen years, I wouldn't have lost my wife. My daughter might have lived."

"You're pinning your daughter's death on the wrong man," Flanagan coughed, pushing himself up to his knees, "If anyone's responsible, it's you, not me."

Smith kicked Flanagan in the side, "It was you. You killed her, and now you'll pay."

"With money? Flanagan answered, coughing and spitting. "Figures."

"No," Smith replied, backing away. "With your life. You and the counselor here."

"What's Hisle got to do with this?" Flanagan croaked, still trying to get his breath.

"Does the name Thomas Mueller mean anything to you?" Monica asked Hisle, standing back, calm.

Hisle nodded. "TOM Trucking."

"Good memory," the woman replied. "You took that case for those bitches. They lied about my father, calling him a pervert, making the jury look at him that way, having the newspapers report about him in that way."

"I offered to settle it," Lyman said simply. "He should have settled."

Monica would have none of it. "You shouldn't have sued him to begin with. You ruined him. He lost everything. *Everything*. You drove him to put that gun in his mouth." Monica glared at Hisle. "Now it's your turn."

Lyman looked resigned to his fate. He wasn't going to plead for his life. "Fine, you all have grudges to settle with Flanagan and me. Fine, settle them then. Do what you're gonna do. But what about the girls? Why hurt our girls?"

"The girls get us you, and they get us money, blood money," Monica said coldly.

"But what about our daughters? They did nothing to you, nothing," Flanagan pleaded, still on the ground, but now up on all fours. "We're the ones you want. *Let them go.*"

"And quickly," Hisle added, pleading, begging. "My daughter is diabetic. She's in danger now, every minute counts for her."

"Just make the call," Flanagan added. "You have us. You have what you want. Let them go."

"When we're done." Smith answered harshly, waving to the dock. "Get on the fuckin' boat." Then to David he said, "Grab the bags out of the van."

Flanagan picked himself up, spat, and followed Hisle down a short flight of rickety wood steps and onto the old, weathered pier. The large river cruiser was tied at the end, its bow pointing out of the channel and onto the river, which was visible through the end of a narrow, tree-lined channel to the right. A small box was placed at the boat's side, allowing Hisle and the chief to climb on board. "Go down the companionway," Smith ordered, "and into the bathroom."

"You think they'll even let the girls go, Charlie?" Hisle asked once the door was closed. He was leaning against the wall, his hands bound and clasped at his waistline.

"I don't know," Flanagan replied as he sat on top of the vanity. He winced as he used the inside of his right forearm to lightly feel his ribs where he'd been kicked. He was having some trouble breathing. Leaning back, taking small breaths, he said, "I just don't know. The look in Smith's eyes scared me."

"I saw it too," Hisle replied and then snorted. "I guess we both really pissed them off, huh?" Lyman lifted Flanagan's shirt up to inspect his ribs while the chief held up his bound arms.

"I suppose we did," Flanagan said and winced as he tried to take in a deeper breath. "Bastard broke my ribs."

"I suspect he did. He kicked you good," Lyman added and then sighed. "So where do you think we're going."

"You know the river better than me. What do you think?"

Hisle leaned against the wall and thought for a moment. "I'd suspect we're going north."

"Why?"

"Less boat traffic up that way, north of Stillwater, up toward the rail bridge maybe."

"There's a lot of boats on the river, aren't there?"

"Yeah. There will be a big fireworks display in about...." Hisle looked at his watch, "an hour or so."

Flanagan smiled wryly and shook his head. "They'll cap us all right. Right during the rockets' red glare. The sound of the gun firing will sound like fireworks."

The two men sat in silence for a few minutes, feeling the acceleration of the boat into open water.

"I can't believe this is happening," Hisle muttered sadly.

"We're not dead yet."

"I don't sense the cavalry charge coming," Lyman replied. "Face it, Charlie. Your boys know who these guys are, but they have no idea where *we* are."

37

"It's that simple."

8:22 PM

"You're sure about this connection?" Burton asked Peters as they made their way down the steps to the basement of the Department of Public Safety.

"Yes," Peters replied. "McRyan has been working this today. Frankly, I thought he was crazy, but that's Mac. He gets going on something and he can't be stopped. It reminds me of that PTA case. The guy simply won't take no for an answer. Anyway, he unearthed this connection between Brown and Mueller and thinks it's worth pursuing. I want you to take a look at it, but with the chief and Lyman missing, we need to move fast."

"Sounds pretty thin," Burton replied as Peters stopped at a metal door and took his keys out of his pocket. "I mean, this Brown name comes up on a criminal case and this Mueller is what, a fellow inmate? That's pretty weak." Burton followed Peters into the conference room.

"IT AIN'T WEAK, IT'S DEAD FUCKIN' ON!" Riley roared as he threw Burton into the cement wall. Rock moved in with a knee to the gut and then threw Burton back across the metal interview table, where the agent slid across, into and then over two folding chairs, and smashed hard against the far wall. Riley picked a dazed Burton up, slammed him into the chair, and emptied the agent's pockets of cuffs, keys, weapon, wallet, two cell phones, and a hotel key card.

"Better talk now, John," Peters said casually, sitting on the corner of the table as Burton tried to catch his breath. "Or I'm going to let these two animals see if they can put you through these cement walls. And," Peters added, crossing his arms and looking around the room, "nobody's going to hear you down here. The room's soundproofed."

"I don't know what you're talking about," Burton spat. "I'm gonna have all of you...."

Riley backhanded Burton out of the chair to the floor. "If you ever want to breathe free air...."

"Fuck that!" Rock yelled, grabbing Burton by his shirt. His bright white eyes bulged in his dark black face. "If he ever wants to get out of this room *alive* he better talk."

"I'm an FBI agent...."

"Do I look like I give a shit!" Rockford yelled and threw the agent against the wall. He punched Burton in the belly again and then tossed him back over the table. Burton pushed himself up to his knees, trying to catch his breath.

"John, John, John..." Peters said shaking his head, a smile on his face. He crouched down to Burton. "How much longer you want this tune-up to last? I mean, these two live for this shit."

"Where's Duffy? I want you to get Duffy in here," Burton demanded, gasping for breath.

"Duffy isn't interested," Peters said. In fact, Duffy had considered the evidence and made himself conveniently scarce. "I'm not getting anyone for you," Peters continued. "We have you cold."

"With what? You ain't got shit on me," Burton panted.

"*Ohhhh yes we do*," came another voice "How was the Ranger up in Forest Lake last night?" Mac asked, his voice booming over the speaker on Peters' cell phone.

The look on Burton's face spoke volumes. "How?"

"We're just that good," Mac answered in a mocking tone. "At the Ranger you met up with Smith Brown. The man who you partnered with to sell drugs sixteen years ago. The man who, because he never rolled over on you, forced you to help him with this. The man who has the chief and Hisle. The man you're going to give us and I mean right fuckin' now."

"Or what?"

"Or you never leave that room alive," Mac replied flatly. "It's that simple."

Burton looked up at Peters, "You wouldn't...."

"It's no big thing," Peters said conversationally. "You simply go missing. A little cement around your ankles and we dump you in the Mississippi. The only way you leave the room alive," Peters stated, "is if you tell us where Brown has Flanagan and Hisle."

"Maybe we can make a deal," Burton replied, on all fours on the floor, trying to play his last card. "I can help you find the girls. I don't know where they are, but I can...."

"We have the girls," Mac answered.

Burton's jaw hit the floor. "How? How is that possible?"

"We've known since the safe house yesterday that someone was working this from the inside, you piece of shit," Riley growled. "You have no leverage to deal." Riley picked Burton up and threw him over to Rock.

"WHERE ARE THEY? TELL US NOW!" Rockford yelled. He grabbed the back of Burton's pants and ran him into the adjoining bathroom. He stuffed Burton's head in the grimy toilet. "Tell us where they are, or so help me God...." Rock pulled Burton's head back.

"But I don't know anything...."

"The hell you don't," Rock growled, pushing Burton's head back down into the water. After twenty seconds, he pulled his head up. "WHAT'S IT GONNA BE?"

"Okay! Okay! Okay!" Burton yelped.

Rockford picked him up and put him into a folding chair at the interview table. "Where? Where are they?"

"I don't know for sure," Burton answered. Rockford raised his hand. "I don't know!" the agent yelped, cowering. Almost whimpering, he repeated, "I don't know."

"What the fuck do you know?" Rock demanded, grabbing Burton's shirt and pulling the man's face close to his.

"That Brown was going to drive them out to the St. Croix River, to some channel between Bayport and Stillwater he said."

"Then what?"

"They have a boat, a big boat. They're going to go somewhere up the river."

"Where?" Riles demanded, leaning on the table.

"I don't know," Burton answered. Rock released him, and Burton buried his face in his hands. "I just don't know. Other than north, I don't know. Brown had a spot that mattered to him, but I don't know where. He didn't tell me that part."

"Were they planning to go ashore somewhere?" Mac asked.

"I think so. He said there was a spot important to him. A place he used to go. I can only assume that meant going ashore."

Peters stood on the other side of the metal table, flipping through the contents from Burton's pockets. He held a cell phone in each hand. "Odd to have two cell phones, isn't it?" he asked, eyebrow raised. "One of these used to contact Brown?"

"Yes," Burton replied, nodding.

"Will it be on?"

Burton nodded. "I'm not supposed to call him unless it's an emergency. If I call him with an emergency now, he'll likely...."

"Kill the chief and Hisle," Riles finished for him.

"But...."

"But what?" Peters asked.

"He's supposed to call me in about fifteen minutes."

"We could get a fix on that phone then." Riles said hopefully.

"I don't think you can," Burton answered. "He won't call me on the phone number I have for him. I have that one for an emergency, if I needed to contact him. Otherwise, he's contacting me with disposable cell phones. It's a different one every time. He's been using a phone once and then dumping it."

"A different phone everytime?" Rock asked.

"That's right," Burton answered. "I don't see how you could get a real fix on it. At least not in the timeframe you need."

"Well then," Mac started, still listening in, "you best get him to explain to you where he is on the river, in as much detail as possible so that we can find him."

"I'll try."

"You better do more than that," Riles responded. "Do you have any idea what this boat looks like?"

Burton shook his head. "I really don't other than it's a pleasure boat, good size, it would have to be."

"Why's that?" Rock asked.

"Because he can't have the chief and Hisle up on deck," Mac answered. "He'll have them down below and will only bring them up when he comes ashore. Until then, he'll have them stuffed down below. Riles?"

"Yeah."

"Get on a chopper and get out there," Mac ordered. "I'm on my way."

"To where?" Riles asked. "Here?"

"The river," Mac answered. "My boat is docked just north of Stillwater. I'll be on it in less than ten minutes. We need to find that boat. And Burton, you better come through if you want to get out of that room."

38

"That's our boat, Mac."

8:42 PM

Brown stood to the left of Dean and admired the flotilla that was now gathering around them, awaiting the start of Stillwater's massive Fourth of July fireworks display. By the time the show started, sometime between 9:30 and 10:00 PM, there would be hundreds of boats running from a half mile south of the famous lift bridge to another quarter-to-half mile north of the town.

The mass of boats included a variety of sizes, from the Showboat Paddle Boats to yachts, sixty-foot cabin cruisers, houseboats, cigarette boats, speedboats, pontoons, and even a boat made out of a tiny sports car. All were full of revelers, the music roaring and alcohol flowing. In addition to the boats, the decks of the bars and restaurants that lined the river were packed to the rooftops with partiers ready for the show. The city riverfront park was covered with lawn chairs and blankets, not a patch of green to be seen.

It was a festive atmosphere and also a good one to get lost in, the congestion increasing by the minute. Most drivers were smart enough to float on either the east or west sides of the river, leaving something of a lane up the middle of the river to allow traffic to move in either direction. But it was closing, the clumps of vessels metastasizing on the north and south sides of the bridge. While it made maneuvering through the channel a slow and tedious process, it also provided camouflage as they moved north.

They approached the historic lift bridge. During some summers, a cruiser of their size might have had to wait for the lift section to open. However, the past winter as well as the summer had been unseasonably dry. Consequently, the water level was down, and Smith cruised easily underneath the steel bridge. Five minutes later, they were able to slowly accelerate as the traffic thinned.

Clear of town, Smith left Dean at the wheel and went back down the companionway to the cabin beneath. Flanagan and Hisle were locked in the bathroom. Monica sat at the small table, counting the bricks of money.

"How does it look?"

"Good," Monica replied, thumbing through the stacks. "The bills are non-sequential, and it's all there." David was taking the bricks and stuffing them into separate smaller nylon shoulder bags.

They had their running money. In a little over an hour they would all be making their way to the Canadian border and toward a new life, leaving Minnesota behind forever.

Smith checked his watch and then took a cell phone out of his pocket. He dialed Burton. Burton answered on the fourth ring. "How are we doing?" the kidnapper asked.

"Fine," the FBI agent answered quietly. "The police are running around with their heads cut off, frantic that they can't find their chief and Hisle. It's almost comical, really. They're quite sheepish that you made Flanagan and Hisle disappear under their noses as you did."

"Good," Smith replied.

"Where are you at?"

"We've moved through Stillwater and past most of the traffic clogging that area. We're clear now and heading north to where the St. Croix starts to narrow."

"How long until you get to your spot?"

"We have about fifteen to twenty minutes before we get there. It's pretty far north. We have to get past all the campers."

"And your cargo?"

"Hisle and Flanagan are locked up for now. We had a little fun with them already with more to come soon enough. What of you?"

"I don't have a fan club, that's for sure," Burton answered. "No chief, no Hisle and now, no girls." Burton replied flatly. "But this was to be expected."

"You have more than held up your end. I will send you a package in a month or so." Smith hung up.

"Does that give you an idea of where they are at?" Duffy asked over the radio. He stood next to Burton, who was now cuffed to the metal table in the basement interview room, under the watchful eyes of Double Frank and Paddy.

"Shit. They're well north of us already," Mac answered on his radio as he revved the engines on his boat and quickly backed out of his slip from Charlie's Marina. He pulled out into the sea of boats congregating just north of the Stillwater lift bridge.

"Pat, what's your position," Mac asked into the radio.

"We're flying over Bayport now and the river. The wind is from the west so the pilot thinks we can mask our approach if we come from the east, at least to start."

"Copy that," Mac answered as he was breaking free from the clogged area around Stillwater. Lich and the Stillwater police chief were downstairs in the cabin, scrutinizing boat traffic through binoculars. "Dick, what can you see?" Mac asked.

"I've got four or five still heading north," Lich answered. "They're pretty far in the distance. We need to get up there."

"I can take care of that," Mac answered, pushing the throttle down, opening up the horses on the powerful inboard motor. To his left stood Jackie Fornier, a Stillwater cop who changed from her uniform into a tight white T-shirt and pair of khaki shorts. She'd let down her shoulder-length brown hair and looked, for all intents and purposes, like the woman out for a little holiday boat ride—except, of course, for the Glock-17 on the floor between her feet. Next to it was a duffel bag that contained vests, Mac's Sig-Sauer, extra clips, and two Remington twelve-gauge shotguns.

"You'll look strange using the hand-held radio," Fornier said as she handed Mac the earpiece for his radio.

"Thanks," Mac answered as he put it in and checked it. It was working. Mac put his hand back on the throttle and eased it down just a bit more. His father bought the boat, aptly named *Simon Says,* nearly twenty years ago at an estate sale for a young couple who died without any family. For years, Mac mockingly called the powerful, white-and-teal-painted craft the *Miami Vice* boat. It wasn't a practical boat, it was a cigarette boat. The compartment below the cabin was small and cramped, and the seating area up top seated only six people. But Simon McRyan had not always been a practical man. He liked toys and speed. Right now, Mac was glad of it.

Well north of the city, Mac settled in a hundred yards behind a houseboat with five people on the top deck. "How about this one?" Mac asked, pretty much knowing the answer.

"Negative," Lich yelled. "Nobody fits."

Mac passed to the left of the house boat at a moderate speed. He kept a close eye on his depth finder. The St. Croix north of Stillwater had an uneven bottom, and one could easily beach a boat on a sand bar. He had done it once many years ago, paying more attention to the girls in their bikinis on the back bench of the boat rather than to where he was going.

A larger river cruiser was next, up another two hundred yards. As he approached from the starboard side, he could see a man and woman up top. Mac eased up on the throttle some, trying to get a better view. Burton had said that Smith had a large cruiser, although he was short on details. However, the man was short and stocky, almost round with thinning gray hair, which didn't fit any of the descriptions. The woman was taller and blonde, and when she gazed back in Mac's direction he saw that she was young and didn't look anything like Monica Reynolds. The vessel's name was *Bull Market,* and Mac suspected that she was either the man's daughter or trophy wife. In either case, it wasn't the vessel they were looking for. Mac checked the depth finder and blew on by.

There were two more boats in the distance. The next was a cigarette boat with two large men at the wheel. "Dicky Boy, what do you make of the next one?"

"Maybe. Get me a little closer."

Mac leaned into the throttle and began to close the gap, but it soon didn't matter. Their target slowed and turned right into a cluster of cruisers and pontoons beached along a sandy island in the river. The island was full of tents and campers setting off their own fireworks. Brown would not be going there.

Smith came back up to find no river traffic ahead of them and little traffic behind. A cigarette boat was in the distance, perhaps three or four hundred yards back. Smith put the glasses on them. A man in a golf shirt and baseball cap and a brunette in a tight shirt were cruising north, a couple looking for open water and maybe a secluded place to celebrate.

They were approaching a left turning bend in the river, and Smith turned to check their path. The steel-arched train bridge appeared a half mile in the distance, towering two hundred feet in the air over the river.

"Dean, let me take over, will you," Smith said. "I'd like to drive the last leg."

Dean stepped back and Smith took control, his left hand on the wheel, his right resting on the throttle.

It was 9:17 PM and the sun was getting low. To the east, the darkness was moving in and the cliff walls soon blocked the remaining sunlight. It would be completely dark in twenty minutes.

There was one more target ahead of them, well in the distance. "Express cruiser ahead," Fornier said. "It's a big one, at least a thirty-footer. Nice boat."

"Burton said a large boat," Mac added as he once again pushed down on the throttle, up to twenty five miles per hour now, gradually closing the gap to about two hundred yards.

"Dick?"

"Get me a little closer," Lich replied.

Mac closed the gap a bit more. He could see one man and now another.

"That's our boat, Mac," Lich bellowed. "There are two men up top."

"I see them."

"One is large, muscular, dark hair. I'm only seeing him from the back, but a big guy," Lich reported. "If we assume that's a Mueller, the other man may be Brown. Mueller is six three. Brown is six foot, and

I'd say there's maybe a three-inch height difference between the two. Wait ... He's got the glasses on us here, be cool."

It was getting darker, but Mac saw the man looking their way in the dimming light, binoculars up. He eased back just slightly on the throttle and turned to Fornier and smiled, "Come close to me."

She did and Mac put his arm around her, pulling her close, kissing her on the head. "Does this mean we're going steady?" The female cop asked, putting her arms around Mac's waist and laughing.

"My girlfriend might object. But I'll definitely buy you a beer for being a good sport," Mac answered, putting on a smile. But his gaze remained straight ahead on the man looking in his direction. After a minute the binoculars came down, and a moment later the man turned away.

"Mac, that's Brown," Lich yelled excitedly.

"You're sure?"

"Hell yes. I had a good look at the face for a few seconds when he took the binoculars down. I know it's getting dark, but that's him."

Brown was now steering to the left around a bend in the river and disappearing from their view. Boat traffic was only allowed to go north maybe another mile before they reached a sign that prohibited motored boats from going further upriver. Mac dialed Riley. "We've got them, Pat. They're in a large express cruiser. They are about a half mile south of the train bridge. What's your position?"

"We're a half mile or so east of the river, about a mile southeast of you. Where do you think he's going?"

That was a good question. He looked to Fornier. "What do you think?"

She bit her bottom lip, kneeled down, and pulled a map out of her backpack on the floor. She looked at the detailed layout of the river and then looked up at the shoreline. She pointed back down the east side of the river. "He can't go much farther north, and there's no place to beach on the west side. The cliffs go right into the water, no beach, no privacy. He'll need those things."

"Same on the east side," Mac answered.

"True, except for here," Fornier pointed to a small patch on the east side, just south of the train bridge. "The cliffs are still there, but there's a beach back there, completely surrounded by trees. Coming in from the south, you have to wind your way in a little to get back there. He'll have to be careful, and he'll never get completely to shore, but heck, he wouldn't want to. He'll have to moor that sucker in the water, which will take him some time. But if you can get back there, there's a place to camp. I did it once a few years ago."

"How far back in on that little channel?" Mac said, pointing down to the map.

"A couple hundred yards," Fornier answered. "But it's isolated, away from the crowds, so if you think their intent is to…."

"Kill them," Mac finished for her.

"Right. It would be a good spot. If anyone heard gunfire, they'd just assume it was fireworks, especially on the Fourth of July."

"Of course, if we come from the same direction, we'll be sitting ducks."

"Maybe," Fornier answered, looking at the map. "But if you come from the north instead…."

"You mean go past their position, up to the rail bridge…"

"Right," Fornier nodded. "You have more of a straight shot from there. You have to plane it out, trim it up pretty high, but this kind of boat…."

"Could do it," Mac nodded, a plan coming together in his mind. He dialed Riley. "Pat, here's what I need you to do."

39

"Now! Now! Now!"

The chief felt the boat make a slow turn to the right, the throttle easing back and then into neutral before once again easing forward very slowly. The chief and Lyman both looked at their watches. They'd been traveling for maybe forty-five minutes to an hour.

"When they open that door, do we come charging out?" Hisle asked. "It might be our only shot."

Flanagan held up his bound hands. "It's our two to their four, and they all have guns. If we rush them, they'll just shoot us."

"So we just let them kill us?"

"I don't know," the chief replied. "I don't like sitting back, going down without a fight. But there's one thing to keep in mind. If we try something, they might not release Shannon and Carrie."

"You think they will release them?"

"I have my doubts. But that's our only play at this point."

Hisle snorted and shook his head. "So to save the girls, we bite the bullet."

"You lawyers are always good for the gallows humor," the chief replied.

The boat came to a stop, and the two men shared a look. Whatever was to happen was going to happen soon.

"Well then," Hisle said, "I guess this is the end of the line. A hell of a way to go, eh Charlie?" Lyman stuck out his hand, a wry smile on his face.

The chief grasped his hand and shook it. "It's always been a pleasure, Lyman."

Smith picked his way through the channel, but it was harder to maneuver in the dimming light. He beached prematurely, approximately one hundred feet from the shoreline. "Shit," he said.

"Ah don't worry about it, we just gotta walk a little farther," Dean said. The Muellers both climbed over the sides to secure the boat and then sloshed to the shore. They started a fire on the beach to help create the camping illusion. The fire started and the boat secure, Dean and David climbed back aboard, and joined Smith and Monica down in the cabin.

Smith took his .45 off the table and nodded for Dean and David to do the same. "They might try to rush us," Smith whispered and then nodded to Monica.

She undid the lock to the bathroom and yanked the door open. Flanagan and Hisle remained seated in the bathroom. Smith waved them out with the .45. Flanagan exited first, grimacing as he slid off the vanity. Hisle followed, lifting himself off the toilet seat. Neither man said a word. The lead kidnapper looked to David, who started up the companionway steps. "Follow him up the steps," Smith ordered.

Mac stayed as far to the west side of the river as he could and cruised past the mouth of the cove that Brown's boat had entered. He could see the large boat slowly working its way into the channel. Not wanting to draw attention, at least not yet, Mac continued a half mile farther north, passing beneath the hulking steel train bridge. Then he turned around and idled a few minutes in the river. Mac, Lich, Fornier, and the Stillwater chief all slipped on their vests and checked their weapons. Mac had his Sig-Sauer, Lich his Smith. Fornier and the Stillwater chief each had their sidearm. Fornier slid a new clip into hers.

"You always like a big gun?" Lich asked, cracking jokes even now.

"Yours isn't big enough for me. I'm sure," was the tart reply, and only Mac saw her smile. "You think these guys will throw down?" she asked Mac.

"I can't believe they wouldn't," Mac answered. "They've come this far. They're not going to stop without a fight."

Everyone was locked and loaded. Mac started south, "Riles, are you in position?"

"Copy, Mac, we're just west of you."

Mac slammed down the throttle and raced back under the bridge, angling the bow to the left, toward the river's east side. Everyone crouched down behind him and braced themselves. Five hundred yards from the mouth of the channel into the little bay, Mac gave the order.

"*Now! Now! Now!*"

Struggling through the knee-deep water, Smith pushed toward the shoreline with Flanagan in tow, followed by Monica and Hisle. The two Muellers were further back, still in waist-high water. The kidnappers each had a gun in hand and a nylon bag of ransom money over their shoulders.

The fireworks show had started in Stillwater, accompanied by the occasional smaller blast from campsites south of their position. Then there was a different thumping sound.

Smith looked up.

The chopper dropped out of nowhere, painting them with a blinding light.

"Get to shore! Get to shore!" Smith yelled, firing up at the chopper.

"Mac, veer right, veer right. They're all out of the boat to the left side of the cove!" Riles screamed. "The chief and Hisle are second and fourth form the front!"

Mac could hear the gunfire as he buried the throttle. "A hundred yards, we're coming in the right side," he yelled. "Hang on. It's gonna be rough!"

Mac ducked his head down just over the steering wheel. The boat planed on the top of the water, the prop just under the surface as he exploded into the cove beneath the chopper. Brown's boat bobbed forty-five degrees to the left. The *Simon Says* hit a sandbar just beneath the surface, skipping into the air. "Hold on!" Mac yelled as the boat bucked left and, hit the water hard, mowing down one of the Mueller brothers just short of shore.

Mac pulled back on the throttle and pulled the wheel to the right just before the boat skidded hard into the shoreline, throwing everyone hard forward. The boat listed hard to the right, creating cover. Mac threw himself over the port side and scrambled to the bow as Lich and the Stillwater chief jumped out and worked their way to the stern of the boat. Fournier was right on Mac's hip.

At the bow, Mac saw Brown moving to the right.

"Dean! Dean!" David wailed at his brother's limp, floating corpse.

"Come on! Come on!" Smith yelled. Already on shore, he opened fire on the boat, trying to cover. He glanced right. Hisle and Flanagan were forty feet back in the water, hands still bound, but high-stepping toward the cigarette boat. Smith had pivoted slightly right to fire at Flanagan when his own body jerked hard to the left. He fell to the ground, a searing pain in his left upper arm.

Mac's second shot hit Brown. He pushed himself under the bow and looked left. The chief and Hisle were running right at him. "Come on! Come on!" Mac yelled. He saw Monica nearly ashore, directly behind Flanagan and Hisle, firing. One shot caught Lyman in the back of his right leg, sending him face-first into the water.

Mac rolled once to his right and emptied his clip. One shot hit the woman in her right shoulder, knocking her back and exposing her whole body. Another shot hit her torso and blew her backward into the water. The chief stumbled past him, under the bow and to the cover of the other side of the boat.

"Go, Mac, I've got you covered," Fornier yelled, firing.

Mac fished Lyman out of the water and dragged him the last twenty feet to the safety of the boat. Mac heard Lich yell, "He's down! He's down! They're all down!"

The whole thing was over in less than twenty seconds.

"Mac!" the chief yelled. "The girls, we don't know where the girls are."

"Relax, Chief," Mac replied with a broad small smile on his face as he leaned back against the boat. "We have them."

"But..." the chief was astonished. "How? Boyo," the chief started smiling, grabbing Mac by the scruff of his neck. "How in the *hell* did you do it?"

"I'll tell you later," Mac answered and then called Riles. "Pat?"

"Mac, everyone all right?"

"Yeah. Lyman's hit in the back of his right leg. We're going to need to get him out of here," Mac reported. He pulled out a heavy-duty Swiss Army knife and cut the chief's and Lyman's hands loose. Then Mac rolled Lyman onto his stomach and cut his pant leg away to get a look at the wound. The hole was on the outside of the right thigh.

"How bad?" Lyman grunted, grimacing in pain.

"I've seen worse," Mac answered as Lich handed him a hankie and he applied pressure. "We should get a tourniquet on this," Mac said as he started to loosen his belt. "There should be a first aid kit in the boat," he said to Fornier. "It's down in the companionway. There should be towels down there as well, grab them."

Fornier climbed into the boat.

"You've got help coming, be there any minute," Riles reported and then said, "Wait a minute..." and then there was a pause. "Mac!"

"What?" Mac answered, tightening his belt around Hisle's upper thigh.

"I don't see Brown."

"What?"

"Brown. I don't see him. He went down by the woods, but now he's gone."

40

"Game. Set. Match."

Mac crawled to the bow and peered around it. Smith Brown was indeed gone. He must have gone into the woods.

"I guess we're not done yet."

"What?" Lich asked. "I thought you hit him."

"I did damnit. I put him down. But now the fucker's gone," Mac answered. "Riles, paint the woods with the search light."

The chopper turned its nose toward the woods on the other side of the clearing. "Riles, do you see anything?"

"Negative, Mac. We see nothing."

Mac had already decided his next move as he slipped a new clip into his Sig Sauer.

"We're all going," Lich said, knowing his partner, grabbing additional shells for the shotgun out of his pocket, and pushing them in. Fournier checked her Glock-17 and the Stillwater chief his smaller Glock-9.

"Give me a gun," the chief ordered. "I'm going with you."

"You sure you're up to it?" Lich asked.

"Fuck you. Give me your piece of shit backup piece," the chief ordered.

"This?" Lich asked as he pulled up his pant leg to show an old Smith & Wesson six-shooter. The chief grabbed it from the ankle holster, popped open the cylinder, and checked it and then snapped his right wrist, which pulled the cylinder back in place.

"What about Hisle?" Fournier asked.

"I'm fine," the lawyer answered, looking at his leg. "Help will be here soon enough. You go catch that bastard."

Mac didn't need to be told twice. He looked toward the group, "Ready?" Everyone nodded. Mac grabbed the radio. "Riles, we're heading in."

"Mac, wait ten seconds and you'll have help from the Wisconsin side, the St. Croix County sheriff. His name is Kolls." Mac looked back to his left, and three boats pulled into the small cove. The first one in the water was the sheriff himself. He was quickly followed by a crew of deputies. All had vests on and their weapons drawn.

Mac immediately went to the sheriff. "Sheriff Kolls, we have one on the move in the woods to the north. He was hit, left shoulder I think, and is injured."

Kolls smiled and pointed to the cliffs. "Not to worry son. There's no way out of here except through us or if he wants to swim." The sheriff then looked to the rest of the men. "I want us in a line, moving straight north. Let's flush him out."

"The man's name is Smith Brown. He is armed and dangerous," Mac added. "He has a .45 and will use it. He just threw down on us."

"So be careful," the sheriff added.

The group moved into the woods in a line. Mac took the chief and moved to the far right of the skirmish line, working their way to the cliffs. Five minutes and one-hundred yards into the woods, Mac started to wonder. "Chief, did you overhear anything from these guys as to what they were going to do after, you know...."

"They capped us," the chief answered, a wry smile on his face. "They didn't share anything with us if that's what you're asking. I assumed they would cap us and then take the boat back out."

"Right," Mac answered, moving forward. The brush was getting thicker, with logs and branches strewn on the ground. Despite the flashlight in the chief's hand and others close by, the woods were getting darker and darker. Mac had trouble seeing more than a few feet in front. He stepped onto a large log and jumped off and hit a tree in front of him.

"Ow. Shit that hurts."

He'd banged into a thorny tree branch that had dug into his left thigh. Looking down he could see blood coming through a hole ripped in his khakis.

"Let me see," the chief said, bending down to look at the leg, putting his flashlight on the hole. "Hmm. That's a nasty gash you've got there boyo."

Sheriff Kolls approached and inspected the thigh. "Stitches for sure. There's a first aid kit back in the boats. You should go get that taken care of."

"I want to finish this," Mac protested.

Kolls shook his head. "We've got this. It's just a matter of time, trust me."

Mac and the chief hung back as Kolls and the rest of the skirmish line moved forward.

"It felt like a knife going into my leg," Mac said, flexing his leg.

"I imagine it did."

The two slowly walked back toward the campsite and boats.

"It's hard to maneuver in here with no light, these trees, logs, and bushes all around," Mac said. "I can't imagine Brown doing it, wounded in the shoulder, that black ... bag ... over ... his .... holy shit. How did I miss that?"

"Miss what?"

"I must be really tired."

"Miss what boyo. Spit it out."

"Chief, they had the bags of money with them, right?"

"Yeah, so?"

"They weren't going back to the boats."

The chief got it. "They had a different out."

"Yes, they did. You know what Monica Reynolds bought at that hardware store in Wyoming?"

"What?"

"An extension ladder. An extremely long extension ladder," Mac answered, already moving back toward the camp site. "I'm betting Brown went up. They had that extension ladder. It's probably not far from the campsite."

With their flashlights lighting the way, Mac and the chief picked their way back toward the campsite. Fifty feet short, Mac's light flashed across it. He stopped and moved closer and there it was: a streak of blood at shoulder level. Mac moved his light further left and noted two more streaks of blood. The chief saw them as well.

Mac pushed that direction. It was fifty or so feet to the base of the cliff. He looked up.

"Look there boyo," the chief said, pointing to the right into the soft sand at the base of the cliff. "Those prints look fresh."

"That they do. He doubled back on us," Mac answered already making his way back south, toward the camp. He went twenty feet or so and the prints turned left into a narrow crevice, perhaps ten feet wide, which carved its way deep into the cliff face. Mac and the chief, weapons drawn slowly moved into the crevice, which curved slowly to the left. Fifty feet in, they found the extension ladder. Fully extended, the ladder reached nearly thirty feet up to a ledge.

"Cover me," Mac said as he stuffed his Sig in his pants and climbed the ladder, his left thigh burning with each bend of his leg and push up off a ladder step. At the top, Mac saw a narrow path that weaved its way further up into the cliffs. Mac waved the chief up.

Once the chief reached the top, Mac radioed Riley.

"Riles, do you copy?"

"Go, Mac."

"Brown doubled back. I've just climbed an extension ladder and I'm on a ledge some thirty or forty feet up into the cliff. You won't be able to see me. The chief and I are going to work our way up to the top. Get up top with the chopper, see if you can see Brown. He's either out or will be coming out up there somewhere. Also, radio the sheriff and clue him in. Brown must have a vehicle waiting up there. We're going to need ground troops and vehicles up there."

"Copy, Mac."

Brown had managed to put the duffel bag of money over his right shoulder and let the strap run diagonally across his body so that the bulk of the bag rested on his left hip. Nonetheless, it was a struggle to make his way up with only one arm. The pain shot through his left shoulder with every step up the narrow path. The shoulder would require attention soon. The wound was a through and through. He had a handkerchief stuffed in the front wound but he could feel the blood seeping into his shirt from the exit wound in the back.

He could hear the sound of the chopper flying overhead. He looked up and saw the search light sweeping up toward the top. The police must have realized he doubled back on them. He needed to get to the top.

He was at an optional point in the path. There was straight ahead or a steeper and narrower path to the left. David and Dean had gone straight ahead two days ago while he and Monica had gone left. Either way would get him to the top of the cliff and to the waiting pickup truck. The left path was longer but offered more cover at the top as the path exited into the dense woods. To the right, the path was shorter but the opening at the top was exposed and he would have to run some twenty or thirty yards to reach the cover of the trees.

Mac took the point, with the chief following. Every so often, along the narrow cliff walls, Mac noted a blood smear.

"You must have hit him good," the chief said. "He's draining a lot of blood."

Mac and the chief approached a fork in the path. They both knelt down and each scanned with their flashlights. There were footprints in either direction.

"Riles, have you seen anything at the top?" Mac asked.

"Negative Mac. Nothing yet."

"How about a vehicle? Truck? Car? Anything?"

"Negative. There's a small clearing up here but the woods are really dense, Mac. We've swept them, but we can't really see down to the bottom in most places. Brown could be going through there, and I don't think we could see him."

Mac looked to the chief. "Are you alright with splitting up?"

"Yes," the chief answered.

"Okay, I'm betting he went straight," Mac said. "That looks flatter and that would be easier with his shoulder and carrying that bag. Besides, my Sig is better than that antique your carrying."

"Fair enough," the chief answered. "Remember though, the son of a bitch has that .45. He has nothing to lose at this point. He will not hesitate."

"Neither will I."

Smith reached the top of the path. He'd made the right choice. Through the dense woods he could see the searchlight of the chopper, maybe one hundred yards to his right, scanning the area where the other path reached the top. All he had left was a narrow path, perhaps one hundred yards long to the pick-up truck, which was covered with a camouflage tarp.

He started down the path, jogged thirty yards, glanced back and saw him.

The chief reached the top of the path and met Brown's eyes, and the barrel of the .45. He raised the Smith.

The end of the path emerged into a clearing on the top of the cliffs. Mac looked up to the chopper.

"Shit."

Brown went the other way. There's no way Riley would have missed him. He immediately turned back to his left where the chief's path would have come out of the cliff. The exit of the chief's path would have been into the dense forest. Then he saw the muzzle flashes.

"Riles, shots fired at ten o'clock! Shots fired at ten o'clock!" Mac yelled as he ran into the dense woods and toward the muzzle flashes.

The chief got two off before he ducked for cover, as Brown unloaded his .45 causing shards from the trees to rain down upon him. The shots stopped, and the chief looked to see Brown was running down the path. The chief pushed himself up and gave chase, firing.

The chopper was overhead scanning the path as Smith ran as hard as he could, even as one, two, and then three shots went by. The chopper must have seen the muzzle flashes for Flanagan's shots as the light was behind him now. The truck was within reach, another thirty yards. But he needed to stop Flanagan first or he wouldn't be able to get the tarp off and get away.

The chief was shooting on the fly. Then he saw Brown turning around with the .45, standing in the middle of the path, exposed. The chief set his feet.

Smith's leg buckled as Flanagan's shot grazed his right leg. He was hit, but it didn't put him down. It was nothing like the wound in his left shoulder. Flanagan was trying to fire again, but nothing was coming out of the gun. He was out of bullets. Slowly Flanagan's arm dropped to his side and a resigned look appeared on his face.

"Flanagan, that must be an old Smith you're holding there and you've had your six. You're finished," Brown yelled as he raised the .45.

"But I'm not!" a voice yelled from behind him.

Smith turned around to see Mac McRyan, with bloody arms and face, feet set, gun pointed right at him.

"Put it down, Brown!"

Brown started to raise the .45.

Mac didn't hesitate.

He hit center mass three times.

Smith Brown was blown flat on his back.

The chief walked up to Brown and kicked the .45 away. Brown spit blood out of his mouth, laboring to breathe, laboring to speak.

"You … may have … got me. But you won't … find … the girls."

A blood-filled smile crossed his face.

"I lost my daughter … because of … you. Now you … will know … how it feels."

The chief kneeled down and looked Brown in the face and smiled.

"My boys, they found the girls."

Brown's eyes went wide with disbelief.

"No … it's not … it's not possible. You're … lying." Brown said, spitting more blood.

"No we're not," Mac answered, standing over him now, blood streaming down his left cheek, the duffel bag of ransom money in his left hand. "We dug them out of the ground at O'Brien State Park a couple of hours ago."

"They're alive," the chief stated. "You failed."

"And we know about Burton," Mac added. "He sold you out. He broke in two minutes."

Brown's shook his head, "N … N … No," he said, the blood running out of his mouth. Death was seconds away. Mac held up the duffel bag, smiled and uttered the last words Smith Brown would ever hear.

"Game. Set. Match."

41

"It's five o'clock somewhere."

JULY 5TH

4:48 AM

It took a little over two hours, and he was dead tired, but Mac gave Heather Foxx everything, or just about everything.

He looked like hell, like death warmed over he said later. Sally, watching from behind the camera, remarked that he looked ten years older.

"But that's fine," Heather said. "It makes the story that much more dramatic. People will see what you put into it, how hard you went after it. The big scar on your face. The whole 'never say die' and 'against all odds' thing. It'll be great."

"If you say so." Mac hated interviews. But in this case, it was the least he could do. Heather had saved the chief and kept her word, kept the story close until it was done. She had lost the story of the girls' rescue to another station—that broke while she was interviewing Mac. But she was the first with the whole story, and she had it in time for the morning news program. By the end of the day, her face—and Mac's—would be on stations across the country, she predicted.

"Sorry Mac, the story is just that good."

"Great," was his wry reply. "But I'm done, right? I don't have to do any more of this?"

"Not with me. I imagine many of my brethren will be seeking your time."

"Not if I can help it," Mac answered, yawning. He could barely stay awake; his body was shutting down.

The Bureau was none too happy, not that he cared at this point. They weren't happy that one of their men had been the mole, although that wasn't out as of yet. Heather held back that element of the story, at least for now. The FBI seemed even more aggravated about the interrogation technique used on Burton. The director was flying into town to personally meet with the mayor, as well as the chief and Peters, blustering about an explanation and investigation. Peters said he and the chief weren't worried about it.

"Fuck the FBI," Peters snorted. "Besides," he added. "If the almighty director makes a big stink, we'll have Heather go with the whole story."

"She'll play ball?" Mac asked.

"Hell yes," Peters responded smiling. "She feels like she's one of us now, a 'copper.' She'd like nothing more than to go with it, but we're willing to work with the Bureau on it. But if the Fibbies make a lot of noise and don't play ball, we'll cut Heather loose. She'll have a field day."

"How's Duffy doing?"

"We're covering for him. The company line is, he had no idea what we were doing." Peters whistled. "Man, he is *pissed* about Burton. Ed Duffy is a company man. He believes in the Bureau. He'd have joined in on Riles and Rock's fun with Burton if he could have."

Mac needed sleep and he had a hospital bed at North Memorial. The hospital bed wasn't provided as a courtesy. To get to Smith Brown he'd had to run through thick woods, low branches, and thorny bushes. As a result, he was full of deep scrapes and bruises. He required stitches in five places, particularly for the fleshy rip in his left thigh and a gash along his left cheek. The cheek scar, depending upon how it healed, might require some plastic surgery. The thigh wound was thick enough that the emergency room doctor was worried about infection. He wanted Mac to stay in the hospital for a few hours to monitor his recovery. Until the leg wound healed, he would have to walk with a cane.

The emergency room doctors also checked for wood ticks. He'd been in the woods a lot, and the last thing he wanted was Lyme disease. However, the little bull's-eye bite was nowhere to be found on his body.

Mac cleaned up, put on some clean clothes, and jumped into bed and crashed. Sally woke him with a kiss a little after 10:00 AM. It took a few minutes to shake the cobwebs loose, but the smell of eggs, bacon, and toast, even if it was hospital eggs, bacon, and toast, brought him back to life. He skipped the coffee—he had lived on it for the last four days—and instead gulped down refreshing glasses of ice water and orange juice.

Half-way through his breakfast, the doctor checked in. There was no sign of infection in the thigh wound. However, the face wound was another story.

"You'll have to give that one a week or so to see how it heals. Ten stitches tends to leave a mark. You might need a little clean up on that."

The doc left and Mac resumed eating his hospital breakfast. As he finished the last of the eggs, there was another knock on the door. Mayor Olson stuck his head in.

"Detective McRyan. I was wondering if I might have a moment with you and Ms. Kennedy?" he asked politely. He was by himself. No staff.

Mac looked at Sally who shrugged her shoulders.

"Sure. Why not."

The mayor slowly walked over to the bed. The smugness and arrogance of the past few days, in reality the past several months, was gone. The man looked tired, with razor stubble and dark circles around his eyes. Not only that, he looked a way Mac had never seen him look—humble. Hizzoner stuck out his hand.

"Well done, Detective, well done. Thank you."

Mac was surprised, and it must have showed. He slowly extended his hand to the mayor's.

"I suspected you might feel that way," the mayor said, giving Mac a firm handshake. "Given how I've treated you and your cohorts the last while here, I owe you an apology."

"Thank you, Sir," Mac replied, stunned at what he was hearing. "Why the change of heart?"

"Lots of reasons," the mayor said as he sat down in a chair by the bed. "You certainly bailed me out. I put Burton in charge of the investigation. I walked the chief and Hisle right into the trap. I would have had their blood on my hands. You saved my ass."

"Bailing you out is not why we did what we did."

"Oh, I know that. It was just a byproduct," the mayor replied. "I'm probably the last person you were worried about. However, what I realized is that by putting Burton in charge and creating this level of distrust between the department and me, that made what you had to do that much harder. I'm sure that if we trusted one another, that if we had a better working relationship, I wouldn't have been putting up road blocks to prevent you from doing what you do so well. Instead of keeping things from me, you could have come to me with your concerns about someone working this thing from the inside. I could have helped. I could have provided resources. But you didn't trust me, did you?"

Mac shook his head.

"Well that's on me," the mayor said quietly. "That's all on me."

"You can understand I'm a little surprised to be hearing this," Mac said.

"I imagine you are. Unfortunately, it took something like this to happen to make *me* see the light. It didn't hurt that the chief and I had a good heart to heart a couple of hours ago. He lit me up pretty good about my office's relations with the force, and he was one-hundred percent right. I haven't been supportive. I've been anything but. Well, that's going to change. It'll start at a press conference in a couple of hours. Peters and I will be handling it. I will be offering my praise and thanks for a job well done."

"I think I can speak for Riles, Rock, Lich, and everyone else. We all appreciate it."

"Good," the mayor said. "Of course, once all the euphoria from this dies down, we're going to have to deal with some stuff."

"Such as?" Mac asked, a little wearily.

"Burton and the FBI for all the obvious reasons. Burton has already hired a lawyer, and the bureau is squawking about how we accessed various records."

"I've got some ideas on how to deal with all that," Mac responded.

"The chief thought you might and I was hoping you would," the mayor answered with a tired smile. "I'm all ears."

"I wouldn't worry too much," Mac said confidently. "We have Burton and the bureau by the short hairs. I think we'll be able to make them see that."

The mayor smiled. "Good. We've been on opposite sides long enough. I'd like to see us on the same side."

"Let's get together in the next day or two and talk that through."

"Fair enough," the mayor answered, pushing himself out of the chair. Once again he extended his hand, which Mac took without hesitation. He walked over to Sally and extended a hand to her as well. "Ms. Kennedy, I know you helped out quite a bit as well. Thank you."

"You're welcome, sir."

"Help this guy get better," the mayor said, pointing at Mac. "We're going to need him."

"I will. Thank you."

The mayor looked back at Mac, smiled one more time and walked out of the room.

"Well, how about that?" Sally said, shocked. "Do you think he meant it?"

"We'll see," Mac answered, always more interested in action than words. "He's a politician, so I take anything a politician says with a grain of salt. But he seemed genuinely contrite and his apology seemed heartfelt. Time will tell."

Sally came over to the side of his bed and sat down and looked him in the eye.

"What?"

"I want to say something," Sally said smiling and then she pecked him on the lips.

"What?"

"I loved watching you in action the last twenty-four hours. You're gifted, honey. You really are. You would have been a great attorney, the way you see and perceive things. You'd have been a great trial lawyer. But as a cop, as a detective, you're doing what you were born to do. You're doing what you *should* be doing. I wouldn't want you to do anything else."

Mac returned the smile now. It always hurt him that his ex-wife thought what he did was beneath him and most certainly her. She never appreciated the sacrifice of the job or the ability required to do it. But now he was with someone who loved him and was proud of him. It felt good, as good as anything he'd done over the last four days. He pushed himself up and kissed her on the lips and hugged her.

"God, I need a vacation."

"Now would be a good time," she answered quietly, her head buried in his chest.

The door to his hospital room blew open and the Boys, Uncle Shamus, Peters, Summer Plantagenate, the chief, and Lyman all came barreling in. Lich, of course, didn't miss a beat.

"God, it looks like the fuckin' Hallmark Channel in here. You two arm in arm, looking deeply into each other's eyes. I think I'm going to get all teary eyed," his partner said as he pulled out a hankie and mockingly dabbed at his eyes.

Mac pushed himself out of bed. The chief came up and gave Mac a big bear hug, "Well *done,* boyo. Well done."

"I've told this to all of these guys," Lyman said, waving his cane toward Lich, Riles, and Rock. "Anything you ever need. Anything, you just tell me. It's yours." The lawyer pumped Mac's arm vehemently in a handshake. "I mean it. Thank you, thank you, *thank you,* Michael."

"Well Lyman, let me tell you about my boat." Everyone burst out in laughter.

"Done!" Lyman exclaimed.

Mac turned serious. "How's Shannon doing?"

"I think she'll be okay. You boys got to her just in time."

"Can she have visitors?" Lich asked.

"She's pretty beat. I think she'll be able to handle visitors tomorrow, and I want all you boys here. I know she'll want to thank you."

"How's Carrie, Chief?" Mac asked.

"Fine, just fine Mac. She asked me to bring you up, all of you up."

"Let's go then."

Carrie Flanagan indeed looked fine, at least physically. It would be the mental part that would be the problem. No doubt she'd have nightmares for a while. Two days in the coffin—the term she used for it—would do that. She was already talking about the need for counseling as if she was looking forward to it, ready to put the whole thing behind her. After a half hour, she started to look tired, so everyone began to file out. She asked Mac to stay behind.

"I told Shannon you'd be coming," Carrie said.

Mac just nodded.

"I told her you and the Boys would never give up. You'd keep looking until you found us, that you would do anything to find us."

"That's right."

"And you did."

"We all did."

"Will there be trouble? I heard something about the FBI guy."

"That's nothing for you to worry about, honey," Mac said, smiling, and then converting it to an evil grin. "We've got the Bureau by the short hairs."

"Thanks," Carrie said, sitting up to give him a hug and a kiss on the cheek. "Thanks."

Mac smiled as she lay back down. He pushed her hair away from her eyes. "You get some rest. I'll come by and see you again tomorrow."

Carrie nodded and rested her head back on her pillow.

Mac grabbed his cane and limped out of the room to find the whole crew waiting in the hallway. "So, what's next?" he asked, a huge grin on his face.

"Is it too early to celebrate?" Lich asked.

"I tell you what it's too early for!" Riles answered.

"What's that?"

"Stupid questions," Riles answered as he smacked Lich in the back of the head. "Is it too early to celebrate? Cripes, what's a matter with you?"

"It's five o'clock somewhere," Mac exclaimed. "I say we go to the Pub."

"Who's buying?" Rock asked.

"Lyman," Mac answered smiling, putting his arm around Hisle. "You just said anything we need, right?"

"That's right."

"Well right now, my friend, I need a bloody mary."